Sexy, prot...
Innocent, prov...
Powerful sex...

These are the ingredients to

Whirlwind
Weddings

Allison Leigh *takes a gorgeous successful man back to his home town and he comes away with more than he bargained for! While* **Carla Cassidy**'s *hero is determined to keep his eye on an adventurous princess who, secretly leaving her home, could easily run into trouble.*

We're proud to present

SILHOUETTE SPOTLIGHT

a second chance to enjoy two bestselling novels by favourite authors every month— they're back by popular demand!

Whirlwind Weddings

ALLISON LEIGH
CARLA CASSIDY

SILHOUETTE®

*Silhouette Books, Eton House, 18-24 Paradise Road,
Richmond, Surrey TW9 1SR*

WHIRLWIND WEDDINGS © Harlequin Books S.A. 2005

The publisher acknowledges the copyright holders of the
individual works as follows:

Married to a Stranger © Allison Lee Davidson 2000
The Princess's White Knight © Harlequin Books S.A. 1999

Special thanks and acknowledgement are given to Carla Cassidy.

ISBN 0 373 60230 8

64-0805

*Printed and bound in Spain
by Litografia Rosés S.A., Barcelona*

Married to a Stranger

ALLISON LEIGH

ALLISON LEIGH

started early by writing a Halloween play that her primary class performed for her school. Since then, though her tastes have changed, her love for reading has not. And her writing appetite simply grows more voracious by the day.

Born in Southern California, she has lived in eight different cities in four different states. She has been, at one time or another, a cosmetologist, a computer programmer and an administrative assistant.

Allison and her husband currently make their home in Arizona, where their time is thoroughly filled with two very active daughters, full-time jobs, pets, church, family and friends. In order to give herself the precious writing time she craves, she burns a lot of midnight oil.

A great believer in the power of love—her parents still hold hands—she cannot imagine anything more exciting to write about than the miracle of two hearts coming together.

For my daughters.

Live your dreams.

Prologue

All he'd wanted was a kiss. A simple kiss.

So how on God's green earth had his life gotten so out of control in just one week over something so simple?

Tris rolled his head against the cushioned seat and looked across the aisle of the custom-fitted jet. Hope was still asleep. She certainly had no head for alcohol.

His jaw was so tight it ached. He had earned himself a doozy of a headache, too. But he knew it wasn't from champagne, or whiskey or anything even remotely alcoholic. He'd barely choked down the few toasts they'd had at the reception—half a glass of champagne wasn't anywhere near enough to set this pain in his head to throbbing.

No, his headache had begun a little over a week ago, he knew. Brought on strictly by himself.

He shoved his fingers through his hair and closed his eyes. But the sight of the woman stretched out on the long seat across from him was firmly burned into his brain.

Hope's toffee-colored hair had fallen loose at some point on the drive to the airport. When he'd carried her onto the private jet, the long, thick waves had clung to his shirt, flowed over his arm and streamed behind them in the night breeze. Now, they lay tangled and gleaming over her shoulders, off the couch, nearly touching the carpeted floor.

He'd slipped off her narrow-heeled shoes and set them on the floor beside her. Her dress—so obviously an antique that he knew women who'd have given their eyeteeth for the ankle-length garment— had worked its way up her shapely calves. With one knee drawn upward, the fabric pulled in a taut stretch of beige-tinted lace over the back of her thighs and her derriere.

She was a total innocent, and lying there, so soundly asleep, she was temptation personified.

Temptation. That's what had gotten them into this mess in the first place. Tris should have known better than to flirt with temptation. God knows *she* didn't have enough experience to fight the blistering sparks between them.

But he was experienced. And older. And he should have known better. His heart might not be programmed for love and happily-ever-after, but he was on a first-name basis with the desires of the flesh.

Tris could feel the plane banking. There was no point in looking out the little oval windows. It was pitch-dark out there. Dark above, dark below, dark all around.

Even this luxurious main cabin of the plane was dark, except for one small lamp burning near him. It cast enough glow to highlight the lace dress and glossy hair of the woman across from him.

He wasn't sure how long he sat there, legs sprawled out before him, his chin resting on his steepled fingers. It could have been one hour or three. But finally, Hope sighed deeply and shifted. Her hand tumbled off the cushion and grazed the carpet. The light glinted on the platinum rings—one plain and one studded with a trio of excruciatingly perfect diamonds—circling her ring finger.

The rings *he* had put there.

She turned her head and pushed her thick hair out of her eyes. She blinked drowsily and he figured her vision was probably blurry, because her eyeglasses were sitting on the round side table beside his seat.

Comprehension slowly dawned in her eyes. He waited, knowing just when that memory clicked into place, because she breathed in sharply and yanked her feet off the cushion to sit up.

"Where are we?" Hope pressed a trembling hand to her head.

"More than halfway to Paris."

Her shoulders seemed to sag. "I drank too much," she murmured. "I've never—*Oh, God. What have we done?*"

Tris would have been amused at the panic rounding her violet eyes if he hadn't been wondering the same thing. He rarely acted impulsively. And even his actions over the last few days had been fairly deliberate. He trusted his instincts, listened to his gut because it rarely failed him.

But now, sitting here in this private jet equipped with every comfort known to man, from a whirlpool tub and a down-covered bed, to a fully equipped kitchen, to an array of computerized equipment that could run a small country if need be, his instincts had fully deserted him.

All because of this violet-eyed temptress.

"What have we done?" he repeated. He'd taken the easiest path of solving her problem. "We've stopped the gossip about us, effectively removing any reason for you to lose your teaching job."

That's *all* they'd done.

The irony burned. He'd started out thinking he'd like to taste her soft-looking lips. That was all.

He still hadn't kissed her. Not really. That quick, off-centered glancing of lips earlier that day didn't count.

He hadn't gotten a kiss. He hadn't "gotten" anything that everybody in town and beyond seemed to think he'd been "getting." It was almost laughable.

Tris picked up her eyeglasses and leaned forward, handing them to her. But in the end, nothing about this situation was laughable.

Particularly the fact that the young woman slipping the gold-rimmed glasses on her nose had—less than twelve hours ago, stood where he'd long ago vowed never to stand—in front of a minister, promising to "love, honor and cherish."

He hadn't gotten a kiss.

He'd gotten a wife.

Chapter One

Eight days earlier.

"I think that's plenty, darlin'. If you don't mind."

Hope Leoni blinked, dragged her eyes from the deep blue gaze of the man sitting at the counter across from her. And realized she was pouring coffee all across the counter.

Well, not precisely across the counter. But it was overflowing the thick white coffee cup, the utilitarian saucer beneath it, quickly pooling around the base. Worse, it flowed into a rich brown river that ran straight to the edge of the counter and into the smoky gray sweater the man wore, creating a large spot where he'd been leaning against the counter edge. Now he sat back with a muffled comment.

Her cheeks burned and she hastily set down the glass coffee carafe and grabbed a cloth from behind the counter, mopping up her mess. "I'm so sorry." She mopped, sopped, wiped and tried not to stare when, with a spare movement, he yanked the sweater over his head and tossed it onto the stool beside him. She dragged her attention from the plain white T-shirt that remained, hugging his broad shoulders, only to realize she was equally distracted by the thick gold hair that tumbled over his forehead. "I don't know what I was thinking—"

He, the man...the blond god with a face that could make angels weep...put one hand over hers, stopping her motions. "No sweat, darlin'."

She didn't know which made her blood flow faster until it zipped along her veins with a fevered frenzy—the touch of his hand atop hers, or the casual endearment murmured in his low voice. The schoolgirl fantasies in which he'd been the star seemed as recent as yesterday. "I, uh, I'm not usually so clumsy. I can't believe I—"

"Hey." His long, long fingers encircled hers. Slid around her hand, beneath it; square, warm palm meeting hers. Warm. Dry. Hard.

Every sound faded—the dog that had been barking half the morning from where it was tied up outside the sheriff's office a few doors down, the tractor mower that somebody was running over at the high school, the music from the radio on the shelf in the corner.

All of that faded. She could hear her pulse, thundering in her ears. Could hear her breath, slowly easing past her lips. She could hear the soft chink of his gold wristwatch as it bumped the counter beneath their hands.

"Relax," he said in that voice that hypnotized. "Nobody's going to fire you over a little spilled coffee. Certainly not Ruby, who's got a heart bigger than Wyoming."

At the mention of Ruby, owner of Ruby's Café and, more importantly, Hope's grandmother, some of Hope's scattered senses returned. She tugged her hand, relieved and disappointed all at once when their hands separated. She picked up the damp cloth, rubbing her palm against the wet, rough, terry cloth. "I'm well aware of Gram's generosity."

"Gram?"

Hope pulled her gaze from his mouth. From the way it tilted at the corner when he spoke as if he were perpetually amused. "Ah…Ruby. You know… she's my grandmother. I'm Hope. Hope…Leoni."

He nodded, giving her the impression that he was absorbing every nonsensical syllable she uttered. Which was, of course, ridiculous.

Men who looked like this man didn't hang on every syllable of the very ordinary Hope Leoni. Only he was nodding, his eyes thoughtful. "That's right," he said. "Ruby did have a little granddaughter she was raising."

"I didn't think you'd remember that." Again, she forced herself to look beyond the mesmerizing way his lips shaped his words—to take in the thick, burnished blond hair, the sapphire-colored eyes that even dark circles beneath couldn't dim, the sharply angled jaw. The astounding width of his shoulders.

"You, um, don't visit Weaver very often." Hope felt her cheeks heat all over again.

When he'd moved away from Wyoming, she truly had been Ruby's "little" granddaughter. But that hadn't kept her or any other girl growing up in Weaver from developing a crush on the Wyoming boy who'd made good.

"Well, I'm here now and it's nice to meet you, officially, Hope Leoni. Tristan Clay." He shifted and stuck out his hand, obviously waiting.

Hope swallowed, placing her hand in his. She was almost prepared for the jolt, but still her breath audibly caught and her cheeks burned. "You, too, Mr—ah, Clay."

His smile widened gently but there was something daunting about his impossibly steady gaze, so intensely blue among thick lashes that were surprisingly dark for someone so blond and golden. "Tristan'll do."

She swallowed, far too aware that he still held her hand engulfed in his much larger one. "I suppose you're here for your father's wedding. The whole town is buzzing with excitement."

Finally, finally, his lashes lowered. His thumb brushed across the back of her hand. "This town buzzes with excitement when the lone traffic signal turns red. Do you work here all the time, Hope?"

She knew she should pull away her hand. But his thumb made that gentle little swirl again and she couldn't bring herself to move. "Yes," she breathed. "No. I mean, I work here during the summer. When school starts, I'll—"

His expression didn't change. "School?"

"I teach at the elementary school. Kindergarten through third."

"Lucky kids. Married? Engaged? Going steady?"

She swallowed, nearly choking. "No."

Again that smooth, gentle swirl against her hand, the faint tilt at the corner of his mouth. "Why not?"

Her fingers curved. She tugged again and had the impression that he wanted to smile when she pushed her hands into the front pockets of her pink waitress uniform. "No particular reason," she answered, hoping that her trembling nerves didn't show in her voice as badly as she suspected. Except she'd have to be asked on a date again before she could worry about marriage proposals. "You?" His smile widened a bit, and he shook his head. Her cheeks flamed hotly. Of course, in a town as small as Weaver, news would have spread like wildfire if he had settled down with one woman.

He was Tristan Clay, the youngest of the Clay brothers of the enormous Double-C cattle ranch located some twenty miles away from town. He was rich, golden-beautiful and successful even without his family's holdings, which were reportedly the largest in the state. He'd developed some type of software when he'd been younger than she was now that had revolutionized the industry. Had dated famous women, danced in Europe with princesses and slept in the White House.

When Hope had been in school, every girl in town had dreamed of capturing the interest of Tristan Clay on his rare visits to his family's ranch. It didn't matter that he was grown and gone and the schoolgirls were just that—girls. The articles about him in the newspapers or magazines years ago had been clipped, savored in scrapbooks or tacked up on bedroom walls.

Hope had so envied her friend, Jolie, who had been allowed to pin up her favorite articles about her latest heartthrob. Gram had refused to let Hope attach anything to her bedroom walls other than a landscape or a print of the Last Supper. As if by doing so she'd be able to prevent Hope from turning into the wild child her sister Justine had been.

But Gram hadn't known about the clipping Hope had had inside her geometry book. The one of Tristan, when he'd made the papers about some high-tech espionage he'd foiled. His appearances in the news had dwindled to nothing over the last six or seven years—a fact that had roused its own share of curiosity—but Hope knew, to her everlasting embarrassment, that her private hoard of clippings were still packed away somewhere in her closet.

And now, here *he* sat, across the counter from where she stood, with his intense blue gaze steady on her face as if there was no place else in the world he wanted to be.

Ridiculous, of course. Tristan Clay was just killing time until he headed out to his family's place.

Yet, he *was* here in her grandmother's café, wearing blue jeans that were washed soft and nearly white. The dark gray crew-neck sweater he'd worn had looked like cashmere. But he'd dumped it on the stool with no regard for the coffee soaking it. And if she wasn't mistaken, there'd even been a small hole in one of the cuffs that had been pushed halfway up his golden-brown, sinewy forearms.

For a self-professed computer geek, his body looked both lean and hard. Her cheeks heated once again at her wayward thoughts. Since when did she speculate on the hardness of a man's body? *Not since you were a silly teenager, mooning over an article clipping about a man completely out of your league.*

Now her ears were burning, too. She swiped a loose strand of hair away from her cheek, nudged up the nose piece of her glasses and made a production of looking at the round clock high on the wall at the end of the counter.

It was three-thirty and the café was supposed to close at two every day until it reopened at six. But Hope had left the front and back doors propped open to take advantage of the lovely June afternoon while she prepared for the supper crowd.

It wasn't the first summer she'd spent working in her grandmother's café. It wasn't likely to be the last. But come the fall, Hope would begin her second year of teaching at Weaver Elementary and her mind had been filled with plans of that. And the relief of it, because she'd known the vote of the three-person school board to keep the school open at all had been terribly close.

She'd come out of the kitchen, her head filled with school projects and ideas, only to find Tristan sitting at one of the counter stools. His arms had been folded across the shining surface, his wide shoulders hunched tiredly. She'd begun telling him they were closed, but he'd looked up and Hope had been lost in the intensity of his eyes.

Tristan had been gone from the area for so long

that he probably didn't remember that Ruby's Café
closed after lunch. Yet telling him that was quite
possibly the last thing on this earth that she'd
wanted to do.

She now cast around for something intelligent to
say. But could only think of the same topic she'd
brought up earlier. "So, you're here for your father's wedding next Saturday?"

He nodded and shifted on the stool, finally blinking his eyes and glancing away. But only for a moment. One moment when she could breathe normally, and then he looked at her again, and she
simply forgot how. She nudged at her slipping
glasses, then pushed her hands into her pockets once
more. "I've met Gloria Day." She felt the tips of
her ears go hot at the way the words seemed to blurt
out of her. "She's very nice. I, uh, hope your father
and she are very happy."

He nodded, not replying. His long fingers
wrapped around the cup and he tilted it, as if to
drink. Hope automatically reached for the coffee pot
and refilled his cup. "Did you want to see a menu?"
She ignored the fact that she was due at her friend's
house in less than ten minutes. She'd promised to
watch Evan, Jolie's son, while Jolie and Drew Taggart drove to Gillette.

"I remember when Ruby used to just write the
specials on that chalkboard over there." Tristan
glanced at the square board that was propped on a
high corner shelf.

"She still puts the specials on the board." Hope
pulled a menu from beneath the counter and slid it

across to him. "But we offer more these days. I could fix you a sandwich or something."

"Coffee, tea or me?" Tris wanted to retract the suggestive words as soon as he said them. But they were already out there and hectic color was staining the waitress-teacher's cheeks. Personally, he found the blush charming. How many women did he know anymore who blushed?

But he'd obviously embarrassed her.

"No. I guess not." He was oddly disappointed. She wasn't at all his type of woman. Hell, she looked barely old enough to vote, much less be a teacher. Besides, the only energy he had right now was expended simply by lifting the coffee cup to drain it of its life-giving liquid. He set the empty cup down, closed the menu and pushed to his feet, dropping a few bills on the counter as he did so.

He wondered when he'd become so jaded that he couldn't recognize a naive girl when he met one. Not that he expected to see her again. He had a week to catch up on his brothers' lives, then there was the wedding to get through. After that, he was due to meet Dom to finish up the case that had kept them all occupied far longer than anyone had expected, thanks to the mess made by a love-sick fool on their very own team. He didn't have time to dwell on Hope's innocent appeal. "Thanks for the java." He headed to the open door. "It was just what I needed."

"You're quite welcome."

He looked back at her painfully polite words. Her ivory cheeks were nearly as pink as the uniform-dress thing she wore. Behind her gold-rimmed glasses, her eyes were wide and so violet they looked like crushed flowers from the lilac bushes that bloomed around the big house at the ranch. If it weren't for the glasses, he'd have figured that she was wearing some colored contact lenses to achieve that vivid color. But they were obviously the genuine article.

He cupped his hand tightly around the metal edge of the glass door as his attention drifted from her eyes to the rosy fullness of her lips. To the gentle, rounded curve of her jaw and the smooth line of her throat where the delicate links of a fine gold chain disappeared beneath the ill-fitting uniform. Behind him, a dog barked and he reeled in thoughts that could get him arrested in some states. Apparently, he wasn't as beat from the last week as he'd thought. "Give my regards to your grandmother."

"I will." Her tongue peeped out, leaving a distracting glisten on her lower lip. "It was nice meeting you."

"You too. Hope."

The color in her cheeks flared again, but she smiled. And he found himself smiling back.

Then he heard his name being called, and turned to see his oldest brother, Sawyer, standing on the street a few yards down. He absently waved at his brother, still looking back inside the café. Feeling disappointed that Hope had turned away, busy with something at the counter.

"Thought you were coming in next week."

Realizing that he was wondering how far her toffee-brown hair would reach down her back if it weren't twisted into that thick, roping braid, Tris deliberately stepped away from the doorway toward Sawyer. Okay, so he took one more look into the café before he did. What was the harm in looking? He was a man. She was a woman.

And his brother was the law now. Tris felt a smile growing on his face as his brother walked closer. The only indication of Sawyer's new status as the sheriff was the star fastened unobtrusively to his leather belt. Except for the billed cap with a naval insignia that he wore, Sawyer looked much the same as the other men in the small rural town he now served. Well-worn blue jeans and a work shirt. "I was," Tris finally answered with a grin. "You're missing the Stetson and spurs."

Sawyer shrugged, tucking the bow of his dark sunglasses in the collar of his shirt. "Left the spurs at home. Rebecca likes 'em, you know," he said blandly.

Tris chuckled. "You wish. How is my newest doctor-in-law?"

"My wife is beautiful and totally in love with me. You can save your charms for someone else." Sawyer leaned his back against the hood of a pickup parked at the curb. "You're early."

"So you already mentioned." Tris looked back toward the café when he heard the soft jingle of a bell. All he saw, though, was the door closing. The blinds had been drawn across all the windows. "Cafe still closed during the afternoons?"

"Regular as rain."

"She didn't tell me," he murmured.

"Ruby?"

"Hope." He felt his brother's look. "What?"

Sawyer just shook his head. "What do you do? Some kind of chant that brings women running?"

"All I had was a cup of coffee." Ordinarily, Tris would have shrugged off his brother's taunt without feeling a shred of defensiveness.

"Yeah, well, I know you. Hope teaches at the elementary school. Everyone in this town looks on her as their daughter, or their sister. So keep your mitts off."

The fact that his brother seemed to think he needed the warning burned. "Thanks for the enthusiastic welcome home, bro."

Sawyer's expression didn't change. Because he was the oldest of his brothers? Because he was the sheriff? Because he was one of Squire Clay's sons and had picked up an endless amount of Clay nosiness along the way?

"Hope Leoni is," *sweet, unbearably sexy and way too innocent,* "of no interest to me," Tris said dismissively. Maybe if he said it with enough conviction, he'd make it true.

Hope's fingers crushed the paper bag holding the rolls she was taking out to the Taggarts, when she heard Tristan's voice, easily carried around the side of the café on the warm summer breeze.

She yanked open the door of her little green car and tossed the sack onto the passenger seat. "Of course you're of no interest to him," she muttered under her breath. She tossed her braid over her shoulder and pushed the key into the ignition, starting the engine with a roar. She threw it into gear and zipped around the side of the café, jouncing out onto Main.

In her rearview mirror she could see Tristan and the sheriff standing on the sidewalk talking. "Men like Tristan Clay don't have interest in women like you." *Men in general don't have interest in you.* Most of the town still considered her Ruby's "little" granddaughter.

She was a fully qualified teacher. She'd moved into her own house and, despite the barely hidden reluctance of the school board, obtained the teaching position at Weaver Elementary. She didn't know what was worse—still being thought of as a teenager, or knowing that every move she made was measured and compared against the actions of her mother who'd had the temerity to be an unwed mother, twice, or her sister, who'd had to leave high school because of her wild ways.

Maybe she should accept the next time Larry Pope asked her out. He wasn't a bad guy, after all. In fact, as the math teacher at the high school, he was respected and well liked. Maybe if she dated him a time or two, the town would see that she *wasn't* her mother or her sister.

But surely that wasn't a good enough reason to go out with a man? To prove she could date without bringing shame to her grandmother the way people seemed to believe her mother and sister had? Larry was nice, yes. He just didn't make her forget her own name when she looked into his...his...what color *were* Larry's eyes? Whatever color they were, they weren't the deep blue that Tristan Clay's were.

She made an impatient sound. Yes. The next time

Larry Pope asked her out, she'd accept. It wasn't as if there was a line of men beating down her door. It wasn't as if she was "of interest" to any male other than Larry Pope.

She hit the brakes abruptly, nearly passing the turn-off to the Taggarts' place.

Several minutes later, she pulled up in front of the partially completed log home that her friends were building. As soon as she stopped the car, the door flew open and Evan tumbled out, racing toward her. "Auntie Hope," he squealed, launching his five-year-old self with considerable enthusiasm at her legs. Hope laughed, swinging the boy in a circle, before settling him back on his feet.

He beamed, gap-toothed, back at her. There was another male who was interested in her after all, Hope thought wryly. Only he was seventeen years her junior and had a seven o'clock bedtime. "Come on, you," she said cheerfully. "Let's hustle your folks along so we can finish writing your surprise story for your mom's birthday."

And maybe, while they were at it, she could rid herself of foolish thoughts about Tristan Clay.

Chapter Two

"Here. Hang these bows from the banister there."

Tris heaved a sigh and lowered his arm that he'd laid across his eyes in a vain attempt to block out the light. "I didn't think it possible, but marriage has actually made you *more* bossy," he complained, looking up at his sister-in-law, Emily Clay. She'd been raised with Tris and his brothers after her parents had been killed when she was little. But she'd legally become a Clay when she'd married his brother, Jefferson. And now they even had two kids.

"And time has only made you more lazy. Move it." Emily nudged him with her foot. "What *are* you doing lying here in the living room on the floor, anyway?"

"Trying to sleep," he muttered. "So stop sticking your foot in my ribs."

She crouched down beside him, propping her arms on her knees. Her long brown hair slid over her shoulder, rich and dark as coffee. A thought which immediately brought to mind Hope Leoni of the pink cheeks and sweet smile. He squelched a groan and concentrated on Emily, who was speaking to him, her eyebrows raised with curiosity. "You're *trying* to sleep on the floor here in the living room because…?"

"The couch is hard as a rock." He yawned and dropped his arm over his face again. "And because Gloria's daughters are using the guest suite downstairs."

"What about your old bedroom upstairs?"

"Full up with packing boxes from Gloria's house. I'm told they were going to be gone by the time I was expected to arrive next week, but I have my doubts."

"The couch in Matthew's office?"

"Too short. And the rec room downstairs has paper doves and bells on every surface." He flexed his fingers. "Doves, for God's sake."

"It's for a wedding shower, ding dong. You *could* have stayed with Jefferson and me, you know. We've got room, even for a big dope like you."

Tris knew that. He also knew that he could have bunked with Daniel or Sawyer, too. But staying at the main house of the ranch, the "big house," as they all called it, had seemed the easiest choice. Whether or not his father ever said so, Tris knew that staying at the big house was what Squire expected. Available bed or not.

He sat up, rubbing a hand across his jaw. He needed a shave. He'd stayed at Sawyer and Rebecca's place in town until nearly midnight. "What time is it? Where's Squire?"

"Nearly two in the afternoon and he better be in town visiting the barber. Jaimie says you came in late last night, crashed out here and haven't risen since. Hung over?"

"Listen runt, I haven't had a hangover in a month of Sundays." Hell, he rarely drank more than an occasional beer anymore. His days of excess had long passed.

"Then what? You sick?"

"No," he said tolerantly. Em had been his best friend since they were bitty, so he made allowances for her that he ordinarily wouldn't have. "Sleepy. It's not a crime, last I checked."

Her pansy-brown eyes narrowed. "I also heard you've been circling Hope Leoni. She's a little—"

His "allowances" only went so far. "I don't go around jumping the town virgins," he said abruptly. "You know, if my love life was as *active* as everyone seems to think, I'd never get any work done."

"And that work is…?" Her expression softened and she smiled peaceably. "Never mind. I learned just how close-mouthed you Hollins-Winword dudes are from my darling husband. Now, about these bows."

Tris shook his head. "No wonder Jefferson finally succumbed to you. You're worse than water torture."

Her eyes danced. "That's right. And only because I love you will I warn you that the dove-decorated shower is set to begin in less than an hour. There'll be about twenty-five women trooping through this house, and I really don't want to explain your presence on the floor. Might ruin your classy image."

Tris made a face, but rolled to his feet. He rubbed Emily's head, deliberately messing up her hair the way he'd done when they were kids, and headed upstairs, grabbing his duffel from where it still sat inside the dining room doorway.

He'd take a shower, then dive into a gallon of coffee. *Then* he'd consider hanging damned bows from the banister for his sister-in-law. Maybe.

Only, when he came out of the shower, considerably more alert and marginally more presentable in clean jeans and shirt, he could hear a horde of women chattering and laughing as they arrived. If he wanted coffee, he had to go down there among all of them to get it.

Not that he was ever averse to being among women. As far as Tris was concerned, it was one of the more pleasurable places to be. But this was a *wedding* shower.

Frankly, the whole notion made his skin itch.

He waited an interminable twenty caffeine-deprived minutes before he went downstairs to the now-empty kitchen, and the coffee pot that he prayed would be hot and full, as usual.

It was, and he stood there at the counter, singeing his tongue as he downed two fast cups, frowning at the playpen that sat on the floor on the other side of the table next to the wall. For now, it was empty of babies even though the family was full of them these days. Emily, Jaimie and Maggie had all had a baby within the last six months.

He shuddered, poured a third cup of coffee and carried it with him through the mudroom and outside.

The sun was bright. Warm. The air filled with the rich scent of mown grass. Across the gravel road separating the big house from the outbuildings and corrals, horses grazed and Matthew's retriever chased a butterfly.

He squinted and poured more coffee down his throat. He was glad his brothers were busy with the hundred chores required every day to keep the place running. It meant that they were thoroughly busy, and Tris could find another place to grab a few more z's, undisturbed.

He slowly wandered around the side of the house, past lilac bushes heavy with blossoms and immediately thought of Hope's striking eyes. He stifled an oath. He'd learned a lot about Miss Hope Leoni while he'd been hanging out at Sawyer's place the evening before. She was a paragon of virtue; an apparent candidate for sainthood.

Which meant the vivid dream he'd had about her that had awakened him around two in the morning was even more ill-advised.

He went up the front steps of the wide porch. Sighing with anticipation, he lowered himself onto the swing, propped his feet on the railing across from him, and dropped his head onto the wooden swing back.

Oh yeah. This was it. He yawned, scratched his

jaw, and closed his eyes. This was the kind of break he needed. No noise, no tourists, no unexpected disasters at work. No wedding nonsense.

No damned dreams about innocent school teachers with violet eyes.

"Shhh."

"Is he sleeping or is he dead?"

"His feet are *big*. They're even bigger than Daddy's, and I can put *both* my feet in his boot!"

"Girls, quiet down. You'll wake him."

"Do we have to share our juice with him? I don't think we have enough for him. My mommy says Unca Twistin has a 'normous appa...appa—"

"Appetite."

"Yeah. That."

"I'm sure he doesn't want any juice. Come on now, we're going to have our picnic over there by those three trees. Remember?"

"But what if he *does* want some?"

"If he does, we'll share with him. It would be impolite not to."

"But—"

"Sshh. Over to the trees before we wake him."

Tris gritted his teeth, staring at the group of little girls, and one big girl through slitted eyes. "Too late."

The little girls, his nieces, jumped and scattered as if he'd grown three heads. The big girl, however, nudged up her gold-rimmed glasses and blinked with dismay. "I'm sorry. I didn't expect you to be out here sleeping, or I'd have talked the girls into having our picnic elsewhere."

His coffee was cold. He finished it off, anyway, then pulled his feet off the rail and sat forward. "I didn't expect to see you here, either."

Hope moistened her lips. "Well. Sorry to have wakened you." She hefted her caramel-colored wicker basket more firmly between her arms.

He was wakened all right. "What are you doing here?"

"Having a picnic with the girls."

"No, I mean why are you with the kids and not at Gloria's shower?"

"I'm watching the children. Well, these guys, anyway. The babies are with their moms."

"Why are you doing this?"

"Because I was asked to." She shook her head as if the answer was obvious.

"How old are you, Hope?"

She looked over her shoulder at the children who were crossing the gravel drive toward the grass on the other side. "Nearly twenty-three. Sarah, honey, wait until you get to the grass before you take off your shoes," she called.

Nearly twenty-three. Hell. How many women did he know who claimed to be nearly any age but one at least a decade younger than was true? And now he had the hots for the babysitter. *Had* he ever had a babysitter? He tried to remember. Couldn't. Not enough coffee in him yet.

"I'll watch the girls," he said abruptly. They were sweet little things, and he liked playing the uncle. It was as close a relationship to kids as he intended to get. "You go join the women," he finished telling Hope.

"I'm hardly dressed for a wedding shower."

Which only brought his attention to the golden length of calf she displayed below the fringe of her knee-length, cut-off blue jeans. He'd have remembered if he'd ever had a babysitter with legs like that.

"Go on back and go to sleep," she was saying, and he dragged his attention upward, over denim worn thin and...did she have to wear such a baggy T-shirt? The obnoxious lime-green cotton hung around her hips, frustratingly loose and boxy. *The babysitter,* for cryin' out loud!

"But, um, thank you for the offer anyway." She smiled shyly and turned to follow the children.

He gave himself a mental shake. Sleep. That's what he needed. Then he wouldn't feel so...hell, what did he feel? Off balance?

He yawned again, watching the graceful sway of her long braid as she walked away, joining the children.

J.D. and Angeline belonged to Daniel and Maggie. Leandra was Jefferson and Emily's. And Sarah, the youngest, was Matthew and Jaimie's. They all circled around Hope as she joined them and set them to work, spreading a bright yellow sheet.

He smiled faintly, though, when the girls didn't dig into the feast—they were too far away for him to see exactly what it was. But he recognized what the little girls preferred over the food when dozens and dozens of small, opalescent bubbles started floating over their heads, bobbing, swaying, popping.

Even Hope was blowing bubbles. He rested his

arms on the rail and watched her purse her lips, blow
and set a wiggling, wobbling train of soap bubbles
into the afternoon breeze. She certainly wasn't shy
when she dealt with the children.

He narrowed his eyes and pictured her face should
he follow them. She'd probably stare at his feet or
his left ear, and she'd turn white, then red. And all
the while he'd be thinking he'd like to see her when
she wasn't wearing that baggy T-shirt that hid her
curves from prying eyes like his.

God. He sat back in his chair and pressed the
heels of his palms against his eye sockets. He was
every bit the lech that his family seemed to think he
was.

But even that knowledge didn't take him back
inside the house. No, he propped his feet back on
the rail and continued watching Hope. If the way
she kept sneaking looks back toward the house now
and again was any indication, she was doing some
of her own watching, too.

"I thought I saw you driving a green car yesterday."

Hope whirled around at the voice behind her. She
was waiting in the kitchen of the ranch house for
her ride back to Weaver. By the time she'd shep-
herded the girls back to the big house, the shower
guests had departed. That's what she got for letting
the little ones talk her into walking all over crea-
tion—and the Double-C had plenty of interesting
places to explore.

Now, Tristan was looking at her with his incredible eyes, waiting for an answer and she wished,

cowardly, that the children were still with her instead of their parents.

"Yes, I have a car," she admitted. "But I rode out here with Dr. Rebecca."

"And where is Dr. Rebecca now?"

Hope curled her fingers over the back of one of the chairs at the enormous oval table that sat in the center of the big kitchen. "She was called away on a house call."

"So you need a ride home, then."

"Jaimie is going to drive me."

"Jaimie drives like a bat out of hell. I'll take you."

Hope's stomach jolted. He was far more harmless when he was sleeping. When he was wide awake and watching her from beneath heavy lids, he was totally devastating. Totally daunting. Why would he offer to drive her? It wasn't as if she was "of interest" to him. "Jaimie has already offered."

"You really prefer to ride with the speed demon?"

Hope swallowed. "I—"

"Stop tormenting our guest," Jaimie chided sailing into the kitchen and poking her brother-in-law in the back. "And I haven't gotten a speeding ticket in months."

"That's 'cause your daughter calls the sheriff *uncle*," Tris countered dryly. "I want to go by and see Drew Taggart anyway. There's no point in all of us driving into town."

Hope folded her hands together and wished she'd driven herself. But Jaimie looked her way, eyebrows lifting. And Hope forced herself to shrug as if it didn't matter in the least how she got back home.

So she found herself sitting beside him in the close confines of his rental car as he drove along the gravel drive toward the main gate of his family's ranch. With each vibrating turn of the tires, Hope felt herself growing more uncomfortable. She was wrinkled and sweaty and her unmanageable hair was working loose from its ordinarily tidy braid. He, on the other hand, made his faded jeans seem like a sinful sight; and she swore she could still smell the freshness of his shower on that golden skin.

She stared out the window and banished thoughts of Tristan and showers.

He hadn't turned on the radio. It was just the two of them and the sound of the tires. And Hope felt more tongue-tied than she'd ever felt in her life.

Considering she'd spent most of her life tongue-tied, that was quite a feat.

"Would you like to grab some dinner?"

She turned and looked at him, her lips parting soundlessly.

"Is that a yes or a no?"

He wasn't asking her for dinner. He couldn't be. Why *would* he? He was only driving her home because he'd been going by to see Drew anyway. "I don't…ah, no. Thank you."

"Why?"

She stared fixedly out at the passing landscape. "Excuse me?"

"Why won't you have dinner with me? We could grab a steak at Colbys."

"Why?" She glanced at him long enough to see the corner of his lips deepen.

"That was my question."

She folded her arms. She didn't like being teased. "I have plans."

"Big date?"

Her cheeks burned. "Is that so hard to believe?"

He smiled faintly. "Not at all."

It ought to be, she thought silently. The last time Hope had been on a date, she'd still been in college. And she may have entertained thoughts of agreeing if Larry Pope asked her out again, but that occasion hadn't actually occurred. "I have to wash my hair."

He raised his eyebrows. "In other words, you're not interested."

"No," she blurted. "I mean, I...I do have to wash my hair. Church is tomorrow."

His smile widened wryly. "Naturally. It's been a while since I've been thrown over for shampoo and conditioner."

Hope closed her eyes and wished for the drive to be over.

When they finally entered the official outskirts of town, Hope started to tell him where she lived, but without any prompting at all, he drove straight to the cozy little house she rented across the street from the park and the high school.

"Sawyer told me," he said, as he parked in her narrow driveway.

Hope shoved open the car door, just glad to be home and certainly not willing to wonder why Tristan and his brother had even discussed the whereabouts of her home, but Tristan caught her arm before she could escape. Her throat tightened and she looked over her shoulder at him. "I appreciate the ride."

Because he couldn't help himself, Tris looked into her eyes.

They were the purest violet he'd ever seen, so dark he could barely distinguish the pupil from the iris. And the whites were whiter than any white that had ever existed. Annoyance and amazement churned inside him. A few days' dalliance with this girl-woman was out of the question. He knew it. So why did he ask her for dinner? And why did it bug him to his core that she'd refused? "Eyes as clear as yours just don't exist," he murmured.

Her eyebrows popped up. "Excuse me?"

"I'll bet you've never had a hangover. Never crossed the street against the light. Never stayed up later than you should."

Color suffused her cheeks. "I *have* been to college."

"Sweet pea, compared to the places I've been, that doesn't mean diddly." His voice lowered. "Never had an impure thought."

Her eyes flickered and she hurriedly climbed from the car. Her thick braid bounced in counterpoint to her hasty steps as she walked away from him.

Let her go.

He swallowed an oath along with the common sense that told him to leave well enough alone. He caught up to her as she pushed open the front door of her little white house. The place was as neat and tidy as she was, with precise rows of summer flowers in the beds lining the sidewalk. He closed his hand around her elbow, pulling her up short before she could shut the door in his face.

"Wait."

Her chin tilted, but her eyes wouldn't meet his.

"Why? So you can make fun of me some more?"

"I wasn't."

She didn't answer. The way her soft lips twisted was answer enough.

He frowned. The bones in her elbow felt fragile. He slid his hand up her arm, curving around the taut flesh, feeling the flex of healthy muscle. Of skin that was smooth as satin against his fingertips. "I have to go back to Paris after the wedding."

She blinked. Hesitated. "Congratulations."

"It's business," he dismissed. "I travel a lot." Too much, he thought vaguely. "I'm not going to be here for long. Why won't you have dinner with me? I'm harmless."

Hope's lips parted and she looked down at his fingers circling her arm. Harmless? Hardly. This man was built for harm. Harm of the heart. "I don't—"

"Want steak. That's okay. Pizza, then."

"Why are you doing this?"

"Man's gotta eat." He didn't smile. "Woman's gotta eat, too. What's your favorite food?"

She frowned. "Chinese. I don't—"

"We'd have to drive a ways to get that."

His thumb swirled against her arm. She looked up at him. "Tristan—"

"Maybe I like the way you say my name."

Her throat knotted. Shivers crept down her spine and broke out on her arm where he would surely feel them. He probably thought she was insane standing there shivering in the warm early evening. "I'm a mess from this afternoon," she whispered thoughtlessly.

Tris looked at her lips. They were perfectly sculpted, impossibly soft-looking. Everything about her was soft. Her voice, her eyes, her skin. "Take a shower," he murmured. "I'll wash your back." He wasn't entirely joking, he realized. But he grinned, trying to look harmless despite his thoughts which were miles away from harmless.

"Colbys," she said abruptly, tugging her arm out of his grasp. "It'll be a zoo at the pizza place. I'll meet you there in a half hour." Then she hastily stepped into the house and shut the door right in his face.

Tris stared at the closed door. "I'll be damned," he murmured. Then he laughed softly, feeling better than he had in weeks, and turned around on her postage-stamp-sized porch. Across the street, the park stretched out, vibrantly green. The high school looked the same as always. And down the street and around the corner was the old elementary school. Where, among her students, shy Hope would laugh and smile and teach.

Too bad he'd be long gone from Weaver by then. He'd have enjoyed seeing Hope in her element.

He'd just have to figure a way in the next few days to get her to look him in the eye with those incredible eyes of hers. To scale that mile-high shyness of hers so that when he kissed her—he wasn't sure when he'd decided it was something he *was* going to do—she wouldn't run away.

She'd kiss him back.

The kiss was definitely something he looked forward to. Probably more than was good for either of them. But it would be *just* a kiss. What would be the harm in that?

Chapter Three

"Would you like wine?"

Beneath the cover of the varnished wood table top, Hope's fingers twisted together. "No, thank you." She didn't drink. Hadn't ever had a hangover, just as he'd said earlier.

She watched Tristan, who sat across from her in the dimly lit booth. He showed no surprise that she'd declined the drink. Of course he wasn't surprised.

The only surprise was that she was sitting here in Colbys, which served food but which everyone still considered a bar, with Tristan Clay. Hope had been to Colbys dozens of times in her lifetime. Never once had the booths seemed so cramped. So shadowy. So intimate.

Tristan was reading the menu he held open between his hands. His fingers idly tapped the corner of the padded vinyl folder and Hope closed her eyes for a moment before focusing on her own menu. She shifted and her knee bumped something solid and immovable beneath the table. It wasn't the table. It was him. She quickly angled her knees away from his and stared blindly at the menu. What was she doing here?

"Decided yet?"

She looked up as Tristan closed his menu and sat back in the booth. "Excuse me?"

His eyebrow peaked. "Do you know what you want to order?"

She nodded and shut her menu with a snap. She didn't. But she wasn't going to sit there like an idiot staring at words that her distracted mind wouldn't read. She chewed at the inside of her lip. Rearranged her flatware and drained her water glass.

He closed the menu and set it to the side of the table, folding his arms over the surface of the table. He seemed suddenly to loom over her from his side, but the portion of her brain that still functioned knew it only seemed that way because he was so tall and his shoulders so wide that he easily filled more than half of the bench on his side of the booth.

A fact that did nothing to prevent her from pressing her spine more firmly against the seat behind her. Or from reaching for the chain at her throat and running an inch of it back and forth between her thumb and forefinger.

His gaze was unwavering, but she was certain that he wanted to smile. She felt her entire body go hot with embarrassment. She dropped her hand to her lap.

She wished that Newt Rasmusson, the owner of the place, would hurry up and take their orders—despite the fact that she didn't know what she wanted—so at least that interruption would draw Tristan's focus away from her.

"Want to dance?"

The jangle that shot through her was *not* a leaping, internal YES! It simply wasn't. "No one is dancing," she pointed out faintly. Her fingers sought the chain necklace once again.

"So?"

"There's no music."

He glanced down at the table. "If you don't want to, Hope, just say so."

"I didn't mean—"

His lashes lifted and she saw, then, the amusement there. Her lips tightened and she angled her chin up a notch. She gathered up her purse and started to slide from the bench. No matter how breathless she became just from looking at him, she wasn't going to sit there and be his evening's entertainment. He'd already found more than enough about her to tease. "This was a bad idea," she said aloud. Her voice shook, but at least she'd spoken up. "Thank you for the ride back to town earlier."

Without looking his way, she hurried toward the entrance, bumping her hip against an empty table as she went. She tugged the strap of her shoulder bag higher on her shoulder and blinked rapidly. She pushed through the door, nearly crying with relief when she made it out onto the street without embarrassing herself even more than she already had.

Though how that would be possible, she couldn't

be sure. "Idiot," she muttered under her breath. She drew in a long breath and started down the street in the direction of her house. It wouldn't take but a few minutes to walk. No longer than it would have taken her to walk *to* Colbys in the first place if Tristan hadn't been sitting on her little porch when she came out, ready to drive them despite her assertion that she'd meet him there.

"I guess you weren't hungry, after all."

She whirled, her braid flying. Her lips parted, but no words came. And that frustrated her even more. She shook her head and turned again, but Tristan caught her arm. His fingers circled her elbow; not tightly, but with enough insistence that she stopped again. Or maybe it was the tingling heat spreading out from her elbow along the rest of her arm. Her voice broke free. "Tristan, don't."

He stepped in front of her, oblivious to the two cars that slowly drove down the main street. His shoulders blocked the red glow of the setting sun. "Am I so objectionable that you couldn't stand one more minute of my company?"

Her fingers curled around her purse strap. "I don't like being laughed at."

"Nobody does, sweet pea." He let go of her elbow and brushed his thumb over her white knuckles. "The only one I was laughing at was myself," he said quietly. "Please. Come back in and have dinner with me. I won't ask you to dance if you don't want me to, but I can't promise not to try talking you into a game of pool."

She didn't want to be charmed by him, knowing how easily he could accomplish it. *Was* accomplishing it. "What about Drew Taggart?" she asked, faintly desperate.

"What about him?"

"You wanted to look him up."

"I'll catch up to him later. There's plenty of time."

"But you told Jaimie—"

"You'd have been racing down the road with her at the wheel if I'd just told you, flat out, what my reasons were for offering you that ride."

He didn't wear boots like most of the men in Weaver did. Not cowboy boots nor heavy work boots. He wore scuffed athletic shoes. She stared at them so fiercely that she spotted the tiny place at the toe of one shoe where the leather had begun to wear through. "And what were they? These reasons that would terrify me so?"

"I'll tell you, but you have to look at me first."

Her cheeks heated. She darted a look into his face.

He tsked, and she jumped when he tucked his knuckles under her chin and lifted it. Nervousness knotted in her chest. "I'm looking at you."

"At my chin," he murmured. He touched the nose piece of her glasses, inching them back up her nose, and surprise lifted her gaze to his for the briefest of moments.

But it was long enough for her to be caught, unable to pull her gaze from his. They were so blue, his eyes. As if a midnight sky had been trapped in his irises. She suddenly felt warm, her senses trapped in some odd time warp where everything moved slowly. She didn't even blink when he took a step closer, wrapping his other hand around her free elbow. Her hands brushed his hips and she pulled them back, clasping them together against her chest.

"That's why," he murmured.

His thumb was doing that maddening swirl-thing on her elbow. "I d-don't know."

"Yes, you do, Hope."

"No—"

"Don't be afraid of me."

"I'm...not." She swallowed. "I'm not."

"You're trembling."

"I—"

"So am I."

"Stop this. You're making fun. You told your brother you weren't interested in me. I overheard you."

"I'm interested all right," he murmured.

She shook her head abruptly. Her protest was as ineffectual as her mushy resistance when he drew his fingertips along her forearms, capturing her hands. He pressed her palms to his chest. And, oh God, she felt his heart. Thundering through the fine cotton of his Hawaiian print shirt as fiercely as her own heart pounded.

"You're doing that to me, sweet pea." His soft words stirred the loose tendrils of hair at her temples. "You have been since the coffee in the café. Maybe I didn't see that it was any of my brother's business, but that doesn't mean it's not so."

"No."

"Yes. That's why I was laughing at myself. I come home expecting nothing but enduring my old man's long-awaited wedding, and find myself meeting a teacher whose violet eyes could make me forget my own name.''

She felt his breath on her forehead, then closed her eyes and held back a gasp when his warm lips touched her temple. Her fingers curled against his chest, grabbing loose fabric. ''We're standing on Main Street.''

His jaw grazed hers, then he lifted his head, untangling her fingers from his shirt front. ''If it bothers you, come back inside with me and have dinner.''

''You said you were harmless. I knew you were lying.'' She frowned as another car pulled along the street and turned into the parking lot behind her. ''What do you want with me?''

He laughed abruptly. ''Are you kidding?''

''You used to date Serena Stevenson.'' She pushed out the words.

His eyes narrowed. ''So? It was a long time ago.''

''She's a famous model!''

''Who is now happily married with two kids, neither of whom are mine, thank the good Lord. What's your point?''

''My face has never stopped traffic.''

''That's because you've probably always been in Weaver where there *is* no traffic.'' He let go of her hands and took a step back. The cool fingers of the evening air slipped between them and Hope shivered.

She hadn't always been in Weaver and she knew good and well that guys who looked this good didn't seek out Hope Leoni because of her physical attri-

butes. Only she couldn't for the life of her think
what Tristan hoped to gain by pursuing this.

Which brought her squarely back to the assumption that he was merely amusing himself. His heart
may have seemed to thunder in tempo with hers. But
in all likelihood it had just been her muddled senses.
Which were quickly clearing again, thank goodness.

"I think you should go see Drew," Hope suggested. "He and Jolie are building a place a few
minutes outside of town. I watch their little boy
on—"

"Good evening, Hope. Tristan. I'd heard you
were back. For the wedding, I presume?"

Hope looked desperately at the sidewalk underneath her feet, wishing it would open up and swallow her. But it stayed dismayingly solid. She
wrapped her hands once more around her purse strap
and turned around to face Bennett Ludlow, the head
of the school board. The man had left his parked car
and stood on the sidewalk behind them.

"Yes," Tristan said abruptly, barely sparing the
other man a glance. "I'll drive you home, Hope."

His hand touched the small of her back, igniting
a warm, melting glow.

"You mean you two were here together?" Bennett's white teeth smiled, but Hope knew the older
man too well not to see the wheels clicking inside
his brain. He was undoubtedly wondering the same
thing Hope was. Why?

"Not really," Hope answered quickly. "And I
think I'll walk home. It's such a lovely evening."
She didn't dare look up into Tristan's face again.
Every time she looked into his eyes, her sensible

brain simply ground to a halt. And the last thing she needed was to look as muddled as she felt with Bennett there to witness it.

She wondered if she'd ever be able to forget that she'd been hired last year as a last resort because no other more qualified teacher had been available.

She smiled vaguely at both men and hurried across the street.

"She's not your usual type, is she, old boy?"

Irritation bubbled beneath Tristan's calm as he watched Hope reach the sidewalk on the other side of the street. He looked at Bennett. The attorney was as much a part of Weaver and the surrounding community as the Clays. More so than Tris, in fact. Because Bennett had returned to Weaver after college and Tris had not. Not that they'd ever had a lot to do with each other since Bennett was more Sawyer's age than Tristan's. "Should I be flattered you think you know my 'type,' Bennett?" he asked lazily. "Didn't think you cared."

Bennett's face tightened. "Before they moved away from Weaver, Gerri and Justine Leoni always were after a nice meal ticket, but I'd hoped that Hope had more sense than her mother and—"

"Go on inside and enjoy a steak," Tris smoothly interrupted. "Double-C beef, you know," he added as he started after Hope. "Can't be beat."

Certainly not by the failing spread that Bennett's parents had once run, long ago. They'd sold out to the Double-C more than twenty years earlier. As far as Tris knew, Bennett had hated the Clays ever since. And though Tris didn't give two hoots and a holler what Bennett thought or said about them, having that cap-toothed blowhard look down his nose at the Leonis—Hope in particular—was more than Tris could stand.

Hope. She was running away from him like the dogs of hell were at her heels. He wasn't so conceited that he believed all women found him irresistible. But he was wholly aware that Hope felt the same drugging attraction that he did, whether she admitted it or not.

He wanted her. Badly.

Seducing virgins was the one thing over which Tris drew the line. But a kiss was not a seduction.

He wanted to kiss her, and he knew she wanted it, too. But what had him going after her now was not the irrefutable urge to taste her lips, but the hurt in her eyes she hadn't been able to hide.

He quickened his step and caught up with her just as she was turning the corner toward her house. The hem of her white and purple flowered dress flared out behind her.

"Hold up there, sweet pea."

She looked over her shoulder once, but kept walking.

He swore silently and lengthened his stride, stepping in her path. She sidestepped, but he wasn't dancing. He closed his hands over her shoulder and she stopped cold. His gut tightened even more at the silvery trail wending its way down her sculpted cheekbones. "I'm sorry."

Her chin angled. "Don't flatter yourself."

He thumbed away a tear drop. "What are they for?"

"My shoes are pinching my feet," she said flatly. Red color flooded her cheeks.

Little liar. He hoped she never played poker. That milky pale skin of hers would give her away every time. He looked down at the confection of narrow straps and tiny heels gracing her feet. They were shamelessly feminine, sexy shoes and not at all what he'd expect her to wear with that ill-fitting sack of a dress. He crouched down, circling her ankle with his palm.

"What are you doing?" She pressed her palm to his shoulder, but he still managed to lift her foot and slide off the supposedly offending shoe. That was the nice thing about the element of surprise. He confiscated the other shoe, too, then swept her up into his arms.

She gasped, her eyes as wide as a child's. "What are you doing?"

"It's my fault your feet are hurting," he explained reasonably, looking down into her shocked face. "I said I'd give you a lift."

"A ride," she sputtered faintly.

He shrugged and turned up her street. He didn't dare think about how comfortable she felt in his arms, even squirming and kicking her legs the way she was. "What's the difference?"

"Well, one is in a car," she hissed. "Put me down before someone sees us—oh, fabulous."

"Hope? Is everything all right here?"

Hope smiled back at the openly curious question issued from a very pregnant woman who was watering a row of flowers in her yard. Tris noticed, however, that Hope's smile was frantic around the edges. "How are you feeling, Brenda? Your baby should be here any day now, right?"

"Next week," the other woman said. Her eyes were suspicious. "You sure you're okay?"

"She's fine," Tris said easily. "Stepped on a stone." He kept right on walking.

Even though he held Hope squarely in his arms, he could feel her straining as if to reduce the contact between their bodies. "Brenda Wyatt is one of the biggest gossips in the county," she muttered. "She's probably already heading to her phone to spread the word."

Tris cut across the corner of Hope's green lawn and carried her up the steps. A glance over his shoulder told him that Hope was probably right. Brenda-the-Blab was gone, and the screen door at the front of her house was swinging in the faint breeze because it hadn't caught the latch. "People in this town have always gossiped."

"Yes," Hope agreed tightly. "And half the time it's been about one of the infamous Leoni women, whether it was my mother or my sister." She leaned over and pushed open her front door. "Put me down."

Tris turned sideways and carried her into her living room. The furnishings were as uncomplicated as he'd expected: long lines and soft pillows, all in soft colors that reminded him of deliciously cool ice cream cones. "The only gossip I ever heard about your mother or your sister was that they were beautiful." He settled her on the couch where an enormous orange cat slept in a ball. "There. You're down."

"They were beautiful. Justine *is* beautiful. She's the kind of woman you should take out for steak."

"How is Justine, anyway? I haven't seen her in years." What he remembered about Justine was that she'd been, well, *popular* was the polite term. Before Justine and her mother had left town, she'd been ahead of him in school several years, but that hadn't meant that Tris hadn't appreciated her sultry appeal.

"She's in Washington State, now."

"Married?"

"Three times. And the people of this town thought she'd never find a husband with her wild, wicked ways," Hope quipped, but the sarcastic tone failed and she just sounded defensive. "Of course, she's divorcing number three, so maybe they had a point."

Tris sat on the couch, too, and Hope popped up like a golden-crisp slice of bread flying out of a toaster. He stretch his legs comfortably. "What does she do there?"

"She works in a bank. We don't talk much. She's older than you are." Hope had walked across the floor to look through the sheer, butter-yellow curtains that covered the big picture window overlooking her front yard. "Oh, nuts." She abruptly turned away from the window, drawing her eyebrows together.

"What's wrong?"

She shook her head and turned on the floor lamp that stood near the window. Bright light flooded the room, banishing the lengthening shadows. "Gram is driving up."

"Ruby? I haven't seen her in ages."

Hope glared at his left ear. "You don't understand at all, do you?"

Whatever was turning Hope's eyes to panic, he couldn't guess. But he understood all too well that the light was shining from behind Hope, turning her white sack dress with the tiny purple flowers into a *translucent* sack, barely veiling the long legs and hourglass curves beneath.

He ordered his heart to start beating again and inhaled slowly.

Hope's wiry grandmother walked right into the house without knocking. Her sharp eyes focused on Tris, then turned to Hope. But that one look left him feeling like he was fifteen again and had been caught making out with Suzette Lipton in the alley behind Ruby's Café. He was relieved he was sitting on the couch with the distance of the entire living room between him and Hope.

"I've had five calls at the café, young lady," Ruby said briskly, "all wanting to impart the news that my granddaughter was seen dancing down the middle of the streets with *him*. Now, I want to know what is going on!"

Tris laughed abruptly, which earned him another stern look from Ruby. He waited for Hope to explain, to defend herself, to tell her grandmother she was a grown woman who could do what she wanted if she chose, but Hope said nothing. She just stood there, looking at her grandmother with dismay emanating from every pore.

He rose and joined Hope, automatically sliding an arm around her shoulders, instinctively trying to support her. To alleviate the expression of dread darkening her eyes. "I carried her from the corner to this house," he said evenly. "Her feet were hurting her." He'd never felt strongly about explaining himself, and he didn't, even now. But he really hated the look on Hope's face. Really, really hated it.

It wasn't a comfortable realization. Because Tris never hated anything. He never hated and he never loved. He never felt that strongly one way or the other about anything. Except, maybe, his work. He was certainly a believer of the passion of the body, but he left all that passion of the heart to others.

Ruby's lips tightened. She propped her aging hands on her hips and ignored Tris. "Hope, you know how people in this town talk. Why would you do such a thing—right out in the street like that?"

"Ruby," Tris interrupted. He knew good and well that Hope's feet had been just fine. "Forget about it. There's no harm done."

Hope shook her head and turned away from her grandmother, pulling away from the arm that Tristan had tucked disturbingly around her shoulder.

"Young man," Ruby said sternly, "have you been gone from this town for so long you've forgotten how it operates? The only thing my granddaughter has is her reputation, and you come blowing into town for a few minutes of entertainment and destroy it without blinking."

"Gram!" Hope fastened her hands around her grandmother's arm and tugged her gently to the door. "Tristan was only being…kind," she said. "But he's going home, now. So you can go back to the café and tell everyone that nothing is going on."

"Hope, you're so innocent, girl. You wouldn't know a wolf in sheep's clothing if he bit you on the nose."

"Gram!" She couldn't bring herself to look at Tristan. She pulled her grandmother out the front door. "You are embarrassing me," she whispered under her breath.

"Everyone knows he lives in the fast lane—has ever since he earned all that money making fancy computer things," her grandmother said sternly. "If you're not careful he could take advantage of you just the way Justine and Gerri were."

"Tristan Clay's not the least bit interested in me that way."

"Ha!" Ruby headed down the path. "Open your eyes, girl. That man has got one thing on his mind, and sore feet is *not* it!"

Hope groaned and turned toward the door. She chewed the inside of her lip and prayed fervently that Tristan hadn't been able to hear her grandmother's outlandish worries.

She reached for the screen door and pulled it open, catching her breath when Tristan stepped right in front of her. Her fingers clenched over the door handle.

"Your grandmother is right." His face was hard, his jaw tight. And there was no trace of amusement in his heavy-lidded blue gaze. None at all. "I'm not interested in sore feet."

"Tristan, please. My grandmother is being ridiculous, I know that. I know you don't feel that way about—"

"I didn't say I didn't want to have you in my bed, Hope. I do. But no matter how much I want that, sweet pea, I don't intend to...deflower you. You're safe from me."

Chapter Four

*N*othing was going right today.

Hope's blow dryer blew a gasket or something, which meant that her hair was wet when she twisted it into a knot at the back of her head. She knew it looked even more unappealing than usual.

Of course, if she'd stuck to her guns the evening before and refused to join Tristan for dinner, Hope's hair would have been dry by the time she needed to leave for Sunday worship.

Even afterward, if she hadn't spent half the night swinging on a pendulum, she would have tended to business. But no, she'd paced around her small house, feeling astonishment. She'd rearranged her living room furniture twice, feeling disbelief. She'd yanked weeds under the moonlight in her backyard, feeling a fearful excitement.

So, her house was spotless, her furniture ended up right where it had been when she'd started and her garden was immaculate. But her hair was still a mess until morning.

Now, it was a wet, albeit clean, mess.

After the blow dryer had died, her iron—apparently sympathetic to the dryer—had shorted out, too. Her cotton dress was still presentable. Barely. Having to chase after Simon, her cat, at the last minute hadn't helped the dress. She'd been hot and frustrated by the time she finally coaxed him out from the bushes where he liked to hide.

At least she'd caught him before he'd prowled down to Brenda Wyatt's house. Brenda's husband hated cats, and Hope wasn't sure if her runaway cat would escape unscathed the next time he was caught eating Brenda's nasturtiums.

She could have driven her little car to church, but she knew there would be no parking left. And now, by the time she'd cut through the neighborhood and walked up the front steps of the church, she could hear the congregation inside already singing and she quietly slipped into the empty pew in the rear, fumbling a hymnal out of the rack. She dropped it and it thudded loudly on the floor just as the music ended.

It seemed as if half the town turned to look and see who'd made the racket. She smiled weakly and sat, feeling around with her hand for the hymnal, but it seemed to have scooted up under the pew ahead of her.

She still felt eyes watching her, and she wished

that she'd just taken the hint when the dryer died and stayed home.

Except if she hadn't shown up at church the way she had done every Sunday of every month of every year she'd lived in Weaver, she'd have ten people trooping by her house later to find out why.

After she'd come down with the flu last year when Ruby was in Washington visiting Justine, Hope's visitors had brought homemade soup and fresh flowers and crossword puzzles. She didn't think having visitors this time would be such a blessing.

The hairs on her neck prickled.

She blinked and saw Jolie staring at her pointedly from her seat on the aisle a few pews ahead. Hope frowned, shaking her head slightly.

Jolie rolled her eyes and subtly jabbed her thumb out. Hope followed the direction and stared, stunned at the sight of Tristan sitting there in church. There was no mistaking the back of his head; she'd never known anyone with hair that brilliantly golden.

She hurriedly closed her mouth and glanced at Jolie. Her friend was smiling, knowingly. Hope frowned at her, hoping Jolie could read her expression that there was no earthly reason to connect Hope with Tristan's once-in-a-blue-moon appearance at worship.

Feet shuffled and Hope dragged her attention to the service, as she stood with the rest of the congregation and read the gospel lesson. But her mind wasn't on the words. It was on the man three rows ahead of her.

When the service was winding down nearly an

hour later, Hope's attention still remained on Tristan. He hadn't turned around once to see her, and she told herself that she was relieved.

But she *was* sitting in church, and the lie tore at her. When the congregation rose once again to sing the last hymn, Hope quietly backed out of the church. If she ended up with calls from Gram and others that afternoon, it would be better than standing there visiting after the service, pretending that she didn't care two hoots that Tristan was around.

She pressed her hand to her forehead. She was a blooming fool, that's what she was. Creating ridiculous fantasies in her head.

Standing just outside the church doors, Tris watched Hope scurry away. It was definitely becoming too familiar a sight, he decided. He stopped and greeted the minister briefly, complimenting the man on his sermon even though he would've been pressed to recall the topic. He'd been too preoccupied with the young woman who'd sneaked in late to sit a few rows behind him.

"Guess no good deed goes unpunished," Sawyer said softly, mockingly, behind him.

Tris slid his sunglasses on and ignored his brother. So what if he'd come to church only in the hopes of catching Hope for a minute or two? What was more above-board than running into each other at church?

"Tristan, you're welcome to join us for dinner this afternoon," said Rebecca, repeating the invitation that he'd already declined once. "I know Ryan wants to have a chance to talk your ear off about his new computer.''

Tris tugged on the bill of Ryan's ball cap. ''Maybe later. But don't hold up the meal if I don't show.''

Ryan grinned and darted off to join his friend. Sawyer slid his arm around Rebecca's shoulders and snorted softly. ''Tris, if your rental car is seen in town anywhere this afternoon other than at our place, the remaining half of this town that hasn't been talking about your *stroll* down the street with Hope yesterday, will be. Leave her alone.''

''Sawyer, don't pick on Tristan like that.''

''He's a big boy, Bec, and you don't know what he's like with women.''

Tristan's good humor was fading fast. ''And you're so sure *you* know?'' he asked Sawyer. ''I thought you were a big believer in the innocent-'til-proven theory.''

''You haven't been innocent since you were fifteen,'' Sawyer replied dryly. ''You're gonna do what you're gonna do no matter what anyone says. Just...remember where you are.''

Rebecca was making a face. ''Sawyer's a fine one to talk.'' She stretched up and kissed Tristan's cheek. ''Maybe we'll see you later,'' she said calmly, then looked at her husband. ''Ryan is going home with Eric for a while,'' she said softly.

Despite his annoyance, Tris felt a smile tug at him as Sawyer cast his wife a long look, then smiled slowly as they walked away. He pulled the car keys out of his pocket and started toward the small, still-congested lot. Most of the cars belonged to people who'd driven in from the outlying areas, since the town itself was small enough to walk pretty well anywhere.

But, as he approached his car, he realized that a van parked crookedly in the lot was responsible for the holdup. He shook his head faintly and cut between two pickups. He wanted to go by Hope's place. Maybe he could talk her into going for a drive. They could invite Drew and his wife if it would put Hope more at ease. He knew she and Jolie were friends—

"Mr. Clay, is it true that you and Ms. Leoni are living together?"

He jerked around, gravel grinding under his boot and came face-to-face with a microphone and an enormous camera. "What the hell?" The microphone shoved closer and he pushed it away. "Get out of my face."

"You've been out of the public eye for nearly seven years now." The strident female voice wasn't discouraged. "You were on the road to success the likes of which we've only seen in Bill Gates. Has the pressure been too much for you? Are you moving back to this quaint little town where you came from? Do you still speak with Serena Stevenson? She moved recently to San Diego, and it's known that you own property there. Does she know of Ms. Leoni's pregnancy?"

Tris grabbed the hand that held the microphone and pulled, yanking the hair-sprayed, brittle reporter close enough to see the flicker of unease in her calculating eyes. But he suddenly became aware of the hush around them, of the intrusive camera not two feet away from him. He clenched his jaw and slowly released the reporter's wrist. He stared hard at her. The reporter was on a fishing expedition pure and simple, and he'd already given her more reaction than she deserved. "No comment."

Every fiber in him wanted to shove the words back down the reporter's throat, but he knew better. So he turned away and yanked open the car door, sliding behind the wheel. It had been many years since he'd had to deal with the media, but he hadn't forgotten the lessons he'd learned.

Serena had been an expert at drawing the press's attention, but then, as a high-priced fashion model, she'd wanted it.

He barely kept himself from gunning the engine. The van—he realized now it belonged to the news crew—was still blocking the driveway and he turned the wheels sharply and drove over the grass, jouncing over the curb and out onto the side street.

In his rearview mirror, he could see the cameraman jogging toward the van. He swore softly. There was no way he could go by Hope's place now. They'd likely follow him.

"Pregnant," he muttered, shaking his head. He'd have to make a few calls and find out who on earth had instigated the story. It would've had to be someone right here in Weaver spinning tales. It must be the slowest news day in history for a crew to drive down from Gillette on such a sorry excuse. His profile these days was so low it was nonexistent.

Turning the car out of town, Tris grimaced. There were some days when nothing went right.

Unfortunately, back at the big house, he had no

doubt that wedding fever continued reigning supreme. If he went back now, he'd be expected to tie bows for his sisters-in-law, or trim back the lilac bushes or, God forbid, help Matt and Dan with the chores.

Didn't seem to matter that the Double-C had year-round hands now, and had done for some time. When a Clay boy put his foot on Double-C land, he was expected to carry his weight. Tris held that belief, too. He was just sick to death of the wedding noise.

It was one thing for the women to talk about it. That was a female kind of thing. But it was another thing for his brothers to jabber about it, too. And if it wasn't Matthew, Daniel and Jefferson as well if he was around, gnawing on the chew toy of happiness that their women had brought into their lives, then it was the old man himself wanting to know when Tris was ''gonna grow up and stop playing with his damned computers.''

Which meant, in Squire-speak, ''When are you gonna move back home where you belong?''

Tris was glad his cantankerous father was finally getting married to his sweetheart. Gloria Day was a great lady. She'd stood up to Squire right from the beginning, when she'd been his nurse after his heart attack. She had grit, and Tris admired grit.

He still wished that Gloria and Squire had eloped or something, rather than wait until summertime when Gloria's daughters were finally out of college.

If they had, Tris wouldn't be here in Wyoming now, and some damned fool reporter with nothing better to do wouldn't be speculating on his relationship with *Ms. Leoni.* He wouldn't have run into Hope at all, for that matter.

Swearing under his breath, Tris pulled a U-turn right in the middle of the highway and drove back toward Weaver. He didn't let his family dictate his actions and he'd be damned if he'd let some idiot reporter do it, either.

He drove past the now-empty church parking lot and tracked down Jolie and Drew at the pizza parlor, where Evan was tumbling around in a big cage with a bunch of colorful baseball-sized plastic balls. Jolie grinned like a fiend when he joined them, and she quickly scurried off to the phone when he casually mentioned Hope's name.

Colbys had been a bust, and church hadn't been much better. Maybe the third time would be the charm.

The restaurant was packed with the after-church crowd. Ryan and his friend were there and Tris— glad of a reason not to be caught watching the door in case Hope *did* show—joined the two boys at the video-game machines.

One of the games was new, he noticed with amusement. There was even a line of kids waiting to play it. He left Ryan and Eric and stood off to the side, watching the player—a girl of about nine or ten, probably—stare fiercely at the screen, one hand clenched around the joystick, one hand hovering over the button controls.

She needed to relax the joystick, Tris thought absently. She wouldn't make it to the third level if her reactions were slowed by that too-tight grip. And the third level was where he'd programmed the dragon to appear, set on stealing away the princess who guarded all of the magical secrets that the player needed to uncover.

Tris slowly turned his head, looking toward the doorway. Hope stood there, and from his vantage point, he could see her eyes drifting over the crowded tables until she found Jolie and Drew. She still wore the pale pink cotton dress she'd worn to church, and with her hair screwed back into that mind-numbingly tight bun, Tris couldn't decide if she was trying to look fourteen or forty.

It didn't matter. He'd known women who seemingly wouldn't draw a second glance from a gnat and women whom the world considered its most beautiful. The surface was only so much trappings, and the woman inside held the wealth of her nature—good or bad. Sometimes both.

Underneath Hope's girl-woman exterior lay what? Innocence? Certainly. Passion? Very probably.

He headed toward her, watching her head lift like a wary animal sensing danger. Her fingertips crept to the necklace that she seemed to wear as a talisman.

He caught the pained look she directed at Jolie, but he kept walking toward Hope. She looked from side to side, then firmed her shoulders and looked him straight on—in the chin.

"I'm not the wolf set to gobble down the girl," he murmured. "So I hope you won't run away from me again like you did this morning."

"I wasn't—oh, I knew I should have gone with Gram instead of coming here."

"Where's Gram?"

"Gone to a quilting show."

"Do you quilt?"

"No, but—"

"Then why go?"

"Because...because the quilts are beautiful."

"I don't doubt it. Several quilts at the ranch were made by my mother. Doesn't mean I want to go looking at a room full of 'em."

"*You* weren't invited," she said, "so I guess you don't have to worry about that."

He smiled faintly. "What worries *you?* What I told you yesterday?"

Her cheeks filled with color. "You shouldn't talk that way. Someone might overhear."

Which reminded him soundly of the reporter and cameraman. "And start to speculate on when the baby is due?"

Her eyes widened. So he told her briefly about the incident. "I wouldn't worry about it much if I were you. There's no story for them here. Nothing will come of it."

"But they asked you right out if I was...um, uh—"

"Pregnant," he supplied. "And it wasn't exactly a question. They just wanted a reaction from me on tape."

"And there were still people in the parking lot who overheard it?"

He shrugged. "The van blocked the drive so nobody could get out. I don't think you need to worry about it, sweet pea, but it is remotely possible that you might get a call for an interview or something."

"Because I'm supposed to be having your baby," she said flatly. "Well, Gram is going to love that."

He touched her shoulder, wishing she'd relax. "It's all bull, Hope. Ignore it. Or, if the reporter does happen to call, give her an earful if it makes you feel better. I'm telling you, though, they'll lose interest, if they haven't already, the second a hotter story comes along."

"Why were you—" She frowned and looked around her, lowering her voice again. "Why were you at church in the first place?"

"Why do you think?"

Her eyes glanced up at him and away. "Seeking forgiveness?"

"Seeking you."

Her throat worked. "You didn't even know I was there."

He nudged her out the entrance they were blocking, and along the sidewalk a few feet. "You arrived exactly twelve-and-a-half minutes into the service, sat in the corner of the back row and left during the first verse of the last song."

"Hymn."

"Whatever. Do your shoes pinch your feet today?"

"What?"

"Let's walk. We'll stay right here on Main, in full view of anyone who cares to look."

"But I thought you were here for pizza with the Taggarts."

"I wouldn't want to impose on them. Walk with me, Hope."

She drew her eyebrows together. "I *do not* understand you. At all."

"If we stand here for one second more," he leaned closer so only she could hear, "I'm going to kiss you regardless of who is watching through the window." He watched her slender throat work. And decided that he wasn't sure he wouldn't *anyway.* "It won't matter that there is no reporter around to spread the word—the gossip-mill of Weaver will do the job quite well on its own."

He could see the indecision in her eyes. "If I promise to keep my hands to myself?" he added blandly.

She huffed and started walking briskly down the sidewalk. Tris hid a smile and easily caught up with her.

They walked for several minutes, passing people now and again. Some familiar to him. Some not. But they all greeted Hope and eyed him closely.

Almost as closely as Hope did when she looked sideways at him. "Are you bored or something?"

Amusement lightened his mood. "Not at all. Surprising, actually, because I've never been all that big a fan of small town life."

"You never had small-town life," she pointed out. "You lived well outside of Weaver on an extremely busy ranch."

"Close enough. Went to school here in town."

She shook her head. "That's not what I meant, anyway."

She was walking so fast, they'd already come to the corner that turned onto her street. He caught her hand and crossed diagonally to the park. The play

equipment was deserted, and he tugged her along
with him to the swings. He grabbed one and jiggled
it invitingly. "Then what?"

She stared at the swing. Then at him. "You want
to *swing?*"

"*You* do."

"No, I don't."

He shook the swing again, making the curving
seat bounce and the chains clank. "When was the
last time you rode a swing? Come on. You know
you want to. I saw you playing with my nieces yesterday, remember? Any self-respecting kindergarten-through-third grade teacher who can blow the
mean bubbles you did *definitely* wants to swing in
the park on a sunny Sunday afternoon."

The smile on her face was unwilling, but it was
there. "You're a nut."

"So I've been told. Come on. Up and at 'em."

She turned and, gathering her dress around her
legs, sat on the swing. He heard her suck in her
breath when he pulled the swing way back and let
it fly. Again and again he pushed, watching her legs
stretch out before her as she soared way, way, up.
Then down and back and down and up.

Her laughter floated on the breeze. "I think
you're bored, and flirting with someone like me is
just a way of passing the time for you," she called
down to him.

He stepped to the side of her swing. She didn't
need him behind, pushing. She was flying all on her
own. "What do you mean, someone like you?"

Down and back. He saw her roll her eyes. "You
know what I mean."

He caught the chains, dragging the swing to a shuddering halt and wrapped his arms around her waist. Only because of her startled grip around the chains did she remain in the seat of the swing. Her bare calves were all but straddling his thighs. "So you want to pretend that there is no attraction between us."

Her lips parted. "I—"

"And pretend that you weren't trembling yesterday in my arms." He drew her an inch closer.

"Don't. Somebody might see."

"What? Two people in broad daylight in the park?" A few more inches closer and she was as high as his waist. It took all of his willpower not to close his hands around her thighs and pull them right around him. And maybe that was why the fire in his gut burned so unbearably bright. The fact that he wouldn't.

Because she was right. Someone might see them. And though they were respectably public, the urge to pull her softness against him—to let her know just exactly what he felt for "someone like her"— was intimately private.

He forced a smile and pushed her and the swing back so far that he could step under it. He let go and she went shooting up into the sky and the moment passed.

Leaving them just a guy and a pink-dressed woman and a swing. Which was fine with him, Tris reminded himself. Exactly the way it should be. The only thing it could be for a man who was as incapable of love as the computers he designed.

Chapter Five

Tris propped his elbows on the gleaming surface of the bar in Colbys and looked around. The bar was packed. Seemed as if half the state of Wyoming had turned out for Squire's bachelor party.

He stifled a sigh and lifted the glass, throwing back half the drink with a grimace. He started for the pool table where Daniel had been reigning, and absently pulled a cue from the rack on the wall.

Jefferson looked over his shoulder at him when he stopped behind him. "Dan's cleaned up," he said.

Tris smiled faintly. "He usually does." Dan was whistling tunelessly, pocketing the money he'd won from the other players before racking the balls again.

By the time he was finished, Sawyer and Matthew had joined them. Matthew broke, and the game was on. And still, Tris felt about as celebratory as a turtle. When it was his shot, he leaned over the table and missed a shot he should have made in his sleep.

"You're not still hung up on the mess Beaudreau made of the Pirelli deal, are you?" Jefferson spoke quietly.

Tris shoved the pool cue back in the rack on the wall. The truth was, he hadn't thought about the case awaiting him in Paris in days. And having his older brother bring up the sticky situation just proved that Jefferson wasn't as out of the loop of Hollins-Winword as he'd have everyone believe. "We got it under control before I left."

"Then you're still thinking about Hope Leoni."

He turned his back on Jefferson, ignoring his observation. But his brother, the one he'd probably been closest to, didn't let it go so easily and followed Tris over to the bar. "Give it a rest, would you?" He glared at his brother and picked up his drink. "I swear, I'd rather hear you wax poetic about marriage and kids."

Jefferson wasn't deterred, even though he smiled faintly at the poetic thing. Nobody had ever accused Jefferson of being talkative. "She's a sweet kid. The story of you pushing her on the swing in the park has made the news wire."

"Not quite," Tris countered. It was an exaggeration, but only slightly. "And I haven't seen Hope since Tuesday, so just drop it."

He'd finally managed to have a meal with Hope—at Drew and Jolie's place while she babysat for young Evan. He'd shown up with cartons of Chinese that he'd had to drive fifty miles to get. She'd looked at him like he was crazy, but she'd let him in. She'd heated the food in the microwave, and the two of them had played video games with Evan until the little boy was ready to fall asleep with the controls in his hand. Drew and Jolie had arrived soon after, and Tris had driven out to the ranch. Pure and simple.

"This big, bad wolf is staying well away from the town virgin." Even if he had been driven from his own bed in the middle of the night after that "pure and simple" evening because he couldn't get the woman out of his head.

Jefferson leaned his elbows on the bar. "It's hard to have the hots for an innocent young woman," he murmured. "No pun intended."

"What is hard," Tris said between his teeth, "is having everyone in this damned town thinking they know some dirty secret about Hope and me. *Nothing* has happened between us." If you didn't count the thoughts he'd had, that was. "Christ, Jefferson, even you warned me to behave around her. Like I couldn't figure that out for myself."

"Well, kid, you haven't exactly been known for your restraint. Em says you had women coming and going when she lived at your place. Must've been your pretty face."

"Em talks too much," Tris muttered, lifting his drink. If he hadn't earned a bloody fortune designing computer programs when he'd been younger than Hope, he would never have been in the position of having women throwing themselves at him at every turn. All he'd wanted back then was to do his own thing, coming up with stronger, more-powerful, less-expensive software. His fledgling company had taken off like a bullet, bringing him money and women. Then more money and more women. Then, on a whim as much as anything—mostly because he'd needed something challenging to keep his mind off the callous way he'd hurt one woman in particular—he'd hacked into one-too-many systems and found himself in a whole other kettle of fish.

He couldn't believe after all these years that his name was once again being stuck in an ongoing news story—that of the former tycoon who was corrupting the schoolmarm. The reporter had even gotten hold of Tristan's old school records, as if the randy behavior of the adolescent was being relived by the grown man.

"You should've known better than to try to meet her at church," Jefferson murmured.

Tris turned and gestured at Newt for another whiskey. "I went to church because I wanted to hear a good sermon."

Jefferson snorted. "Blatant lies don't get you into heaven, kid. You even chased her around town, ending up in the park."

"We weren't doing anything wrong." The film crew had caught only a hazy shot of Tris pushing Hope on the swing. "I can't help it if that crazy reporter is pushing us as the next great... Hell, I don't even know what they're pushing."

"They're speculating on whether the good girl can tame the bad boy, or whether the bad boy is ruining the good girl. Same thing everyone in town is wondering."

"It's none of their damned business," Tris said

irritably. The reporter hadn't stopped after the park swing incident, and had caught Hope just yesterday. "If Hope had only locked herself in at the café instead of trying to beat them home, the only thing the cameraman would have been able to film would have been the exterior of the café." Instead, footage of Hope—head bowed against the questions being pelted at her by the reporter as she ran away down the street in her pink waitress uniform—had been seen in one form or another on everything from the local news to a syndicated gossip show.

"You're accustomed to dealing with the press— at least you used to be. Hope isn't. Where is she, anyway?"

Tris looked down at his drink. "Home, I think." He knew she wasn't at Ruby's because Jolie had told him so when he'd called to talk to Drew.

Thanks to posting some key hands at the gates of the Double-C, the reporter and her crew hadn't been able to get near the ranch. And Colbys was locked up tighter than a drum tonight against any unknown faces. But Hope? What the hell had he done to protect Hope?

Not one damned thing.

Tris hated it all. He hated feeling so strongly about anything, and he hated the fact that he hadn't been able to help Hope in the slightest. Or perhaps it was just his conscience nagging him because he'd brought all this down on her head. Because he had the "hots," to use his brother's ironic word.

Jefferson ought to know, since he'd had it bad for Emily for years before he'd ever made a move. Because Em was younger. Innocent.

There was a severe difference, though, Tris knew. He tossed back another shot of whiskey and absently noticed that the lights around the room were starting to blur. Thank goodness the women were at their own party—a nonalcoholic one—and would pick up the men to go home later.

He frowned. Difference. Right. The difference between Jefferson and Tris was the fact that Jefferson had loved Emily all along. Tris, though, didn't love any woman. He might enjoy sleeping with them, and he was damn sure he'd really enjoy spreading Hope's toffee-colored hair over a pillowcase and tracing the trail of her necklace down to her breasts. But that was sex. Not love. He didn't love her. He couldn't love her.

It wasn't in him to love anyone. He'd designed impenetrable computer systems; as impenetrable as one could be anyway. He knew computers inside and out. Hell, he had a computer chip for a heart. Isn't that what Serena had accused him of years ago?

She'd been right.

Tris had teased Hope, flirted with her because he liked seeing that rosy blush rise in her cheeks, and he'd wanted to taste her lips. Now she had Wyoming's own version of paparazzi hounding her.

He had to see her, he thought fuzzily. He had to fix it. He looked over at Jefferson—blinked when he realized his brother wasn't even sitting on the bar stool anymore, but had returned to the pool game. Tris focused on the exit he could see through the kitchen and headed for it.

* * *

Hope checked both doors to make sure they were locked, then all the windows to be certain the shades and curtains were drawn, before she let herself relax enough to take a quick shower. She'd never felt so unnerved in her life. In less than a week, her life had become a circus sideshow. All because of Tristan Clay.

If only she could make herself be angry with him. Lastingly angry, that was. The kind that would stick. Rather than the kind that dissipated the moment she looked at his ridiculously handsome face. It didn't even have to be in person. All she had to do was see his image on the television screen in some old story the media had dug up from years ago and her anger drained away. She was left feeling lightheaded and limp and remembering the moments on the swing in the park; remembering the statement he'd made even before that.

Tristan Clay wanted boring Hope Leoni.

It boggled the mind. It agitated her tummy. It left her warm and aching and altogether edgy and even a soothing shower failed to alleviate any of it.

She was just combing out her wet hair when she heard the thump at the rear of her house. Her heart raced. If it was that reporter, she was going to call the sheriff whether he was still at his father's bachelor party, or not. She set down her comb and turned the light off in her bedroom, then crept down the hallway.

Another thump made her gasp aloud.

She sidled into the kitchen. The back door was locked. She'd checked it twice. But as she watched, the knob started turning. The door creaked, the door opened, she heard a soft oath and a large, dark shape loomed in the doorway.

Hope screeched and reacted. She grabbed the cordless phone off the wall and launched it directly at the body and darted down the hall toward the front door, intent only on getting out of the house as rapidly as possible.

She only made it as far as the couch in the living room when an iron arm clamped around her waist, halting her flight. She kicked out, but her feet were bare. She'd have kneed him—for it was a *he* she was certain—only he had her from behind. She used her elbow sharply, earning a muffled grunt. And then she lowered her head, sinking her teeth into the back of the pig's hand—

"Dammittohell, Hope!"

He let her loose and she tumbled over the arm of the couch, falling inelegantly to the floor. Then suddenly, the light was on and Tristan was staring at her from across the room, his hand on the floor lamp near the front window.

Hope adjusted her glasses and stared. "What on earth are you doing?" She pressed her hand to her heart, willing it to stop thundering.

"Getting my hand bit off," he growled. "Couldn't you hear me calling your name?"

She drew the folds of her cotton robe closer together and scrambled up from the floor onto the couch. Her heart still felt ready to explode right out of her chest. "All I heard was a few thumps, and then you were breaking into my kitchen." She drew in a hard breath. "Are you *insane?*"

"I didn't break in," he said, rather more clearly

than necessary. "I—well, mebbe I picked the lock," he admitted. "I came to rescue you." He smiled.

"Rescue me from what?"

"The pap-razzi." He frowned, looking around the living room.

"I *thought* you were that hideous reporter," Hope muttered. She pushed her hair out of her eyes and focused more clearly on him. He wore black jeans and an ivory shirt that flowed smoothly over his broad shoulders. "You shouldn't be here."

He nodded, utterly serious. Then abruptly sat on the arm of the cushioned chair beside the lamp. "I know. I'm a sorry SOB. It's all my fault." He squinted at her. "I knew your hair would reach your...ah...fanny if it wasn't braided. "

Hope flushed from the roots of her hair to that other part he'd just mentioned. She felt the heat just flood through her like a switch had been thrown on. "You're drunk."

He frowned. Sighed. "No. Not much." Then he smiled faintly. "I found the right house from the alley side."

She almost smiled, completely forgetting that she was going to tell him he had to leave. It was nearly midnight. "You...ah, didn't tell anyone you were coming here, did you?"

He shook his head, holding up his hand. "No more'n I told anyone about Tuesday at the Taggarts. Scout's honor."

She stood and tightened the sash on her ankle-length robe. She knew Jolie and Drew weren't likely to gossip about Tristan's unexpected visit while

Hope was watching Evan. "Were you ever a boy scout?"

He grinned wickedly. "Whatdya think?"

She groaned and turned toward the kitchen. She closed the back door that had been left open, hung up the phone that had miraculously remained intact and started a pot of strong coffee. When she turned around again, it was to find Tristan standing just a few feet behind her. She sucked in her breath, pressing her hand against her heart. "Stop sneaking around on me!"

"Sweet pea, I'd never sneak around on you," he said distinctly, giving the words an entirely different spin that made her cheeks heat all over again.

She frowned severely. "Have you eaten?"

He shrugged. "Sure."

"When?" She stepped past him toward the refrigerator, dragging her eyes from the waist of his jeans that looked as if they hung just a little too loosely from his hips. "Oh, for goodness sake, Tristan, you're swaying. Sit down before you fall on your face." She yanked open the door and pulled out the roast that she'd made in the Crock-Pot earlier that day.

His eyes followed the food. "Please don't be a good cook," he muttered.

He was half-drunk, she reminded herself. "Okay, I won't. But I can't be expected to drive miles to pick up Chinese if I'm not inclined to cook or order pizza here in town." She *was* Ruby Leoni's granddaughter, after all, and had grown up in her kitchen. She sliced off a thick wedge of beef and scooped vegetables on the plate, heated the whole lot in the microwave while the coffee finished perking, and set the meal in front of him at the table.

Without a word, he picked up the fork and dove in. But when she started to leave the kitchen, intent on donning something more suitable, more sensible, than her pale-green robe, he caught her wrist and tugged her back down to the seat beside him. "Stay with me."

Hope yanked her robe over her knees. "You shouldn't be here, Tristan," she said again.

He didn't disagree. Just popped a tender piece of carrot into his mouth. "I should've known you could cook," he said eventually, when his plate was scraped clean and the lingering bleariness had nearly been eradicated from his eyes. "You'll be a perfect wife for some lucky guy one day."

Hope swallowed and retrieved the coffee pot to refill his cup. His eyes met hers. She stopped pouring and set the pot on the table. "According to the six o'clock news yesterday, half the state apparently thinks I'm going to make *you* a perfect wife." She couldn't believe the bold words had come from her own lips. If the surprise in his sapphire eyes was any indication, he couldn't believe it, either.

"But I'd make the worst husband. I didn't mean to bring this all down on your head, Hope," he said quietly. "I just—hell, I just wanted to spend some time with a pretty woman."

Her fingers twisted the ends of her sash into knots. "I'm not pretty. I'm not…anything. That's why everybody is making such a fuss. Because you're so—" She couldn't finish that. Not without bringing fresh mortification upon herself. He was wealthy, spectacularly handsome and decidedly mysterious since he'd disappeared from the public eye. She was…none of those things.

"That reporter is Brenda Wyatt's cousin, you know," she said, instead. "That's how this insanity began. Brenda was probably on the phone the minute she realized it was Tristan Clay carrying the hometown nobody down the street."

"You need to look in a mirror more often, sweet pea, and get rid of this notion that you have no appeal." He stared into his coffee. "You can stay at the Double-C until the reporter-from-hell loses interest."

Hope swallowed.

"Nobody gets on the property who doesn't belong there," he continued.

"I still have to help Gram during the week," she countered, even though she knew Gram could get one of the high school kids to help her out. He'd made the offer only because he wanted to protect her. It was impossibly sweet. But even contemplating the notion shook her to the core. "I won't let that reporter person make me hide," she added.

He smiled faintly. "Grit. Good for you."

"And you'll be gone soon, anyway." She didn't like thinking about that just yet, but it was a fact. "They can hardly make a, uh, a romance—sleazy, or a fairy tale—out of anything when you're not even here. Right?"

"Brenda Wyatt's kid is gonna be born with two heads," he said, rather than answer.

"Don't be mean." She nibbled the inside of her

lip. "Destined to become a gossip columnist is far more likely."

He stared. Then barked with laughter.

Hope couldn't help but smile. But then his eyes touched on her lips and she swallowed, staring down at the edge of her robe that her fingers were nervously pleating.

He cleared his throat, then drained the rest of his coffee. "Thanks for the meal. I think I can walk a straight line, now."

Feeling awkward, Hope managed a smile. "You can probably slip back into the bachelor party with nobody the wiser." She wanted, desperately, to ask him why he hadn't just stayed at Colbys where she'd heard a veritable feast had been planned for the party-goers.

He didn't look very enthusiastic about the suggestion, however. "Mind if I finish the coffee first?"

"No, of course not." She snatched up the pot and reached over to pour it in his cup, but he moved the cup toward her at the same time, and the hot liquid hit the table, splashing the front of his shirt.

He stood abruptly, yanking his sodden shirt away from his abdomen. Hope set down the pot, pressing her hands to her cheeks in horror. "I'm so sorry," she gasped. "I c-can't believe I did that again." She dashed around and pulled at the top button. "Take it off so I can get the stain out before it ruins your shirt."

"Don't worry about it."

"Please, it's the least I can do."

He raked his fingers through his hair, disheveling

the thick gold mass. "Sweet pea, taking off my shirt isn't a real good idea."

"Don't be ridiculous. It shouldn't take long for me to rinse out the stain."

Tris ignored the lingering scorch of the coffee that had burned through the shirt against his stomach. The burn ignited by Hope's fluttering fingers tugging at the collar of his shirt was another matter. "Hope."

"What?"

One look into her violet eyes and he knew she was just one big bundle of nerves. Another weight clanged into place on his conscience. One of her hands crept nervously to her gold necklace. He deliberately lifted his gaze from the beguiling shadow in the vee of her robe lapels. It didn't even bear thinking about what she had on beneath the cotton. Or didn't.

He touched her necklace with his fingertip and she went abruptly, painfully, still. "You always wear this," he murmured. "Don't you?"

Her long throat worked. She nodded. "Since I was twelve years old and snooping in Gram's attic for her dresses from Italy when she was young. I, uh, I found it in a jewelry box."

When he hooked his finger beneath the fine gold links, he was even more aware of the satiny texture of her skin beneath. Warm and fragrant with the lilac scent of her. He slowly drew the chain upward, watching the pulse beat visibly in her throat, feeling his own drum heavily in response.

The chain was long. Long enough to lay nestled between her breasts, he realized with a silent groan.

And at the end of it hung a skin-warmed wedding band. Too large to be a woman's, he noticed. "And this? You found this, too?"

She caught her lip between her teeth. Then exhaled audibly and stepped back. Not too far back, however, because he still held the ring.

"Gram told me it was my mother's. That she'd been saving it for the love of her life."

The ring was plain, with no inscription, and was large enough to slide over his finger. "And now you're saving it for the love of your life?"

She lifted her shoulder, not answering. But he knew he'd guessed accurately. He let go of the ring and it settled against her robe. "Do you miss her?"

Hope turned away, busily mopping up the spilled coffee. "It's hard to miss what you never knew. She died when I was two. That's when Gram brought me back to Weaver to live with her. Justine was already out on her own by then."

His mother had died in childbirth with him. Only when it was late at night and he was trying not to think about a violet-eyed temptress would he admit that he missed his mother. Missed never having known her.

He still felt guilty deep down in his gut for even existing. Which was something he wouldn't think about no matter what the circumstances. "So Ruby stepped in, becoming the mother you'd lost," he concluded abruptly.

Hope nodded. "Will you let me clean that stain, now?"

Because it seemed so important to her, he flicked open the buttons and shrugged out of it, handing it to her. She avoided looking at him and disappeared into a little room off the kitchen. The laundry room, he assumed.

He took his plate and flatware to the sink and rinsed them, then wiped up the last bit of spill from the floor. Hope still hadn't emerged and he scrubbed his hands over his face.

He could go now, but appearing at the bachelor party without his shirt was probably not a good move.

Hell, he hadn't been making good moves since he'd arrived in Weaver last week. And he was supposed to be a fairly intelligent guy.

He tilted his head, hearing an odd scraping sound. His first thought was that someone had followed him. But then he dismissed it. Paranoia on his part wouldn't help anything.

Suddenly, Hope reappeared. "Did you hear that noise?"

"Yeah."

She huffed and darted past him, opening the kitchen door and looking out. "Simon? Simon are you out there?" Huffing again, she shut the door and stepped around him into the hall.

"Who the hell is Simon?" He followed.

"My cat." She dashed aside the curtains on her front window. "Darnitall, he got out through the window again."

"If that's a problem, maybe you should shut it," Tris murmured, standing to the side and looking over her head at the side-sliding window.

She frowned, sliding it the few inches until it was closed once more. "I do. He opens it."

"A cat who opens windows. Now *that* is interesting news for Brenda-the-Blab's cousin."

Hope turned, froze for a second when she found him standing right behind her, then moved over to the front door and yanked it open. "Yes, well, Simon seems to have a thing for the Wyatt's flowers, and I'd better find him before Brenda's husband does." She gathered the long folds of her robe around her and went out into the dark.

Tris closed his eyes, hoping like hell that Brenda's cousin wasn't camped out in some ridiculous vantage-point at the school or park across the street. He strode after Hope, catching up to her quickly. "I'll find the cat."

She was looking toward the Wyatt's house, where the flowers grew profusely against the fence. "I know the spot he goes to."

He physically turned her toward her own house. "I'll find the cat," he repeated. "You're wearing a robe."

Her lips parted. She looked down at herself, then nodded and hurried back toward the light shining out her front door. He could hear her muttering to herself as she went. "Stupid, stupid, stupid," she was saying.

Tris watched her until she entered her house. Then he blew out a long breath and crossed the lawn of the house next door to the Wyatts'. He crouched down, peering through the foliage and fence. "Simon," he grumbled. "Get your tail outta there before we all get caught."

The beast didn't appear. Naturally. But it did let out a howl loud enough to wake the dead. "I hate

cats.'' Tris followed the sound of the meowing back
between the two houses. He looked around, and seeing nobody—no shifting shadows that might indi-
cate someone—stepped over the white pickets. His
shoes squished in the slippery mud and he slid, grabbing onto the first thing he could. The leafy plants
came right out of the ground in his fist just as his
hip banged hard against the fence. He barely caught
himself from landing butt-first in the mud. And still,
nobody came running from either house to see who
was making the racket.

Shoving the uprooted plant back into the mud,
Tris gave the fence a good shake, relieved to find it
held firm. All he needed was to have to own up to
knocking down a fence in the middle of the night
and he'd complete the picture of being a teenager,
sneaking around in the middle of the night with his
buddy, Drew, when they were supposed to be back
at Drew's house, sleeping soundly. If any of Coleman Black's guys could see him now, nobody at
Hollins-Winword would ever take him seriously
again.

The moon was high and bright and Tris eventually found the cat huddling under a plant, chewing
merrily away on a flower. He scooped up the feline,
for which he earned a stinging scratch, hopped the
fence and jogged back to Hope's house, holding the
cat out at a safe distance.

Hope had left the front door open and he wiped
his muddy shoes before going inside. He pushed the
door shut and held out the cat to Hope. ''Put a lock
on the window,'' he suggested dryly, watching her
bury her nose in the cat's tabby-orange ruff.

"Thank you for finding him," she said gratefully. The cat jumped out of her arms, sidled around her bare feet, looked up at Tristan disdainfully, then hopped onto the couch where he turned a few circles and settled himself in the corner. "Simon thanks you, too."

"Oh yeah, I can tell," he said dryly. He wondered if the bachelor party was still going on. He'd been at Hope's more than an hour.

"You've scratched yourself," Hope murmured, her eyes distressed.

Tris looked over at the cat.

"Simon? Now I really feel awful. Let me get something to clean it up." She turned in a whirl of green cotton and damp hair and was back in seconds, a gauze pad in one hand and a bottle of rubbing alcohol in the other.

"It might sting a bit," she murmured and pressed the wet pad against his rib where the cat had left his "thank you."

Tris sucked in his breath. "A bit?" He laughed and winced all at once and caught her dabbing hand before she could torment and torture him even more. "It's fine, sweet pea. It's late and I should go. Why don't you give me my shirt and I'll—"

"Oh! Yes, yes, of course." She held the gauze and the alcohol close against her and scurried away again.

He must be out of his mind, he thought, shoving his hands through his hair as he followed. She came out of the kitchen, shirt in hand. Her eyes flitted nervously over his chest, then away.

He took the shirt from her and yanked the damp

fabric over his shoulders, not bothering to button it. The hall seemed too narrow, her lilac-scented body too close. In some portion of his mind, he knew he should get out of there. But when he reached out and threaded his fingertips through the damp hair at her temple and gently drew the dark locks away from her ivory face, he couldn't for the life of him think why.

"Tristan," she whispered, her gaze finally flying to his. "You have to go."

Knowing she was right didn't help his conscience any. Nor did it prevent him taking a step nearer to her. "No one knows I'm here, sweet pea, except your fern-eating feline," he said.

She pressed her lips together. Sighed softly. Her hands lifted and pressed against his chest for the briefest of moments before she gasped and yanked them away, tucking them behind her back as if she'd done something wrong.

He could still feel the imprint of that brief touch just as vividly as he could feel the cat-scratch stinging from the alcohol. He ran his thumb along her cheek. Cupped his hand over her shoulder, feeling the supple skin through her robe. "I'm sorry about the reporter. I thought the press would've lost interest in me years ago."

"It's not your fault."

"And you're too generous." He settled his thumb on the center of her lower lip, watching her eyelids flicker, then fall. Heard her catch her breath. She'd be generous in bed, too. The sure knowledge dragged at him.

He gently pressed with his thumb and her lips

parted. Her hand closed over his forearm. He lowered his head toward hers, absorbing the scent of her, the warmth.

The ringing.

She gasped and scurried away into the kitchen to grab the ringing telephone.

Tris gritted his teeth, pressing his hands against the wall. He was a dog. Every bit as bad as the news stories slyly implied. He beat down the fire in his gut that urged him to go after her, to take the phone off the hook and to sweep her down the hall to the bedroom he could see at the end.

A bedroom with a narrow, girlish bed, complete with a big, worn, stuffed rabbit sitting against the ruffled, pink pillows.

He silently cursed himself to hell and back. The sight of that bed did what nothing else had been able to do—douse him with cold reality.

He had no business seeking her out in the middle of the night. She was a hometown girl with "innocent" all but tattooed on her forehead, and he was leaving town again after the wedding, in just a few days.

She was sitting at the table, obviously finished with her phone call, when he went into the kitchen again. She just stared at him.

"I should go."

She nodded.

He left the way he'd come—through the back kitchen door. When he stepped out onto the little porch, his wet shirt clung to his chest, cold though the night air was still warm. A lover's-night warmth.

He stood there, on the outside of the door, feeling her on the other side. He slowly buttoned the shirt.

After a long while, he heard the lock click into place behind him.

He sighed. And walked away.

Chapter Six

"What did you do to that girl?"

Tris barely heard Sawyer's demanding question. He was too busy following Hope out the door of the sheriff's office. She'd arrived not two seconds earlier to deliver Sawyer's lunch order from the café. But the sight of Tris, sitting there working on Sawyer's computer, had turned her right around on her heels, barely taking time to drop the brown bag of food onto the straight-back chair just inside the door.

He stepped out onto the sidewalk just in time to see the end of her braid streaming behind her as she darted into the café a few doors down.

"Think before you run after her," Sawyer cautioned, joining him. "Every time you even *look* in the direction of the café, you send the grapevine into apoplexy." He shook his head. "Wish you'd turn off the love 'em and leave 'em mentality for just one week. She's got to stay here when you're gone. Is it worth a few hours of tangled sheets?''

Tris had felt like sludge ever since he'd heard Hope turn the kitchen lock on him last night. He'd also heard plenty that morning at breakfast because he'd missed the end of the bachelor party and had ended up hitching a ride back to the ranch. He didn't need to hear that another family member thought he'd seduced Hope.

Not one of them knew what was going on between them. What *wasn't* going on between them.

Ignoring Sawyer, he started down the sidewalk. When he entered the café, he felt at least a dozen pairs of eyes staring him down. He focused on Ruby, standing behind the counter, her short, white curls practically vibrating off her head as she furiously scrubbed the counter. There was no welcome in her bright eyes. None at all.

All conversations had ceased. Tristan's footsteps sounded loud as he crossed the floor. ''I want to talk to Hope,'' he said to Ruby when he reached the counter.

Her aging, wrinkled face tightened. ''What for?''

Hell. He didn't want to upset Ruby. She was part of his childhood. Coming to the café for her delicious pecan-crusted cinnamon rolls; chocolate malts that were so thick you couldn't suck the ice cream drink through a straw; handing over his report cards when she demanded to see them on report card day. ''Ruby,'' he said quietly. ''You know I don't want her hurt, either.''

Her lips tightened. But he could see in her eyes

that she was softening. "She'll be with me at the wedding," she said. "You can see her, then."

"Gram."

Tris looked over to see Hope standing in the swinging door that led to the kitchen.

Ruby huffed and tossed up her hands. As soon as the swinging door closed, with Tris and Hope in the empty kitchen, he heard a half-dozen conversations start up again out in the dining area.

He pushed his hands into the pockets of his jeans. "Why did you run out of the office like that?"

"Because I'm a fool," she said. "But you shouldn't have followed me."

"You know," he mused softly, "I've never much been one for following the expectations of others. If I had been, I wouldn't have struck out on my own at eighteen with nothing but determination and dreams swimming in my head. Why did you run out like that? Are you upset about last night?"

She wouldn't look at him and he couldn't believe the wave of frustration that buffeted him. "Dammit, Hope, what is it? Don't you know by now that you can talk to me?"

"Tristan, please, you should go. Just trust me. Go."

"Look, I'm sorry about the ruckus over our...friendship...but I'll be damned if I'll let a bunch of gossips dictate my actions. I thought you felt the same. That's why you refused to hide out at the Double-C until I leave town again."

Her eyes wouldn't meet his. "I was talking then about that reporter. *Her* stories—" Her voice shook, but when Tris started toward her, she held up a hand, her expression pleading. ''—not about my own friends and family.''

''People who should know you better than that.''

''You just don't understand,'' she whispered.

''Then help me to!''

Her lips pressed together. ''Your reputation is already settled in gold,'' she began, clearing her throat, but her voice was still husky. ''People think you're larger than life. The more supermodels you dated, the better. The more money you earned, the happier people here were. You're admired as much for the things people whisper about behind their hands as you are criticized. It's not the same for me.''

His hands curled. ''I'm just a guy, Hope. It shouldn't be any different for me than it is for you.''

''Calling you 'just a guy' is like calling the Double-C a little cow kennel. Just stop, would you?'' Her eyes pleaded. ''Maybe you feel some…passing fancy for me, but I know just as well as everyone else in this town that *that* is all it is. Maybe you're so hung up over your daddy's wedding that you're desperate for some diversion, but I can't be it! Not anymore.''

''I'm not 'hung up' over Squire's wedding,'' he denied flatly. ''And maybe I'm used to…having women in my life. But the women in my life are just that. Women. Who expect as little from me as I expect from them.''

Hope's lips parted. ''That's horrible.''

''That's life, sweet pea. My life, anyway. And maybe I want to kiss you more than is wise—hell, I *know* I want to—but I can control myself, which

I'd think you'd know after last night. You don't have to run away from me like I'm ready to jump your bones at the first opportunity, regardless of our surroundings.''

''I don't!''

''What was that about at Sawyer's office, then?''

''Bennett Ludlow's office is next door to the sheriff's office,'' she finally said, as if pushed beyond endurance. ''And frankly, if I want to keep my job, I don't want him seeing you and me within the same *block* of one another.''

''Bennett is a jerk. He always has been.''

''He controls my career. Which he reminded me of very clearly last night when he called!''

Anger curled darkly through him. ''That was Bennett on the phone last night?''

She turned her back on him, pressing her palms against a stainless steel table, and nodded.

''He often call you in the middle of the night?''

''As often as you visit.''

He deserved that, and a part of him applauded her for saying it, even if it stung. But, God, if Tris was too old for Hope, then Bennett was even worse. The guy was old enough to be her father. ''What did he want?'' The last he'd seen, Bennett had been at the bachelor party.

She didn't look at him. ''To tell me that he's called a school board meeting for Monday morning.''

''Why?''

''To fire me, I suppose.''

He stilled. She was too calm.

''On what grounds?''

"Moral misconduct."

He walked over to her. Physically turned her around to face him. "Excuse me?"

"It's in my teaching contract," she said flatly. But her eyes shimmered with tears.

"You haven't done anything!" Not with him and damn sure not with anyone else.

"That doesn't really matter, does it? Everyone thinks I have. The news people think I'm your latest…lover. Gram is afraid I've fallen into my mother's footsteps. The school board, Bennett included, thinks I'm c-carrying on inappropriately. You know, my mother and Justine had to move away from Weaver when Justine was in high school because she was supposedly having an affair with an older man. But nobody ever seemed to blame the guy, whoever he was. They just considered my sister a tramp and that was that."

"That was years ago, Hope."

"Yes," she agreed. "But memories are long in this town, and I grew up hearing the stories."

He swore.

She closed her eyes. "Please, Tristan. Just go now."

She looked fragile and young and frightened. "I'll make this right, Hope," he promised. Anything to take that look off her face.

"You can't. There is nothing to be done."

"So you're just going to let them fire you. With no cause. You're just going to give up."

"What would you have me do?"

"Fight them!"

"With what?" She stared at her hands. "I'm a

Leoni, Tristan. It wouldn't matter if I became a nun, there would still be people in this town who would believe, simply because of my mother and sister, that I was seducing the priests!''

''All this because I carried you down the street?''

''All this because Bennett saw you at my house last night. It was late and you were half-naked, to use his words, and I wasn't exactly wearing jeans and sweatshirt, either.'' She wearily pressed her palm to her forehead. ''On top of everything else…''

''He's not going to fire you.''

''You can't stop him, Tristan. You're not even a resident here, anymore. And your family, as…well, as influential as they are, none of them sits on the board, either. This is my own battle.''

''Which you won't fight!'' He shook her gently. ''This is ridiculous. Tell them to shove it where the sun doesn't shine. You can move somewhere else, have some freedom to live without the people around you judging you. I'll help you find something.''

''I don't want to move somewhere else.''

He realized she meant it. He could see it in her swimming eyes and he felt even more like pond scum.

''I might have been born in Colorado, but Weaver is my home,'' Hope said shakily. ''And I love it here. My Gram, she's been everything to me. I don't even remember my own mother, except for the photographs Gram has and the ring I wear on my necklace. I have friends here. People who care about me. People *I* care about. The ones who are gossip-

ing...they don't mean to be hurtful. They just...this
is a small town. Everything that happens here seems
to carry more importance or more significance than
it would elsewhere. You live in California, and people probably don't bat an eye at the women who
come and go through your front door. But here, it's
different.''

The tears had slipped over her lashes and the sight
twisted his guts into knots. He didn't even bother
correcting her assumption that he had a revolving
door where women were concerned. ''I'll talk to
Bennett.''

She smiled sadly, dashing a hand across her
cheek. ''He can be decent enough when he wants,
but we all know he has a grudge against anyone with
the last name of Clay. Your talking to him wouldn't
help. But I appreciate the gesture.''

She appreciated his gesture. The politeness knifed
through his soul like a hot poker. He tugged her
closer and folded his arms around her shoulders. She
was so stiff he could have snapped her into two
brittle pieces. Then suddenly, she drew in a breath
that shuddered through them both.

''It's such a mess,'' she said against his chest.

He pressed his lips to the top of her hair. ''I'll
figure something out, sweet pea. I started it, and I
will stop it.'' He thought briefly of the case he'd
cleaned up before he'd arrived in Weaver. It had
taken nearly a week to untangle the mess an associate had made, but he'd succeeded. Hell, he always
succeeded.

Despite the fact that he considered Hope's options
far more open than she did when it came to Weaver

and her teaching position, it was now his *own* mess to clean up. He'd start by untangling the web of gossip one strand at a time until Hope's reputation was as pristine as ever.

And he'd have to do it before Bennett's damned meeting on Monday morning.

* * *

"Gracious, he *is* a handsome one. It's no wonder people talk about him so much. When he was a boy he was impossible to resist. So sad he never had a chance to know his mama. She was a real lady. Never said an unkind word about anyone."

Hope was climbing from the car and nearly dropped her keys, she was so surprised. "You haven't said one nice thing about Tristan in days," Hope murmured, looking at her grandmother across the roof of the car. Her grandmother who had insisted that she come to this wedding, no matter what. Her grandmother who had pushed a lace dress into Hope's hands and insisted that if she hadn't done anything wrong, as she claimed, then she couldn't avoid the wedding by acting as if she were ashamed.

Gram patted her fresh curls and adjusted her white purse over her elbow. "He's not all bad. And you do like him, don't you?"

Hope closed the car door, not answering. Most of the town was expected to turn out at the Double-C ranch to attend Squire Clay's wedding to Gloria Day. Hope would have avoided it altogether if not for Gram's insistence that if Hope didn't attend, Gram wouldn't either. It was emotional blackmail, but it was effective. Ruby had known Squire for years. Naturally, she wanted to be present for the wedding.

So Hope had donned her grandmother's antique dress, knowing that Gram had presented it purely as a bribe, since she knew how much Hope loved her old dresses. And she'd driven them out to the ranch with the specific intention of avoiding Tristan Clay at all costs.

Only there he was. Standing by the corner of the big, imposing house. Perhaps it was the lilac bushes behind him, vivid with lush blooms and glossy leaves that made his black tuxedo seem even blacker. And perhaps it was the black fabric that fit him like he'd been born to it that made his hair look even brighter, even more gilded.

All she knew was the sight of him made her feet simply take root in the gravel beneath her.

There were dozens of cars already parked in the drive and it was some distance to the house; yet Tristan turned his gaze unerringly in her direction.

Hope blindly shut her car door when her grandmother crunched around the car to tuck her hand through Hope's arm. "Let's go, girl. The chairs are filling, and I want to get a good seat. You know, I heard that Gloria's dress comes all the way from London, England. Have you ever heard such a thing? We've got dressmakers right here in Wyoming. That Squire always did spoil his women. Hard on his sons, but, gracious, he loved his wife. And I haven't seen anything quite as sweet as him, good-looking coot that he is, courting Gloria.

"Sure is nice and tidy that Gloria is working here in town now with Dr. Rebecca. We're getting right

metropolitan with a doctor and a nurse. Gloria called
me last week, you know. To make sure I'd made
that appointment with Dr. Rebecca.''

''Did you?'' Hope murmured absently. But her
grandmother's chatter was effective, allowing Hope
the willpower to drag her gaze from Tristan to look
at the rows and rows of white chairs that had been
set out on the front lawn. Swags of airy white tulle
swayed in the faint breeze, and lilacs and white
daisies festooned the chair at the end of each row.
A good portion of the seats were already occupied,
and those that weren't soon would be, once the clus-
ters of standing guests seated themselves.

''Next Wednesday,'' Ruby replied as they luckily
found two seats near the front. Hope folded her
hands in her lap, absently listening to Ruby chatter
to the guests around them, as naturally as if the cra-
ziness of the last week had never occurred. Maybe
it hadn't. Maybe Hope had built it up in her mind
to be worse than it really was.

Or maybe it was just that her grandmother had
had plenty of practice at holding her head up when
other people were gossiping about her family.

Hope tucked her keys in her tiny, useless purse
that held only a minimum of essentials and
smoothed the dress over her knees. At least the
chairs faced away from the house, she thought.
Away from Tristan.

Bennett and the two other members of the school
board stood on the far side of the chairs on the other
side of the aisle. She felt her face burn, knowing
they were watching her.

Jolie and Drew and little Evan Taggart arrived,

and Hope felt herself relax a little. Evan hugged her enthusiastically before his daddy nudged him into a chair. Jolie, who looked as bright as a sunflower in her yellow dress, slipped into the seat beside Hope and leaned close. "You've been busy, my friend. I've been trying to call you since Wednesday."

Hope shook her head. "I wasn't answering my phone."

"That awful cousin of Brenda's, I suppose," Jolie finished sympathetically. "I heard she was gonna get fired or transferred or something from her station over the stories she's been telling." She looked around again and leaned close. "So, is it true? Were you really caught doing the horizontal mamba with Tristan during his daddy's bachelor party?"

Hope stared. "What?"

"I knew it couldn't be." Jolie patted her arm.

"That's what people are saying?" She glanced at her grandmother, praying that Gram hadn't heard *that* particular rumor. She leaned toward Jolie. "Who told you that?" she hissed.

Jolie shook her head. "Half-a-dozen people, at least. I told them they were all crazy."

Hope pressed shaking fingers to her lips. She wished more than ever that she'd stayed home.

"Excuse me, Jolie. Hope? I need to talk to you for a minute."

Hope's hands knotted. She looked up at Tristan, who was leaning over, one hand extended to her. *Horizontal mamba.* Please, God, let him not have heard that. Painfully aware of Bennett and his companions watching, Hope shook her head.

"It's important," he said, when Ruby turned and

saw him. "There's not a lot of time before the ceremony begins."

Hope knew that if she dared to look around, she'd find everyone's attention focused on them. Staring. Waiting. Probably thinking she'd throw herself uncontrollably at Tristan in a fit of passion that, as a Leoni, she'd be unable to contain.

"Perhaps you should, girl," Gram patted her hand.

Thoroughly rattled, Hope looked at her grandmother. "Gram—"

"You're a good girl," Gram said softly. "It'll be all right."

Hope looked from her grandmother to Tristan. His face was expressionless except for the muscle ticking in his jaw. He was angry, Hope realized with a start. She was mortified, and he was angry. She moistened her lips and rose. She didn't take his hand, however, and his lips thinned.

He stepped out of the row and waited for her, then tucked his hand at the small of her back; right below the small gathered bow at the center of the scooped back. She felt the grazing contact right down to her toes.

But when he started toward the house, Hope shook her head violently. "We can talk out here."

"Fine." But still, he took her elbow and walked along the side of the house, well away from the gathering guests. "Why didn't you tell me about Bennett's plans to close the school?"

Hope's stomach dropped. "I didn't think about it."

"Bull," he said smoothly. So smoothly and

fiercely that shivers danced over her skin. "You were thinking about it all along. *That* is why you are so afraid of losing your job. Because if the school loses another teacher, Bennett and his side-kicks can close it. The kids will have to be bused to Braden, thirty miles away."

Hope didn't reply. He'd obviously learned the full facts from someone.

He pushed one hand in his pocket. "I can't believe you would just sit back and let Bennett do this."

"I wasn't going to just sit back," she blurted tightly. She'd been doing nothing but worrying and thinking and planning since Bennett's middle-of-the-night call. "But until I can meet with the board the day after tomorrow, I won't even have an opportunity to defend myself officially against their charges."

"What were you planning to do then? Lay yourself across the conference table as a sacrificial lamb, begging their mercy for committing whatever sins they've come up with in their tiny, judgmental minds?"

"Once you're gone, things will die down." She hoped that was the case, anyway. "I'll move back in with my grandmother, if it becomes necessary. And if worse comes to worse, I've called a friend from college who may be willing to move here for a year and apply for my job. If she agrees, hopefully the board would hire her and the school can remain open." It wasn't the best of plans, but it was the only thing she'd been able to come up with.

"Bennett is not going to hire anyone," Tris countered flatly. "He's so mired in paperwork trying to bring about the consolidation of the two schools in Weaver and Braden that I'm not sure he could stop it if he wanted to."

She paused, unease making her queasy. "How do you know that?"

"I made it my business to know. Given opportunity, Bennett's going to pounce." Tris looked over his shoulder at the man in question. Bennett was watching, his expression unreadable at the distance. "The rub is that the board is within its rights to act. Not about firing you because of this moral sh—stuff. But closing the school. Weaver has the students and Braden has the teachers, but Braden's facility is nearly brand new, top of the line, so the argument is that our kids will benefit more by going there, than shuffling *them* here."

Hope chewed her lip. Nodded.

"And thanks to my…association with you, he figures he's got the momentum now to push it over the hump."

"If it hadn't been this," she waved her hand, since there weren't any words adequate enough to describe the absurdity, "it would have been something else. Some other teacher he took to task, some reason to close our doors."

"We need to clear your name."

Hope shook her head. "I'm not worried about that. I'm worried about my kids in the fall."

"I figured." He drew his hand out of his pocket and held it out. "This will shut their mouths. If not for good, then at least long enough to give me some breathing room to stop Bennett's plan."

She looked at the square black jeweler's box sitting on the palm of his hand. "I don't understand."

"We're getting married."

Her jaw loosened.

Tristan's thumb flipped open the box and the diamond rings inside glinted whitely under the sunlight. "Once you're my wife, no one will have any cause to speak ill of you. And Bennett can take his morals and shove 'em u—"

"No!" She reached for the box and snapped it shut. Hiding the impossibly beautiful rings from sight.

"Yes. We will do this. Here. Today."

"Your father is getting married today!" She frowned up at him. "Are you drunk again?"

"Sweet pea, I've never been more sober in my life."

"But you don't love me!"

She caught something in his eyes. Something sad. "It's the only way I can right what's wrong," he said. His impassive voice held none of the fleeting expression she'd thought she'd glimpsed in his eyes.

"Is that so important?"

He rubbed his thumb over the box. "It's what I do, Hope. And I won't let you, or the kids who go to school here suffer because I didn't think beyond my—because I thought flirting with a very pretty, sweet young woman would be harmless."

She *wasn't* pretty. And still, Tristan stood in front of her, a jeweler's box in his hand, expecting her to marry him. To protect her. Her chest filled with panic and too many emotions to name. But mostly panic. Oh, yes. Panic. "People would know it was only for show," she pointed out, struggling for breath. "You…you said you were going to France after the wedding. And I would still be here. That would be just one more thing with which they'd take exception. It may seem quaint and old fashioned to you, but I do think this area of the world expects wives to live *with* their husbands… Gads, I can't believe I'm even discussing this. It's crazy."

"It's the perfect answer. And you can come to Paris with me. Once my work there is done, we'll go to my place in California. You can spend the rest of the summer there. I've got a number of social engagements that I can't get out of. You can go with me, or just lay around on the beach or by the pool. Whatever. Then, if you still want to teach here in Weaver, you can come back in the fall. Or arrange for your friend to come, after all. Either way, Bennett will have a hard time pushing through the school closure. He'll have a full roster of teachers again, and the funding is still in place."

"Of course I still want to teach at the school. It's all I've wanted since I was six years old, attending first grade there myself!"

"That's your choice." There was a fine white line surrounding his mobile lips. "I realize I'm no prize, but as my wife, your options *will* be open, Hope."

As his wife. Wife. "No." She shook her head violently. Not a prize? That was proof that this wasn't really happening. "I have to join my grandmother, now. Everybody is sitting down, and the minister is over there waiting with your father and brothers. We're attracting too much attention."

He caught her hand in a gentle, inescapable grip. "Hope."

She drew in a panicky breath, feeling desperately close to tears. "We can't get married. We can't. We…uh, we…we don't have a license!"

He tucked his other hand inside his lapel and drew out a folded sheet. "I called in a few favors," he said, handing it to her.

Hope twisted her hand free and unfolded the document. It was *her* name typed on the license. *His* name. And it was signed and stamped and looked utterly official. "No."

"It's the only way, Hope."

She pushed the wedding license back into his hand and curled her fingers into a fist, as if by doing so she could prevent him from sliding that theoretical ring onto her finger.

Only this wasn't theoretical. It *was* happening, and it was very, very real.

Beyond Tristan's shoulder she could see the string quartet set up off to the side of the white chairs; could hear the lilting strains floating on the afternoon breeze. The groom and Tristan's brothers were all lined up, too, obviously waiting for him before they moved to the head of the aisle and awaited the arrival of the bride.

She thought about the day of Gloria's wedding shower and the little girls she'd watched. Of Evan. They were only a few of the children who would have to be bused thirty miles beyond Weaver to a school that offered every physical advantage, but was still miles away from their own home.

Once the school closed, Hope knew it was unlikely that it would reopen. Weaver would begin to die away, just like so many other small towns died away when their young ones grew up and left. Never to return.

"What will Gram think?"

His expression didn't change one iota, but she knew. "Oh my! Gram knows, doesn't she? That's why she insisted I come today." She flicked her ankle-length skirt. "And this dress."

He didn't deny it. "Marry me. Right here. Right now."

Barely able to breathe, she stared at Tristan's outstretched palm. A million thoughts whirled through her mind. The clipping inside her old geometry book. The tiredness in Tristan's eyes the first day when he'd appeared in the café and the amusement that day in the park. The Chinese food cartons he'd stuck in her hands the night she was watching Evan.

She pressed her hand to her head, feeling dizzy from the thoughts. Or maybe it was just his presence that made her dizzy.

Not certain she'd ever draw a sane breath again, Hope placed her shaking hand in his. "All right," she whispered, "I'll marry you."

Chapter Seven

Squire and Gloria hadn't planned to share their wedding day. But when Tris escorted Hope through the back of the big house, tugging her unresistingly into the living room where his future stepmother and a bevy of excited women waited, he had to admit that Gloria accepted the news with typical equanimity, though he received some strongly shocked looks from his sisters-in-law.

But he couldn't worry about what they thought. Getting Hope through the ceremony and her signature on the license afterward was his focus. There'd been another way to stop Bennett, but after speaking with Ruby that morning, Tris couldn't bring himself to do it. Marrying Hope was the far easier thing to do. He'd been honest when he'd told her that they'd figure out the rest later.

Seeing that Hope, pale and shaky, was being ca-
pably taken under the wings of the other women as
they rearranged floral bouquets and such, he headed
out the front door and down one side of the two-
hundred white chairs. He joined the men and met
the minister's eyes.

The other man nodded imperceptibly at the string
quartet, and the guests suddenly hushed.

Tris was aware of the close look he received from
Squire when he moved next to him, where Sawyer—
as best man—had been designated to stand. But he
ignored his father and concentrated on the opened
doorway of the big house.

His nieces all came first, looking like cherubs in
white and yellow ruffles as they solemnly dropped
their flower petals from their matching baskets along
the way. Then Maggie and Emily and Jaimie came
out of the doorway, stepping gracefully down the
steps, followed by Rebecca, who was Gloria's boss
now, as well as her friend.

And finally, Hope appeared. Even across the
yards, her eyes focused on his and with every fiber
inside him, Tris willed her to walk surely down the
aisle. To hold her head up, because she hadn't done
one damned thing wrong—was in fact so good inside that she was marrying a man who was nowhere
near as good as she in order to save something far
more important than just a job.

He watched, impassive, as Hope moved forward.
She looked lovely with her thick hair twisted at her
nape and that old-fashioned-looking dress barely
skimming her curves like some movie star of the
twenties. But the only thing similar to the other

women in the wedding party was the cluster of flowers she carried in her hands.

She did walk gracefully down the steps of the big house. And she did walk up the aisle with no shred of nervousness showing, except maybe the trembling of the flowers in her hands.

He stepped forward, meeting her part way along the aisle to tuck her shaking hand around his arm where no one could see and she looked at him with eyes glazed by panic.

Because of what people would think or say? Or because she knew somewhere inside her that she was marrying a man who would never love her?

He walked her the rest of the way, to stand beside his father and heard the collective gasp of the guests as it began to dawn on them what they were seeing, when she didn't move off to the side as the other women had done.

He ignored the avidly curious looks he knew they were receiving. And he ignored the "good thing you're doing right by that girl," his father grunted in his ear.

The guests didn't know whether to stare at the sight of Tristan and Hope, or enjoy the lovely picture Gloria made as she glided down the aisle after her daughters, Belle and Nikki. Gloria's dress was violet in color, Tris noticed, thinking the color matched Hope's eyes.

Then, Gloria joined Squire, and the four of them turned to face the minister.

"Dearly Beloved," he began.

"And to the bride and groom—*both* sets of them—may they have as much happiness and love in their lives always as they do today.''

Hope listened to Sawyer Clay's toast with disbelief. Tristan had pushed a crystal flute of champagne into her hands several minutes ago and she'd already drained it. A white-coated waiter had immediately replaced it with a full one. As if it were against the rules for the bride—either one of them— to be seen without a full champagne glass in her hand.

She smiled and murmured nonsensically at the stream of people who passed by offering well wishes and expressions of surprise. Even Bennett managed a tight smile when he lightly kissed her cheek and briefly shook Tristan's hand before moving on to Gloria and Squire. Tristan leaned down to murmur in Hope's ear, ''If I didn't know better, I'd say he looked almost relieved.''

Hope dragged her thoughts from the ceremony that had passed in a blur. Except for the moment when Tristan slid the perfectly fitted wedding set on her finger. That was perfectly clear in her thoughts. The way he'd lowered his head over hers and pressed an impossibly gentle, but much too brief, kiss on her lips was even more clear. She frowned up at Tristan, his question finally sinking in. She swayed a little at finding him standing so close. ''Who?''

''Bennett,'' he said.

''Frustrated at being thwarted is more like it,'' Hope dismissed. ''Assuming this plan actually succeeds.'' She turned blindly to receive the next guest's best wishes.

It seemed to take an interminable amount of time for all the guests to make their way along the receiving line. But Hope realized about halfway through that the more champagne she drank, the easier it became. That, plus the steady wall Tristan made beside her as he kept her tucked close against him. She wasn't even aware of leaning against him, letting him take more of her weight, until he slipped the champagne flute out of her hand and set it on the tray of a passing waiter.

"Enough for you, I think," he murmured. "Come on. We have to cut a piece of cake, dance a time or two, then we can get out of here."

They headed toward the cake table, where another ribbon-bedecked cake knife had appeared to join the first. They cut and fed each other a morsel and smiled dutifully and even laughed at the toasts directed at Squire and Gloria and at them.

And when the sun was starting to drop toward the horizon, the string quartet was replaced by a live band and the dancing began.

Closing her eyes, pressing her cheek against Tristan's chest, Hope could almost make herself believe that it all was real. That she'd married the man of her dreams, that he'd married her because he couldn't bear to live his life without her.

"But it's not like that," she murmured sleepily. Not for her mother, not for Justine, not for her.

"What's not?"

She blinked up at Tristan, focusing until she saw only one of him. "You did plan this with Gram, didn't you. She told you about the school."

"Yes."

"She says you'll break my heart." Hope heard the words come out of her mouth with a kind of fascinated, dulled horror. "But today she said you always were hard to resist. She's almost always right."

Tristan pressed his hand gently against her head. "Stop worrying."

"Okay." She closed her eyes and listened to the swaying beat of the mournful love song. He danced beautifully. He did everything beautifully. Even rescuing the abruptly tarnished reputation of the plain, hometown girl.

"May I?"

Hope craned her neck around to see Squire Clay waiting to cut in. Before she could blink, Tristan had surrendered her to his father—her father-in-law, she realized with panic—and was now dancing with Gloria.

"I won't bite you, child." Squire took her hands and simply began guiding her around in an easy waltz, since she seemed incapable of moving on her own.

Hope started to speak, but didn't know what on earth to say. Had he heard all the gossip, too? It seemed likely. "I'm sorry." The words burst from her.

His pale, ice-blue eyes were sharp, but not unkind. "For loving my son?"

"I—" What could she say?

"You do, don't you?"

She moistened her lips. "I, um, I married him," she said weakly.

Squire turned her in a slow circle and her head

swam dizzily. "He sure in he…sure did surprise us all. Too bad he didn't give me a clue what he'd planned. His mama had a cameo that she wore on our wedding day. Would'a looked right nice on your dress today. Passed on from her grandmother—last name was Tristan."

If his easy tone was meant to relax, it was failing miserably. Hope concentrated on the studs of the man's shirt. He wasn't quite as tall as his youngest son, but he was still nearly as broad in the shoulder and made an intimidating, imposing sight. "I imagine you expected more for him," she said shakily.

"More?"

"Someone more, ah, suitable."

He smiled slightly, reminding her strongly of Tristan. "I believe he's made the perfect match. Just like his old man has."

Hope blushed. If only that were true. They circled the dance area marked off by the twinkling lights a few more times, then Hope found herself with more champagne and more dancing with each one of Tristan's brothers.

They were an intense lot, but as quietly kind as Squire had been. Nevertheless, Hope was impossibly relieved when she wound up with Tristan once again. So relieved that she unknowingly curled her fingers into his collar and rested her head on his wide chest.

"You've charmed my family," he murmured. "I've been getting warnings from all sides to treat you right."

Hope focused on his words. "You really didn't tell them, then. The real reason?"

"It's nobody's business but our own," he said shortly. He whirled her in a smooth circle, bending her over his arm with a flourish as the song died.

Her head spun when he straightened. "Oh my."

His arm around her shoulders held her upright. "Flattering to know you have to get tanked to get through this," he murmured in her ear.

She made a face. "I like that champagne. I've never had you—*it*, I mean—before, you know."

"I figured."

The music began again. Low and slow and yearning. More couples crowded into the area between the round banquet-style tables. Hope's senses swam. "You smell good."

"You smell good, too," he murmured. "But remind me never to let you have more than one glass of champagne again."

"Okay." She breathed the word. Somehow or other, her hand had reached the back of his neck and she pushed her fingertips luxuriously through his hair. It felt as wonderfully thick and silky as it looked.

"Behave yourself," he murmured.

"I always behave myself." She suddenly had to enunciate carefully. "That's what I do. You're a protect-or. I'm a behave-er."

She felt his chest rumble with a soft chuckle. And for the first time in what seemed like days, she smiled, too. Because dancing with Tristan really was an experience she'd never thought she'd have. And it was one that she intended to tuck away in her heart to relive later on.

Once Tristan returned to his world and she was

left in hers, everything would be normal once again. That was when she'd remember the feel of his fine tuxedo jacket under her cheek and the heavy beat of his heart underneath that. When she'd think about the stars that had begun to shine overhead and the romantic sounds from the band, and the champagne that bubbled giddily in her veins.

When things were normal once again. When she was just plain old Hope Leoni, kindergarten-through-third-grade teacher. And this wedding stuff was just a dream.

It wasn't a dream.

Hope leaned across the carpeted aisle of the jet, took her eyeglasses from Tristan and shoved them in place. Moving too fast made her dizzy, though, and she cursed the champagne that several hours earlier she'd blessed.

"We'll get an annulment," she said abruptly. It didn't matter that Tristan seemed to believe they'd done the right thing in wedding one another—that by doing so, her reputation was protected and the school was out of danger for now. She must have been out of her mind to agree.

Tristan had leaned back in his high-backed, leather chair and his head was no longer within the circle of light cast by the lamp on the table beside him. "No."

Her hair was everywhere. She yanked it over one shoulder and roughly braided it. But she didn't have anything to fasten the end. Goodness knows what happened to the hair pins she'd used earlier to an-

chor her chignon. She braided anyway. Then left it
hanging over her shoulder. "We have to."

"Why?"

"Because it was madness for us to resort to this
in the first place!" She winced at the way her raised
voice resonated unpleasantly inside her skull.

"You don't have much of a head for champagne."

"I don't have *any* head at all when it comes to
you," she muttered. "Oh, Tristan, *what* have we
done?"

"I could explain again," he said dryly, "but I
think we've beat that one to death already."

She pushed to her feet, swaying for a moment. "I
can't believe you'd joke at a time like this."

"Meet the real Tris Clay." He propped one foot
on his knee. "Nice enough until you get to know
him. Then, you find out he's all surface and no substance."

Hope blinked. "More jokes." She folded her
arms and started pacing. She pressed her fingertips
to her forehead. "Where are we going?"

"Paris, sweet pea. How much *do* you remember,
anyway?"

Her restless pacing stopped. "I don't even have
a passport!"

"Taken care of."

She peered at his shadowed face. "Excuse me?
Don't you need, I don't know, my birth certificate
and photo and…and stuff?"

He nodded.

Her lips parted. She couldn't think what to say.

She wasn't even sure she *had* a copy of her birth certificate— "Gram," she realized aloud.

The plane hit a bump, and she swallowed an abrupt surge of nausea that made her completely forget everything. She pressed her palm flat against her tummy, biting her lip. Tristan rose, saying something unrepeatable under his breath, and hooking his arm around her waist, hauled her along the plane. Toward the rear? She didn't know, didn't care, because he pushed open a door and nudged her inside and at the sight of the commode, Hope slammed the door shut in his face and lost her lunch.

She washed her face and sat weakly on the edge of the bathtub. A bathtub on a plane? She stared at it as if she expected it to disappear. But it didn't. It stayed right there, solid as could be underneath her rear.

It was so ridiculous, as ridiculous as this whole situation. She didn't know whether to laugh or cry.

But the tears clouding her vision told her the decision for that had already been made.

She sucked in a hard breath, scrubbing furiously at her cheeks. She might be shy, but she wasn't a cry baby. And she *had* agreed to marry Tristan. It wasn't as if he'd held a gun to her head and forced her to say "I do."

If anything, he'd been remarkably sweet. In a…a forceful kind of way.

The idiocy of that had her rising to her feet. She splashed cool water over her face and reached for the velvety thick towel hanging on a gold bar beside the sink. Her fingers pressed into the ivory thickness. She'd never seen a towel so outlandishly plush.

Shaking her head gingerly, she dried her face and hands and carefully hung the towel back exactly as it had been. Then she swallowed and pulled open the door, breathing a little easier when she didn't find Tristan hovering outside.

He—or someone—had turned on some very low music. The plane was enormous, she realized, as she slowly padded back along the hall. Her own little house would have easily fit inside it. There was even a staircase leading up to another floor. Floor? She swallowed and peered up the curving metal staircase, but she couldn't see anything up there. Just thick shadows interspersed with an odd, greenish glow.

A low murmur drew her along the hall. When she rounded a curve in the interior wall before the hall widened into the same area where she'd awakened, she realized that Tristan was talking on a phone.

He was sitting in that same big, leather chair. Only this time he didn't look relaxed and amused. She hovered in the hallway. He sat with his elbows on his thighs, one hand shoving through his gilded hair and the other clenching a phone to his ear. He seemed to be staring at the floor between his squarely planted, polished boots.

Even his shoulders looked weary.

Hope quietly backed along the hallway, and slid down that odd, curving interior wall until she sat on the floor. She stared down at her dress—the beautiful lace dress that was the color of dairy cream tinted by coffee. She had told Gram the dress was more suitable for Justine's exotic beauty than for her, with its flyaway sleeves and plunging back, but Gram hadn't agreed. Now she knew why.

Hope sighed. She had hadn't had much chance to speak with Gram at the reception. Ruby had left on a promise to take care of Simon, long before Tristan and Hope had finally departed.

Her head ached as she tried to recall the exact details of that departure. Mostly, it was one big blur. She didn't even remember boarding this extraordinary plane.

"...Dom, I know it wasn't in the plan, dammit, but there's nothing I can do about it. I'm bringing a friend, so get used to it. Just make bloody sure to clear the suite. And clear your schedule to take her around the city...yes, you will, because I'm telling you to. Take her sightseeing or something—just keep her busy."

Hope tried to blot out Tristan's voice, but she couldn't. No more than she could forget the sight of him, hunched over like he wanted to tear his hair out by the roots. She drew up her knees and carefully tucked the dress over them. Why couldn't the low music be louder so that it blotted out that roughly impatient voice?

"Has anything ever distracted me from the job? Or *anyone* for that matter? Nothing has changed. Trust me."

Hope lowered her forehead to her knees.

What a mess.

Chapter Eight

White-gold sunlight speared through the tall windows, cutting across the bed with its mound of pillows. The billowy duvet was tangled in a pale blue heap at the foot of the bed, tumbling halfway off the mattress onto the carpet. Hope stood in the doorway of the adjoining bathroom, tightening the belt of the pristine white terry cloth robe she'd found hanging in the closet, and looked at the disheveled bed.

She, alone, was responsible for the bed getting into such a state. If she had thought Tristan had created a whirlwind through their wedding and reception and the flight, it was nothing compared to the rapid activity she'd experienced when they'd landed. Three men had surrounded her and Tristan the moment they stepped off the plane. They'd barely looked sideways at her, but the way they deferred to Tristan was telling.

After a hair-raising car ride, Tristan had hustled her through a discreet side door of an elegant looking hotel and swept her along with him onto an elevator where he'd punched in some sort of code on a keypad on the wall. Then he'd left her alone in this high-ceilinged, sumptuous bedroom.

She didn't have a clue what room he'd left his ragged black duffel in—if he'd even remained in the hotel, that is.

She'd fallen into bed even though the sun was still above the horizon, slept restlessly and risen again to a sun that was bright and full.

"The wedding night of every girl's dreams," she murmured aloud. Not that she wanted anything different, of course. Did she? She was married to a stranger. Was it any wonder that she felt unsettled?

Hungover, she corrected. That's what she was. Pure and simple. The shower hadn't helped. She tucked her wet hair behind her ears and wandered across the acres of carpet. The fact that the pastel toned carpet was comfortably worn didn't detract from the beautiful floral pattern. The tall windows opened onto a small, iron-railed balcony, and she slowly pulled open the doors. Then she stepped out into the sunlight to a view of a formal garden that was so beautiful she could have looked at it for hours.

The garden was idyllic, but the noise hovering in the air was anything but. Cars. Lots and lots of cars going every which way with no discernable pattern.

She sighed and folded her arms on the rail, tuning

out the cacophony. She suspected it was late morning, but her internal clock was so discombobulated she couldn't have sworn to it. What she did know, however, was that she had no desire whatsoever to put on her coffee-tinted lace dress. Yet it was the only item of clothing she had—except for the lone robe that she'd found.

As thoroughly as Tristan had planned for every contingency, he hadn't thought to stop and collect some of her clothes before whisking her off for their "honeymoon." Even her Gram hadn't come up with some sneaky way of doing that.

Her stomach rumbled and she went back inside, reluctantly closing the windows against the view, but it was so much quieter when she did so. She pulled in a deep breath, opened the bedroom door and stuck out her head. "Quiet as a tomb," she muttered. But somewhere there should be a phone, and room service, with any luck. Her high school French lessons seemed a long time ago, but she figured "coffee" was fairly universal.

Maybe, along the way in her search she'd even find the man she'd married.

She stuck her head in one opened door after another. Tristan had called it a "suite," but as far as Hope was concerned, she felt like she was the only person on the entire floor. She found several other bedrooms, all unoccupied and well appointed, though none quite as lavish as the one she'd used.

She didn't find a phone. But she did find a kitchen. A fully equipped kitchen. A fully *occupied* kitchen.

Hope swallowed against the breath that jammed

in her throat and pressed a shaking hand to her stomach. "Well," she said, feeling positively ill, "I seem to have found the kitchen, the phone *and* you."

She watched Tristan slowly turn toward her and the woman he was with—the woman who had been tangling her red-tipped talons through his blond hair until Hope spoke, raised one raven eyebrow. "Plucking them young these days, aren't you, darling?"

Hope's jaw tightened, and she wished that she'd put on Gram's dress after all. Anything would be better than standing there—wet hair, bare feet and shapeless robe—in the presence of this glossed-to-perfection woman.

Her photo probably accompanied the dictionary's description of *chic,* Hope thought despairingly.

"Shut up, Dom." Tristan waved an absent hand at the table where a tray of fresh fruit and pastries sat. If he felt at all odd that Hope had found him with another woman's hands in his hair, he didn't show it by so much as a blink. "Come on in, Hope."

Lovely. *This* was Dom. The Dom who was supposed to make sure Hope stayed busy. She nearly turned around and headed back the way she'd come. But the glint of superiority in the other woman's eyes stopped her and her feet carried her forward, instead, to the seat Tristan had indicated.

"Did you sleep well?" he asked, pulling out one of the other chairs and straddling it.

The words came out before she thought, just as her gaze skimmed once again over that woman. "Did you?"

The woman laughed softly. She smoothed her lily-white hand over Tristan's denim-clad shoulder, and then held it out toward Hope. "I'm Dominique Marchand," she introduced herself in a faintly accented voice. "Welcome to Paris. Tris doesn't usually bring women here. He doesn't have that much sentiment in his soul."

"Enough, Dom."

Hope wondered at the irritation in Tristan's voice. She wanted to shake the woman's hand about as much as she wanted to kiss a snake. A lifetime of Gram's good manners made her do so. But it was brief, and afterward, beneath the cover of the table, Hope smoothed her hand across her robe as if to wipe away the contact.

She also wondered whether Dominique meant Tristan didn't bring women to Paris in general, or didn't bring women *here*. Why would he need to? He obviously had *Dom*. Sentiment or not. And it was clear that he hadn't mentioned their marriage.

Her throat was tight, but the room itself seemed to wait for her response. "Thank you. Is this a hotel, Tristan? It seems more like an apartment building or something."

"A hotel," he said, shooting the other woman a look that Hope couldn't interpret. "But I'm here a lot and keep this floor available for my use year-round." He nudged the platter toward her. "Once you've eaten, you'll probably want to call your grandmother. I've got some work that will keep me busy for quite a while, but there's plenty to entertain you. An indoor pool and the garden in the courtyard. Shops nearby. We're just off the Champs Élysées.

Dom will take you around the city if you want to do some sight—''

"I'm sure I can occupy myself," Hope interrupted. She reached for a croissant, even though her appetite had ground down to nothing, and stood. "You and your friend needn't worry about me." She turned to go.

"Hope, hold on—"

"Let her go, darling, can't you see she's—"

Hope didn't hang around to hear the rest. *"By all means, darling,"* she mimicked under her breath as she strode along one hallway, then another, trying to find her way through the mazelike floor plan to her bedroom. "Working. Right." Finally, she saw the right door.

"Talking to yourself?"

"Oh!" Hope's foot slid on the cold marble floor and she scrambled for balance, dropping the croissant her clenched fingers had smashed. "Where did you come from?"

Tristan smiled faintly and pointed a thumb over his shoulder in the opposite direction. "Through there." He reached down and scooped up the croissant.

Hope yanked the sash of her robe tighter and sidled around him into the bedroom. "Well. Excuse me."

"Not so fast, sweet pea." He prevented her from closing the door with the flat of his hand.

She released the door, backing away toward the tall windows. "It's your hotel…*floor*. What did you do? Buy it?"

"Sort of. Does that bother you?" He stepped into the room and slowly pushed the door closed.

Feeling every bit the ninny she was, Hope shrugged. She wished he'd left the door open. With it shut, with her bed still tumbled from her restless sleep, she felt buffeted by a nagging sense of intimacy that was so far from reality it nearly made her laugh. Or cry. "Not at all," she denied. "I, uh, I thought you had to work."

He left the croissant on the nightstand and brushed off his hands. "I do. What's wrong?"

Everything. She hid her hands in the pockets of her robe. "I think I, um, made a mistake."

"You did?"

"*We*. We made a mistake." His steady gaze unsettled her. "We *have* to get an annulment."

"No."

"Why not? You surely don't want to be married. I…was weak when I should have stood on my own feet and told Bennett to take a flying leap."

"Bennett will get his," Tristan murmured. "And you're not weak, so stop talking that way. We're married. It's done."

"We, but…we…we don't even know anything about each other! We've never even kissed!" Her cheeks felt on fire. "For…real, I mean."

"Is that an invitation?"

She swallowed and backed away. "No!"

He smiled faintly. "Didn't think so." Then he blew out a slow breath and dropped down onto the foot of her tumbled bed, casually resting his forearms on his thighs. "You're sure now? We *are* married."

Hope frowned severely. That's all she needed. Falling for her husband who apparently had a "Dom" at his beck and call.

"Relax, sweet pea," he said after a moment. "What do you want to know?"

Did Dominique usually use this room? Where had he slept last night? "I don't know!"

He rubbed his jaw, then ran his fingers through his hair. "I'm thirty-four, have all my own teeth and know how to sew a button back on a shirt if it pops off. I'd rather listen to the sound of silence than most any music around, and I hate green beans. Does that help?"

"Don't joke."

"Trust me, sweet pea. The green bean thing is no joke."

She huffed and turned her back on him, escaping onto the small balcony. She stared blindly down at the garden, wishing she had the slightest notion how to handle him.

She wrapped her hands around the rail, and the rings on her finger clinked against it. She wore Clay's wedding band, but she was still a Leoni.

Tristan moved to the rail beside her. "I know this isn't how you expected to spend the rest of your summer," he said quietly, "but if you let yourself, you might enjoy it here. It's Paris."

City of light. City of love. The place where he kept an entire hotel floor available for his use. She stared straight ahead. "Of course."

"Dammit, Hope." He pulled her inexorably around to face him. "Tell me and I'll try to fix it."

"Fixing things is what got us here in the first place."

"So let's make the best of it. I know you've never been to France before. Look at this as a vacation."

"With no clothes?" she burst. "I don't know what kind of vacations *you* take, but I prefer to be dressed on mine! I don't even know how long we're supposed to be here."

He frowned.

"I know you don't pack much—the size of your duffel bag gave that away, but didn't it occur to either you or Gram that I might need something besides that dress?"

He shook his head and nudged her inside. "We didn't have a lot of time to attend to details like that," he said smoothly. "We'll just get some new things for you."

She felt something inside her lift; like a balloon slowly being filled with helium.

"Dom lives to shop. She'll get you fixed up right away."

The helium rushed out with dizzying speed.

"Too bad you're so much taller than she is, or she could give you a few of her things to tide you over while you shop." Now that he apparently figured that all problems were solved, he spoke quickly, as if he'd spent enough of his precious time on this latest little snag.

Hope slowly twisted the rings around her finger. She was only an inch or so taller than Dominique, but the other woman was so excruciatingly thin it would have taken two of her to equal Hope's healthy curves. "So, does Dominique stay here in the hotel, too?"

He nodded, pulling open the door. "Think you can stand wearing your dress for another hour or two?"

Did she have any other choice? "Is this ordinarily her room?"

"What?"

"Dominique. Is this her room?"

"No. Why?"

Hope wished she had enough courage to ask the rest of her question—if Dominique's room was also his room. But she was afraid of the answer. "I didn't want to put anyone out," she said instead. "I'll get dressed now."

He paused for a moment, then nodded again. "Come and find us when you're ready."

Hope shoved her fists into the side pockets of the robe and waited until he'd left, closing the door once more behind him. *Find us.* Just how much of an "us" were he and Dominique?

She wore his rings, though there had never been the slightest discussion about him wearing hers. Had he wanted to wear one, Hope felt sure he wouldn't have overlooked the detail. Which most likely meant the omission was by choice. Instinct had prevented her from offering the one on her necklace—mostly because she couldn't have borne it if—when—he refused it. Even during the wedding ceremony, the minister hadn't looked at Hope as if she was supposed to produce a ring for the man she was impetuously marrying. But what did it matter? What did the rings mean? For her, a cease-fire to the rumors back home in Weaver. But for him? She was merely one more detail in his life about which she knew absolutely nothing.

She was so far out of her depth it scared her. But what scared her more was the depth of her instant dislike for the raven-haired Dominique. And if Tristan thought he could foist her off on Dom, he was dreaming.

That may be the kind of life he led away from Weaver, but she didn't have to accommodate it. The force of her decision left her feeling lightheaded. But at least it was *her* decision.

She straightened her shoulders and strode into the connecting bathroom where she'd left her dress hanging behind the door.

"What do you mean she ditched you?" Tris stared at Dominique.

His associate lifted one impeccable shoulder. "I turned my back for a few moments and she was gone. Poof."

"You're an expert in surveillance," Tris said tightly.

Dominique shrugged again. "Darling, she is a grown woman. She'll find her way back here when she's ready. I still don't know what you brought her here for, anyway. I've got better things to do than babysit your little girlfriend. I'm supposed to be surveilling Pirelli's mistress, not yours. And you've got to break Pirelli's latest computer code so you can do your magic in their databases before Billy and Franco blow their covers and end up dead. We're still behind schedule thanks to Marc." Dominique's obsidian eyes were sharp. "He was thinking about a woman, too."

Marc's mess had nearly gotten Franco—one of Hollins-Winword's best agents since Jefferson's retirement several years earlier—killed once already. It had taken both Coleman Black and Tris to derail that particular disaster without sacrificing eighteen months of work on a case that would put a nasty little terrorist named Abe Pirelli out of illegal arms trading for good. Once they had been satisfied that Franco was safe, Cole had returned to Connecticut and the main control center located there. "Marc's wife left him," Tris reminded.

Dominique's eyebrows rose. "Ooh. *La petite fleur* is having quite an effect on you, darling. Two weeks ago you wanted to strangle Marc yourself, and now you sound almost…ah, *sympathique?* Marc should have known better than to get married and not leave the agency. We all end up divorced."

"Did you say something to upset Hope?"

"*Non.* We were shopping, I told you. Though she kept insisting on picking up those trinkets for her kids rather than finding some clothing for her that doesn't resemble a sack. She looks too young to be a mother, I think."

Tris wanted to shake her. He pushed her into the seat he'd just vacated. "Watch the monitors," he said tightly. "If I can trust you not to turn your back on them."

Dominique pouted. "Darling—"

"Shut up, Dom." He walked out on her, closing the security door that kept the existence of the control center from a chance discovery by any curious hotel staff. Dom was good at her job. The best. She had been able to ferret out details about her targets that had been invaluable to their successes. But the woman was as annoying as a splinter stuck under your thumbnail. He didn't know how Cole stood her. But then, Cole was in Connecticut, wasn't he? Putting plenty of distance, on a regular basis, between him and the woman who occasionally shared his bed, if not his life.

He went downstairs, stopping only long enough to speak with Henri, another H-W agent who also served as the hotel's concierge, before heading out onto the narrow, street. If Hope returned before Tris did, Henri would take care of her. The man was a pillar of reliability and discretion, which was why he was so suited to his cover. Only the H-W agents who used the hotel as a base knew the true purpose of the hotel. The guests who returned year after year—the wealthy, the famous, the privileged—gave their loyalty because the exclusive hotel offered the height of elegance, service and privacy. Which kept anyone from noticing the other activities that occasionally occurred within its historic walls. Activities spanning everything from being a safe house to an occasional prison to a crash zone for operatives going to and from their various gigs.

Tris quickly walked through the streets, searching every shop, every café, for a glimpse of his errant bride. He didn't think she'd have quite the nerve to try the metro. And she had no money that he knew of—he'd told Dom to make sure Hope got whatever she needed. But then, he'd have never thought she'd deliberately evade Dom, either.

Dammit. This was all his fault. The rumors. The wedding. The fact that Hope was all alone some-where on the streets of Paris, probably chewing the hell out of her soft inner lip, and hanging on to her gold necklace like a lifeline.

He stopped on the corner, absently noticing the chatter and the clink of glasses from the people sit-ting at the little umbrella tables of yet another out-door café.

When he found Hope and made sure she was okay, he was going to strangle Dom.

"No, please, Henri. There is no need to call my...Monsieur Clay. I'll just go on up to my, ah, room."

"Monsieur Clay was very clear. He insisted." Henri was inflexible as he picked up a sleek black phone and punched in numbers. "Perhaps *made-moiselle* would like to leave her packages with me and have some refreshment?"

Hope looked over at the elaborately engraved windows that separated the restaurant from the rest of the minuscule lobby. Henri was as excruciatingly polite and courteous as anyone she'd ever met. But she also knew that the man had no intention of let-ting her up to Tristan's floor until he'd phoned.

She sighed and left him with the boxes and bags she'd collected on her afternoon adventure. She'd occupied herself just fine once she'd gotten rid of Dominique, she reminded herself cheerfully, as she entered the restaurant. That woman had been pa-tronizing to the point of rudeness, telling Hope point-blank that if she hoped to ever get Tristan "in her bed,'' she'd better lose the doe-eyed country-girl act.

While Dominique had been aimlessly browsing a narrow rack of touristy T-shirts, Hope hadn't felt the least bit guilty for stepping into a crowd of laughing students, following them out of the shop and down the street.

Once on her own, she'd bought gifts for Gram and Justine and Jolie and Drew. She'd found delightful souvenirs that she would give to her class when school started in the fall. And for herself, she'd found a selection of relatively inexpensive T-shirts, a few pairs of capri pants and some underthings. She only hoped it was enough to get her through until their trip was over, because the next time she went out, she wanted to see the sights that were to be had *outside* of the expensive shops.

Her feet ached and she felt like she was positively wilting from having walked for what seemed miles. But inside, oh inside, she was beaming. Not even the small table she was escorted to in an oppressive corner near the swinging door of the kitchen was enough to dim her enthusiasm.

She smoothed her finger over the useless purse, biting back a smile as she looked at the linen-covered table. But the credit card she'd carried inside had been far from useless. And shopping in Paris was like nothing else in this world. She couldn't wait to try the metro and—

''Where the hell have you been?''

She jumped and looked up at Tristan standing in front of her table, wearing an annoyed expression. ''Henri called you.''

"You've been gone hours."

"There was a lot to entertain me."

He wasn't amused. "Did you get lost?"

"No!"

"Then where have you been?"

"Shopping. Wasn't that what you wanted me to do? Stay busy and out of your hair while you worked?"

He stared at her as if he didn't recognize her, then wedged his tall body into the other seat at the table. "You had no money," he gritted. "You didn't even have the telephone number here in case something happened."

She flipped open her purse and pulled out her credit card. "Plastic," she said flippantly. "Good all around the world, and I didn't even have to know the exchange rate. And I left a trail of bread crumbs so I could find my way home."

"Nice, Hope. Joke. In the meantime, I've spent most of the afternoon looking for you, instead of getting the work done that I've come here to do."

She hated the wave of guilt that swamped her at that. "No one asked you to go hunting for me as if I were a lost infant." She nudged up her glasses and smiled calmly. "As you can see, it wasn't necessary, because here I am. Safe and sound."

He sent away the approaching waiter with an impatient look. "What would you have had me do? Ignore your little disappearing act?"

"I'm surprised you noticed *what* I was doing while your friend is around tangling her long fingernails in your hair and calling you *darling*."

"Dom is an associate," he said impatiently.

Her tongue kept running away from her. "You sleep with all your female associates, then?"

His lips twisted. "Better them than the men."

"Oh!"

"This wasn't like you, Hope." He grabbed her hand and folded his fingers around it and just that easily the bubble of nerves and irritation and shaky confidence that had spurred her along all afternoon wobbled. Hard. "I can't help, if I don't know what's going on. Talk to me."

Hope tugged on her hand, and she folded it over the other hand in her lap. "I just would have appreciated it if you'd warned me what to expect when we arrived here."

"About what? The hotel? You knew I had to work."

"About…Dominique." She felt his narrowed gaze on her face and looked to the side at the other patrons. Couples mostly. Lovers. The whole city seemed to be filled with them. In the shops, at the cafés, on the sidewalks and in the streets. People strolling arm in arm, heads bowed together as if they shared some sweet secret known only to them. "It was a bit awkward, you know. I realize our, ah, marriage is purely for show, but it was still odd to be wearing your rings while you sent me off shopping with your lover."

"Lover?"

"I suppose I can understand why you didn't tell her we were married in Weaver. Might have cramped your style."

"Lover?"

"Why do you keep repeating it? Are you afraid

someone here in the restaurant didn't hear you the first time?''

"Sweet pea, Dominique is most definitely *not* my lover. And I think my boss Cole—the guy who is— might take exception to your insistence otherwise. I didn't tell them because it's none of their business. Marriages aren't real popular in my business, and I thought I was saving us both some grief.'' He leaned over the table, wrapping his hand behind her neck and inexorably tugging her close. "You're sounding remarkably jealous.''

She forgot her curiosity over what that "business" was at that last remark. "I am not jealous.''

He ignored her protest. "Perhaps you *would* like our marriage to be a little less for show and a little more in deed?'' He didn't let go when Hope tried to turn away. "God knows you entice me. More than any female I can recall. I'd certainly like to get the kiss I wanted that got us into this mess. And I'd definitely find it no hardship to take you into my bed. But you'd be the one ending up on the short end of the deal, so consider yourself lucky that I have a few decent cells left in me.''

It was not the first time he'd said something like that. She remembered his caustic words on the flight—that he was all surface and no substance. She'd dismissed them at the time as another indication of the dry amusement that always seemed to hover beneath his surface. But now, with his lips a hair's breadth from hers and his strong fingers shaping the curve of her skull beneath her loose braid, she wasn't so sure. "Why would I be on the short end?'' she whispered.

His lids lowered, and she could *feel* the touch of his gaze on her lips. She thought her heart might well stop.

And then she didn't care, because he leaned that tiny bit farther and covered her mouth with his.

Hope had been kissed before. The first time when she'd been twelve and Jolie's brother had dared her into it one afternoon after school. But she'd eventually learned about the legacy left behind by her mother and by Justine, and Hope had kept her kisses to herself lest she bring any more embarrassment upon Gram. Until she'd gone off to college and met Johnny Mueller. He'd gotten past her defenses, all right. But even he hadn't made her tremble to her toes. He hadn't tasted of dreams—dark, dangerous dreams that sucked at her soul until she couldn't tell where she stopped and he began.

Tristan's fingers angled her head and she willingly went, forgetting that they were in that dark, overly warm back corner of the restaurant; forgetting that they were in a public place; forgetting that they were married only to put the gloss of respectability back on her name.

And when they finally broke apart, her breath tumbled past her lips and she swayed unsteadily. He rested his forehead against hers, sucking in a hard breath. "That's why," he said roughly. "I'd take everything you've got to give and it'd be a hell of a ride, but when we finally landed, you'd be left with nothing. You'd give me your heart. I can see it in your eyes."

Hope drew back and he let her. "Would that be

so bad?'' She smiled quickly, awkwardly, painfully. ''You said it yourself. We *are* married.''

He brushed his thumb over her lips and his lashes shaded his expression. A muscle ticked in his jaw. ''It wouldn't be bad for me. I'm the most selfish guy I know. I'd take it all. But I don't have anything to give back.''

She looked down at the table. He wasn't selfish at all. And despite Dominique's taunt earlier, Hope knew that Tristan possessed plenty of sentiment. ''Because I'm just a plain girl from Weaver and you're the golden-haired guy who keeps an entire Parisian hotel floor at his disposal.''

''No. Because you have a heart to give, Hope. And I don't.''

Chapter Nine

All told, they spent nine days in Paris. Hope learned to ignore Dominique's sharp humor on the few occasions they ran into one another, and to adjust to Tristan's undeniable capacity to focus himself. Since the…episode in the restaurant, Tristan hadn't given Hope one single glimpse of the man who had kissed her as if she was his salvation.

Of course, he was usually working at whatever it was he did in that room he'd thought she hadn't noticed; and when he wasn't working, he was preoccupied and tense. In fact, all of his associates, who came and went at all hours of the day, were tense.

But on one occasion when Hope had mustered some courage and broached the subject of Tristan's "business" with him, he'd shrugged and offered some pat explanation about computer programming

that she hadn't believed for a moment. If it weren't
for the fact that she knew just how deeply his hon-
orable streak ran, she might be worried about what
went on in that secret room. She wasn't worried, but
she was curious. She had no intention of asking
again, particularly since he'd made it plain that he
wanted to keep the fact of their marriage separate
from his work. If Hope wasn't going to go out of
her mind, she had to get out of the hotel and away
from those men and women who came and went,
barely glancing her way as they went about their
business.

With Henri's help and advice, and armed with a
phrase book and guide to Paris, she'd discovered all
the beauty and magnificence of the Louvre; lost her
cheery beret to the gusting wind high atop the Eiffel
Tower; and strolled along the Seine where artists
painted and children played. She sat and had her
portrait done in charcoal, because she couldn't resist
the charming young artist who'd laughed her way.
But she'd hidden the small canvas away in her suite
because she didn't consider the rendition to look
anything like her, and felt silly that she'd spent her
money on something so frivolous.

She explored the garden outside the hotel, and
lounged by the crystal-clear indoor pool. It was all
beautiful and all wondrous but none of it matched
the promise of spending a rare moment with the
stranger who was her husband.

It wasn't wise to fall for him, she knew. He was
confusing and difficult and had told her flat out that
there was no future for them.

He hadn't kissed her again. But that didn't mean

she hadn't relived that moment over and over again. That she hadn't puzzled over his claim at being heartless. Goodness, a heartless man would have *left* her to face alone the rumors of their nonexistent torrid love affair. A heartless man wouldn't care about the schooling of the town's children. A heartless man wouldn't have requested the concierge of their hotel to see that every whim of Hope's was met.

That tidbit had obviously made the rounds beyond Henri, too, because Hope hadn't been seated at that dinky little table in the rear of the restaurant again. And to prove her own stupid sentimentality, Hope had wished she *had* been seated back there.

Then, just that morning, Hope had opened her bedroom door to Tristan's abrupt knock and he'd told her they were leaving the next day. Early.

She'd nodded and promised to be ready.

But, instead of turning on his heel and heading off to do whatever it was that put those new lines in his forehead and beside his mobile lips, he'd looked at her for a long moment, pushed a wad of French currency into her hands and told her to get a nice dress. Because they were going out that night.

So there she was. On the night of their ninth day in Paris, dressed in an outfit that the salesgirl in the exclusive shop had assured Hope was *très magnifique.*

With Tristan nowhere in sight.

When she'd thumped her knuckles on the seemingly solid wall that hid the secret room he disappeared into for hours on end, she'd gotten no answer.

Nobody came and went. Even Dominique hadn't been around with her acerbic humor.

Eight o'clock ticked past. Then nine. Finally, at half past, Hope gathered her purse and the light wrap that went with her little slip of a dress. If she stayed in the suite, she knew she'd drown in the despair that plucked at her with greedy fingers. She'd look in the mirror yet again, see the stranger staring back at her, and convince herself that no matter how much paint she used or what fancy dress she wore, she would never be a match for her gloriously handsome husband.

Husband. What an overstatement. He was the familiar stranger who had signed his name below hers on the marriage license he'd magically produced.

When she stepped out of the private elevator, the appreciative gleam in Henri's eyes went a small way to restoring Hope's flagging confidence. He kissed the back of her hand and gallantly escorted her into the restaurant. But Hope didn't think she could face sitting alone at one of the little round tables, so she went instead to the ornate bar and slipped onto a gilded seat. Henri ordered champagne for her despite her faint protest, told her again that she looked *très belle,* and returned to his post.

Hope warily wrapped her fingers around the glass that was set before her. She looked over her shoulder through the window at Henri. He smiled and tilted his head, obviously waiting for Hope to drink. She sighed and lifted it to her lips. The sparkling, golden liquid burst to life on her tongue and she closed her eyes.

Drinking champagne alone in a bar. Well, wouldn't Gram be proud of her now?

"I'm sorry I'm late."

Hope whirled. Tristan stood behind her, looking as spectacular as he had on their wedding day. Obviously it wasn't the tux that had taken her breath that day, because now he wore black trousers and a thin black sweater that clung to his broad shoulders. He was riveting.

Impossibly handsome or not, she had waited an hour and a half for him, she reminded herself, as she twirled the crystal between her fingers. She had spent all afternoon at a French-speaking hairdresser armed with nothing more than her phrase book and a terribly shaky determination to show Tristan that she could be…what? Like Dominique?

"The kiss of death," Tristan observed, watching her slowly sip.

It was the wrong choice of words. Hope couldn't prevent herself from looking at "their" little table in the back of the room. She set the glass on the bar and turned her back on it. She didn't want to be like Dominique. She wanted to be a normal woman, a kindergarten-through-third-grade teacher. She wanted the man she'd married to not look upon her as some needy little thing whom he had to protect.

"You look lovely," he murmured.

"Don't let the shock throw you."

He tilted his head, narrowed his eyes, and gave an exaggerated sniff.

"What are you doing?"

"Trying to figure out what is in the air that has affected you so."

She adjusted the filmy narrow scarf where it looped over her elbows. "I don't know what you mean."

That amused Tristan. "I don't know what you mean," he parroted. "Have you been taking lessons from Dom?"

"If you're going to be insulting, I'll go out by myself."

Tris eyed her, wondering when he'd blinked and his sexily shy sweet pea had been replaced by this sexily quick-tongued young woman. "You would, wouldn't you."

She nodded and slid off the stool. Tris nearly swallowed his tongue. He'd known she was curvy, of course. A man who enjoyed women as much as he did didn't reach his age without having some clue about what women could hide under baggy clothes. The dress she'd worn the day of the wedding had only hinted, and the thigh-length T-shirts and snug pants that stretched just past her knees that she'd taken to wearing over the last week hadn't been much better.

This dress—this confection of black silk that covered her from neck to knee—yet didn't—wasted no time at hinting. It announced. Loudly and boldly and tauntingly.

"Something wrong?"

She was pure woman from the top of her gleaming, toffee hair down to her toes, encased in high-heeled shoes that screamed sex. She was mesmerizing. And even more slender in the waist than she had been when they'd left Wyoming—and she'd been plenty perfect then.

He realized he didn't know exactly what she'd done during her days when he'd been tiptoeing through the bowels of Pirelli's computer systems, carefully planting the identities that would ensure the safety of his colleagues, and in turn, hundreds of others. "I'm hungry," he said truthfully.

Somehow she'd managed to make her violet eyes look even deeper and more entrancing—yet avoiding the overt look that women like Dom preferred, which also made him realize that she hadn't worn makeup at all before this. "You've done something with your eyes."

Her eyes flickered, but she didn't look away. "Is it just awful? Gram would say I was painting myself up like Justine if she saw me like this."

"Your Gram would say you looked like a beautiful woman," he countered. Ruby Leoni had obviously said a lot of things to her granddaughter. But one important truth she'd kept from Hope, and he didn't know if he agreed with her reasoning or not. But then he wasn't in any position to judge.

Hope was drawing the ends of the scarf through her fingers. "If you're hungry, perhaps we should eat," she said. "Or are we being joined by your associates?"

He shook his head, wondering if she was even aware of the motions of her hand on the scarf. Caressing.

He made himself think of the work—it was a hell of a lot easier on his nerves. The Pirelli case was coming along. His team had done its job, and now it was up to the guys in the field. Tris wouldn't likely be involved again unless there was a hitch in the extraction; otherwise, he'd be around for the debriefing when the dust settled and Pirelli was out of the illegal arms trade and on his way to an eternity in prison. Tris would make his final report, head back to his place in San Diego where he'd continue designing software for computer games until Cole contacted him with the details for their next op. Then he'd be on the move again.

It might take a week. It might take a few more. But Tris knew from experience that he wouldn't be at home for more than a month before something new came up. At least, that was what he'd done dozens of times over the last ten years. This time when Tris headed back to San Diego, he'd be taking along a passenger.

His wife. Yet not his wife.

A woman who tied him in knots simply with the way she absently toyed with that filmy black scarf.

"Tristan? Do you want to go, or not? Because I'm perfectly capable of occupying myself. There is a nightclub I passed the other day that I want to visit and—"

He slid his hand up her back and she went silent. "If you think I'm going to let you loose on the club scene here, you're dreaming."

"I'm of age and reasonably intelligent," she sputtered. "I've managed to keep myself safe over the past nine days."

"Thank God. But you're a walking invitation to men in that dress." He escorted her past Henri who smiled benevolently at them as the liveried doorman awaited their exit.

"I didn't buy this dress to gain attention from

strange men,'' Hope said. ''I bought it to please my-self.''

''Does it?''

She glanced down at the dress. ''I've never owned anything like it. Even Gram's dresses from when she was young don't compare to this. It's—''

''Almost worthy of the woman who fills it.'' He wrapped his arm around her shoulder, only, he reasoned, because they were crossing the uneven street and she wore heels that were so high he wondered how she could walk at all. She stiffened for a moment, then relaxed.

''It's so beautiful here,'' Hope sighed long moments later as they rounded a corner and the golden glitter of the Champs Élysées at night was laid out before them.

''It has its points,'' Tris murmured, watching the way the streetlights reflected on Hope's eyeglasses. ''Nearsighted or farsighted?''

She glanced up at him, then away, and he realized that the veneer of confidence she'd acquired was not so thick, after all. ''I need them for driving.''

He stepped in front of her, uncaring that they were in the middle of the sidewalk, blocking the other people who were out strolling. ''You're not driving now.'' She lifted one shoulder in a shrug, and the filmy wrap slid down her arm.

''So?''

''So,'' Tris yanked his gaze up from her shoulder, ''let's try it without them.'' He slipped the gold frames off her nose and tucked them in his pocket before she could protest. ''If you walk into the Seine accidentally, I'll let you have them back.''

Her fingers lifted to her neck, and he knew that she wore her necklace under the black band of fabric that circled her throat. The dress started there, high on her neck and cut a sharp angle downward, covering everything except the whole of her shoulders and arms and a painfully tantalizing slice of flesh when she lifted her arm. It was simple and owed every bit of its appeal to the astonishingly perfect figure beneath.

"But I always wear my glasses," Hope protested faintly.

"Not tonight." He didn't want her hiding behind the protection of her eyeglasses.

"Afraid someone will see you with old four-eyes?"

Tris tucked her hand under his elbow and started slowly along the famous thoroughfare. "Nobody here knows me or cares about me." Certainly no reporters desperate for a story.

"Henri does. He says you don't eat enough when you're here. And Dominique."

"Henri is a fuss-pot, and we go way back. And Dom, well, who can explain Dom? She's brilliant and a pain in the neck."

"She's beautiful."

"If you care for the type," Tris agreed blandly. "Cole is welcome to her, I say."

They walked along in silence and with each step Tris tortured himself by focusing on the feel of her breast brushing against his arm.

"You were never involved with her, then? Ever?"

"I've kissed you more than I've kissed Dom," Tris murmured.

"But, you've...ah...kissed lots of women."

He looked down at her head. Her hair was twisted into an intricate knot on her head, but several long strands had worked loose. Or perhaps she'd left them dangling at her nape and her temple to drive him around the bend. "A few," he answered absently, not sure if she'd been making a statement or asking a question. "But I don't get involved with women—not the way you're implying." Not anymore.

"Ever?"

"I'm the computer guy, remember? So tell me, who was your first kiss?"

"Jolie's brother."

"You must've been pretty young. He died when he was fifteen or so, didn't he?"

Hope nodded. "He kissed me on a bet," she said after a moment. "To see if I was as...easy as Justine's legacy implied."

There was nothing but acceptance in her voice. No old anger, no hurt. Nothing. He pushed his free hand in his pocket. "Anyone since?"

She tilted her head and looked up at him sideways. "Other than you, you mean?"

He slowly grinned.

She rolled her eyes and slipped her hand from his arm, walking ahead. Tris watched her from behind, following along. He wondered if she had the slightest conception of how she'd blossomed here in Paris. He wondered if she knew that when she reached up to push a pin back into her hair, he could see the outer curve of her breast. Just the narrowest glimpse of velvety skin.

Mostly, he wondered why she hadn't answered him.

He caught up to her. "So was there anything in Paris that you wanted to see or do that you haven't?"

She shook her head, pushing in that pin yet again. "No. I'm sure Henri kept you well informed of my daily excursions."

Not enough to give Tris some advance warning of Hope's heart-stopping transformation. "Does that bother you?"

"Not as much as it bothered me to have you assign Dominique as my official keeper."

"I didn't do it to hurt you, Hope."

She nodded. "I know." She turned around and looked back up the avenue, ablaze in lights. "You were just doing what you do. Taking care of things. Protecting things."

"You're not a thing, Hope."

She looked down, and he followed her gaze. She was twisting the wedding set around her finger. "Sure I am. I was something else you were protecting. I suspect Henri thinks I'm just someone under your protection."

He frowned. The only protection she needed was *from* him. "I know you've called Ruby a few times. Everything okay back home?"

"Yes. Brenda's cousin-the-reporter came back and wanted to get interviews from the wedding guests, but Gram says everyone has closed ranks against that sort of thing. Even Bennett, oddly enough. Soon after, I guess, she was assigned to a food column. Now, everyone in Weaver is talking about how romantic it was, you sweeping me off my feet the way they think you did.'' She wouldn't look at him. ''Too bad they didn't do that before the wedding. You wouldn't be saddled with a wife you don't want.''

''I'm not saddled, Hope.''

Her lips moved, but her expression was too solemn for it to be a smile. ''Well. That's kind of you to say.''

And she didn't believe him for a second. He drew in a long breath. This was getting too deep. ''You had a club in mind?''

Hope nodded and pointed.

''All right then,'' he said smoothly. ''Let's get moving before I decide I'd rather stand here and keep you to myself.''

She shook her head, clearly disbelieving.

He could have convinced her easily enough. All he'd have to do would be to pull her into his arms, taste her lips again, and he knew they'd both forget the nightclub. They'd forget everything except each other.

But if he ever wanted to have a restful night's sleep again—something he figured *would* return in time if he didn't rock the boat too badly—he knew he couldn't go there. Not after that kiss they'd shared. The kiss, he was beginning to fear, that had been worth every minute of inconvenience and disruption it had caused—both before it had occurred, and after.

So it was definitely time to stop thinking about it,

he told himself roughly. He grabbed Hope's hand and strode toward the club.

It was crowded, but Tris was big and people just naturally stepped out of his way. He also knew the owner, so it wasn't long before he and Hope were inside where the music throbbed through their bones. There was every manner of dress inside and for a moment, Tris let himself see the place through Hope's wide eyes—bodies crushed together on the dance floor, cocktail waitresses wearing next to nothing serving everything from martinis to ginger ale.

Hope looked up at him, and he leaned down to hear. "Toto, I don't think we're in Kansas anymore."

But there was only sparkle in her eyes and Tris smiled. She was still the same woman he'd pushed on a swing one Sunday afternoon. There wasn't one logical reason they should have much in common, but he liked her. When he wasn't silently cursing them both for the want that ate at him from the inside out, that was. "Want to dance, or eat?"

She slipped the wrap off her arms and left it on the high stool she'd been using. Looping her fingers through his, she tugged him toward the dance floor. Her eyes flashed when she looked at him over her shoulder. "I want it all," she laughed. "Every last little thing!"

The fire in his blood leaped through every single pore. How in the hell was he supposed to resist her like this? It was hard enough when she had her schoolteacher persona firmly in place. Hard. There was a laugh.

Thank God the music was loud and fast. It meant he could keep the space of an inch or two between them. Because holding her against him right now would be an education for them both.

He couldn't remember the last time he'd gone clubbing. Probably not since Serena. She'd loved the nightlife in California. She'd said she'd loved him, too. But his dysfunctional heart had been untouched. Just as it had been when, a few months later, she'd left.

He wasn't human, she'd accused at the end. Her reasons were valid, the most valid in the world, he knew. She'd been deeply hurt and he hadn't been able to lie and tell her she was wrong about him.

In the minuscule, shifting bit of floor Hope had found among the revelers, she lifted her hands above her head, whirled to the music and showed Tris that when it came to his violet-eyed temptress, his humanity didn't count.

He was just a man who wanted to capture that whirling dervish and swallow her smiles and taste the skin that warmed her necklace underneath that drive-him-mad dress.

She suddenly danced close, and even among the throng he could smell the subtle scent of her skin; feel the warmth of her flesh; taste in his mind the bead of moisture that had formed at her temple. "What do *you* want?" she asked breathlessly.

"I want it all," he said, settling his hands on her shoulders, feeling the scorch of her bare skin against his palms. All his good intentions at that moment mattered not at all. He was just a man. And she, right or wrong, was his wife. ''Every last inch of you.''

Her lips parted. He groaned. And took them.

Chapter Ten

Over the edge of his laptop, Tris glanced at Hope. Again. She was still peering out the window, and he wondered what was so fascinating about watching the wings of the jet cut through the layers of cloud. Or, maybe she just couldn't stand to look at him.

He'd lay bets on the latter.

When he should have been finalizing his report for Cole, he continued watching Hope's profile. The smooth, clear forehead. The nose that was cut just a little short at the end, saving it from an aristocratic elegance and giving it more personality. Smooth, rounded jaw with just a hint of stubbornness—the grit she displayed more easily since he'd virtually left her to sink or swim in Paris.

He should have known she and Dom wouldn't

become bosom buddies. Dom didn't exactly relate well with other women.

Well, Hope hadn't sunk. Not that he'd expected her to. She'd swam, she'd burst from the water in a miraculous spray of water. She'd blossomed. She'd soared.

"Think you'll miss Paris?"

Hope looked over at him, surprised. And why not? He'd barely spoken to her since they had left the hotel. Hours ago. They'd boarded the plane, and Tris had immediately buried his nose in work.

"It was unforgettable," she answered after a moment. Her attention turned again toward the window. "Almost like a *real* honeymoon," she murmured. "Except nobody but you and I knew we'd even exchanged vows."

Score for the lady.

It had been approaching dawn when Tris finally flagged down a taxi to take them back to the hotel. It wouldn't have taken a lot of effort on his part to gain an invite into her bedroom once they'd arrived. She'd had champagne again, she'd been bubbling with energy after their evening, and she'd been so tempting he'd had to nearly chew off his own tongue to keep from pursuing her.

He'd seen the confusion clouding her eyes when he'd kissed her chastely on the forehead and nudged her into her bedroom. Alone.

"I like home better." Hope's voice drifted slightly above the hum of the jet engines and he had to strain to hear.

"Weaver?"

She nodded. She rested her chin on her arm.

"Have you been to California?"

"No."

"Ever wanted to go?"

"Doesn't matter, does it? I'm going."

"Well, hell, Hope. All this enthusiasm of yours might just knock the plane off course. Be careful, would you?"

She looked at him again. "Why don't you like Weaver?"

"Who said I don't?"

"You rarely visit. It looked to me like you got on with your family just fine. What other reason is there?"

His thumb tapped his keyboard. "I don't dislike Weaver."

"Then it must be your family. Your dad, maybe? Because he married again? I know that bothered you."

"No," he said with exaggerated patience, "it didn't bother me. I'm not into weddings. Most men aren't, you know. My family is fine. They've got great lives. But that's their lives. Not mine."

"Married and starting families, you mean."

He watched her. "Why are you going on about this?" There was a small vein pulsing in her milky-pale temple.

"Remember last night when we were walking? Before we went to the nightclub?"

"It was less than eighteen hours ago, sweet pea. I remember."

"We were talking about you protecting everyone."

"Well, not exactly."

"Yes, exactly." She moistened her lips but didn't look at him. "I don't know at all what kind of work you were doing in Paris. But everyone deferred to you, you know."

"I'm not the boss. Cole is."

"Maybe so, but he wasn't there, was he? Everyone from Dominique to Henri to the garçon in the restaurant to the men who escorted us to and from this plane—they all looked to you for direction before making a single move."

If Cole had his way, Tris would eventually take over Cole's job as head of Hollins-Winword. Tris was even beginning to consider it himself. Mostly for the challenge. As usual, his interest in a job only went so far before he needed new ground. And it wasn't as if he had a personal life he'd be sacrificing for that life. "What's your point? You want me to give you the rundown on how I make my living?"

She moistened her lips, swung her knees around on the couch-style seat and wrapped her arms around them. "No. If you wanted me to know, you'd tell me."

"What if I was some kind of, I don't know, international jewel thief or something?"

"Oh, please. You'd never do anything…nefarious."

So she didn't know him so well, after all. "When I was twenty-three, I shut down NORAD's power grid. Hacked into the National Security Agency. Rerouted a couple of planes. Airforce One among them."

Her eyes blinked. Shock visibly rippled through her. "Oh my."

"It was either go to work for them or…"

"Or?"

"…or go to jail," he said flatly. What the hell was he doing? He didn't talk about his work. Not even Jefferson, who had been on the H-W payroll as a field agent for years, had known until just a few years ago that Tristan was even *part* of H-W, much less why. God knows he'd never felt inclined to admit getting nailed by the Feds eleven years ago. But if he hadn't been caught, Tristan's particular skills wouldn't have been made known to Coleman Black. Cole wouldn't have then negotiated for Tristan's services from the government, and God only knows what he'd have been doing since then. Punching out license plates, probably.

"Why did you do it? And what about your company? T-Comp, wasn't it?" Her voice was faint.

"I did it because I could," he said. "And my business was real. It made me a passel of money, particularly when I sold it." He'd made so much he'd never need to work another day in his life. But where was the fun in that?

"So you work for the government now? Is that why you're so secretive?"

"Not exactly."

Her soft lips compressed. "*Not exactly* seems to be one of your favorite phrases. And you're changing the subject again. You do that a lot when you don't want to answer something personal."

"It's not personal to tell you about my hacker days?"

She lifted her shoulder in a decidedly Parisian way. "You're legal now, right?"

"I'm not in danger of going to jail."

"Why doesn't anyone know about this? My life is an open book in Weaver—even if some of the people write their own passages on my pages. I've never heard *anything* about you like this."

"No reason you would. My work is confidential in nature."

Her eyes studied him and he felt a ridiculous urge to squirm in his seat. "You're protecting people," she murmured after a moment.

He shook his head, looking again at the open computer on his lap. "Don't start weaving fantasies about it," he advised. "It's not that interesting."

"Does your family know?"

"That I'm not that interesting? You bet."

"Do they know you keep those rooms in Paris?"

"They know I travel a lot."

"But not why."

She couldn't possibly know what a distraction she was, he thought. Not just her conversation, but her entire being. He'd been a knot of need ever since the nightclub. Hell, since well before that. Since a hometown café. "Does it matter?" he finally countered.

Her eyes narrowed and she ran the tip of her tongue thoughtfully along the edge of her pearly teeth. Her hair was pinned up with some sort of clip, and she wore a baggy white T-shirt with a picture of the Eiffel Tower running up the center. Snug, bright-red pants hugged her legs, ending just below her knees. She looked like a kid. And he wanted this version of her just as badly as he wanted the woman he'd left outside her bedroom door.

"Yes," she said after a moment, "it does matter."

"My brothers are aware of the general thrust of my work," he finally answered. "But we don't usually sit around yakkin' about it."

"The general thrust being *protection.*"

Thrust. Hell of a word to choose. He was slipping. His eyes lingered on her legs. "If you like."

"Which brings me back to my point." She moved her palm over her ankle. "Who protects you?"

He lifted his eyebrows. "Am I in danger?"

She grimaced. "Maybe from the people who sneak in and out of that secret room of yours in Paris."

Tris held back an oath. He'd known the likelihood of keeping Hope totally in the dark about the control center had been slim. He'd just hoped that she'd be preoccupied enough with exploring the city that she'd pay no mind to what else went on in the hotel. Shows how much he underestimated his wife. Under that good-girl, virginal exterior lay a mind that was plenty sharp. "They're my associates. I'm not in danger."

Despite the work he did for Hollins-Winword, it was the people who depended on his expertise who regularly walked their lives down the center divide of jeopardy's road. He tiptoed through cyberspace; peeking here, planting there. Creating identities, removing all traces of others. Rerouting, reconnoitering, reinventing. He did it to protect people like his brothers, Jefferson and Daniel and even Sawyer, to some extent—who'd spent years scattered out there trying to bring justice to a world where justice was a scarce commodity. Tris wasn't a dangerous guy. But he *was* single-minded. And the second time he'd gotten into the NSA system, he hadn't been caught. So he'd introduced them to a whole new set of system safeguards.

"That's not what I meant, anyway," Hope dismissed.

"I'm not sure I want to *know* what you meant," he murmured dryly. Truthfully.

She rubbed her hand up and down her bare calf. "I don't want you to share details of your work with me unless you *want* to. What I meant was who do you go to when you need protection?" She made an impatient sound and rose, pacing back and forth in front of him. "Who guards your heart, Tristan? Your fears?"

He was silent for a moment. "I told you already that my heart doesn't function that way," he said flatly. "And if I have any fears, it's more in the area of knowing we're alone on this plane except for the crew up there in the cockpit and there is a king-sized bed in that bedroom behind you just waiting to be messed up."

She stopped dead in her tracks. He hadn't returned her glasses to her yet, and he watched her eyes widen and look away. "There was a nice-sized bed in my room last night at the hotel, too," she said huskily. She looked at him again, a little frown pulling at her eyebrows. "I think you say things like that just to shut me up."

He smiled slowly.

"And you smile that way—all wicked-like—because you think it'll scare me off."

He dumped the computer on the table beside him. "If you're smart, it would."

"Don't you let anyone get close to you, Tristan?"

"Sure." He raised one eyebrow. "You want to come over here and sit on my lap? I won't object."

"You are impossible."

"And you are every inch a woman with all the needs to apply nicer labels on what is, essentially, a basic thing." Impatience ran through him. "Men want sex. Women want love. And they'll turn and twist it every which way from Sunday in order to convince themselves that sex *is* love."

"Who was it that twisted it on you?" Her eyes were flower soft.

"Nobody."

"Your brothers love their wives. Your father loves Gloria."

"I never said they didn't."

"So it isn't as if you don't believe in love. You just don't believe in it for you. That's so typical."

Tris smiled faintly. "I believe I'm being insulted."

"Maybe you are."

"And this, after I've sacrificed my sacred bachelorhood for you."

"No one asked you to," she said seriously. "You cared about the school, too. But you'll have it back—your sacred bachelorhood, I mean—soon enough."

The school was the farthest thing from his mind just then. "Why is that?"

"Because we're going to get an annulment."

"I've already told you that's not going to happen."

She propped her hands on her hips. "There are two of us involved here, you know."

"An annulment should occur only when a marriage hasn't been consummated."

Her cheeks went pink. "Well, there you go. No problem there."

He slowly pushed out of his chair. "You really don't believe that I want to take you to bed."

Now, her cheeks were red. Her soft lips compressed. "No," she blurted. "No man ever has."

"Who was the idiot who convinced you of that?" She didn't answer and he felt murderous. "Did you love him?"

"Did you love *her?*" she countered, her eyes pained. "The woman who twisted sex and love on you?"

The silence stretched between them. "You *wanted* me to follow you into your room last night," he finally said.

"I—Yes," she admitted, casting him a defiant look.

He'd never understand women. They were the most confounded creatures ever put on Earth. "If you want to have sex, just say so, Hope. Convince me that you understand that's all it can be, and I'm game."

She exhaled noisily. But her cheeks were nearly as red as those snug little half-pants she wore.

He pushed to his feet and grabbed her hand, pulling her toward the bedroom.

She gasped and dug her bare feet into the carpet.

He hid a smile and looked back at her. "Changed your mind so soon?"

Her chin angled and her eyes snapped. "Aren't you afraid I'll be so overcome that I'll burden you with my profession of undying love?"

"You'll be overcome all right," he murmured. Any minute now she'd tell him to take a flying leap. As well she should. His behavior was abominable.

But he had to get her to stop thinking about making love. He was thinking about it enough for *both* of them. His good intentions only went so far and right now, they were miserably thin.

It was his own fault. He should have continued keeping her at a safe distance instead of recklessly suggesting last night's "on the town" activities.

She toyed with her necklace. "Is this your plane or does it belong to the people you work for? The 'not exactly' government."

Where was she going with that mind of hers now? "Mine."

"Do you usually travel with women?"

"Hordes," he smoothly lied. "I have a regular flying orgy going on up here."

"I don't believe you. I think you haven't been close to a woman in years," she countered. "If ever at all."

It was a few bytes too close to the truth. He wondered warily why it was that Hope was the one who saw it. Not his associates, not his brothers, not even Emily. Only this girl-woman who had apparently dived impetuously into the woman side of that equation while wandering the streets of Paris.

He deliberately drew his finger along the fine line

of Hope's jaw. "I'm not out of practice, if that worries you. But if you've changed your mind about pursuing this, say the word."

She was blushing from her forehead to her toes. "Not at all," she assured him. Her chin tilted, challenging.

A war of wills, he thought, intrigued more than he wanted to admit. "Did you ever play 'chicken' when you were younger?"

He could see her mind busily processing. "I had more sense," she said, her tone lofty. "Are you suggesting that I have less nerve than you?"

"I'm sure of it, sweet pea. You're the one who has never done this before. Right?"

Her soft lashes narrowed, leaving a slice of violet gleam that, if he'd been a fearful man, would have made him distinctly uneasy. She moistened her lips and stepped closer to him. So close that her soft curves grazed against his chest. He could feel the warm rise and fall of every torturously slow breath she drew.

"Right," she murmured silkily. Her head tilted slightly. "Are you too warm?" She reached up and drew her fingertip across his forehead, feathering the hair at his temple. "You feel—" she sighed, and he felt the punch of it to his gut "—feverish."

He caught her hand. The steady, dull roar of the plane engines hummed around them, enclosing them in their own private world. He stared at her and she stared back. He knew she was as acutely aware of their absolute privacy as he. "This isn't a game," he warned. "It's not swings in the park. It's not champagne in Paris, and my control is in short supply. I know what I want, Hope. Are you sure you know what *you* want?"

Yes. Your heart. Hope looked up at his fingers, manacled so impossibly gently, around her wrist. She'd been half in love with him even before the day she spilled coffee on him in the café. He'd been the hometown boy who'd had the world by the tail. He'd been the stuff of girlish fantasies, the white knight who rescued the damsel in distress.

But who was the real Tristan Clay? The man who wore a tuxedo as if born in one, who'd spoken fluent French in the nightclub the night before? Or this man who wore faded jeans, athletic shoes with a hole building above his toe and a yellow-and-purple tropical print shirt that was saved from garishness only because it was so faded?

Either way, he'd been the man who had pushed her on the swing in the park. Who had surprised her with Chinese food and played video games with a five-year-old boy. But he was so much more.

She could see it in the lines fanning out at the corners of his sapphire eyes. Eyes that held so much of the feelings that he claimed his heart didn't recognize. A heart that protected others, but refused protection for itself. He was a mystery to her, yet she felt like she knew him better than she knew herself.

She looked down to see his free hand curled into a fist at his side. She reached for it, slowly sliding her fingers around his wrist, in the same way he held her. She didn't know if it was his pulse she felt against her thumb or her own.

Or maybe their hearts were both pulsing slowly, heavily, one in tempo with the other.

She swallowed, not with nervousness but with the sureness of putting her trust in a man whose entire being was focused on caring for those around him. Even if he couldn't admit it.

She met his gaze, feeling the warmth of that intense blue deep down inside where she trembled and ached for something she'd never known. "I want the same thing you want," she said, and her voice shook only a little. "Right here. Right now."

Her chest felt tight, her skin burning beneath her clothing. She could barely breathe, waiting. Waiting, while he looked at her, his eyes full of something she couldn't put a name to no matter how hard she tried.

And when he did move, it was almost in slow motion, his eyes flickering over the fingers that she couldn't wrap all the way around his larger, masculine wrist. But the slowness was deceptive and in less than a blink, he'd reversed the positions until he held that wrist, too.

She flexed her fingers, her hands held aloft—away from him, away from her.

"Why?"

One simple word. One complex question. She searched for words, but none came. "I—"

He exhaled a sharp breath and tugged her wrists, pulling her hard and tight against him. "Never mind," he growled. "I don't care."

Her head fell back under the onslaught of his lips against hers. She could feel every imprint of his long fingers as he spread them around her waist, up her back. Then she gasped, breathing his breath, when he lifted her right off her feet.

"Hold on." His lips moved against hers and she wrapped her arms around his neck. "I won't drop you."

"I know." She'd never felt more secure in her life. More alive. More sure. She felt his hand on her hip, on her knee, pulling her thighs alongside his strong hips. She tore her lips from his, pressing her forehead to his shoulder. Then he was moving, and she closed her eyes tightly. Oh, please, if this was a dream, let her never awaken.

The soft click of the bedroom door closing was not a dream. The give of the mattress under her bare feet was not a dream when he settled her there, standing, looking down at him.

She moistened her lips, pressing her hands against his shoulders, adjusting to the reversal of heights. Weak sunlight shone through the porthole windows on the other side of the bed, enough to make strands of his burnished hair gleam like it had been dipped in liquid gold. The glisten drew her trembling fingers like a magnet, and his hair felt cool and heavy and slick as satin.

He stood there, a muscle ticking unevenly in his jaw and let her fingertips explore. The shape of his head. The curve of his ears. The bridge of his sharp blade of a nose. The mobile curve of his lips.

Oh, his lips.

His lashes lowered and she felt his hands on the hem of her oversized T-shirt. Then he was drawing it upward. She tilted her head, moved her arms and the soft, warm cotton fell to the floor.

She could hear him breathing. Felt his eyes like a physical caress on her breasts that, until this exact moment, she'd always cursed. His hand smoothed up her bare arm, shaped her shoulder, followed the edge of white satin, the necklace that dipped into the valley between her breasts. Her mouth went dry, and her eyes felt heavy.

His palm slipped over one aching peak, so lightly she might have imagined it. "Please," the word sounded on her lips without volition. Her fingers curled against his shoulder, grasping the washed-soft fabric. She didn't know for what she begged, only knew that his hands came up along her hips, tightening, soothing, tormenting.

His gilded head moved, and his lips touched her collarbone. Tasted her shoulder. Breathed against her breasts, warmed her skin through the thin fabric that separated them. Hope's knees went to water. "Tristan—"

"Sshh. It'll be all right."

She sank her teeth into her lip, sucking in her breath when he flicked the center clasp undone and peeled back the bra.

"Perfect." He flattened his palm against her spine and drew her toward him. Her flesh sang, bloomed, swelled. Felt perfect, only because of his kiss so reverent, the tip of his tongue so sinful. Hope pressed her cheek to his hair, gasping for breath. Her head spun with madness.

Then he was pulling back, leaving her swaying. But only for a moment—a moment when he yanked at his shirt and sent it flying. Then he was lifting her from the mattress, holding her against him, her breasts grazing his hard, sinewy muscles as he slowly lowered her feet to the carpet.

She was weak. Her grasping hands reached for purchase, found his belt loops, felt the sharp intake of breath he gave when her hands brushed against him. He suddenly covered her fingers with his hand, stilling her trembling.

"If you wanna stop, say so now," he gritted. "After this, you're mine."

Hope's lips parted. She struggled for speech. But words wouldn't come. She drew her fingertip over his ridged abdomen. Felt his muscles leap. She leaned forward, pressing her mouth against his chest.

He sighed deeply, and folded her against his chest. The contact made her head reel, her flesh seeming to soften and mold to his harder angles. She felt his hands on her hair, releasing the clip and her hair tumbled down her back, over his hands, around them. A moan rose in her throat when he threaded his fingers through the long strands, slowly wrapping his fists in it.

She wasn't sure who was trapped. Her or him. She wasn't sure it even mattered.

Instincts were all she had, and she reached for the metal button at the waist of his jeans. He went still and she looked up, seeing the grimace on his face. Uncertainty accosted her. He smiled faintly, but it wasn't with amusement. His eyes were dark, intense. He released her hair, and it slid over her shoulders, her breasts. "Keep going."

Her lips were dry. She swallowed and he made a soft sound, tilting her chin up with his thumb. His lips traced hers, his tongue teased. Her head fell back under the pressure, and the uncertainty faded as if it never was. She tugged at his jeans, and the button popped loose. It sounded as loud as a cannon in the stillness, and she couldn't help jumping.

He smiled faintly against her lips, and it was like sending champagne bubbles straight to her bloodstream. A breathless laugh rose in her throat and she pressed her palms flat against his abdomen, running them with ever increasing delight up his torso, exploring every ridge, every broad plane. His flat nipples tightened against her palms and she murmured in amazement.

"You're gonna be the death of me," he muttered with half a laugh. With one hand he yanked back the bedding and tumbled her onto the mattress. She saw him reach out, without looking, and rummage in the drawer of the nightstand. Hope's smile faltered at the evidence of his preparedness. But then he was kissing her again, her breath becoming his and his becoming hers and she forgot to care. Their clothes disappeared as if by magic.

His long legs slid along hers, his hands tormented, soothed and tormented again. She was surrounded by him, by his heat, his scent, his touch. And still, every nerve inside her screamed for more. His back was hot and flexed under her searching fingers, his shoulders were wide and roped with muscle. And there, oh, there, she could feel him against her.

And just when she didn't think she could possibly live another moment without *something,* he stopped. A sob burst past her lips. "Please—"

He pushed up on his arms, his head bent over hers. "I don't want to hurt you."

"You won't." Tears collected in the corners of her eyes. Oh, she loved him.

He growled something under his breath and pressed.

Her lips parted. He stopped. She arched against him, mindless with need.

His back bowed and he lifted her against him, swallowing her involuntary cry with his kiss. She didn't know where she left off and he began. Her senses fragmented, stunning her. She cried out his name.

Tris groaned, feeling her come apart in his arms, convulse against him. She was silken and hot and she was tight and every curve fit him like never before. She was living hope, and he couldn't stop, couldn't wait to make sure she was all right, couldn't do anything but take everything she gave and gave.

He pressed his face into her toffee hair and gave up the notion that he'd ever been in control around her. Then she pushed her fingers through his hair and pressed her mouth to his, shaking, arching. Breathless sounds of need in her throat, and still she gave.

Her name screamed through his brain.

And he was lost.

Chapter Eleven

"I've never brought a woman on this plane," Tris admitted against her ear a long while later. His fingertips slowly trailed along her spine, content for the moment to indolently caress each little ridge under her satin-smooth skin. "Only you."

She was draped over his chest, her body sweet and warm and lax. "Your well-stocked drawer suggests otherwise," she murmured.

"Cole's sense of humor," he admitted blandly. "Been there, unused for a long while. Let's hope there's not an expiration date or something."

Her eyes drifted shut. "Thank you," she murmured sleepily.

"For what?"

"Making me your wife," she whispered.

Tris didn't answer. But she didn't notice, because she'd fallen asleep.

He stared into the shifting shadows of his airborne bedroom, absorbing the warm weight of her snuggled against him; absorbing the clean scent of her hair that spread over them both as she slept.

She was his wife. It was true.

Making love to her was like nothing he'd ever experienced, and the knot inside his gut told him that it wasn't because he'd been alone for years.

It was because she was Hope.

Kindergarten-through-third grade teacher.

Who saw enough to ask stinging questions about protecting his heart.

He could make love to her for the next millennium and never tire of her. He knew it with everything inside him.

But that didn't mean he had the heart to love her.

Against him, she made a soft sound. Satisfied. Sexy.

He closed his eyes and gently nudged her onto the bed beside him. It was better to leave now, than lay there with her, waiting for the inevitable urge he would get to escape. It would come. It always did, but he'd never before dreaded it.

He'd do exactly what he'd warned her of that first day in Paris. He'd take everything she had to give, and in the end she'd have nothing.

God help him, he didn't know what he could do to change it. He was a pathetic excuse of a man that he would take what physical pleasures she offered, knowing he was incapable of giving back the emotion she deserved. He'd married her to save her from one hurt, only to risk her heart in another way.

She sighed again, her hand sweeping along his hip, staying him when he would have left the bed. ''Don't go,'' she mumbled, her hand gliding over his chest to settle over the spot where his heart beat. ''I'll protect you,'' she murmured.

Tris went still. He looked down to find her violet eyes watching him. Her fingertips felt like burning pokers against his chest, and his heart, that unfeeling organ, jerked like an engine about to fire.

Time seemed to stand still as he waited—waited to see if he felt something there; something that would tell him he wasn't the inhuman freak he'd been accused once too often of being.

He felt Hope's gaze and the urge to get out of there, now, right this second now, slammed into him. And it wasn't anything like the ''morning after jitters'' he'd detested so much that he'd simply stopped getting involved with women that way. This was pure hell and just getting out of the bed wasn't anywhere near enough distance to put between them.

But where could he go? He left jumping out of planes to thrill-junkies like Jefferson.

Her lashes lowered over her eyes and he saw the long, smooth line of her throat move when she swallowed. She shifted on the bed and the tangled sheet didn't quite follow, barely sliding over one creamy hip.

Tris sat up, fierce want tangling with that mighty urge to escape. He knew he should look away, that his frank regard of her was probably unsettling her, despite what had just occurred. But he couldn't.

Innocence still shone from her face, but her beautiful, full breasts were peaked, wantonly inviting. Then she slowly drew up her left leg, her knee bending; slender, arched foot gliding on the mattress.

She could have been a model for an ageless painting—wanton innocence. The white sheet draped diagonally over her hip, revealing but not revealing. Her skin shone like a pearl, cool to the glance, but he knew if he touched her she'd be warm. As Tris watched, Hope touched the necklace.

But now, she didn't work the chain back and forth between her thumb and forefinger as she did when she was uncertain. She let the necklace lay, and watched him through her lashes as she slowly, so slowly, followed the gold links with her fingertip.

He wondered why the top of his scalp didn't explode from the blast of heat that rose in him.

She wasn't uncertain at all, he realized. She was seducing him with nothing more than the slow glide of her fingertip along a necklace that held—of all impossible things—a wedding ring.

"Why?" he asked.

Her soft lips curved faintly. Her fingertip reached the man-sized ring at the end of the necklace and began inching upward once again. He braced his hand on the mattress and decided abruptly that his efforts at keeping the sheet bunched at his own waist to protect her sensibilities was laughable. She was the one who was shocking him to his soul.

"You are my husband," she finally said.

"You knew I didn't intend for us to end up like

this when I proposed." His eyes roved over her re-
clining form.

"Because I was too young and too innocent for
someone like you."

"Because you believe in happily ever after."

"And you think you don't."

"Women want more than I have to give."

"*I* want more than you can give, you mean."

He knew it for a fact. "You deserve more."

She nibbled her lip for a moment, sending rockets
through his nerves that were already frayed and shot.
Then she lifted her hand, palm upward.

"I don't read palms."

She didn't smile. Her hand didn't drop. Just extended toward him. Vulnerable. Open. Accepting.
"You deserve more, too, Tristan," she said quietly.

Maybe he did. But he'd given up, years ago, expecting the same things out of life that other people
took for granted. He'd never quite felt like he op-
erated on the same level as the world around him.
He saw problems, figured them out and corrected
them. He could practically read some people's
thoughts just from watching them from a distance.

But he'd never felt what they did. He'd tried.
God, he'd tried. There had even been a time when
he'd been with Serena twelve years ago that he'd
thought…perhaps.

Before marrying Jefferson, Emily had lived right
in his house for several years in California. She'd
been his best friend. She knew him about as well as
anyone could and even with her he had felt a chasm
between the emotion that could easily have been

there but wasn't. Which was just as well, since Em had been in love with Jefferson since she was a kid.

And still Hope's palm reached out toward him. Not grasping for him. Just waiting.

His chest felt tight. He looked out the porthole windows, saw nothing but the stream of white clouds. "I don't know how to love," he said abruptly. "I'll use up all of yours and leave you with nothing."

She blinked slowly. "Did it occur to you that I'm not offering you my love? That I haven't offered you the ring on my necklace?"

He looked at her, then. Brave words. Her violet eyes were practically swimming with emotion. He recognized love, even if he was incapable of feeling it himself.

And still her hand was there. To take, or not.

His wedding rings were on that hand even if he'd been unable to reciprocate by wearing a ring himself. He knew that there would never come a day that he wouldn't make certain that Hope was provided for. No matter what came later, she'd never be out of his life. Not completely. "I'm a wealthy man," he said.

A faint line appeared between her eyebrows. "So?"

"So you'll never want for anything. You can take Ruby sailing around the world if you choose. Move to San Francisco or Manhattan or Paris or Nantucket."

"Gram doesn't like boats since my grandfather died on one when they were still practically newlyweds, and I live in Weaver, which is exactly where

I want to live. Stop thinking you need to salve your conscience.''

"I'm not. You're my wife. You need to under-stand what that means. You'll inherit a sizeable es-tate someday."

"I didn't marry you for your money."

"I know that." He avoided her extended palm and reached for his jeans. He hitched them over his hips and moved across the bedroom to the intercom that connected to the cockpit. He buzzed, confirmed their flight status, and turned to look at Hope once more.

She'd sat up, and her hair flowed around her shoulders. Both her knees were drawn up under the sheet, and her hands were wrapped around them.

No longer extending toward him.

He told himself he was glad.

He *was* glad. It was better for her. Better for him.

"You married me because you were between a rock and a hard place with the school board," he said. "I put you in that place so it was only right that I get you out of it."

"Very accurately stated," she murmured. She pushed back the sheet and reached for her clothing. She dressed, not looking at him. "And I apparently married the pot of gold at the end of the rainbow, too. How nice."

He felt like scum. Not only because of his words, but because he didn't bother trying to turn his eyes from the sight of her. He couldn't have managed it had he tried.

She raked her hair back from her face and looked around. He handed her the clip. He wanted to tell her to leave it down. But knew he had no right to do so. "It's better that we keep things clear between us, Hope."

"I'm perfectly clear," she said calmly. "You're the one who is all muddled up inside, focusing on things that don't matter so you don't have to face the things that do." She stepped past him and pulled open the door. "I think I'll go sit up in the cockpit for a while. Will your crew mind very much?"

His jaw was tight. "No."

She smoothed her long shirt over her thighs. "You think I'm going up there to get away from you."

"Yes."

She shook her head, looking up at him with eyes whisper soft. "I'm going up there so *you* don't have to get away from me." She lifted her hand and he very nearly jerked when she touched her fingertips to his chest, right where his heart didn't beat with the emotions everyone else on earth seemed to have the ability to feel. "Do you still want to know why?"

She wasn't talking about the cockpit. She was talking about making love with him. About giving him her virginity. Her innocence. Her love.

"Yes." It was a bald-faced lie. He didn't want to hear what she had to say. He didn't want it on his conscience. Wasn't sure he could bear it.

She idly tapped her finger against his chest. She smiled softly. "Liar."

Then she turned on her bare heel and walked through the main cabin toward the front of the jet.

* * *

Their landing in San Diego was considerably different than when they'd arrived in Paris. There was no group of stone-faced men to greet them. No limousine. No floor of a hotel, no Henri.

Just a sizeable, graceful house that was what Hope figured must be the quintessential California dwelling. Tristan pointed to it when it came into view as they drove up a narrow, curving street.

The house sat well above street level and in the fading, gentle light of early evening, it looked entirely welcoming. A brick walkway and steps led up to an enormous black door in the center of the cream stucco structure. The roof was brick-red Mexican tile and the windows were arched. It was beautiful. And not at all what she'd have expected of Tristan, given the sketchy details she knew about his life. It was large and elegant, yes. But it was still in a neighborhood with other houses. It wasn't surrounded by fence or anything. It was, she thought with surprise, a regular house.

He thumbed a button, and the garage door opened. He drove the pickup that had been parked in a private lot at the airport right inside the garage. The door lowered behind them, momentarily throwing them into darkness. He shoved open his door and climbed out, hitting a switch on the wall that controlled an overhead light.

Hope swallowed and told herself to keep it together. The last thing Tristan needed was for her to be the weak-kneed Nelly he'd rescued by virtue of a wedding ring. She didn't know what demons dwelt inside him, but that they were present was not in question.

He'd made love to her as if they'd never have another day together on earth, and then he'd denied the emotions that she knew with every fiber of her soul he *did* feel. Just as she knew with every fiber of her soul that he wouldn't—couldn't—recognize it.

Maybe their marriage was a mistake. But Hope couldn't regret it. Not because of his wealth, or Paris or private jet. But because, when Tristan looked at her with his eyes ablaze with azure flame, she felt beautiful. She felt brave. She felt like a butterfly who'd been set free from a stifling cocoon.

The door beside her opened, and she looked up at him. She could see the shadows under his eyes and wondered when he'd last slept.

"Home sweet home," he murmured.

Hope slid off the seat and moved away from the truck while he retrieved his duffel and the suitcase Henri had produced for her to pack the purchases she'd made. She looked around the enormous garage.

Alongside the pickup were two motorcycles and on the other side of them was a sleek, wicked-looking convertible sports car. An expensive-looking racing bicycle, a surfboard and an assortment of other sporting goods were hanging from heavy-duty hooks. "Looks like a sporting goods store in here," she commented. He had every piece of equipment she could think of, but it all looked new. Unused.

He glanced around at the items, staring at them as if he'd never seen them. "Guess it does," he agreed blandly.

He shouldered the truck door closed and carried their bags around the truck and up three steps. There he punched in a code on a panel beside a door before opening it and waited for Hope to enter.

She stepped past him into a laundry room that was so typically familiar it made her immediately feel less like she'd tumbled down yet another rabbit hole.

He followed her into the room and she continued forward, entering a spacious kitchen. Well, it would have been spacious if not for the large electronic video game sitting between the table and a white-tiled breakfast counter.

On the table was a foot-high stack of hardback books, a computer printer and several other pieces of electronic equipment that she couldn't even hazard a guess at their purposes.

She eyed the mess. Did he ever stop working? Other than the days in Weaver before the wedding, and their last evening in Paris, he'd never once relaxed. Always with reports, paperwork, charts on which he scrawled indecipherable notes and symbols. She was fairly certain she'd seen him with at least three different laptop computers; one had looked similar to the one that the school had purchased last year for her classroom and one had been as slim as a narrow pad of paper. ''Cozy,'' she commented.

He grunted, dumping their bags onto the nearest surface, which happened to be the top of the video game. ''I wasn't expecting company,'' he said. ''I'll call the cleaning service in the morning.''

She folded her arms, looking around the kitchen. There was a dead fern sitting next to the stove. The

phone on the wall rang stridently, startling her. But
he ignored it and gestured for her to follow him.

They entered a high-ceilinged, tiled hall that separated the kitchen from a great room, beyond which
she could see what looked like an atrium, complete
with trees and pots of plants.

"Pool is through the jungle over there," he said.
"My office is at the end of this hall. There's a bathroom down here and four upstairs, plus bedrooms.
Take your pick. I've gotta make some calls, then I'll
see about scrounging us up some food."

Hope nodded. His expression was already distracted as he headed for the office he'd spoken of.
Obviously, he wasn't plagued with the vividness of
their so-recent lovemaking the way she was when-
ever she looked at him.

Well, what did she expect from a man who had
shut off his feelings?

She returned to the kitchen and opened the refrigerator door. Two long necks and a moldy block of
cheese. She sighed and opened a few cupboard
doors. She found cleaning supplies in the laundry
room and set to work. Cleaning service. Hah. If she
was going to be here for even a few days, she wasn't
going to sit around by the swimming pool, twiddling
her thumbs.

Two hours later, the kitchen sparkled. She
couldn't do anything about the video game. She'd
tried pushing it more to the side of the room, but it
weighed a ton.

She'd carried her suitcases into the laundry room
and started a load. But that didn't take long, which
left her warily eyeing his leather duffel.

She finally decided she was being ridiculous, so she yanked open the zipper and pulled out a handful of shirts and jeans and plain old white B.V.D.'s.

She moistened her lips and hastily pushed it all in the washer. In the bottom of the duffel was a pad of paper and she pulled it out. Tristan's distinctive scrawl covered the page, but she couldn't begin to decipher the mathematical notations. She set it on the ironing board that she'd discovered was built into a nifty cupboard.

Tristan still hadn't emerged from his office and Hope dusted and mopped. Though the kitchen had been a jumble, the rest of the house was as neat as a pin. Barely used.

She carried their clean laundry upstairs, and decided that Tristan's room surely must be the large one with the wall of video tapes and big-screen television opposite an unmade king-size bed.

She found clean sheets in the hall closet and changed his bedding, smoothing the dark brown comforter up in place. And then, because she was tired, or because she just couldn't resist, she sat down, her hand absently stroking the bed beside her.

There were a few photographs in frames on the shelves among the videos, and impossibly curious about the man she'd married, she went over to look. One was of Emily Clay, wearing a graduation cap and gown. Another was an old black-and-white photo of Tristan's father and his first wife, Hope realized, looking with interest at the woman. Tristan had inherited Squire Clay's extraordinarily chiseled features, the hard, angled jaw and sharp blade of a nose. But Hope could see the resemblance to his mother, as well.

She nibbled her lip, slowly reaching for the frame. "You've been busy."

Hope jumped, shoving the picture frame back on the shelf. Then realized she'd tucked her hands behind her back like she'd been caught snooping. Which, of course, she had been. But it was only a photo.

"I put your clothes on your dresser there," she said, nodding at the neat stacks of T-shirts and socks and jeans. The Hawaiian prints and the plain-Joe briefs. She felt her cheeks heat.

He rubbed his jaw and Hope's fingers tingled as if she, herself, had brushed her hand over the golden-brown stubble shadowing his jaw. "You didn't need to clean," he said abruptly. "I didn't bring you here for that."

"I'm not exactly a guest, either," she pointed out.

He tilted his head in agreement. And Hope, once again, noticed the weariness in his face. In the too-controlled angle of his shoulders when he leaned his hip against the dresser.

"Where did you put your clothes?"

It was a simple enough question, but she felt, suddenly, as if she were treading in deep waters. "The room closest to the stairs," she said after a moment. She'd chosen it simply because of the lovely needlepoint pillows that were stacked on the bed.

"Emily's old room," he murmured.

Hope crossed her arms. Emily Clay was beautiful with deep brown hair that reached past her shoulders and eyes as expressive and brown as eyes could be.

And Hope knew that the other woman had lived here in this house for quite some time before marrying Jefferson several years earlier.

"We were friends," Tristan said quietly, as if he'd read her forming thoughts. "Still are. But that's all it ever was. She only had eyes for my brother."

"You didn't mind?"

His lips twisted. "I'm not tearing myself up with unrequited passion for Em," he assured her dryly.

The relief of that was enormous. Unexpectedly so, and it dislodged her tongue just as unexpectedly. "Then she wasn't the one who—" She broke off, feeling like an idiot.

"Who...what?"

Hope shook her head, waving a hand. "Nothing. Look, is there a grocery store in the area? My stomach is about as empty as it's ever been and I—"

"Hope."

"—could fix us something quick. You look like you could sleep a week and—"

He crossed the room without her having been aware of his moving. One moment he was over by the door, the next he was covering her lips with his. She caught her breath, reaching for his shoulders without volition.

When he lifted his head, she swayed unsteadily. "I've never driven a truck as big as yours, but I'm sure I could manage."

His eyes were amused and her words finally dried. "Sweet pea, after seeing you in action in Paris, I'm positive that you can manage anything you set your mind to. There's no doubt about it."

Her throat constricted. He meant it. Not just about

something as simple as procuring groceries or driving an unfamiliar vehicle. The backs of her eyes suddenly burned.

And it was as if a light snapped off inside him. The amusement disappeared as if it had never been. He let her go and turned away, lifting one hand to the back of his neck as if to squeeze away a pain. "I'll order Chinese," he said smoothly.

Hope didn't know whether to cry or hit him over the head with one of his laptop computers. There was one sitting right there on the shelf, within easy reach. "Chinese would be fine."

He was insistent that he didn't feel the emotions of an ordinary man. It was true—Tristan wasn't an ordinary man. He owned a jet, yet wore very pedestrian underwear. He doodled pages and pages of incomprehensible equations, yet owned an astoundingly extensive collection of Three Stooges videotapes. He made love but insisted it was only the meeting of two bodies.

He was a man of complete contradictions, and he had faith she could do whatever she set her mind to. And since that first real, unforgettable kiss they'd shared at that cramped little table in the hotel's restaurant in Paris, Hope now finally accepted that there was only one thing she wanted in life—capturing Tristan's heart as thoroughly as he'd captured hers.

She also knew the odds of that happening were on a par with the world turning flat.

Chapter Twelve

Tris hung up the phone and rubbed his eyes. God, he was beat. The Pirelli case was a wrap, all parties safe and accounted for. This was the time he was supposed to feel the high of accomplishment. The satisfaction of justice being served.

He didn't know what he felt.

A soft sound at the door to his office drew his attention. Hope stood there, a wooden tray in her hand.

He felt completely frustrated, he thought, with no small amount of unpleasant humor.

"I brought you some lunch," she said.

Over the past week, she'd taken to bringing him a meal in the middle of the day. Today was no exception. She'd deposit the food she prepared and leave him with a meal he ate out of necessity, and a desire he dared not quench. "You didn't have to."

"So you've already said," she countered. She walked across the room and set the tray on the side of his desk. Thick slices of homemade bread and chunky chili guaranteed to singe the taste buds off his tongue. Just the way he liked it. "I can't help it," she continued. "You stay holed up here in your office all day long. I feel guilty. I need to cook something to eat for myself, anyway. We can't eat out for every meal."

"Wanna bet?" Tris broke off a piece of bread. He knew for a fact that his kitchen didn't have a bread-making machine. Emily had had one, but she'd taken it with her when she'd gone back to Wyoming for good. Hope made this bread the old-fashioned way with her own hands. Mixing, kneading, shaping. He knew. He'd watched her when she hadn't been aware of it.

She rolled her eyes and tucked her hair behind her ear, heading once more for the doorway. "Well, I didn't mean to disturb your work."

Tris watched her, frowning suddenly. "You've cut your hair." It didn't reach the curve of her seductive rear anymore. It hung loose in a glossy thick curtain, but it only fell to the middle of her back.

She looked over her shoulder at him. "A few inches."

"What on earth for?"

"You were the one who arranged that personal shopper and the day at the spa. Obviously, you expected me to do something with my appearance."

"Your appearance was fine," he said impatiently.

"I just thought you'd enjoy it." Didn't all women like that primping sort of thing?

Her shoulder lifted and she smiled faintly. "I did." She waved her hands. "My nails are glossed, my face has been de-something or other, my body's been buffed and—"

Her words continued, but his brain took a short circuit when she mentioned buffing her body. He jabbed the spoon into his chili and thought about the least appealing thing he could. "There's another charity thing tonight."

"Oh. All right. You seem to get invited to a lot of these things. That dinner the other night. And the auction."

"I'm on a few boards," he muttered. "You don't have to go tonight. It'll be just more of the same. Too many people jammed into too small a place, too much noise, smoke, booze."

"I don't mind."

Of course she didn't mind. It didn't matter what curves he threw her way, Hope handled it all. Usually with a sweet smile and touch of pink in her cheeks that generally won over even the most jaded of his acquaintances. "Nah. I think we'll both skip it tonight," he said, wishing he hadn't brought it up in the first place. What the hell was wrong with him?

She returned to his desk. "What is it for?"

He watched her fingertip trace along the corner of the wood surface. "Chalmers House," he murmured. He'd been good. He hadn't touched her since that one kiss the day they'd arrived.

"You told me that was your favorite project," she

said. "It's a crisis center for abused women and children right?"

He nodded absently. He'd kept his hands to himself, and she'd kept her hands to herself.

It was killing him.

"You seem to support a lot of programs that help women and children."

"Tax deductions," he dismissed.

"Right. It's not a crime to want to help others, you know. You paid an astronomical amount for that painting at that charity auction the other day, because you knew the money would go toward such a good cause."

He'd bought the painting, donated by a local artist for the auction, benefiting a center for the homeless, because he'd seen the way Hope's attention had lingered on the wintry landscape. Because he'd liked her stunned surprise when he'd handed it to her. "Did you and that shopper lady find a swimsuit?"

She blinked. "Well, yes."

He pushed aside the food and stood. "Go put it on. I'll meet you out back."

"But I—" Her cheeks went pink. "All right."

He watched her go, a swish of long hair and cheery red shorts and shirt. Maybe submerged in the cold water of his tree-shaded pool he could get rid of the constant heat riding in his gut for her.

Hope's hands shook as she pulled on the one-piece bathing suit over which Julie, the "shopper-lady," had raved. Once she'd pulled the narrow straps over her shoulders, Hope looked at her reflection in the wide bathroom mirror and wasn't so sure.

For one thing, it was black. Not just black. It was shiny black. A shiny black that shrieked "look at me." It was a one-piece, but the legs were cut so high on her hips that she felt more naked than not. The scoop top seemed too low, and Hope tugged and pulled as much as she could.

She'd bought the suit with some vague notion of lying out and getting a bit of a tan. Or rather, Tristan had bought it. He'd made the arrangements with the shopper for the clothing that now filled the closet and drawers upstairs in the bedroom Hope was using, and that had been that.

Hope started to pull her hair into a ponytail, but decided to leave it loose. If she pulled some of it in front of her shoulders, it helped cover some of that bare skin. She didn't need to add feeling naked to her unsettled stomach.

Aside from the few charity functions they'd been to, Tristan hadn't deliberately sought out Hope's company since they'd arrived. That he would do so now, today of all days, wasn't something she wanted to examine too closely.

She left her necklace on the dresser and, at the last minute, dragged one of the over-sized T-shirts she'd bought in Paris over her head.

Feeling better, Hope slid her feet back into her casual sandals and went downstairs. He was already in the pool, and Hope hauled in a shuddering breath as she walked out of the house.

His hair was darkened by water, making his sapphire eyes seem even more vivid. And those vivid eyes watched her steadily as she walked over to one of the cushioned lounges. Her knees felt shaky, and she gratefully sat on the edge of the lounge.

"Put on some sunblock," he said tersely. "Bottle is on the table there."

He disappeared beneath the surface of the glittering blue water, and she watched his water-wavery form travel the entire length of the pool without once coming up for air.

She absently reached for the bottle and applied some lotion to her legs. The bottle dropped from her slippery hands when Tristan surfaced by her toes, sending a cascade of water droplets over her feet.

"Ready?"

"Ah...I'll just lay here." She managed to smile even though she felt like a ninny.

He flattened his palms on the textured surface around the pool and pulled himself smoothly out of the water onto the edge. Hope's stomach clenched, and she blindly reached for the bottle she'd dropped. He was so bare. Too bare.

His wet hand closed around her ankle. "Come on in. Water's not too bad, today."

His thumb swirled over her instep. "I'm sure it's fine," she said breathlessly. "But, uh, I...don't... don't swim."

"Don't, or can't?"

His lashes were spiked together with water. She tore her gaze from his eyes only to have it land on that broad chest. That broad, bare, tawny chest. "Can't," she said, trying for another safe thing to look at. It wasn't his legs, dusted with hair and defined by long, roping muscles. She settled for the hand he'd flattened on the cement beside him. But even that was very near the dark blue swim trunks he wore.

"You don't know how to swim? Why didn't you say so earlier?"

The corner of his lips curved gently, and he pushed to his feet, pulling her up, too. "Come on." He headed toward the other end of the pool.

"Tristan, really, I don't care all that much about swimming."

He ignored her and stepped into the water where there were long, shallow steps leading down to the bottom. Hope hung back, but he held out his hand, palm up. "It'll be fine," he assured her. "This is the shallow end. Only three feet or so."

Shallow. Maybe the water was, but with Tristan she'd been out of her depth since the beginning. A knowledge that didn't stop her from putting her hand in his and stepping down onto the first step. He grinned and she took another step, just to see that smile again.

Before she knew it, her feet were on the bottom of the pool and the chilly water was lapping high around her waist, dragging heavily at the T-shirt.

"Let's get rid of this." Before she could protest, he tugged the shirt up and over her head, tossing it with a wet slap onto the side of the pool. Then his gaze drifted over her, and she thought she heard him mutter something under his breath. But he merely put his hands on her waist. "You're not afraid of the water?"

She shook her head, her thoughts numb.

He stepped further into the pool until it came up to Hope's chest. "Let your feet float up."

She swallowed. Tall trees surrounded the pool, and it suddenly seemed terribly private—utterly silent except for the rhythmic slap of the crystalline water. She lifted her feet, felt his arms slide under her and found herself floating on her back. "Oh!"

He smiled slowly.

She floated on her back. She floated on her stomach. He held her by the hands and towed her to the middle of the pool where even he couldn't reach the bottom, and she kicked and splashed. She watched the deep lines in his forehead ease.

And she fell in love with him all over again when he threw back his head and laughed.

When the phone rang a short while later, she swallowed a sigh and told herself not to be too greedy. He climbed from the pool and grabbed up the cordless unit that sat on the umbrella-covered glass table.

Tris couldn't take his eyes off Hope. She was standing in the shallow end near the side and as he watched, she bent her knees and tipped her head back into the water. Her hair floated around her in a glorious cloud.

The black swimsuit molded her in such perfection that his palms itched. Torture, insanity. Holding her in his arms, their water-slicked legs brushing against each other.

He wanted his wife.

But it wasn't fair to her. That *want* without love.

Swearing under his breath, he turned his back on the distracting sight and answered the phone.

* * *

"People who say women change their minds a lot haven't met you," Hope murmured. She was trying to fix the crooked black bow tie that circled Tristan's pristine white collar. But he kept fidgeting, reminding her strongly of one of her students who couldn't wait to go out for recess and play. "First you say you want to go to this thing tonight, then you say you don't. And now we're going again. If you don't like these benefit galas, why do you agree to go? You can donate your money and time without the parties, can't you?"

"It's expected," he said flatly. "You should know about expectations."

Hope stifled a wince and calmly finished his tie. She stepped back and pretended to objectively study his appearance. What she saw with her eyes was a strikingly handsome man. What she saw with her heart, however, was a tense, overtired man who gave two-hundred percent of himself for others, but refused to let anyone give to him. For the briefest of time that afternoon he'd relaxed, but the phone call had put an end to that.

Deciding his tie was too straight to use as an excuse to touch him, she turned away, gathering up her wrap from where she'd left it lying over the gleaming banister.

"That's the dress you wore in Paris," Tristan said behind her. "Why didn't you get something new? I thought that personal shopper was supposed to—"

"I like this dress." She had dozens of outfits now, all nipped and tucked and fitting her like she'd been born to them. She'd shopped. She'd explored the sights that San Diego had to offer. She'd expended rolls and rolls of film at the Wild Animal Park and the zoo.

She supposed it was every girl's fantasy life come true. Within the confines of his office, Tristan made a call and people came trotting over to do his bidding.

Fantasy or not, Hope knew she'd never been so alone. The phone calls she'd gotten from Justine and Gram that afternoon when Tristan had once again shut himself in his office had only underscored it.

"It does suit you."

She frowned, then realized he was still referring to her dress, and looked down at herself. "Thank you," she murmured. "Perhaps we should go? I think we're already late."

He didn't reply and Hope looked at him. His jaw ticked rhythmically. "Tristan?"

"You don't have to go tonight, you know."

"So you've already said. If you don't want me going, just say so."

"I didn't say that."

"Then what's the problem?"

He watched her for a moment, and then turned and slung his tuxedo jacket over his shoulder, heading for the interior door of the garage. "There isn't a problem," he muttered.

Hope held her breath for a moment until her stomach stopped jumping around like a bouncing ball gone mad, then followed.

They took the Porsche. Tristan left the top in place, because of her she felt certain. He wouldn't say so, of course, but he'd be aware of the time it took to put her long hair up into the twist that she'd copied from a photo in one of the hairdresser's books. That was just Tristan.

It was nearly dark by the time they arrived at the beach-front home where the party was being held. Cars lined the narrow road, but there was a valet, and Tristan left the car and keys with the young man, then escorted Hope toward the coolly modern house.

The doors were open and music blasted from inside, underscored by chatter and laughter. Tris handed over the engraved invitation, and they stepped inside. Hope swallowed the nervousness clutching her throat. She realized her fingers were clinging to his arm and carefully loosened her frantic grip. She felt his eyes on her, but kept her attention on the glittering group of people crammed into the house. And after a moment, she felt his hand at the small of her back as they entered.

After the first gala, Hope had gotten used to the vaguely shocked expressions of the people who greeted Tristan when he introduced her as his wife. She'd learned how to smile and avoid direct answers when one sleek woman after another had arched their eyebrows and asked how she'd manage to land such an elusive fish. She'd also realized, after that first gala, that Tristan was even less enamored of those public events than she.

Predictably, he was surrounded by a half-dozen people as soon as they realized he'd arrived. Hope calmly let them edge her out of the way, and started weaving in and out of people toward the buffet table she'd glimpsed.

Someone stuck a glass of champagne in her face, and she automatically took it as she looked over the sumptuous buffet. Shrimp and crab. Caviar and little golden toast points. Crudités, cheese, crackers. Chocolates, tiny cakes.

"I hope you see something to your taste."

Hope looked up, and the champagne sloshed over the edge of her glass when her hand jerked. She'd only seen the woman on the covers of fashion magazines, but Serena Stevenson was even more breathtaking in person. She blinked and looked blindly down at the buffet. It was as much a work of art in its display as anything. She picked up a napkin and dabbed the drops of alcohol from her hand. "It's magnificent."

"I'm glad you think so." The other woman smiled even more brightly, her face positively lighting up. Hope's stomach dropped, and she knew who had stepped up behind her even without that signal. She stiffened when Tristan dropped his fingers over her shoulder. "Hello, Serena. Still throwing the best parties, I see."

"Tristan, I am so glad you came. It's been too long." Serena stepped forward in a cloud of expensive perfume and reached up to kiss his cheek. Then she turned again to Hope and held out her hand, her smile seemingly genuine. "And this must be your new wife I've been hearing about. I'm very happy to meet you."

Hope shook her hand. Even in her beautiful Parisian dress, she felt like a dowdy goose next to such a graceful swan. Fortunately, Serena didn't linger.

Serena Stevenson was the hostess.

Hope set down her glass.

"Something wrong?" Tristan's lips brushed her ear again, sending shivers dancing down her spine.

He'd known they were coming to Serena's house. He'd told Hope that she didn't need to accompany him, but she hadn't taken the hint. She shook her head, not looking at him. "Noisy," she shouted.

He nodded, and she watched his eyes stray yet again to their hostess, who was circling the room like some beautiful, exotic bird.

Hope's head suddenly pounded. From the noise. From the cigarette smoke. From the sight of her husband being unable to tear his eyes away from a woman with whom he'd once been involved.

Standing in the center of the crowded room that looked as if it had come out of an architectural magazine, Serena started speaking eloquently about the efforts supporting the crisis center where she'd been helped herself as a child many years ago. And now that she'd returned to San Diego she was determined to see that others continued to be aided as she had been. And when she held out her hand and Tristan stepped forward, Hope made herself focus. Hearing just enough to know that he'd made some enormous endowment that would ensure the center would operate in the black for years to come.

All around her, people were clapping.

Nobody even noticed when Hope slipped to the back of the room and out the doors that opened onto a veranda with steps leading right down to the sand.

But even on the veranda there were people.

The urge to run down the stairs and keep on running was strong. But she kept her steps slow and measured. When she reached the sand, she removed her high-heeled pumps and started walking toward the softly crashing surf that filled the air with the pungent scent of salt water. The closer she got to the water, the darker it became away from the lights of the house. And quieter.

She reached sand that was hard packed and damp beneath her bare feet and, uncaring of the dress, she sat right down on it, folding her arms around her legs. The pain in her chest had nothing to do with her trek through the sand.

"I told you that you didn't have to come tonight."

Hope didn't look up at Tristan. A part of her was surprised that he'd followed her. But another part had been expecting him. "She's the one, isn't she?"

"The one what?"

Hope frowned, dashing a discreet hand across her cheek. A wave rolled over in a splash of foam, sending water rippling ever closer to Hope's bare feet. "The one who broke your heart."

Chapter Thirteen

Her question hung in the air.

After a long moment, Tristan lowered himself beside her and sighed grimly. "The one whose heart *I* broke," he corrected quietly.

Hope closed her eyes, turning her cheek to rest on her knees. "What happened?"

"Does it matter?"

"Everything about you matters, Tristan," she murmured tiredly. "You're the only one who doesn't realize that."

"We met after I'd started T-Comp. We became involved."

"Lovers, you mean."

"Yes." His voice was flat.

"She still cares about you." Hope had seen it in the other woman's vividly green eyes.

"She is married, Hope. Don't start looking for ghosts that don't exist. We were together a long time ago."

"And now you're back together, supporting a cause that obviously has deep meaning for her."

"I got involved with Chalmers years ago because of Serena, yes. But she moved away to New York and I stayed involved with Chalmers because I believe in the work they do. That's it. Our mutual involvement now is a coincidence. That's all."

"I don't believe you."

"I haven't made a habit of lying to you."

Hope lifted her head and pushed to her feet, brushing at her dress. "Lying to yourself is much more your forte," she said softly. "Why can't you just admit that she once meant something to you?"

He stood also and shoved Hope's pumps into his pocket. "She was beautiful, and the sex was good."

She ached inside. Not only because she could never hope to compete with a woman like Serena Stevenson, but because she felt the knot of anguish inside him like she bore it herself. He'd cared for Serena and for all Hope knew, he still did. "She's beautiful and she looks at you like a woman looks at a man for whom she cares deeply."

Even in the moonlight, Hope could see the fierce angle of his jaw. "Trust me, Hope. She knows me too well for that."

"Why?"

"Because when she lost the baby she was pregnant with—my baby—I was relieved." His words were clipped. "Relieved." He turned away.

Hope covered her mouth. Tears stung her eyes. "Oh, Tristan. I'm so sorry."

"So was she."

"You were scared."

His shoulders visibly stiffened. "I was relieved. I didn't want kids when I was twenty-two. I sure in hell don't want them now."

"But you're wonderful with them."

He snorted. "Says who?"

"I know about the volunteer work you do at Chalmers House," Hope murmured. "You give your money, certainly. But you give your time, too. I heard that you take those kids to the beach, the movies. Horseback riding. That you go by regularly, showing them how to use computers and such."

"Yeah, well, they're not *my* kids."

Hope chewed the inside of her lip and barely kept herself from placing her hand on her flat abdomen. Tristan was a man who didn't leave things to chance. He'd protected her on the flight from France, and only during the darkest hours of night would she admit that she wouldn't be upset if the condom had failed. "Just because you weren't devastated when Serena lost your baby doesn't mean you're unfeeling," she reasoned gently. "Tristan, you were young."

"The same age you are now," he pointed out abruptly. "I don't want to talk about this."

"Why not?"

"Because it doesn't serve any good purpose."

"Talking about feelings serves *every* good purpose."

"Aren't you the little expert, now."

"Have you ever talked about the baby with any-one? Even with Serena?"

"Serena knew exactly how I felt. It's why she left," he said flatly. "She wasn't even showing yet when she lost it, and she knew what kind of a man I was when I didn't share her grief."

Hope took a step nearer to him. "Why didn't you?"

"I don't want a woman having my kid. Okay?"

"Why not?" Going on instinct, she settled her hands on his chest. His heart chugged like a crazed freighter.

"Dammit, Hope—"

"Why not?" She slid her hands around his back, beneath his jacket. She felt his muscles bunch and flex. She let her body form to his unnaturally rigid stance.

He suddenly pushed her away, but his hands on her shoulders kept her from stumbling. "The night of my seventh birthday," he said flatly, "I found my father in his bedroom with one hand wrapped around a half-empty bottle of whiskey and the other holding a Smith & Wesson. Christmas Eve. He missed her so much, I think he was getting ready to eat that gun and it was my fault she was gone. She died having me," he said harshly. "Why the hell do you think I don't want children?"

"My mother died when I was two," she countered swiftly, anger hitting her sharply. For her loss. For Squire Clay's. And for Tristan, who'd been marked by the actions of a grieving man through no fault of his own. "And she *did* die by her own hand because she was so distraught that the man she loved wouldn't marry her because she had *me*. Justine told me so when I was a teenager.'' Hope yanked the chain out from beneath her dress and the wedding ring swung back and forth wildly. ''Does that mean I should never find a man to love? To never have a child?''

''Your mother.'' He spoke so softly she almost didn't hear it. ''I thought Gerri died in an accident,'' he said more naturally.

''When I asked Gram if what Justine said was true, she admitted to me that my mother drove her car head-on into an approaching semi. Gram never talks about it much, but I know she feels that she should have been able to prevent it. I never want to hurt Gram that way.''

He scrubbed his hands over his face, muttering under his breath. ''I'm sorry. I didn't know.''

The anger left as swiftly as it had come, leaving her feeling chilled and empty. ''I'm sorry for what your father went through. But you can't blame yourself for your mother's death any more than I can for mine.''

''I don't—''

''Don't you? You probably blamed yourself when Serena lost your baby, too.''

''Dammit, Hope, don't you get it? If I could have loved Serena, I would have. I tried and it was never there. It wasn't there with anyone.''

Not even you. The words weren't said, but she heard them in his thoughts. ''So you think that just because you didn't love *them,* you are incapable of loving *anyone?* That is such a cop-out.''

He jerked. Stared. ''What?''

"You are so intelligent." Hope couldn't stop the words once they started. "You see things around you and fix them. You try to make life better for others. You do all these wonderful things—you married me and I was weak enough to let it happen when there was probably another way to solve that problem—and you take the coward's way out by convincing yourself that it really isn't your *heart* leading you to do all this in the first place. You claim to be some sort of user. But really, you're just afraid of being hurt like all the rest of us poor souls in the world. Only you won't admit it. You hold yourself off, untouched, uninvolved emotionally because it's safer than putting yourself on the line."

Her words rang out, underscored by the steady throb of the tide. Leaving her breathless and him silent as a stone. Hope let her necklace fall back into place. "His name was Johnny Mueller," she said abruptly.

Tristan's eyes narrowed. "Who?"

"We dated in college. I thought it was love and when he, uh, didn't want to…well, you know, I thought he was being sweet and old-fashioned. Respecting me, you know." Hope looked out at the rolling ocean. It was such a magnificent sight. But it wasn't Wyoming. And she missed her home more than she could say.

She turned away and looked at Tristan. Beyond his shoulders she could see the brightly lit house. "But Johnny didn't want me. He wanted my access in the dean's office to change a failing grade to passing so he could graduate. Johnny was a user, Tristan. That's not what you are."

"A failing grade is small potatoes to things I've done."

"A person whose actions are self-serving is a user no matter what the arena. That's not who you are, Tristan. It's more a description of *me* than you."

He snorted. "You don't have a self-serving bone in your body."

"I married you."

"To save the school."

She moistened her lips. "There was probably other ways to fight Bennett. I was just too rattled to think of them. You sacrificed yourself for me. And I let you."

"Sacrifice," he repeated slowly. "Bull."

"What have you gotten out of this?"

His eyebrow lifted. "Don't underestimate yourself, Hope."

Her skin burned. She crossed her arms around herself tightly. "A few hours of sex."

"Making love."

She scrabbled for composure. "You said it wasn't."

"I lied."

Her eyes suddenly burned. She felt like a breathless racehorse chasing after that ever-elusive carrot. "Then why—" Her throat closed. She swallowed and moistened her lips. "—then why am I sleeping in one bedroom and you in another?"

The question seemed to echo again and again in her thoughts. And with each ticking second, each whoosh of the ocean, Hope knew he wasn't going to answer.

It broke her heart.

"I want to go home," she said after an eternity.

"I'll have the valet bring the car around."

"I don't mean your home, Tristan. I mean mine. I want to go home to Wyoming."

No. The response churned in Tristan's gut. He didn't know if her words were accurate or not. All he knew was he didn't like all this...emotion. It wasn't the love she deserved and he didn't like feeling churned up one bit.

"And before you take control, I'll make my own arrangements to get there," she said. "I'm a grown woman. It's time I began acting like it."

He knew good and well how grown up she was. And it was causing him no end of sleepless nights. "I never thought you weren't capable."

"I know. I was the one who thought it." Her soft lips pressed together and there was a liquid gleam in her eyes. The moonlight? Or tears? "You've helped me learn otherwise. If for nothing else, I'll always be grateful for that."

"That sounds like good-bye."

"It is."

"You're still my wife."

"On paper," she said huskily. "Not in your heart."

"I knew I'd end up hurting you."

She shook her head. "Oh, Tristan. I know I'm just a relatively inexperienced kindergarten teacher and you're a brilliant, worldly man, but even I can see the real truth. The one you're hurting is yourself."

There was an odd calmness on her face that disturbed him more than anything.

"I know what I want for my birthday," she said suddenly.

He jerked. Her birthday. Oh, hell. "It's today."

He should have remembered even though she hadn't mentioned it. It was on the birth certificate he'd gotten from Ruby, after all. The birth certificate that held nearly as many secrets as his own life held.

She smiled and it cut him deeply. Because she didn't seem to blame him for not realizing it.

"Anything," he said gruffly. "Whatever you want, it's yours."

"Go talk to Serena," Hope whispered gently. "Let go of the guilt you feel. Maybe when you do, you'll find your heart isn't as dysfunctional as you fear."

She pulled her pumps from his pocket, turned and walked away.

Tris pressed his palms against his eyes. He swore at himself. This is what happened when he didn't stick with the computers he knew.

She should have shrieked at him for being insensitive. Isn't that what all women despaired of in their men? But, *no,* she'd worried about a relationship that was dead and gone and years past. She worried about who protected *him.*

Yanking the tie loose around his neck, Tris headed toward Serena's high-priced beach house. Maybe Hope was right about that one thing, at least. It was long past time for him to make his peace with her. And once he did, he'd collect his wife and "make" something else.

Only once he returned to the house, Hope was gone.

* * *

Hope heard the door slam downstairs, but continued folding her clothing into the suitcase. She pushed a pair of rolled up socks into one of the corners and dashed her hand across her cheeks as she walked over to the closet and stared at the garments hanging inside. She'd leave the designer gowns, she decided. It wasn't as if she'd have a lot of use for them in Weaver.

But she'd take the black dress from Paris.

It was sitting on the chair by the bed. She'd put it in last because it was still slightly damp from sitting on the beach.

Only by concentrating on such details was she holding together. What she wanted to do was throw herself on the bed and weep for a week. But tears weren't the answer to the mess in her life. So why, then, did they keep leaking out the corners of her eyes, making it hard to focus on the clothing she pulled from the hangers?

She wiped her cheeks again. And pulled out her grandmother's lace dress. Hope's *wedding* dress.

Her hands trembled as she folded it. Through the closed bedroom door, she heard Tristan's distinctive footsteps on the stairs.

The door slammed open and she whirled around, her hands clenching around the dress.

Tristan stood there, his hair looking as if it had been combed by a whirlwind and his tie hanging loose about his unbuttoned collar. The sleeves of his shirt were rolled haphazardly up his forearms and his hands were curled into fists. "You're so anxious to go home that you can't even wait for me at the party? Proving your independence is that important?'' He advanced into the room. "I thought you went back to the house," he gritted. "I looked for you for nearly an hour in that crowd. I had nightmares of you doing something crazy, of hitching a ride or falling for some stranger's line. And then I find out that you got the car from the valet."

"I'm not a fool!"

"I know you're not," he snapped. "You're a beautiful woman who was upset."

"What did you think I'd do? Take your Porsche and drive it into a semi like my mother did?"

He sighed noisily and shoved his hands through his hair. "How do you know that's what your... what Gerri did? That it was deliberate?"

"I told you. Justine told me." She refolded the dress and put it in the nearly full suitcase, then tightened the belt of her robe.

"How often do you talk to her?"

"She called today to tell me happy birthday. Why?"

His shoulders seemed to sag for a moment. Hope could feel his distress like a tangible thing. She wanted to ease it for him more than anything. But she couldn't.

She turned to the suitcase and folded the flap in place, zipping it shut.

"I don't want you to go."

Her lips parted. She braced her hands on either side of the suitcase and closed her eyes for a brief moment. There was no point to the crying relief that his words brought. It wasn't as if he'd professed undying devotion. "I'll have to sooner or later," she said once she was sure her voice wouldn't fail. "That was the intention all along."

"Then go later."

Hope straightened. "Why? Why do you say this now?" She knew she sounded frustrated and hurt, but she couldn't help it. "You don't just change your mind in the middle of the stream, Tristan. You never wanted a wife."

"I never said that."

"You didn't have to. You needn't worry about protecting my reputation any longer. You shouldn't have had to worry about it in the first place."

"I like having you around."

She flipped her hair behind her back and swallowed the fresh pain of that. "Sort of like a pet you're fond of?" she said flippantly.

"Dammit, Hope." His lips thinned. "What do you want me to say?"

That you care for me! If only a little. "Nothing. I just want to go home. Where I belong. My world is Weaver. Your world is…the rest of the world." She pulled the suitcase off the bed, staggering a step under the weight of it. She lugged it past Tristan into the hall, propped it, angled, on the steps and followed it as it practically pulled her down the stairs with it.

She left it by the front door. She'd arranged for a shuttle to pick her up at six in the morning and take her to the airport. It wasn't as stylish a method as Tristan might have used, but it would work just fine for her.

Painfully aware of Tristan descending the stairs, she turned and went into the great room. She should have known he'd follow. Maybe she did know. Maybe she was aching for a confrontation. Something. Anything to expend the tangle of emotions churning inside her.

He entered the room and turned on a lamp. "We didn't have to get married in order to stop the school board from charging you with moral misconduct."

"I know. I should have fought Bennett right from the beginning. Instead, I just let it all happen right around us."

"No." He held out a cream-colored piece of paper. "You only needed this."

"What is it?"

"Your birth certificate. You've never seen it, have you? Every time you had to present it for some reason, your grandmother was with you. She handled the paperwork for you." It wasn't really a question. More an observation.

She frowned, looking at the square document. "Well, yes. I guess so. I never thought about it. You probably got it from Gram for the passport. How did you get that processed so quickly, anyway?"

"Look at it."

She didn't want to. She knew it was silly. But she really, truly didn't want to touch it. Not when he looked so grim. "What? I'm adopted or something?" she joked shakily. "That's why I didn't inherit the Leoni looks?"

He held out the paper.

She swallowed and took it in her hand, but still didn't look. Long ago she'd asked Ruby about her father, but Ruby had become so distressed, Hope had never asked again. She'd never been able to stand upsetting Gram. Feeling her pulse beating inside her head, Hope looked down at the document. There it was. The name of her father.

She couldn't breathe. "No. No, it's not possible." She looked up at Tristan. His eyes were filled with regret. *"Bennett?"*

Tristan nodded.

Hope grappled with the fact. "What did he have in common with my mother? Wouldn't he have been in college? My mother was older—" she broke off. Tristan's expression was even more gentle. And suddenly, Hope knew. She *knew.*

She looked at the document again and there, in the place where it should have said Geraldine Leoni, it had another name entirely. "Justine," Hope whispered.

The birth certificate fluttered from her fingers to the carpet.

Tristan caught her as her knees gave way, and carried her to the couch.

Chapter Fourteen

"I don't know why I'm crying," Hope said thickly a long while later.

"You've had a shock," Tris murmured. He ran his hand down her glossy hair. His shirt front was wet from her tears. Her nose was red, and her eyes were puffy. She was so damned beautiful it made him ache inside.

"I can't believe this is happening. That I didn't know. How could I have been so blind? So stupid?"

"Whoa." He put his thumb under her chin and lifted her face. "How were you supposed to know?"

Her eyes, drowning pools of purple, were beyond pain. "I feel like a fool. Who hasn't looked at their own birth certificate?"

"Someone who's never been given the opportunity to," he reasoned. "I don't think I saw my own until I had to replace my social security card when I was in college. Justine was only sixteen when you were born in Colorado. Gerri and Ruby were only trying to protect both of you.''

''But Justine—God, my mother. We talk maybe three, four times a year. She's practically a stranger to me. She must hate the sight of me.''

''I doubt that.'' He pressed his lips to her temple.

''Then why did they lie all these years? Why didn't Gram tell Bennett to lay off?''

''Ruby's managed to keep everyone in town from needing to see your birth certificate. Probably wasn't hard. Weaver is a small place—they don't usually need that type of ID. Ruby said Bennett doesn't know.''

Hope laughed brokenly. ''How pathetic. He'd just croak knowing that he is my...my—''

Tris brushed his thumb over her lips. ''He'd be proud if he's got any sense at all. There's no love lost between his family and mine, but he's not stupid.'' He smiled faintly. ''What may give him a coronary, actually, is knowing that his daughter is a Clay by marriage.''

Hope's eyes crinkled with humor for a second, but then they filled again. She shifted and pushed herself out of his arms. ''So you married me for nothing, after all. All I'd have had to do was tell my, uh, Bennett, that the girl he was trying to tar and feather was his own flesh and blood and he'd have ceased and desisted.''

''Presumably. But Ruby didn't want you to find out like that.''

''She didn't want me to find out at all! How could

she lie to me all these years? Keep this from me? I'd have surely found out eventually.''

''She loves you. People do odd things all the time in the name of love.''

Hope's face crumpled. ''I know. God, I know. Gram's been everything to me. I'm the first one in her family who finished college, did you know that? She was so proud. What am I going to say to her? What will I say to Bennett? And Justine. Poor Justine. She must have been so scared.''

''Say whatever you want to say. It's your call, sweet pea.''

Hope pushed from the couch, rubbing her hands over her cheeks. ''Why did you tell me this, now?''

He should have known her mind would insist on seeing all the angles. ''To prove that marrying you wasn't the only option. It was just the one I preferred. So don't go around thinking that I made some ultimate sacrifice. I warned you I was a selfish soul.''

Her eyebrows pulled together. ''But…but, why?''

''Because I liked being with you,'' he admitted abruptly. ''And I don't want you to leave, now.''

''Did you talk to Serena?''

His jaw tightened. ''Yes. She *is* happy, Hope. Happier than she ever was with me. And no matter what you think, it is long over between us.''

''If…if I do stay, what, um—''

''It'll be in my bedroom,'' he finished bluntly. ''I want you in my bed, Hope. There's no point in pretending it ain't so. Tried that. Didn't work.''

''I still have to go home to Weaver. School starts in about six weeks.''

He didn't like acknowledging it, but it was staring him in the face. "You really miss it there, don't you? That painting—it reminds you of home."

She was running her fingers along the necklace in that old, nervous habit of hers. "I do miss it. I miss Gram." Her eyes shut, and Tris saw a tear slip down her cheek. "What am I supposed to do now, Tristan? Where do we go from here?"

Tris wished he had an answer. He stood and went over to her, tilting her face toward his. "It's been a helluva birthday," he murmured.

Her hands settled on his chest, fingers tangling in the fabric. "You gave me a gift no one else did," she whispered. "The truth."

"I never wanted to hurt you."

"I know. It's not in your nature to hurt people."

He had to smile. "No matter how much evidence to the contrary, you're insistent on that point, aren't you?"

She slipped her fingertips inside his shirt, touching his chest. The exact spot where his heart thudded, slow and heavy. "Your heart functions just fine," she said softly. "Thank you for being honest." She leaned up against him and brushed her lips against his.

It took every bit of control he had to keep his hands light on her waist. "Will you stay?"

She sighed. Pressed her forehead against his chin. "For a while."

Hearing it, the knot of tension in his stomach eased. He slid his arms around her, swept her into his arms, and carried her slowly up the stairs to his bedroom.

This time, when he settled her in the middle of
his bed and she held out her hand to him, he didn't
ignore it. He put his hand in hers, and lowered himself beside her. She lifted the necklace over her head
and let it go, to puddle on the nightstand. Next, she
unbuttoned his shirt, slowly tugging it from his
shoulders.

Her teeth sank into the tip of her tongue and he
shook his head at that, kissing her, tasting her. He
spread the lapels of her soft robe, discovering her
all over again. The sleek shoulders, the satin-smooth
ridge of her collarbone. The dip of her waist and the
crests of her beautiful breasts. The ticklish spot on
the arch of her foot and the sweet heat between her
legs.

Her hands tangled in his hair and her legs, smooth
as anything he'd ever felt in his life, tangled with
his. She slid over him, her fragrant hair surrounding
them. And her mouth…

"You're killing me," he finally groaned through
gritted teeth and smoothly flipped her onto her back.
His hands held hers over her head and he kissed her,
swallowing her breathless laughter. Still holding her
hands safely, he pressed into her, watching her eyes
go wide, then slowly close on a long sigh of pleasure.

He let go of her hands and she touched his face
with gentle fingertips, murmuring his name. Tris
pressed his lips against her palm and felt his soul
ache when she opened her eyes again and he saw a
tear slip free. "Don't," he whispered against her
lips. He pulled her close, unable to pull himself from

the haven of her body, unable to bear the thought of her crying. "Don't cry."

She wound her arms around his shoulders and opened her mouth beneath his. Her knees brushed his hips and she moved, drawing him ever deeper, ever closer. Her neck arched back, luring his lips. "Don't stop," she moaned.

He felt her trembling. Felt her tension. Felt it, shared it, experienced it. He couldn't stop. Not now. Maybe not ever.

She shuddered and quaked, and Tris couldn't think anymore. He could only feel. Only hang on to the one woman who'd ever made him hope for more.

Her breath rasped in his ear. "I love you, Tristan. I love you. Now. Now."

His jaw locked. Her hips cradled his. He closed his eyes and gave himself over to the passion he could no longer contain. *Now.*

The winter landscape sat propped on top of his dresser. She'd moved it there two weeks ago when she'd moved into his bedroom. Every morning, they wakened to the sight of that small, exquisite painting.

And Tris knew their time was nearing an end. He couldn't imagine moving back to Weaver and she couldn't remain away.

She'd talked to Ruby, he knew.

Her grandmother, probably relieved that the truth was finally coming out, had finally explained what had happened when Justine found herself pregnant and just sixteen years old. Gerri had gone to Ben-

nett's parents, who'd been scandalized by the whole
thing. They'd sold their struggling ranch to the Double-C and tried to pay off Gerri to take Justine away
and never return. To her credit, Gerri had refused
the money, but they had still left town. They'd gone
to Colorado where Gerri had an old friend, and when
Hope was born, Gerri raised her as her own, since
Justine was so young and still behaving irresponsi-
bly. After a year and a half, after all the struggling
to keep her family together on a limited means,
Gerri had thought things were on the upswing when
she'd met a new man she'd been crazy about. But
it hadn't worked out when he'd learned that Gerri
never intended to give up raising her new little
granddaughter.

Ruby insisted that Gerri's accident may have been
just that. An accident. But they'd never know for
certain. And Justine, feeling guilt over the entire ep-
isode, had pleaded with Ruby to continue upholding
the lie that Hope was Gerri's daughter. She wanted
Hope to have *some* stability, and the only chance of
that would be if Ruby took her back to Weaver to
live with her.

In that, at least, Justine had been correct. Because,
aside from Ruby's strictness, she couldn't have possibly loved Hope more.

But Hope hadn't spoken with Justine.

Tris figured that might take a while. But it would
come. Of that there was no doubt. Because no one
had a greater capacity for love and forgiveness than
did Hope Leoni Clay.

As for Bennett, Tris wasn't sure how Hope felt.
She hadn't said, and he hadn't asked. If he could

have solved that problem for her, he would have. But it was something she'd have to decide herself. He had complete confidence that, whatever she did, it would be right.

The fall session at Weaver Elementary was getting closer with every day. And the hotter it became in San Diego as August neared, the more he saw her eyes lingering on that winter landscape.

Cole called him for a new job, and Tris did the unthinkable. He told his boss about his marriage, and he turned the job down. He was in the middle of programming a new video game, and Hope had been helping him with the story behind the action.

In truth, he knew he didn't want to go away just yet. There'd be time enough later. When Hope was no longer with him. When his home was just a house once again. When he was alone. Burying his attention in the bowels of a computer system was a sure-fire way of forgetting that regrettable reality.

The day he wakened and the painting was gone from his dresser, he knew. Hope was leaving. She was going home.

He found her downstairs in the kitchen. Wearing one of his button-down white shirts. The sexiest attire he could imagine her wearing. He stood in the doorway for a long while, watching her move around the kitchen. Even though it was only seven in the morning, there was already a loaf of bread cooling on a bread rack.

Then she looked over her shoulder at him and her lips curved. "Good morning," she greeted. "I thought you'd sleep for hours yet."

"Because a certain violet-eyed temptress kept me awake until the wee hours, you mean?"

Her eyes flickered and pink rose in her cheeks. She turned back to the sink and ran the towel in her hand over and around the fixtures until they gleamed. "I called Gram," she said after a moment.

Tris tucked his thumbs in his beltloops and leaned his shoulder against the doorjamb. "You can take the jet."

She gave him a startled look, then her lips twisted wryly. Sadly. "Do you really read minds," she asked curiously, "or am I just that obvious?"

"There's nothing obvious about you, Hope."

She just gave a little shake of her head, making her toffee waves ripple over her shoulders. "Oh, I think I'm utterly predictable," she murmured so softly he barely heard. "You had a call again this morning from Coleman Black."

Tris pursed his lips. "I turned him down already."

"He said to tell you it was urgent."

"With Cole it always is."

"You should call him." Her eyes drifted to the video game that he'd finally shouldered out of the middle of the kitchen. It now sat against the wall where an empty china hutch had once sat, but was now doing duty as a toy bin at Chalmers House. "Your video games are great fun. But your real interest is the work you do with Cole." Work that he'd finally opened up about and shared fully with her.

"For a woman still wet behind the ears, you're awful full of insight." His tone was teasing.

"I dried behind them this morning," she replied lightly. Then she folded the dish towel and set it on the counter with an air of finality. "Tristan—"

"Don't. Your life is there. Mine isn't. We both know it."

She moistened her lips and smiled. Bittersweet. He saw her twist the rings on her finger. "What about, um—"

"You're my wife, Hope. Together or not, I don't see any reason to change that."

"You might change your mind."

"You might find someone who loves you the way you should be loved."

Her eyes closed for a moment. Her long, lovely throat worked. "Well. I guess I should get dressed. Gram is expecting me before evening."

He could talk her into staying. He knew he could. But every day she'd look at that wintry landscape and wish for Weaver. It would kill him. "I'll drive you to the airport."

Her eyes glistened. "I've arranged a driver," she said huskily. "It's better this way."

Nothing was better. But he nodded anyway, because he could see she needed to do this her way. She passed by him, and he breathed in the scent of her, holding it in his mind. Wondering how long it would be before he forgot it.

Shoving his hands through his hair, he walked through the house, seeing the little signs of Hope everywhere. The jar in the foyer filled with wildflowers she'd picked when she'd talked him into renting horses at the nearby stable. The charcoal drawing of her from Paris, that was such a perfect rendition of the tentative confidence she'd been gaining there, hung on the wall near his office. The oversized paperback book she'd left on the cocktail table in the great room. She'd been studying science project ideas geared toward the primary grades.

Turning his back on it all, he went into his office and closed the door. He didn't go out again until he heard the doorbell chime and knew that the driver had come to collect Hope.

She wore a lilac-colored sheath that ended just above her knees and left her arms bare. Her hair was pulled back in a gold clip. She looked cool and chic and lovely and totally capable of handling anything the world tossed her way.

Including a husband who didn't have the guts to reach out for the love she so freely offered.

Hope looked at Tristan, determined not to break down. She knew she had to leave. Her kids depended on her. Gram needed her. But most of all, it was time for her handsome husband to move out of the limbo in which they'd been tentatively existing. "I do love you." The words came out, even though she'd been determined not to say them again.

His eyes were so darkly blue they looked nearly black. "Call me when you get there."

She nodded, even though she knew she wouldn't. The next move had to be his. "Think Gram will recognize me?" she asked.

He didn't smile. "Your violet eyes will give you away."

She reached for the door. Her cases had already been carried out to the waiting limousine. "Well…"

Suddenly he was next to her, hauling her against

him. Her mouth opened under his and her bones dissolved. She kissed him with all the love in her heart. All the love she prayed was in his.

When he finally lowered her toes back to the tile floor, Hope's eyes were burning. But she couldn't go without touching his ruggedly beautiful face once more. She drew her fingertip along his tight jaw. And prayed with everything inside her that her husband would find his way from the cocoon just the way she had. ''Good-bye, Tristan.''

She pulled open the door and stepped outside.

The sun was just starting to burn through the morning fog. It would be a hot August day.

The limousine was on the street, aligned perfectly with the brick walkway. The rear door was open and waiting.

She held her shoulders straight. And walked toward the vehicle. She didn't look back.

Chapter Fifteen

Tris stared at the little package in the drawer of the bathroom cabinet. A home pregnancy test.

He couldn't breathe. He yanked open the bottom cupboard door and fumbled with the small trash can, pulling it out and rummaging through it until he found the little white stick.

He closed his eyes, slid down to the floor and wondered if he had the nerve to look.

It had been two weeks since Hope walked out of his California house. Two weeks of being unable to sleep in his own bed, instead taking refuge in the room she'd used that first week. The room attached to this very bathroom. Two weeks since he'd answered his phone, checked his e-mail, left the house.

It wasn't pleasant to know he was such a coward. But he realized he didn't know what cowardice was until he sat there, afraid to see what that little white stick showed.

He wished he had a drink. But he'd realized the first week after Hope left that he couldn't live his life in a bottle. It reminded him too much of the night he'd come across Squire.

He stared at himself in the mirror. He looked like hell. He felt worse. Swearing under his breath, he tipped the pregnancy test stick into his hand and turned it over.

Stared. Stared while his muscles went lax and his brain seemed to explode in his head. Stared while it felt as if his chest would crack open from the ache that expanded and multiplied.

His hands shook so badly that the little white stick tumbled to the floor. Face up where he could still see the results.

God.

Tris let out a low groan. Oh, God. Did anything ever hurt so badly? His eyes burned, his vision blurred. Dammit, dammit, dammit. He pressed the heels of his palms against his eyes.

He was such a bloody fool.

He wasn't sure how long he sat there. His knees were stiff and his head ached when he finally pushed to his feet and went into his room. The room he hadn't entered since the day Hope left.

But the shocks of the day weren't over. For on the nightstand, he caught the glint of gold.

Her necklace. With the ring that she'd worn since she was twelve. Tris sank on the edge of the bed and picked up the ring. Despite the burning in his eyes, he turned it, noticing the inscription that hadn't been there before. He tilted it to the light.

You are my heart.

His gut ached, and he knew she'd left the ring for him. That she'd had it inscribed for him. He let out a long, hard breath.

He picked up the phone and started punching numbers. Thirty minutes later, he was in the air, knowing he could clean up on the plane. A chartered chopper was waiting for him when they landed in Gillette, and it took him straight to the Double-C.

The arrival of a helicopter wasn't exactly every-day fare and Tris wasn't surprised to find he had a landing party when he climbed out and gave a thumbs-up to the pilot. The chopper took off once more, and Tris turned to see Squire and Matthew standing there.

"You all right?" Matthew asked.

Tris nodded. Satisfied, Matthew turned and headed for the horse that was ground-tied a safe distance away from where the chopper had landed. Which just left Squire. Tris looked at his old man. "How's married life?"

Squire lifted an eyebrow. "You tell me."

"It's gonna get better," Tris said abruptly. "I've come to get the cameo."

"The one she wore when we got hitched."

Tris nodded. "Yes."

"To give to Hope. It's about time. Your mama would have approved of your choice, boy." Squire slanted a look his way. "Even if she wouldn't have approved of letting your bride come home all by herself for days on end. We've all been making a point of checking on your new bride.''

Tris barely kept himself from rolling his shoulders against the itch that accompanied the censure from his old man. ''I don't think my mother would have approved of you holding a gun to your head on my seventh birthday, either.''

Squire stopped so short, the gravel beneath his boots kicked up a pile of dust. ''What?''

Tris hadn't planned to say that. He also hadn't planned to fall for a woman who was eleven years younger than he was. He hadn't planned a lot of things. ''Christmas Eve. My seventh birthday. You were in your room. You had a bottle of whiskey in one hand and your gun in another.''

Squire settled his gray Stetson more firmly on his head. ''In my hand, son. Not against my head.''

''You weren't thinking about ending it all then? You weren't missing your wife so damned bad that it was almost worth giving in to the pain? You were alone for thirty-four years, Squire. Because I was born.'' The memory of that long-ago day was so clear in Tristan's mind it was as if he hadn't spent all the years since, trying to ignore its existence. His father, who'd made a life out of being unemotional and hard-edged, had had a single track of tears running down his lean, tanned face. ''You told me you were cleaning the gun and sent me back to bed,'' he remembered.

Squire sighed. ''There's a lotta years under that bridge, boy. I remember that night, though. Seemed like the years of missing her sleeping next to me all rolled up together, damned near drowning me in misery. Or mebbe it was the whiskey that was drowning me. But it was my son with his mother's eyes who saved me. Come on. I got something to give you. Besides the cameo.''

Curbing his impatience, Tris followed Squire into the house. They entered through the mudroom in the rear, where the wooden screen door squeaked and slapped shut the way it always had. It was the sound of his childhood, he thought. Squire headed back through the house to the spacious room beyond the wide staircase that he now shared with his new wife. Squire went to the closet and rummaged around one of the shelves, and returned with a hank of white fabric bunched in his hand.

''Your mama was a stubborn woman,'' he said. ''I was mighty mad at her for dying. But more mad at myself because if I had insisted she stay inside instead of going out to the old barn, or if I'd just gone out there for her in the first place, she wouldn't have been out in that snowstorm. She wouldn't have slipped and fallen. It was my fault, pure and simple. And it's only because of Gloria that I've learned to live with it.''

It was more information than Squire had ever offered about the night of his mother's death. ''What was she looking for in the barn?''

''A Christmas present she'd made.'' Squire held up the fabric that he'd retrieved. ''This.''

Tris realized it was a small dress. Sized for an infant.

''It's a baptism gown,'' Squire said. ''For you. She wanted you, Tristan. She wanted all you boys. Don't ever doubt that she'd have changed one thing in her life.'' He handed the small white garment to Tris. ''Think she'd like the idea of your Hope having this, as well as the cameo.''

Your Hope. That's exactly what she was. His hope. For happiness for the future. For a life that wasn't centered around microchips, processors and cables.

His throat tight, Tris managed a grin. ''So, Pop, can I borrow the keys to the car?''

''Could I get a cup?'' Tristan flipped over the down-turned coffee cup in front of where he sat at the counter. Hope swallowed her shock and forced herself to walk across the café to the front door and pull it closed. The air conditioner hummed and she could already feel cool air flowing. ''We're closed in the afternoons,'' she said.

His lips curved enticingly. ''Just one cup?''

She wanted to throttle him. She wanted to put her arms around him and kiss his beautiful, hard face. She rounded the counter and grabbed up the coffee pot. It was cold, but she poured it in his cup anyway.

''Not going to spill this time, huh?''

She clasped her hands together atop the counter. ''No.''

''Good.'' He shifted, then set a folded bunch of fabric on the counter. ''You know, I don't remember what happened to that gray sweater I wore that first day.''

Hope felt her cheeks flush. She'd been sleeping in that sweater every night since she'd left California. Her electricity bill had doubled because she'd been running the air conditioner just so she'd still

be comfortable enough to sleep. "It's around somewhere, I'm sure. I'll have to look for it," she murmured. Then moistened her lips nervously when he
slid one of his hands over hers. Under. Palm meeting
palm.

His eyes, those intense sapphire eyes watched her.
It was as bad as that first day. No, worse. She could
hear her pulse, thundering in her ears. Could hear
her breath, slowly easing past her lips. She could
hear the soft chink of his gold wristwatch as it
bumped the counter beneath their hands.

"Relax," he said in that voice that hypnotized.
His thumb swirled over her hand. "It was just a
sweater."

She realized she was leaning toward him and
straightened like a shot, pulling her hands away
from his. "What are you doing here?"

He smiled slightly and lifted the coffee cup,
drinking slowly as if it were the best coffee in the
world and not a good three hours old and stone cold.
"Not exactly a glowing welcome," he said.

She couldn't smile and joke. Not now. Not anymore. "I'm not pregnant," she said baldly. And
she'd cried for a solid day when she'd learned it.
She'd left California the next day. "If that's what's
worrying you, you can stop."

He set aside the cup and slowly laid a familiar-
looking white stick on the counter. "I know. I never
knew how much I would regret that until I found
this," he replied, his voice low.

"Tristan."

"No. I need to tell you." His jaw cocked. "I

found this, and I wished it had been positive. That you'd been pregnant."

His gaze met hers. His eyes were so filled with grief that her heart clenched. "I started out thinking I could satisfy myself with just a kiss from you," he said gruffly. "One kiss. But a kiss doesn't begin to cover it. I want you to have my baby, Hope."

Hope saw the ravages in his eyes. Her heart squeezed. "Oh, Tristan."

He slid the bundle of fabric in front of her and spread it out. "My mother made this," he said roughly. "For me, apparently. But obviously, I've outgrown it a size or two. So if we're gonna get any use out of it, we'll have to start with something less than six-five."

Hope looked at the delicate tucks and fine stitching of the white gown. She was afraid to hope.

"It's a baptism dress," he said. "You're not pregnant yet, so we'll just have to keep trying."

Her teeth worried her inner lip. "Are you sure?"

His lips twisted. "I'm not saying it'll be the most peaceful nine months of my life, but if you're willing to give it a go, I'm your man."

She touched the dress, her fingers trembling. He couldn't mean it.

"Tell me why you wanted to make love that day on the flight back from France."

"Because I loved you," she said. "And I knew you didn't want to hear those words from me."

"I did. I wanted to hear them. Even when I couldn't acknowledge the stuff inside me, I wanted them from you."

Her heart thundered. "What do you want now?"

"Let me back in your life, Hope. Nothing's been right since you left."

Hope trembled. "Why?"

"Because you pick up where I leave off. Because you remind me that life is more than a computer cable and an uplink. Because you see inside me and have the guts to keep standing right there beside me, despite it all."

He reached over the counter and caught her left hand in his, dropping something in her palm. She looked at it. The wedding ring she'd worn around her neck since she was twelve. She let out a ragged sigh.

"Because I love you," he said softly. "And you know it's true because I've never said it before. Not even to my favorite laptop." He held out his hand. "Marry me."

Hope laughed brokenly. "I already did," she said and pushed the ring onto his finger. "It fits," she whispered.

"Perfectly." His gaze touched on her lips, and then he was folding her hands in his, tugging her close until their lips were only inches apart above the counter that still separated them. "I'll try to cut down on the traveling for Cole," he murmured. "And keep the Paris jaunts to the summertime so you can come with me."

Hope could barely breathe. She pulled back far enough to see his eyes. "Are you sure?"

"I've broken rules in the past, Hope. Maybe if you and I prove that an agent for Hollins-Winword can be happily married, Cole will finally bite the bullet and put Dom out of her misery, too."

Her lips parted. He was serious. Well and truly serious. "Where will we live?"

He smiled slowly. Stealing her breath and her heart all over again. "Here in Weaver, of course. I can't possibly take you away from your students. They're sort of responsible for bringing us together."

"But you don't like living here."

"You pointed out yourself not so long ago that I'd never *lived* here. Not really. And besides, I'm thinking of starting up another company—video games are a real hoot. I'll need an office—probably have to get that built since there's not a lot of buildings here going empty. And some employees. Might mean some new people moving to town. I've got a lot of new scenarios in mind for the programs. But I'm thinking some of the stories behind the action aren't quite right, so I might need some help in that area from an expert in that age of kids—"

"What about your house in San Diego?"

"I donated it to Chalmers House," he said. "Serena's husband is handling it, actually. He's in real estate."

Hope leaned over and kissed him. She felt his lips smile against hers. Then he was lifting her right across the counter, knocking his coffee cup sideways where it spilled. She laughed. And cried. And wrapped her arms around him, loving him more than life itself.

He lifted her hand and pressed a kiss to the rings around her finger. "I love you, Hope Leoni."

"Hope Leoni Clay." She picked up the baptism

gown and held it against her heart. "And I love you."

He smiled into her eyes, and then pulled out a lovely cameo of ivory and the palest of pink. "My mother wore this when she married the old man," he said. "She died too early but he never stopped loving her. Not even now, even though he's finally moving on with his life with Gloria." He pinned it to Hope's collar. "That's how I love you, Hope. Now. Always."

"Oh, Tristan," she whispered. She touched his jaw. A shock of brilliant gold hair had tumbled over his forehead. He was beautiful on the outside. But it was the complicated man inside that held her heart. "You are my dream come true."

His lips lowered over hers. "More than a dream," he amended. "It's hope. Hope, sweet pea. And with you by my side, I'll never lose that again."

Epilogue

A breeze drifted over the land, bringing with it the scent of alfalfa, of horses and cattle and the wide, wide open sky.

For the assembly of individuals crowded around the beribboned bassinet that sat in the sparse shade of a trio of cottonwoods, the breeze brought the scent of peace. Most of them were Clays. But there were a few others. Ruby Leoni for one. And Justine Leoni and Bennett Ludlow who were both keeping a fair distance from one another, but who were behaving for the sake of the daughter and grandson they now openly shared.

Squire Clay looked off to one side of his property. From where he stood, he could see the stand of trees that surrounded the swimming hole his grandchildren used every chance they got. The other direction, too far off for him to see, was the ranch his middle son had bought. Jefferson raised horses. Went his own way, the way he'd always done. But he and Emily and their young 'uns were close enough to home to satisfy Squire.

Matthew had never strayed far. He figured he'd brought enough of the city to the ranch when he'd married Jaimie, and Squire suspected it was so. Nobody had more zest for life than Jaimie, except maybe Matt and Jaimie's two kids.

Daniel was happy as a pup in clover with Maggie and their three. When he wasn't busy with ranch business, he was wearing a hard hat in town overseeing the construction of the new office complex that would house Tristan's new business, as well as an honest-to-God hospital. Only eighteen beds, but it was more than Squire had ever expected he'd live long enough to see. And it was needed, considering the influx of people his son's business was bringing about.

He heard wheels crunching over gravel and turned to see a sport utility vehicle bearing "Sheriff" on the side roll to a stop. The doors opened and Sawyer, his oldest, stepped out, sketching a faint wave before he went around to help his wife out of the seat. Rebecca was so big with the baby she was pregnant with, it was a wonder she didn't just tip over. But even if she did, Sawyer and Ryan were constantly hovering. They'd catch her.

Squire glanced up to the sky. It was the same color as Sarah's eyes had been—the woman who had borne him these five sons who were better men than he'd ever hoped for. Than he'd had a right to expect considering all the things he'd done wrong.

He closed his eyes for a moment, breathing in the smell of this land that had been his life for damned near all of it. When he opened them, he knew who stood beside him. Gloria. His love. The last one he'd have.

He put his arm over her shoulder and marveled again at how well she fit him. They'd been married just over two years and he still had to shake himself every morning to remind himself it was real. "Is the preacher here yet?"

Gloria shook her head. "Not yet. But he will be. He's baptized all the grandchildren. Hope's and Tristan's first won't be one he'll miss."

Her auburn head tilted and she looked at him with her lovely eyes. "Sarah's watching over all this, I think. Think she's satisfied?" Understanding shined in Gloria's eyes. Understanding of the losses and blessings, the pain and the love that all added together to form one person's life.

"I think she'd say everything was just right." He settled his gaze on Gloria. She was the one who'd opened his heart again. "The men of the Double-C have exactly what she wanted for us all along."

Gloria smiled. "Love," she finished.

"Yes, ma'am," Squire said contentedly. "Yes, indeed."

* * * * *

Allison Leigh has new Silhouette Special Edition novels out in August and November 2005.

The Princess's
White Knight

CARLA CASSIDY

CARLA CASSIDY

is an award-winning author who has written many books for Silhouette. In 1998, she won a Career Achievement Award for Best Innovative Series from *Romantic Times Magazine*.

Carla believes the only thing better than curling up with a good book to read is sitting down at the computer with a good story to write. She's looking forward to writing many more and bringing hours of pleasure to readers.

To Donna Julian
who yells at me when I don't have dedications.

Chapter One

He sensed her before he saw her. Her Royal Highness sneaking out of her royal bedroom to get her royal behind in trouble.

Gabriel Morgan frowned as he followed the evocative scent of her perfume down the long hallway that eventually would take him to the living room and the front door of the luxurious vacation home.

The hallway was dark, the house quiet as the rest of the household servants slept. Gabriel heard a thud, then a muffled groan as Princess Serena Wyndham apparently misjudged the length of the hallway and walked into a wall.

Gabriel made no such mistake. He moved with the stealth of a wild animal pursuing prey. Only in this case, his prey was one hundred and ten pounds of utter trouble.

This wasn't the first time she'd attempted to escape the confines of the Aspen family vacation home alone, without her bodyguard. In the months they had been here, Princess Serena had tried to sneak out countless times, and thankfully each time Gabriel had caught her.

He moved into the living room, where the Aspen moon sent bright shafts of ghostly light through the floor-to-ceiling windows. The illumination provided him an easy view of the young woman who crept across the floor toward the front door.

She held a pair of ski boots in hand and she moved slowly, with exaggerated motions in an attempt to make absolutely no noise.

Gabriel waited until she reached up to turn the deadbolt lock. "Going somewhere?" He hit the lights, flooding the room with brilliance.

She squealed and jumped in surprise. Whirling around to face him, she drew a deep breath and Gabriel waited for a display of her royal temper.

"Must you always creep up on me?" Her eyes sparked with obvious ire, the emerald coat she wore a perfect match for their shimmering hue. "Why aren't you in bed?" she demanded. "Don't you ever sleep?"

"Not when you don't," he replied.

She pulled off the ski jacket hood, releasing a spill of red hair, then frowned in irritation. "I was going to step outside for a little breath of fresh air."

"Okay," he agreed. "Just let me get my coat and I'll go with you."

"If I wanted you to go with me, I'd have issued a formal invitation." She dropped the boots to the floor with a thud. She unzipped the ski jacket and shrugged it off, exposing a petite, but shapely body clad in a pair of designer jeans and a bulky beige sweater.

"It's my job to go with you," Gabe said, studiously ignoring how rich and thick her red hair looked against the paleness of the sweater.

"You take your job far too seriously," she exclaimed. She walked over to the sofa and sank down. "I'm going stir-crazy here. It's not fair that my sisters are all off on adventures while I'm stuck here like a baby."

Gabe said nothing, although nobody looked less like a baby than Serena. At twenty-one years old, she might be the youngest of the royal family, but she was definitely all woman.

"Serena, you know your sisters aren't off on lighthearted jaunts. They're seeking clues to your brother's whereabouts."

For a moment Serena seemed to forget her irritation. She leaned toward him, her features soft and wistful. "Oh, Gabe, do you really think it's possible James is still alive after all these years?"

"I don't know. I hope so," he replied.

Prince James Wyndham, the first and only son of Phillip Wyndham, King of Wynborough, had been kidnapped from the town of Aspen twenty-nine years before. Just recently, evidence that he might still be alive and living in the United States had surfaced. Serena and her sisters were determined to discover if their brother was alive and well.

"It would be so wonderful if we could find James

before the celebration of the anniversary of father's coronation.'' Serena sighed, her features softened with longing. ''He'd be thirty years old by now. A big brother.''

Gabe shifted uncomfortably from one foot to the other, unaccustomed to seeing Serena look so subdued and vulnerable. When she looked like this, it made a man want to wrap his arms around her, hold her close and never let her go.

The softness fell away and she glared at Gabe. ''And hopefully he won't be as bossy and overly protective with me as you are.''

Gabe relaxed, much more comfortable and familiar with her irritability where he was concerned. ''Your father expects me to be bossy and overly protective.''

''I don't see why you didn't go with Alexandra and Elizabeth to Arizona, or with Katherine to New Mexico.''

''Both Alexandra and Katherine now have husbands to watch over them, and Elizabeth can take care of herself,'' Gabe replied.

''So can I!'' Serena returned.

Gabe didn't reply. He didn't dare tell her the truth, that of the four princesses, Gabe knew that Serena was the one most likely to find trouble.

Impetuous and willful to a fault, Serena far too often followed her heart and sense of adventure rather than her head and sense of duty.

When the other three sisters had taken off to follow leads about Prince James, Gabe had elected to stick with Serena, knowing that was what King Phillip would want, and Queen Gabriella as well.

Of the four girls, Serena was the one who had inherited not only her mother's red hair and green eyes, but Gabe suspected Serena got her adventurous soul from her beautiful mother as well.

"Do you still want to get some fresh air?" Gabe asked. "I'll take a walk with you if that's what you want."

"Just the kind of thing I dream about…a moonlight walk in the snow with my bodyguard," Serena replied dryly. She covered a yawn with the back of her hand. "I think I'll just go ahead and go to bed." She stood, grabbed her boots and coat and started toward Gabe at the threshold of the hallway.

Instantly he was once again aware of her perfume, a spicy fragrance both arresting and distinct. She stepped so close to him, he could see the tiny flecks of gold that mingled with the green of her eyes. He could feel her body heat, radiating outward to encompass him.

She smiled, a teasing smile that caused a dimple to dance on the left side of her full mouth. "Want to come and tuck me in?" she asked, her voice low and husky.

Although his impulse was to take a step backward, gain distance between her body and his, through sheer willpower alone he remained unmoving, his expression impassive. "Good night, Princess."

For a brief moment, her eyes held the same soft wistfulness they'd had before, then she whirled away from him and down the hallway toward her room.

She paused at her door and turned back to him. "Oh, I forgot to tell you. I've got an interview scheduled at nine tomorrow at a radio station in town. Just another boring publicity engagement." Without waiting for his reply, she went into her room and closed the door.

Gabe narrowed his eyes thoughtfully. Something was up. She'd made her announcement with a studied nonchalance, but he sensed the fidgety energy radiating from her. Besides, all interview requests filtered through him so he could check out the security situation. Laura Bishop, the social secretary for the princesses, would never set up an interview without letting him know about it in advance.

Instead of going back to his room, Gabe stretched out on the sofa where he would be alerted if Serena attempted another escape.

Yes, something was amiss and he had a feeling he'd better be on his toes in the morning. He had a feeling his princess intended to fly the coop, and he had every intention of being by her side.

Serena sank into the airplane seat with a sigh of intense satisfaction. She'd done it. She'd fooled him and very soon she would be on her way to Las Vegas alone, without her handsome, sober bodyguard anywhere in sight.

It had been surprisingly easy. While Gabe had parked the car, Serena had gone into the front of the radio station and out the back door where a cab had been waiting.

Her self-congratulatory smile faded as she thought of Gabriel Morgan.

While she'd been with her sisters, she hadn't paid much attention to their keeper. It had only been since her sisters had left and she and Gabe had been alone in the Aspen vacation home that she'd begun to entertain disturbing thoughts about him.

Lately her thoughts toward Gabe were more than disturbing. During the days, she found herself studying him, wondering about him. And during the nights, she had been having dreams about him, fantasizing an intense, passionate relationship with him.

It wouldn't be so bad if she thought he reciprocated her feelings in any way, but she knew he didn't. He acted as if she were nothing more than a spoiled brat, an immature little girl who needed his presence to stay safe.

She definitely needed to get some distance from him. She needed to get some perspective. Of course she fantasized about him. Other than her father, he was the only male in her life.

A smile once again curved her lips and she slapped on a pair of sunglasses and leaned her head back against the seat.

Las Vegas. It was the perfect place to enjoy some freedom, and in the process she could chase down a lead about James…a lead that had been languishing while she fulfilled her obligations of publicizing the approaching anniversary of her father's coronation.

She eyed the empty seat next to her. Perhaps a handsome young stranger would sit beside her and they would spend the flight time indulging in playful flirting.

Or maybe she'd meet somebody wonderful in Las Vegas. He'd be tall and handsome and he'd fall in love with her not because she was Princess Serena, but just plain Serena, the princess of his heart. She closed her eyes and shivered with excitement.

Surely a couple of days in Las Vegas would put her crazy feelings for Gabe into perspective. And maybe…just maybe…she'd fall desperately, helplessly in love with a man who could fulfill all the romantic fantasies that ached in her heart.

"Going somewhere?"

The deep, familiar voice washed over her with a combination of heat and dread. She opened her eyes and met Gabe's dark gaze. He grinned at her expression of utter disbelief.

He stowed a bag in the overhead compartment, then slid into the seat next to her. Instantly she could smell him. He always smelled like Aspen, like clean mountain air with a whispered breeze of pine.

She snatched off her sunglasses and eyed him in disbelief. "How did you find me? What gave it away? Where did I mess up?" She frowned with irritation. "Tell the truth, you had a homing device surgically implanted in me one night while I slept."

One dark eyebrow rose wryly. "A homing device? Surgical implantation? Princess, you've been watching too much television."

Serena's irritation grew by leaps and bounds. "Of

course I've been watching too much television. That's because I have no life. Eventually, I'll be the oldest living virgin in the world because my body-guard won't give me a moment of privacy."

She flushed hotly, mortified by the impetuous gallop of her tongue. "Just…just don't talk to me. Pretend you don't know me at least for the duration of this flight." She grabbed a magazine from her over-size purse and flipped it open on her lap, embarrassed and determined to ignore him for as long as possible.

"As you like it, Princess," he murmured, then leaned his head back and closed his eyes.

He'd even brought a suitcase, Serena thought as she stared down at the magazine in her lap. He'd known she was catching a flight and had been completely prepared. The man was positively amazing.

She cast him a surreptitious glance. As always, he was the epitome of a well-groomed male. He wore a navy suit with her family crest embroidered on the breast of the jacket. His dark hair was neat, his jaw without a shadow of an errant whisker. With his eyes closed, she had full view of his sinfully long lashes.

Serena's sister, Elizabeth, had once declared that Gabe had bedroom eyes, the kind that made women think of breathless kisses and tangled sheets and heated caresses.

Bedroom eyes and a cold, unemotional heart. Heaven help the woman who falls in love with Gabriel Morgan, Serena thought. She gazed once again at her magazine, more determined than ever to ignore the handsome man beside her.

She'd been so certain she'd done it this time, successfully made her escape from him. How had he known? How had he managed not only to catch this flight, but also to be prepared enough to have a bag packed?

She had to know where she'd made her mistake…had to know so the next time she wouldn't repeat it. "You have to tell me how you knew I was going to try to sneak away," she finally said.

She stared at him, waiting for an answer. He didn't move, didn't twitch an eyelid. She sighed impatiently. "It's only fair that you tell me."

He opened his eyes and gazed at her blankly. "Excuse me, ma'am, are you talking to me?"

Serena grimaced, remembering the last thing she'd said to him was for him to pretend he didn't know her for the duration of the flight. The man was utterly maddening. "Gabriel, please. Just tell me how you knew."

He smiled, a smug, slightly superior smile that made Serena want to scream. "There were a dozen clues that let me know you had something planned. Clue number one…" He shifted in his chair and held up a finger. His leg pressed warmly against hers. "You never set up your own interviews. Laura does that for you.

"Clue number two…" A second finger joined the first. "All morning you vibrated with energy. Every gesture, every movement signaled something was going to happen."

He lowered his hand to his knee. "A word of advice, Princess. While in Las Vegas, you'd do well to stay away from the poker tables. You don't exactly possess a poker face." He grinned. "And you don't bluff well at all."

"But how did you know about the flight? About Las Vegas?" she asked, trying to stay focused on the conversation and not on his overwhelming nearness.

He shrugged. "I called Laura first thing this morning. She told me she'd booked tickets on this flight. Of course, she'd booked two because she didn't know you intended to ditch me and come alone."

Serena nodded thoughtfully. She should have known better than to make all her arrangements through Laura, but old habits died hard and it never crossed her mind to make the travel arrangements herself. Next time she'd know better.

"Now, can I ask you a question?" he inquired.

"What?"

"Why Las Vegas? You could have gone any-where in the country or joined one of your sisters."

Serena frowned. "Remember when Katherine called me and told me about a woman named Betty Jo Parker?" Katherine was one of Serena's older sisters, who had recently married Trey Sutherland, a wealthy CEO in New Mexico.

Gabe frowned. "Vaguely. Doesn't she have something to do with Bill Lewis?" he asked.

Serena nodded. She knew Gabe hadn't followed too closely the sisters' progress in the search for their brother. "Yes, but we don't know what. All we know is that we think Bill Lewis might really be James, and that a woman named Betty Jo Parker tried to reach him at Trey's from a Las Vegas phone number."

"So, you decided to go to Las Vegas and see if you can find this Betty Jo Parker."

"Exactly," she replied. "And hopefully Betty Jo can tell us where Bill is, and hopefully Bill is really James."

"There's a lot of hopefullys in there. You aren't a private investigator, you're a princess," he reminded her gruffly.

"I don't see why I can't be a little of both," she returned. "I've spent the last several months doing every radio and talk show in and around the Aspen area. I have more than done my publicity duty. Now I want to take an active part in the search for my brother."

"Won't your parents wonder what's up when none of you are doing any publicity?" Gabe asked. "That is the reason you gave them for the four of you coming to the States."

Serena waved her hands dismissively. "I've already told Laura to set up some interviews for me in and around the Las Vegas area. I also told her to tell Mother and Father that I'd saturated the Aspen market and thought Las Vegas might be fun."

Gabe grunted and closed his eyes once again. Serena gazed at him for a long moment. Drat, but the man was handsome as the devil.

She wished her father had assigned her a bodyguard who was old, far too old to evoke the kind of fantasies Serena found herself constantly entertaining about Gabe.

She wished her father had hired somebody who didn't have intriguing, haunting secrets in his dark eyes, a man who didn't have shoulders quite so broad, a man who didn't make her knees grow weak with strange emotions that both frightened and disturbed her.

She settled back in her seat and closed her eyes. What she'd told him about wanting to chase down the lead concerning Betty Jo Parker had been true.

However, Las Vegas held an additional draw. Las Vegas...the city of bright lights, fast money and hundreds of wedding chapels.

Wedding chapels. She'd heard that in Las Vegas they came in all shapes and sizes and no blood test or waiting period was required for marriage.

Every year thousands of couples gazed into each other's eyes, spoke their marriage vows and began their lives together as man and wife.

Maybe while she was hunting for the elusive Betty Jo Parker, she would meet a handsome stranger, and in the instant of their eyes meeting, she'd know he was the one for her. Maybe when she finally left Las Vegas, she would no longer be a lonely princess, but rather somebody's cherished wife.

She opened one eye and cast a sideways glance at Gabe. Of course, it would be impossible to indulge in a whirlwind romance, to lose herself in breathtaking spontaneous passion with him as a sidekick.

As the plane engines whined alive, Serena felt a thrum of excitement build inside her. Las Vegas was a big little city. Surely it was big enough for her to lose one handsome, irritating, overzealous bodyguard.

Chapter Two

Las Vegas. Energy surged through Gabe as he stood two steps behind Serena on the automated walkway in the Las Vegas airport.

He had a feeling his time of guarding Serena in Aspen would seem like a vacation compared to this. People clogged the walkways...businessmen, vacationers, honeymoon couples...so many people. Late December was the height of the city's tourist season, and it showed.

Although most of the time his biggest challenge was to guard Serena from herself and her crazy impulses, Gabe never lost sight of the fact that she was a princess and, therefore, a potential target. The Wyndhams were already painfully aware of that reality.

Kidnapping a princess would probably yield a criminal a sizable fortune; holding her hostage for partisan gain would be equally appealing to many political zealots.

And Las Vegas was a hotbed of all kinds of humanity in all sizes and shapes. He patted his gun, nestled in its shoulder holster beneath his jacket. The feel of the weapon assured him, although since being in charge of Serena's safety, he'd never had to remove it from its holster.

He hoped they wouldn't be here long. Serena was determined to find Betty Jo Parker, and Gabe would do everything he could to help her in the effort. Within a day or two he wanted to get Serena back to either the family vacation home in Aspen, or back to her parents in Wynborough.

As a former cop, he'd once prided himself on his investigative skills. But that had been almost four years ago...before a bank robbery gone awry had scarred forever the heart of the man he might have been.

He shook his head to dislodge thoughts of the past and instead focused on the woman in front of him, and the surrounding people. He couldn't help but notice the admiring glances Serena received from the males who passed her.

And why wouldn't she draw admiring, even lustful, glances? The green suit she wore was a perfect foil for her flaming hair. The short skirt displayed a sinful length of sexy legs and hugged her slender, but shapely hips. The bolero-type jacket emphasized her tiny waist and the swell of her breasts.

Gabe frowned. His job would be a hell of a lot easier if Serena would wear plastic garbage bags from head to toe, hiding the curves that seemed to beg attention. Unfortunately, Serena had an unerring fashion sense and knew exactly what styles emphasized her attributes.

A car awaited them outside the airport. Gabe slid into the front seat with the driver while Serena was alone in the luxurious rear interior. "Lucky Diamond Hotel," Gabe told the driver, knowing that was where Laura had made the reservations for their indefinite stay in Las Vegas.

The hotel was one of the new ones on the strip, a monolith of glass and steel that towered against the desert sky. It took only minutes for Serena and Gabe to be whisked by a courteous hotel employee to one of the lavish penthouse suites.

Gabe took the smaller of the two bedrooms, although he knew his nights would be spent on the sofa near the front door where he could hear if his charge attempted to sneak away.

The center room was elegant with plush rose carpeting, expensive furniture and a fully stocked wet bar in one corner. An extravagant bouquet of flowers sat on the marble coffee table, alongside a fruit basket that could feed a small village. Both compliments of the hotel.

Gabe stored his clothes in the closet in the bedroom, then went back into the living room, awaiting Serena's next move.

He walked over to the wet bar and eyed a bottle of scotch, waiting to hear the siren call he'd once not been able to ignore. Nothing. No evocative whispered promise of oblivion, no sweet song offering the numbness from pain.

He fixed himself a soft drink, satisfied that his destructive tendencies were truly behind him. Somehow in the past three years, he'd managed to regain some enjoyment in life and his self-respect.

And much of his recovery was due to Serena's father, King Phillip. Gabe owed his life, his sanity and his renewed feeling of worthiness to the king, and in return, he had pledged his honor and his commitment to that same man. And that was why Gabe took his job guarding King Phillip's youngest daughter most seriously.

"Isn't it magnificent?"

Gabe turned away from the bar to see Serena standing at the floor-to-ceiling window that gave a stunning view of sin city and the surrounding desert.

"There's no place like it on this earth," he replied.

She turned and looked at him, curiosity evident in her gaze. "Have you been here before?"

He nodded, remembering a honeymoon suite, a young woman with laughing brown eyes, and a night of promised love forever. Only in their case, forever had lasted less than six months. "Once," he finally answered. "A very long time ago."

She stared at him for another long moment, as if wanting to pursue the topic further. He wasn't sure if it was his forbidding expression or the edge that had been in his voice that changed her mind.

"I'm starving," she said and looked at her watch.

"You want me to call up room service?" he asked.

She eyed him as if he'd lost his mind. "Do you really think I'm going to spend my time in Las Vegas cooped up in this room?"

"One could only hope," he replied dryly.

"Where's your sense of adventure?" she asked, her eyes sparkling with excitement. She turned back to peer out the window, her body appearing to vibrate with the restless energy he'd come to dread. "Oh, this is going to be such fun," she exclaimed.

"Yeah, fun," Gabe echoed with sardonic amusement.

She whirled away from the window and to the front door of the room. "You know, you're welcome to stay right here and catch a nap or grab some room service. I'm sure I'll be just fine on my own."

"Fat chance," Gabe exclaimed, and followed her out the door.

He wasn't surprised when she found one of the biggest buffets in the world at Circus Circus. As she went through the food line, he walked just behind her, watching in indulgent amusement as she piled food high and heavy on her plate.

From the first moment he'd been assigned as a bodyguard and had watched Serena eat, it had amazed him how a woman so petite could eat like a burly ranch hand. Unlike so many women, Serena seemed not to have to watch her weight. He had a feeling she probably burned excess calories in thinking of ways to aggravate him.

By the time Serena left the buffet line, she had

two full plates of food and hadn't yet hit the desserts. Gabe carried his plate and followed her to a couple of empty tables. As she slid into a chair at one of them, he started to sit down at the table next to hers.

"You might as well join me," she said, and motioned him over with a wave of her hand. He changed directions and settled in the chair directly across from her.

For a few minutes they ate in silence. Gabe watched the crowd around them, trying not to focus on Serena. But his gaze was drawn again and again to her.

She was the most sensual eater he'd ever seen. She took obvious pleasure in each morsel, not hesitating to lick her fingers or run her tongue across her bottom lip to capture an errant crumb.

She'd surprised him when she'd spoken of being afraid she'd become the oldest living virgin in Wynborough. He'd suspected she was a virgin due more to circumstance than any commitment on her part to save herself for marriage.

In the two years Gabe had worked for King Phillip, other than the official dates arranged by the palace, Serena didn't appear to have any special suitor.

Gabe envied the man who would be her first lover. He had a feeling Serena would approach lovemaking as she did everything else in her life…with lustful enthusiasm.

"Hmmm, now all I need to top this off is a piece of that sinful chocolate cake," she said as she wiped her mouth with a napkin.

"I'll get it for you, Princess." Gabe jumped up, suddenly feeling the need to distance himself, not so much from her, but rather his own crazy thoughts where she was concerned.

The last thing he needed to do was to entertain fantasies of himself as her first lover. Harboring any such thoughts made him feel disloyal to King Phillip.

Besides the fact that she was his princess and he was her humble protector, there was also the fact that he'd sworn to himself long ago that no woman would ever again possess any piece of his heart.

He grabbed a slice of the requested chocolate cake and carried it back to the table, the short walk and stern self-admonishment working to put him back in a proper mindset.

"Here you are, Princess," he said as he placed the cake before her.

He sat back down and nodded to the waiter who appeared as if by magic at their table to refill their coffee cups. As Serena polished off the cake, he kept his focus studiously away from her and on the people coming and going at the tables nearby.

She had just finished her cake when an elderly woman who'd been sitting at the table next to them leaned over and touched Serena's shoulder. From caution borne of bitter experience, Gabe's hand automatically went beneath his jacket to his gun.

"I couldn't help but overhear the two of you while I was eating," the older woman said. She smiled, a sweet gesture that wreathed her face with wrinkles. "My William, God rest his soul, used to call me Princess."

Gabe relaxed, sensing no danger. The woman turned to Gabe, her smile deepening. "It's so nice to hear a young man talking so sweetly to his lady. It's obvious the two of you are very much in love."

"Oh, but I'm not—" Gabe grunted as Serena's foot connected solidly with his shin beneath the table.

Serena smiled and grabbed Gabe's hand. Her dimple flashed at the corner of her mouth with her impish smile. "He loves me madly and passionately, just as I love him."

Her thumb caressed the back of his hand, shooting rivulets of warmth up his arm. She leaned closer to the older woman. "He not only calls me Princess, he treats me like one. Don't you, darling?" Her eyes glittered with mischief.

"Oh, that's wonderful." The old woman clapped her hands together in delight. "I hope the two of you have many happy years together, just like my William and I did."

"Trust me, I don't intend to let him go for a very long time," Serena replied and she raised Gabe's hand to her lips. She pressed her mouth against the back of his hand in a sensual kiss. Her gaze never left his, as if she wanted to see what response her kiss would bring.

The rivulets of warmth that had been racing through him ignited into flames. The heat her kiss had evoked was bewitching…addictive.

With a happy nod to them both, the old woman

murmured goodbye, then rose and walked away. The minute her back was turned, Gabe snatched his hand from Serena's, irritated with her for her teasing, and irritated with himself for his response. She laughed, as if aware that he'd not been unaffected by her touch.

"How do you plan on finding this Betty Jo Parker?" he asked, wanting to remind her of the reason she was here and get his own mind away from her kiss.

"I've got her phone number and an address back at the room. But I don't intend to do anything about that today. I'll start the search first thing in the morning." She smiled with excitement. "Today I just want to wallow in the experience of Las Vegas." She pushed away from the table and stood. "And the first thing I need to do is walk off this incredible meal."

Gabe followed her out of the restaurant, trying desperately not to notice the sway of her hips, trying desperately to forget the sweet warmth of her lips against his skin.

She was a tease, a young woman experiencing her first flush of sexual awareness. At twenty-one years old, Serena appeared to be researching the power of her female wiles…and they were powerful.

He frowned with irritation. His biggest problem at the moment was in protecting Serena from herself and her adventurous soul. He hoped that it never came to a situation where he had to protect her from himself.

* * *

She'd irritated him. As Serena left Circus Circus and walked out into the warm desert air, she was aware of Gabe following close behind her, his dark eyebrows pulled together in a scowl. Like an angry pit bull, he looked as if he might take a bite out of anyone who approached too near.

She knew she'd irritated him with her teasing game with the old woman. But it was his own fault. She'd asked him again and again not to call her Princess, but rather to use her name, Serena. But Gabe continued to be proper. A proper, uptight, stick-in-the-mud.

All she wanted was to experience life, not as a princess, but as a normal, healthy twenty-one year old. A normal, healthy twenty-one year old who had spent most of her life desperately lonely.

She halted and waited for him to catch up with her. "I'm sorry if I embarrassed you before," she said.

He eyed her in surprise. "No problem," he replied, but her apology did nothing to remove his frown.

"Is it possible you could lose the scowl?" she asked. "You know, could you maybe look pleased to be here?"

"It'd be a stretch," he returned. "I'm not exactly pleased to be here."

"Why not?" she asked incredulously. "I'd think you'd appreciate the break from the boredom of being cooped up in the house in Aspen."

His dark gaze played over her face. "I'm not particularly happy to be here because I don't trust you at all.''

She worked for an expression of surprise, but it was simply out of her reach. She stopped walking and turned to face him. She knew exactly why he didn't trust her and he had every reason not to. ''Okay...what if I agree to be good for today, if I promise no attempt to get away from you...would that earn a smile?''

To her delight, the corners of his lips turned up ever so slightly and the darkness of his eyes lightened a bit. ''It would have to be a cross-your-heart, hope-to-die kind of promise before I'd really believe it.''

She made an imaginary cross over her heart. ''Cross my heart and hope to die, I won't try to get away from you for the remainder of the day. I promise, and I never, ever break my promises. Now, will you lose the pit bull expression?''

''Pit bull?'' A burst of laughter escaped him. ''Is that what I look like to you?''

The sound of his deep, melodic laughter filled her with warmth.

When he scowled, he was still handsome, but when he laughed, he was absolutely devastating. He made her want to melt against him, curl up in his arms and feel that rumble of laughter vibrate inside his chest.

She felt an unaccustomed blush warm her cheeks. Her thoughts irritated her. Somehow she had to stop her crazy musings about Gabe. He was her bodyguard, and to her dismay, he'd never given her any sign that he wanted to be anything more to her.

"Okay, so it's settled," she said briskly. "For the rest of the day you won't glower and glare at people and you'll pretend you enjoy being here."

"I'll do the best I can, Princess," he replied, amused indulgence lighting his eyes.

"And don't call me Princess," she exclaimed. She took a step closer to him, wondering if it was the desert warmth she felt or his body heat radiating out to encompass her.

She reached out a hand and placed it on his arm. "Gabe, please. I've asked you a dozen times in the past, but it's really important to me that I be as inconspicuous as possible. I don't want people to know who I am. I just want to be a regular person. For the duration of our stay in Las Vegas, I don't want to be Princess Serena. I just want to be Serena."

"I'll do the best I can," he agreed, any smile gone from him. She felt the tension in his arm and dropped her hand. She knew he didn't like to be touched. Any simple touch from her always made his eyes darken and his muscles bunch as if in protest. And that was exactly why she wanted to get away from him, to find a man who'd long for her touch.

"Good, so it's settled. I'm Serena for as long as we're here." She began walking once again, Gabe at her side. She'd promised him she would be good for today, and she'd told the truth. She wouldn't try to lose him. But at midnight, her promise would expire.

"Oh look, a street musician." She pointed ahead of them, where a man with a guitar was singing and strumming, entertaining the crowd that had gathered around him.

Just what she needed, a diversion from her pre-occupation with Gabe. She wiggled her way toward the front of the enthusiastic audience, aware of Gabe trailing in back of her.

She tapped her foot in time to the music and tried to stay focused on the entertainer, but it was difficult to focus on anything but Gabe's body directly behind hers. If she leaned back just a little, she would be nestled intimately against him. She closed her eyes for a moment, weak with temptation.

But she knew what would happen. She'd feel him tense in protest, and he'd quickly step aside, breaking immediately any intimate contact between them.

When the singer ended his song, the crowd began to disperse. Serena had only taken a couple of steps away when a little girl tugged at the bottom of her skirt.

Serena smiled at the child, who looked to be no older than six and had a riotous burst of blond curls all over her head. Serena loved children. She hoped someday to have a dozen of her own.

"Hi, sweetheart," she said to the young girl.

"My mommy says you're a real princess. Can I have your autograph?" she asked. She held out a slip of paper and a pen.

At that moment, the child's mother approached,

an expression of awe on her face. "We're sorry to bother you," the woman said. "I recognize you from the interview you did in *Today's Woman,* and I told my Samantha that you were a princess and perhaps you'd give her an autograph."

"I'd be honored to," Serena replied, although she was dismayed at being recognized. She took the pen and paper the girl held out and quickly signed her name. "There you are, sweetheart," she said to little Samantha.

"Thank you," Samantha said shyly.

"Samantha is a very pretty name," she said and was rewarded by a smile.

"Someday I want to grow up and be a princess," Samantha said.

As the mother and child moved away, Serena stared after them. She sighed and began to walk once again. "Every little girl wants to grow up to be a princess. I wonder if every princess wants to grow up to be just an ordinary girl?"

"Is that what you wish?" Gabe asked.

"Sometimes," she admitted. "I just wish for a little while I could be an average young woman. I wish I could go out with somebody and not have to worry about if he's with me for political gain, or to please the press. I wish…" She broke off, unwilling to share her innermost dreams with a man who was with her because of duty to her father. "Never mind," she said, and waved her hand to dismiss the entire conversation.

She couldn't tell Gabe that what she most wished for was marriage and babies, a life filled with love and laughter rather than pomp and circumstance. And she definitely couldn't confess that when she indulged in daydreams, they always included him.

"What about you? Don't you ever get tired of having no life other than mine?" she asked him. "I mean, if I want Chinese food, that's what you eat. If I want to see a movie, that's what you see. Everything you do revolves around my choices, my schedule."

"That's my job," he returned easily.

"But that's not a life," she protested.

"My job is my life," he said with more vehemence than her protest required. He smiled, as if in an attempt to lighten his intensity. "When I pledged myself to your father and his reign, I gave up all rights to any personal life."

Serena gazed at him for a long moment, seeking answers in his handsome features. But he gave nothing away. Why would a man with Gabe's looks, his obvious intelligence, pledge himself so completely to another and sacrifice all personal choice and freedom?

She walked into a casino and sat down at one of the dollar slot machines. Gabe sat at the one next to her and twirled his chair around so he could survey anyone who might come too near.

She fed a twenty-dollar bill into the slot and twenty dollar tokens clunked into the bin. She'd never been much of a gambler. What she really wanted to do was sit and get to know a little bit more about Gabe. She actually knew very little about the man who occupied her fantasies, the man whom her father had entrusted with her very life. The right moment to ask personal questions had never presented itself. They were rarely alone and the few times they had been alone, she'd found herself ridiculously shy and tongue-tied by the childish crush she'd entertained. But she was no longer a child and she refused to consider that what she felt for Gabe had anything to do with a simple silly crush.

"What did you do before you came to work for my father?" she asked him. She put a token in the machine and hit the button to spin the reel.

"Nothing that would interest a princess," he replied. His voice held a tiny note of tension that let her know he found her question an intrusion.

That didn't stop her from pursuing the issue. "If you won't tell me, I'll just have to guess." She turned her chair and eyed him boldly. "I think probably you were either a gangster or a hit man."

She was rewarded with his burst of laughter and amusement lighting the darkness of his eyes. "A hit man? You have definitely been watching too much television." His laughter died and shadows once again usurped the momentary glow of his eyes. "I was a police officer before I came to work for your father."

"A police officer?" Somehow it didn't surprise her. She had suspected a background in either law enforcement or the military. Her father wouldn't have hired anyone without some sort of professional training.

She gave up all pretense of playing the machine

and instead focused her full attention on him. "Where? I mean, what city in the States?"

"Kansas City, Missouri," he answered grudgingly, as if somehow he were giving away pieces of himself that could never be retrieved.

"Is that where your family is? In Kansas City?"

"What is this? Twenty questions?" he asked, a touch of irritation back in his voice.

"I just suddenly realized that I don't know anything about you," she replied, refusing to be distracted from what had become a mission. "So, is it?" she pressed.

He sighed in resignation. "I don't have any family. I prefer rock to classical music, steak to seafood and action movies to dramas. There, now you know everything that's worth knowing about me." He looked away from her, once again studying their surroundings.

She frowned at him, instinctively knowing there was much, much more to the man than he offered. There were secrets in his eyes, a profound sadness that sometimes radiated from him.

"What was a police officer from Kansas City, Missouri, doing in Wynborough?" She knew part of the story that had brought Gabe to her father's attention.

King Phillip had been about to make a public speech when Gabe, who had been in the audience, spied a man with a gun. Instantly, Gabe had wrestled the man to the ground and gained possession of the gun, saving the king's life. Soon after, Gabe had been offered the position of head of palace security before being assigned as head of the Royal Wynborough Bodyguards.

"I wasn't a police officer anymore when I came to Wynborough." Again, there was an edge of tension in his voice.

"So, what were you doing in Wynborough?"

He hesitated a moment, then replied, "Vacation. I was on vacation."

"Aren't you ever lonely, Gabe?" she asked softly. Didn't he ever long for somebody to hold, somebody to love?

His gaze swung back to her and he emitted a dry laugh. "Lonely? Since you became my charge, I don't have the time and I'm never alone long enough to get lonely."

Serena turned back to her machine and fed in several more coins one at a time as she mulled over his words. It was true, he was virtually never alone, and yet in many ways he was always alone.

She looked at him once again. "I know you spend all your time with me, but you're still alone. I mean, we're together…but not really." She frowned, aware that she wasn't clearly communicating what she really meant.

Gabe's life was every bit as confined as hers due to their stations, hers as a princess and his as a royal bodyguard. He couldn't date, couldn't just take off on a whim and see a movie or eat out. His every move was dictated by hers, and her every move was usually dictated by her duty.

"Don't you ever wish for somebody to share your

heart? Somebody you could tell your dreams?'' Do
you ever think of me? her heart yearned to ask.

"Never," he said succinctly. "Besides—" he offered her a thin smile "—I don't waste time entertaining dreams, and I definitely don't have a heart."

Serena gazed at him for a long moment. She
didn't believe him. She didn't know what his past
experiences had been, but somewhere along the road
of his life, he'd abandoned his dreams and closed
off his heart.

But lost dreams could be found, and a closed
heart could be reopened. Love could accomplish all
those things and more.

She had a feeling that the woman who managed
to tap into Gabe's dreams, to step into his heart,
would be the luckiest woman alive.

What she didn't know was if she was the woman
to accomplish such a task. She didn't know if she
should run from him, escape and fly solo to find the
love her heart craved. Or should she stay with him,
spend time with him, and hope she could be the
woman who would reawaken his dreams, his love.

It was a gamble either way. She fed the last of
her coins into the slot machine and hit the button to
spin the reel. Nothing. She'd never been very lucky
at gambling.

Chapter Three

Gabe hadn't lied to her. He'd lost his dreams a long time ago, and he'd locked away his heart at the same time, building barriers around it that would keep it safe and untouched.

He'd first learned to guard his heart while still a boy. As a foster child, he'd learned not to love too much, too deeply, that nothing and nobody could be counted on forever.

He'd allowed the barriers to drop only once, and the result had devastated him. He wouldn't make the same mistake again.

Serena had irritated him with her probing questions. She'd made him think about people, places and times he didn't want to remember.

As he followed her down the sidewalk once again, he reminded himself that she was young, a complete stranger to tragedy, an innocent to the cruel winds of fate.

She was still young enough to believe in the power of love and the concept of soul mates. She had yet to taste the bitter tang of regret, experience the utter emptiness of loss. And he hoped she never would.

Eventually he knew Serena would probably marry a prince. She would set up a household in a castle with all the trappings of her station, and fulfill the duties she was born for.

He frowned, wondering why the thought of Serena happily married rankled him. It was probably because he knew until that happened, he was responsible for her. And being responsible for Serena was a momentous task.

Apparently his terse reply concerning his dreams and his heart had momentarily stifled her curiosity about him. She'd stopped asking questions and instead had grown quiet and introspective.

There were times when he found her endless chattering rather trying, but her silence worried him far more. When Serena grew quiet, it usually meant she was thinking, and rarely did anything good come from that.

She had been right about one thing. The moment he'd become a royal bodyguard, he'd given up all rights to his own life. He no longer made the decisions a normal man made. His decisions were made by Serena, who set the daily schedule and he merely followed.

He'd learned to snooze when she slept, shower while she showered, and constantly be aware of her and her safety. His every move was dictated by hers and for the moment it was a life-style that suited him perfectly. He had little time for thinking of anything other than his duty to King Phillip and how to remain one step ahead of Serena.

"Oh, Gabe, look!" The object of his thoughts grabbed his arm and pointed to a building across the street. The building, a traditional gray stone chapel, was nearly lost between two towering, glittering casinos.

The only concession to the surrounding tourism and capitalism was a bright gold banner that proclaimed the place Ye Olde Wedding Chapel.

"Let's go inside," she said, her features shining with excitement.

Gabe wanted to protest. He didn't want to enter any chapel for any reason. But, of course, it wasn't his place to lodge any complaint. With a long-suffering sigh, he followed her into the front door.

There was nothing traditional about the lobby area. A sign posted the prices of a variety of different kinds of wedding ceremonies. A refrigerated unit against one wall held fresh flower arrangements, the bouquets in a variety of sizes and styles, with different colored ribbons to match each assortment of blooms.

Dozens of wedding photos decorated the wall opposite the floral display, each with a smiling couple and a bald minister with a bulbous nose.

Serena peeked through the window in the door that led to the inner sanctum of the church. She turned back to Gabe, her eyes dazzling bright. "There's a couple in there getting married right now.'' She grabbed his hand. ''Come on, let's go in and watch.''

Again, Gabe fought a protest, unsure if he wanted to complain about her plan to watch a wedding or reprove her for holding his hand, the connection both warm and unsettling.

They entered through the door and Serena led him to the back pew, where they eased down, their presence not interrupting the ceremony in progress.

Gabe wanted his hand back, but Serena held tight. The minister was reading a section of the Bible, but Gabe had trouble focusing on the man's words. His head was filled with the scent of Serena, the evocative spicy scent that she always wore.

''They probably met in a nightclub several nights ago,'' Serena whispered, her gaze not leaving the couple who had begun to exchange their vows. ''It was love at first sight, and they've spent every moment together since.''

Her hand tightened around Gabe's. ''Maybe he's a school principal and she's a teacher, and they have everything in common and this is the beginning of a wonderful life for them, a life filled with love and happiness.''

''He's probably a hardware salesman from Toledo and she's a waitress. Their marriage will probably last no longer than six months before they both realize this wedding was a big mistake,'' Gabe said. ''These quickie weddings almost never last.'' He stifled a yelp as Serena pinched him.

''You stop it right now, Gabriel Morgan,'' she hissed beneath her breath. She glared at him, her

eyes green crystals of ice. "Don't you dare say another word to ruin my fantasy." She looked back at
the "happy" couple and her features softened.
"Look at them," she said. "He loves her desperately, hopelessly, as she loves him."

Gabe followed her gaze, grudgingly admitting the
two people did appear to be in love. As the groom
placed a ring on his intended's finger, Gabe remembered doing the same in a distant past.

LeAnn hadn't worn white. She'd worn a vivid
pink suit, refusing to be confined by tradition.
They'd married right here in Vegas, the culmination
of an eight-week whirlwind romance. They'd had
six months together as man and wife before fate had
intervened.

Funny, the intense pain that thoughts of LeAnn
had always brought with them was finally gone. He
closed his eyes and tried to conjure a picture of her
in his mind.

Instead of LeAnn's blond hair, his mind filled
with the vision of a cascade of fiery red curls, green
eyes, sparking with fire and passion, and inviting
lips, parted as if waiting for his kiss.

Serena.

Damn. He snapped his eyes open and extricated
his hand from hers. At that moment the minister
pronounced the couple man and wife and the newlyweds shared a kiss.

Gabe looked at Serena, surprised to find her eyes
filled with tears. She caught his gaze and emitted an
embarrassed little laugh. "I know...it's crazy," she

said as she swiped her tears with her fingers. "I don't even know them, but I'm so happy for them."

Oddly, her tears moved him. He pulled a clean handkerchief from his pocket and handed it to her. Serena rarely wept, and it touched him that she could so easily cry tears of joy for strangers. "Don't be embarrassed," he replied. "Lots of people cry at weddings."

"Let's get out of here," she said.

They snuck out of the chapel just ahead of the newly wedded couple and for the next couple of hours wandered the strip, sightseeing with the rest of the tourists. Serena was quiet, her thoughts obviously far away from the glittering casinos with their dazzling designs.

Gabe was grateful when she spied a casino offering a prime rib special, and decided to get a bite to eat.

"You aren't really such a cynic about love, are you?" she asked when they were seated at a secluded table in the dimly lit dining area.

He shrugged, finding it difficult to look at her. The glow of the candle in the center of the table stroked her like a lover, pulling soft color into her cheeks and accentuating the brilliant green of her eyes. "I'm not necessarily a cynic about love, but I do doubt the longevity of quickie Las Vegas marriages."

"But why? Love doesn't know where or in what kind of ceremony you get married."

He smiled. "True, but if I was to make an educated guess, I'd surmise that most of the Las Vegas weddings take place due to lust, rather than love.''

''I'd settle for a little lust in my life at this point,'' she said and gave him a sly glance as if to gauge his reaction.

He knew she expected a stern admonishment. He didn't give it to her. ''Trust me, Princess, lust is vastly overrated.''

She eyed him curiously. ''You sound like you're no stranger to lust.'' She leaned forward, so close the warmth of her breath stirred past the candle flame and caressed his face. ''Tell me who you lusted for…what kind of woman she was.''

Gabe wanted to change the subject, felt the suffocating crush of ancient regrets pressing hard against his chest. He wished there was some way to divert her from the question, but she had the look of a determined hound dog with the scent of prey in her nose and he knew nothing would satisfy her except answers.

He leaned back in his chair and eyed her with studied indulgence. ''She was a gorgeous blonde with big blue eyes and a laugh that made me feel all warm inside.''

Serena nodded, as if to encourage him to confide further in her. ''And did you love her desperately?''

''Madly, passionately,'' he said, trying not to notice how utterly appealing Serena looked. There was a wistful softness in her eyes, a slight tremble to her lips. And in that moment, Gabe wanted her as he'd never wanted a woman before.

''What happened?'' she asked.

He shrugged. "Her parents moved away and she had to go with them. She was only in third grade. I was in fourth."

He watched in satisfaction as the soft wistfulness in her eyes died, replaced by exasperation.

"You're making fun of me," she said. She leaned back in her chair and ran her hands over the napkin in her lap. The tremble of her lips was more pronounced, only this time in hurt.

Instantly Gabe wanted to lean across the table, stroke her arm or touch her face and say he was sorry. But the waiter arrived with their food, and the moment was lost.

Just as well, he thought, as they began to eat their meal in silence. He was beginning to realize that there was no way he could touch Serena and not feel desire. Somehow, she'd begun to crawl under his skin.

Tomorrow they would seek out Betty Jo Parker, then Gabe would escort Princess Serena back to her parents in Wynborough. And once in Wynborough, Gabe would ask for a transfer of duty. In time, he would forget the crazy, inappropriate desire that one certain red-haired minx had managed to stir.

When Serena awoke the next morning, the desert sun had already crept halfway up the sky. "Rats," she muttered as she grabbed the alarm clock on the nightstand. "Double rats," she exclaimed as she saw it was nearly ten o'clock.

Minutes later, she stood beneath a hot shower, cursing the good night's sleep she'd gained. After dinner, she and Gabe had attended one of the Las Vegas shows, a glittering extravaganza that had been both beautiful and entertaining.

However, she'd had found it difficult to stay focused on the merriment on stage. Gabe's presence in the seat next to hers was distracting. He was easily the most handsome man at the show, and she couldn't help but notice the admiring gazes he drew from other women.

She remained aloof throughout the show, still smarting from the way he'd teased her about lust and love. When they returned to their hotel, she'd gone directly to her bedroom with every intention of sneaking out after midnight and experiencing life far away from his domineering, overly protective manner. Unfortunately, her body had betrayed her and almost immediately she'd fallen asleep.

She finished her shower, dressed and blow-dried her hair, then left her room and went into the main area of the suite.

Gabe was there at the table, sipping a cup of coffee and reading the morning newspaper. As she came into the room, he stood and reached for his jacket, which hung on the back of his chair.

"Relax," she said and waved him back down. "I'm not going anywhere or doing anything until I have a cup of coffee."

"There are sweet rolls and muffins there, too," he said, and pointed to the room service cart, then returned his focus to the paper.

Serena poured herself a cup of coffee and grabbed

a huge cinnamon roll, then sat at the table in the chair opposite Gabe.

As she ate her roll, she studied Gabe's features, trying to figure out what it was about the man that so attracted her to him. Granted, he was handsome, with his dark brown hair and chiseled features. But she'd attended royal functions with other handsome men dancing attendance on her. She'd dated princes and dukes, viscounts and barons. For the most part they'd been handsome men with impeccable manners who had bored her to tears.

No, it wasn't just Gabe's looks that drew her to him. It was an aura of suppressed danger that radiated from him, a proficiency in dealing with any and all situations that might arise. More than this, it was the streak of humor he infrequently exhibited, the spark of emotion that sometimes lit his features, and those haunting dark shadows that at times eclipsed the light in his eyes.

He raised an eyebrow at her. "I would think a princess would know that it's rude to stare."

An embarrassed blush warmed her cheeks, but she didn't avert her gaze from him. "And I would think a bodyguard would know that it's rude to remind a princess of her shortcomings."

"Touché," he said, the corner of his mouth curling up in a smile of amusement. He got up to pour himself a fresh cup of coffee. When he turned back to face her, she noticed the top two buttons of his shirt were unfastened, allowing curly dark chest hairs to escape over the top of the crisp cotton confines.

Her mind filled with a vision of her hands dancing in that hair, reveling in the coarse tendrils curling around her fingers, tickling her nose as she pressed her lips against the center of his chest.

"So, what are your plans for the day?" he asked as he resumed his seat.

She shrugged. "I thought I might slip something into your drink, then when you're unconscious I'll ravage your body."

His gaze shot to his coffee cup and he peered at the liquid suspiciously. Serena laughed. "Oh honestly, Gabe, if I ever decide to ravish your body, trust me, I won't want you unconscious."

To her surprise, a deep flush swept over his features. "Your father should have spanked you more often when you were young," he declared.

"My father never spanked me," she protested.

An eyebrow quirked up wryly. "My point exactly."

"Oh, don't be such an old fuddy-duddy," she exclaimed. She stood and walked over to the window. Staring out, she sighed, the long-suffering sigh of a prisoner behind bars seeking elusive freedom.

"Princess, I don't know what you want from me." Gabe's voice was low and controlled. "I can't let you just go off on your own. There could be a kidnapping attempt, or something worse."

She turned to face him. "But only if people know who I am. Your presence makes me obvious. If I was off on my own, nobody would recognize me." She swept her hands toward the window. "There's a sea of humanity out there. I'd just be another tiny little fish.''

''That woman and her daughter recognized you,'' he countered.

''A mere fluke,'' Serena replied. She couldn't tell him what she really wanted from him…that she wanted him to love her, to marry her, that she wanted to bear his children and build a life with him.

He'd never once intimated in any way, shape or form that he had any interest in her other than his royal duty. If she confessed this particular fantasy to him, he'd have her back in Wynborough under her parents' wings so fast her head would spin.

If she couldn't have Gabe, then the next best thing was to lose him altogether and see what other men she might meet. Perhaps her fantasies concerning Gabe grew only out of the fact that they spent all their time together. She'd never know the truth of her feelings unless she gained some perspective.

''I see wheels turning,'' he said, pulling her from her thoughts.

''I was just thinking that it's time to start hunting down Betty Jo Parker. I'll go get her phone number and try to call her.'' Serena went into her bedroom, her frustration still simmering.

Nobody understood the abiding loneliness that ached inside her. As the youngest of the four sisters, Serena had always felt rather lost in the fracas of her family. She knew her parents loved her dearly, and she was close to all her sisters, but they had to love her—she was family.

Just as so many of the men she dated and the

people in her country loved her because she was a princess. Their affection had nothing to do with real love of the person she was inside, beneath her princess crown.

She opened her purse and grabbed the slip of paper that held the information on Betty Jo Parker, then returned to the main suite.

Gabe had buttoned his shirt and slipped on his jacket, and she was grateful that he now looked less approachable. She was a fool to entertain any kind of fantasies where he was concerned.

"So, remind me where you and your sisters are in this search for Prince James." Gabe said. "I must confess, I haven't kept up on all of it."

Serena sat on the sofa near the telephone. "Well, you know that Beulah Whitaker, who used to work at The Sunshine Home for Children in Arizona, found a baby blanket with the royal emblem on it. That's how we knew it was possible James might be alive and had been adopted."

Gabe nodded. "I also know Katherine went to Albuquerque to see if Trey Sutherland's missing partner, the elusive Bill Lewis, might be Prince James."

"And Bill Lewis has disappeared." And Katherine and Trey had fallen madly in love with each other, Serena thought, wishing the same thing for herself. Lucky Katherine.

She shook away thoughts of her elder sister. "We're hoping that if Betty Jo Parker is Bill's lover, she'll know where he is," Serena explained. She stared down at the slip of paper in her hand. A single phone number and address, it held all the dreams and hopes of finding her brother after all these years. What if it was just another dead end? What if they never found out what really happened to James?

"How did you get the address?" Gabe asked.

Serena flashed him a quick smile. "I pulled a few strings with the phone company. Sometimes it pays to be a princess."

"Why don't we just drive there now?"

Serena frowned, unsure how to explain to Gabe the fear that tore at her heart. She was so afraid of another dead end. She wasn't sure why, but a preliminary phone call seemed better than just showing up at the address. "I just think it's better to call first." she finally said.

He nodded as if he'd peeked into her mind and saw her doubts, her fears.

She drew a deep breath and picked up the telephone receiver. She punched in the numbers quickly, then sent a small prayer skyward. The phone on the other end of the line rang once… twice…four times, five times. She hung up after it had rung ten times. "There's no answer."

"Try again later. Maybe Betty has a job," Gabe said.

Serena tried all morning to connect with somebody at the phone number she had. Now that she had made the decision to get hold of Betty Jo Parker, it consumed her. She wandered around the suite while Gabe remained at the table reading the paper. When he'd finished reading, he began to work the crossword puzzle.

At noon they ordered room service and after eating Serena continued her phone duty, calling the number every half an hour.

By four, she was going stir-crazy. Gabe had finished the crossword puzzle and was reading a paperback book while she paced back and forth, stopping the agitated walking only to try the number again.

"Maybe we should just drive over there," she finally said. "We could wait around and maybe catch her as she comes home from work."

Gabe nodded. "I'll call for a car."

Within minutes they were on their way to the address Serena had for Betty Jo Parker. As usual, Gabe sat in the front seat with the driver, and Serena sat in the back.

They left the strip and drove into a residential area with houses and yards that were well kept. Serena realized it was easy to think of Las Vegas as a city strictly built for gambling, but in actuality there was a pleasant city beyond the glittering casinos and pawnshops.

They passed a school, the playground empty as all the children were home for the holidays. Greenery and red bows still decorated the lampposts, lingering reminders of the holiday just passed.

In two days it would be New Year's Eve. The way things were shaping up, when the clock struck midnight, Serena would have nobody to kiss. She eyed the back of Gabe's head. Unless she could sneak a kiss from him.

A shiver raced up her spine as she thought of his

lips covering hers. He would be a marvelous kisser, she knew instinctively. His kisses would be firm, commanding...demanding. She sighed. And midnight on New Year's Eve would probably be the first time in months she'd turn around to find him and he'd be nowhere in sight.

She refocused her attention outside the window, noting that the neighborhood they were now in was less attractive, less well kept than the one they had just passed.

Serena sat up straighter in the seat as the driver pulled to the curb in front of a neat white ranch with hunter green shutters.

Gabe turned around. "You want me to go up and knock?"

She shook her head and opened her car door. "I'll do it."

She got out of the car and approached the front door. A wicker rocking chair sat on the porch, as if bidding a visitor to sit and rest a while. A plastic, glittering sign reading Merry Christmas hung on the door.

Serena knocked and waited. As she heard footsteps behind her, she turned to see Gabe approaching. "It doesn't look like anyone's home," he said.

"Maybe she's taking a nap or cooking dinner and didn't hear my knock," Serena replied.

Gabe knocked on the door, his broad knuckles rapping loudly against the wood. "If she's here, she should hear that," he said.

Together they stood...waiting. There was no answer, no noise inside the house to attest to anyone's presence.

Serena sighed in defeat and looked at her watch. "It's nearly five o'clock. Surely if she's at work, she should be home almost anytime."

"Then we'll wait," Gabe said. "We have the driver for as long as we need him."

Serena nodded, and together the two of them started back toward the car. They had almost reached the car when Serena sniffed the air. "I smell charcoal."

"Somebody must be getting ready to barbecue," Gabe replied.

"I think I'll look in the backyard, see if it's Betty," she said. "Maybe that's why she didn't hear us knocking on her door."

"And I'll tell the driver to relax, that we might be here for a while."

As Gabe went toward the car, Serena walked around the side of the house to the back. Almost immediately she saw the next-door neighbor, an older man, placing steaks on his grill and knew that was what she smelled.

There was nobody on Betty's porch. Serena turned to head back to the front of the house, but paused, her gaze roaming beyond Betty's backyard. Houses and sheds everywhere, and not a fence in sight.

She faced the backyard again and took a step forward…then another…and another. Breaking into a run, she had no plan in mind. She only knew opportunity had presented itself, and she intended to grab it with both hands.

She didn't stop running until she was two blocks from Betty Jo Parker's house. Bending over, she breathed deeply in and out, trying to catch her breath.

She'd done it. Her heart did a jump and twirl in joy. She'd managed to lose Gabe. Oh, eventually she'd find him and they would have to go back to Betty's house to find the woman. But for the moment, Serena was free and she intended to savor every second, every minute.

She consciously shoved away images of a very angry Gabe. She'd face her consequences later... after she'd had a little fun.

Still, as she ducked between houses and sheds, the smell of freedom in her nose and the taste of success in her mouth, her mind was clouded with thoughts of a tall, handsome man who just might kill her when she saw him again.

Chapter Four

It only took a couple of minutes of Serena being out of his sight before Gabe got a bad feeling in the pit of his stomach. It was a feeling he'd experienced before…a number of times since being in charge of Serena, and that feeling rarely lied to him.

Telling the driver to stay put, he raced around the side of the house to the backyard.

Nothing. Nobody. Not a single sign of Serena. "Dammit." The epithet exploded from him, startling the man next door, who dropped his spatula and scurried into his house.

Gabe knew better than to yell for her. Even if she were hiding right next to where he stood and he yelled himself hoarse, she wouldn't answer.

He narrowed his eyes, his gaze sweeping the area, seeking a flutter of her scarlet hair, a wisp of teal material from her blouse. Nothing. There was not a sign of Serena anywhere.

He raced back to the car and got in. "Drive very slowly up and down the streets," he said to the astonished driver.

As the car moved at a snail's pace down the street, Gabe continued to look for his princess. Inside he seethed, not only at her, but at himself.

He should have known she would try something. He should have been prepared. But there had been no sign, no subtle signal from her that any such thoughts of escape were in her head.

Still, it was his job to know. It was his job to stay one step ahead of her. "Dammit," he exploded once again, hitting the palm of his hand against the dashboard.

The driver smirked and cast him a sideways glance. "Lovers' quarrel?"

"Something like that," Gabe replied.

"Ah, she'll come back. They always do. And if she doesn't, then you're better off without her."

Terrific, Gabe thought. Not only had he lost the princess, he was now getting romance advice from a man who insisted on wearing his driving hat backward.

"Just keep driving," Gabe replied. "She can't have gotten too far."

Up and down the streets they went, the driver watching the left side and Gabe watching the right, but there was no sign of Serena. It was as if she'd been swallowed by the very street.

It was nearly six-thirty when Gabe directed the driver to take him back to the hotel. Gabe's anger had grown to mammoth proportions, along with his fear, but there was no point in continuing to cruise the streets.

By seven o'clock, he stood in front of the floor-to-ceiling windows in their suite, watching the darkness of night slowly creeping across the sky.

Nighttime in Las Vegas, and Serena was someplace out there alone. His guts twisted at the very thought. Despite her teasing talk, she was such an innocent, easy prey for a smooth-talking operator.

She could be robbed, raped, kidnapped…every heinous crime imaginable played in his mind, filling it with horrifying details of Serena in trouble.

If anything happened to Serena, it would be Gabe's responsibility to tell King Phillip and Queen Gabriella. Gabe clenched his hands into fists and moved away from the window. If anything happened to Serena, he wasn't sure he could handle it.

He eyed the wet bar, knowing a finger of scotch would take off the edge, numb the icy fear that surrounded his heart. He also knew that to succumb to such temptation would be the end of him and his recently realized self-esteem.

It had been his inability to protect another woman that had nearly allowed him to destroy himself three years before. He wouldn't go down that path again…at least not yet.

He jumped as a knock sounded at the door. Hope filled his heart. She was back and didn't have a key. "Serena…" He pulled open the door to find a bellman carrying a huge bouquet of fresh flowers. Like a balloon losing air, the hope seeped out of Gabe.

"Compliments of the management," the young kid said. "Where would you like them?"

"Put them anywhere," he replied irritably.

The kid placed the arrangement in the center of the table, then left.

Alone once again, Gabe sank down on the sofa, knowing his only course of action was to wait…and pray that eventually Serena would return safe and sound.

The hours dragged by. Gabe alternated between pacing and cursing. He stared out the window, then stared at the door. His mind worked overtime to present him with everything horrible that could happen to one beautiful, impulsive, innocent young woman alone on the streets of Las Vegas after dark.

By nine o'clock he could stand his inaction no longer. He left the hotel and began to wander the streets, searching for Serena. In and out of casinos, through dining areas and into nightclubs, Gabe looked everywhere he thought she might be, but with no success.

His anger faded as fear took its place, a relentless fear that tore at his insides. Perhaps he should contact the local authorities? When should he place a call to King Phillip? Where in the hell could Serena be? Damn her and her need to experience life without the burden of her bodyguard.

By midnight, he was once again in their hotel, riding up the elevator to the room. He'd exhausted every possibility and didn't know where else to look for her. There was nothing else he could do but wait for her return…pray for her return.

In the suite, he didn't bother to turn on any lights. The glitter and color of a million lights from nearby casinos and hotels shone into the windows and gave the room a garish illumination.

He sank down on the sofa and closed his eyes. He knew better than anyone that the world was a dangerous place, with too many guns on the streets and too many crazy people in possession of those guns.

Even a simple trip to the local bank on a sunny morning could turn into a journey into death. All it took was one bank robber with an itchy finger.

He shuddered, and tried to push aside images that had haunted him forever. He didn't want to go back there, didn't want to remember that day.

His eyes flicked open as he heard the sound of a key being inserted in the lock of the door. He remained seated as the door opened and Serena entered.

In an instant, relief fluttered through him, intense relief that momentarily made him weak. She appeared safe. Thank God.

In the next instant, that relief dissipated, replaced by an anger so rich, so huge, it filled him to capacity. Serena turned on the lamp near the door, then jumped and yelped in surprise.

"You scared me to death," she exclaimed. "Why were you sitting in the dark? I didn't see you there." She gazed at him for only a moment, then flushed and sat at one of the chairs at the table.

Gabe said nothing. In truth, he was afraid to speak

to her until he reined in the untamed anger that surged inside him.

She kicked off her shoes and massaged one of her feet, still not looking at him.

"What in the hell have you done to your hair?" he asked, suddenly noticing her hair was woven in one long braid down her back, a style he'd never seen her wear before.

She began to knead her other foot. "It was an attempt to remain incognito. I know my hair is sort of my trademark, so I thought if I wore it completely different, it would keep people from recognizing me." She looked up and offered him an uneasy smile. "Do you like it?"

Gabe wondered if the King would forgive him for throttling his youngest daughter. "Do I like it?" He stared at her in amazement. She'd just given him the most miserable night of his life and now she wanted to know if he liked her hairstyle.

He stood, his anger threatening to erupt. "You are truly incredible," he exclaimed. "You run away from me, stay gone for hours, then waltz back in here and want to know if I like your hair?"

In truth, the style was quite becoming, emphasizing her large luminous eyes and the fullness of her mouth. She looked more touchable with her hair in the casual braid, less like a princess and more like a woman he'd love to make love to. The realization only served to further enrage him.

She sat up straight and frowned with a touch of petulance. "Please don't yell at me."

"I can't help it. When I'm angry, I yell," he exclaimed, then drew a deep breath.

"I'd appreciate it if you'd stop," she returned. The petulance faded and excitement lit her features. "Oh, Gabe, I had the most marvelous time tonight." She stood and took a step toward him. "It was just like I'd always dreamed it would be. Nobody knew who I was. I told everyone I met that my name was Sarah Wynn and I was a salesclerk on vacation from Kansas City."

She took two more steps toward him, standing close enough that he could smell the sweet scent of her, see the tiny golden flecks that mingled with the green of her eyes. She placed a hand on his arm. "I met a wonderful man, and he took me out to dinner, then we danced the night away. His name is Avery Kintell and he's an investment banker from here in Las Vegas."

She'd met a man. A wonderful man. The words reverberated through Gabe's head, serving to stoke the fires of his rage even higher.

He jerked away from her touch. "How nice for you," he said sarcastically. "And while you were dining and dancing the night away, I was back here trying to figure out how to tell your mother and father that they'd lost another child." He didn't mince words. "I didn't know if you'd been kidnapped, or worse."

The light in her eyes dimmed. "I'm sorry, Gabe. I didn't mean to worry you."

"Didn't mean to worry me?" The words exploded from him, his anger unleashed and wild.

"When exactly did you not mean to worry me? While I was driving up and down the streets, wondering where you'd gone, what had happened to you? Or perhaps later, when it got dark and I went into every casino, every restaurant and nightclub in a ten-block radius, searching for you?"

"You're yelling again," she said, her voice tiny compared to his.

"Hell yes, I'm yelling." The words roared out of him. "You need to be yelled at. You don't have the luxury of forgetting who you are…what you are. You're a princess, and because of that you're always at risk."

"I was fine tonight," she countered with a touch of defiance.

"You were damned lucky tonight," he replied. "It only takes one nut, Serena. One crazy person out to prove a point or looking for a king's ransom. What you did tonight was selfish, and self-indulgent, without regard for me, or your parents, or your country."

Tears welled up in her eyes. "I said I was sorry. I won't do it again, okay?"

Gabe wanted to take her in his arms, kiss away the tears his words had created, and the impulse only made him angry all over again. "You're spoiled, Serena. Spoiled and willful, and someday those two traits are going to get you in a world of trouble."

He barely got the words out of his mouth when she turned from him and ran to her room. He fought his desire to run after her, to somehow ease the hurt he'd inflicted.

She needed to think about what he'd said, needed to understand that no matter how badly she wanted to be just a normal, average young woman, she couldn't be.

He sat back down on the sofa and drew a deep breath. At least she was home, safe and sound. All the horrendous scenarios for disaster that had crossed his mind had not come true.

He should be feeling enormous relief, but instead a wave of impending doom swept through him. And he suspected the cause of it was that she'd met a man...a wonderful man.

Serena found her bed through a veil of tears and threw herself across it. Her tears burned hot as sobs escaped from her.

Gabriel Morgan was the meanest, most hateful man she'd ever known. His words burned in her brain. Spoiled. Willful. Selfish and self-indulgent. How could he be so cruel? To say such hateful, hurtful things to her. Was that what he really believed about her?

The thought that he believed her to be such horrid things only served to make her cry harder. She wanted Gabe to like her. She wanted that more than anything in the world.

It took only a few minutes for her tears to be spent. When she was finished crying, she sat up and swiped the last of her tears with her fingers.

She wanted to hate Gabe for all the things he'd said, but in her heart, she knew there was more than a little truth in those words.

She hadn't given much thought to consequences when she'd taken flight from Gabe. Oh, she'd known she would face his ire when she returned, but she hadn't considered all the dire things that might have happened to her.

As she imagined Gabe having to call her mother and father to tell them she'd been kidnapped or worse, her heart constricted. Her parents had learned to live with James's disappearance, had coped with the realization that they'd never see their only son again. But losing another child would be devastating, and Serena would never want to be responsible for hurting her parents in any way.

Swiping her hair from her face, she remembered the way Gabe had looked when she'd turned on the light. His face had been drawn and pale, his hair askew as if he'd run his hands through it a hundred times. He'd looked like a man who'd worried himself half to death. Shame coursed through her.

Gabe was right. She'd been willful and self-indulgent. And as much as she'd like to be normal and average, she would never be anything but a princess and there were certain responsibilities that came along with her birthright.

As much as she hated to admit it, she owed Gabe a huge apology, and a promise that she would never, ever again sneak away from him and go off on her own.

With this thought in mind, she opened the door to her room and peered out into the darkened suite. The curtains had been pulled over the windows and she assumed Gabe had gone to bed in his room.

She crept across the floor of the main area to Gabe's bedroom door. No glimmer of light shone beneath the door. For a moment irritation swept through her, irritation that he could say such mean things, then just go to sleep so easily. She shoved away the irritation, not wanting it to get in the way of her apology and knocked on the door.

"What do you want?"

His voice came from behind her, startling her. She jumped and whirled around. "Where are you?" she asked, narrowing her eyes in an attempt to penetrate the darkness of the room.

The lamp next to the sofa lit. Gabe was stretched out on the sofa, a blanket covering him from the waist down. He was bare chested and as Serena stared at his broad, muscled chest, she momentarily forgot why she'd sought him out in the first place.

She'd never seen him in anything other than his official uniform, the navy suit and white shirt. She'd certainly never seen him half-naked before.

Dark hair dusted the center of his chest and Serena's fingers itched to dance in that hair and feel the warmth of his skin beneath.

"Princess?"

His voice broke her momentary inertia and she flushed with the heat of her thoughts. "What are you doing out here?" she asked.

"What do you think?" he returned, an edge in his voice. "You snuck away from me once, but it won't happen again." He sat up, his dark gaze intense. "You won't get away from me a second time. I'm going to be on you like tread on a tire, Serena."

"That's what I came out to tell you." She averted her gaze from him, unable to think with the distraction of his bare chest. "Everything you said before was true. I have been selfish and self-absorbed, and tonight I took a risk that I shouldn't have."

She paused a moment and snuck a quick glance at him. His facial features radiated cynicism. "I mean it, Gabe. There's no reason for you to sleep out here with one eye open. You won't have to worry about me trying to get away from you again. I promise I won't."

"You'll make my job a lot easier with your full cooperation," he finally said.

"I know." She frowned. "Avery has invited me out tomorrow night and I intend to go, but I don't intend to tell him who I really am." She ignored Gabe's frown. "He thinks I'm Sarah Wynn from Kansas City and I want it to stay that way."

"So how do you intend to explain Sarah Wynn having a bodyguard?" he asked.

"We'll tell him that you're an old family friend, and you couldn't find a date so I invited you to tag along with us." She held up her hands as his frown deepened. "I know it's not a perfect solution, but it will work for the short-term."

He hesitated a moment, then nodded. "If that's what you wish."

"It is," Serena replied. She paused a moment, drinking in the vision he made with his bare chest and slightly mussed hair. What she really wished was that she could curl up on the sofa next to him, feel that beautiful broad chest against her own, be embraced by him and held through the night.

"Was there something else?" he asked.

Again, a flush swept over Serena's face, warming her cheeks. "One more thing. In the morning I'd like to go back by Betty Jo Parker's house. If she isn't home again, maybe we could talk to the neighbors, ask them when she is normally home."

"Okay," Gabe said.

"Well…I guess this is good-night," she said. There was nothing else to say to him. She'd apologized and she'd promised never again to try to escape from him. What she wanted to do was beg him not to think badly of her, ask him to take back the things he'd said. Instead, she went back into her bedroom and closed the door.

As she put on her nightgown and got into bed, she shoved away thoughts of the man who was paid to be with her, a man who'd never given any indication that she was anything but a duty, and instead thought of Avery Kintell.

When Serena had lost Gabe in Betty Jo Parker's neighborhood, she'd figured she would have to walk back to the strip. She'd run without her purse, without money so she couldn't catch a bus or a cab.

She'd lucked out when a little old woman in a luxury car had pulled up beside her and offered her a ride.

"I normally don't pick up hitchhikers," the old woman had said as she'd motioned Serena into the car. "But you look a little down and out."

"My boyfriend and I had a fight," Serena said,

the lie tasting bad in her mouth. "I took off without thinking and didn't grab my purse or anything."

The old woman had smiled and winked at Serena. "Lovers' spats. They're all the same…mostly a waste of time. Make love, not war, that's what I say."

She'd dropped Serena in front of the Flamingo Casino. The Flamingo was far enough away from her hotel that Serena was fairly certain she wouldn't run into Gabe. In the lobby of the Flamingo the management was offering free hors d'oeuvres and cocktails. Serena had been sampling a couple of tiny egg rolls when Avery had approached her.

He was attractive, although not nearly as handsome as Gabe. But he'd gazed at Serena as if she were one of the wonders of the world. As they'd gotten to know each other, he'd hung on her every word, devoting his full attention to her. It had been a heady experience for Serena.

From the Flamingo, they had gone to dinner at a nice Italian place, then gone dancing at an upscale club. All in all, it had been the kind of normal dating evening that Serena had never experienced.

When Avery had kissed her good-night at the end of their evening together, there had been no bells or whistles. It had been pleasant, but not earth-shattering.

Serena supposed first kisses were never particularly earth-shattering. It took time for passion to grow, time for bells and whistles to resound from a kiss.

She closed her eyes, trying to summon a visual

picture of Avery in her mind. She'd liked him…and it had been obvious he was crazy about her. And he had no idea she was anything but a salesclerk from Kansas City.

What she couldn't understand was why her mind refused to produce his image? Why was her head so filled with visions of a dark-haired, dark-eyed man, bare chested on a sofa?

Chapter Five

"I see she came back," the driver said, smirking the next afternoon as Gabe and Serena got into the car for a second trip to Betty Jo Parker's house. "Told you she would." He shook his head and grinned. "Women…we can't live without them."

"Yeah, you're a romantic genius," Gabe replied dryly.

Though a quiet understanding existed between Gabe and Serena now, the air had been tense as they had shared morning coffee, then an early lunch.

After she had gone back to her room the night before, Gabe had left the sofa and gone into his bedroom. Despite the fact that he knew Serena to be willful and impulsive, spoiled and spirited, he also knew she was a young woman of honor. She had given him her promise that she wouldn't try to lose him again, and he knew no matter how great the temptation, she would adhere to that promise.

He'd climbed into the crisp, clean sheets of the king-size bed, anticipating the first good night's sleep in months. But instead of a good night's sleep, his slumber had been disturbed by dreams…dreams of Serena.

In those dreams, her hair had been braided, and he'd slowly unwound it, the silky strands sensually soft against his fingers. And the unwinding of those locks of hair had only been the beginning in a ritual of lovemaking.

With her hair loose and flowing down her back, they had shared a kiss…a kiss that seared his lips with heat and created a raging fire in his veins.

When the kiss ended, she'd stood in front of him and slowly undressed, sliding off the teal blouse to display a wispy white bra that increased the inferno inside him. When the blouse fell to the floor, she unclasped her bra, exposing perfect breasts. Her slacks followed the blouse and bra, leaving her clad only in a pair of silky panties.

With desire surging inside him, he'd reached for her and pulled her down on the bed with him. Again they kissed, her lips the sweet honey he'd always known they would be.

And that was when the dream had changed. Suddenly he was sitting on a chair in the corner and another man was in the bed with Serena. He knew the man was Avery Kintell and at that moment Gabe had awakened, filled with jealousy and yearning with desire for the flame-haired woman.

The unsettling quality of the dream had stayed with him throughout the early morning. As he'd sat across from Serena at the table, he'd tried to shove it aside, telling himself that dreams were nothing more than crazy sleep images and meant nothing whatsoever.

Just because he'd dreamed that Serena was making love to Avery, didn't mean it was going to happen. He would make sure it didn't happen. He wasn't about to let her first love experience be with a man who had picked her up in a casino lobby. But in any case, the bottom line was that it really was none of his business.

"I hope she's home today," Serena said from the back seat of the car, pulling Gabe from his disturbing thoughts. "I really want to get this resolved."

"One way or another, we'll get some information," Gabe assured her. The man who had been barbecuing the day before had looked old enough to be retired. Even if Betty wasn't home, Gabe hoped the neighbor would be and would know Betty's work hours.

Within minutes the car was once again parked at the curb in front of the neat little house. Together, Serena and Gabe walked up to the door. Gabe knocked and they waited.

"The curtains are all drawn and it doesn't look like anyone is home," Serena said with a touch of disappointment.

Gabe knocked again. They waited for a reply and when none was forthcoming, he nodded toward the house next door. "Let's see if the neighbor knows when she might be home."

They left Betty's porch and went to the house

next door, where Gabe's knock was answered by the elderly man who'd been cooking outside the day before.

"Hi, we've been trying to get hold of Betty Jo Parker from next door," Serena said. "But we're having problems catching her at home."

"Course you are," the man replied. "Betty don't live there anymore. She moved a couple days ago."

"Oh no!" Serena exclaimed. "She can't be gone." Serena's voice held a heavy layer of disappointment.

"Do you know where she moved to?" Gabe asked.

"'Fraid not." The old man scratched his head thoughtfully. "Although she did mention a sweet little apartment she'd found on the north side of town."

"But she didn't say anything more specific?" Gabe pressed.

"Think. Surely she said something about her new address…something that would let you know more about where she was moving," Serena said with a touch of desperation.

"Nah, Betty wasn't one of those women who felt the need to spill her guts about her personal life." He shrugged. "Sorry I can't be of more help."

"Thank you, anyway," Gabe replied. Serena nodded, as if too disheartened to speak.

The old man started to close the door, then reopened it. "If it helps at all, last I heard Betty was working down at Harrah's Casino. Maybe you can catch her there."

CARLA CASSIDY
77

Serena's face lit with excitement and a responding rush of desire swept through Gabe. When she looked the way she did at that moment, her eyes all shiny and bright, happiness lighting her up from within, she was incredibly magnetic. A man would have to be completely dead inside not to feel some response to her.

As he followed her back to the car, he accepted the fact that he wanted Serena. He wanted her in his arms, in his bed. He wanted to be the man who introduced her to physical pleasure, the man who'd watch her eyes as they darkened with abandonment.

Along with the acknowledgment of his desire for her came the knowledge that he'd never have her. Another man would experience the pleasure of initiating her in the art of lovemaking.

It was right that it would be another man. She deserved that her first time making love be with a man who loved her. And Gabe would never love her, or anyone else. His heart was completely closed, unavailable to the emotion of love.

They went directly to Harrah's, where the personnel manager told them that Betty was no longer with them, although the manager said he thought Betty had gone to work at another casino, but he couldn't remember which one.

"Maybe I can call the local authorities and see if they can hunt down this Betty Jo Parker," Gabe suggested when they were back in their hotel room.

"Oh, Gabe, that would be wonderful," Serena exclaimed. "Do you really think they'll help us?"

He smiled at her in genuine amusement. She was

truly an innocent when it came to recognizing the power of her position. Despite the fact that in the United States she had no real power or position, he didn't think the Las Vegas police department would alienate a visiting princess. "I'm sure they'll bend over backward to help you as long as we explain the situation."

It took only minutes for Gabe to make the phone call. He got in touch with a Lieutenant Breckenridge and explained who he was and what they needed. Breckenridge was hesitant at first, but finally agreed to do what he could to help them in their search for Betty Jo Parker. It didn't hurt when Gabe mentioned his own background as one of the boys in blue.

As Gabe hung up the phone, a knock sounded at the door. Gabe answered, surprised to see the bellman with yet another bouquet of flowers, this time a dozen long-stem yellow roses. "The gentleman said to send these here for a Sarah Wynn?" He looked at Gabe, then at Serena, who clapped her hands together with excitement.

"Thank you, I'll take them," she said. She took the bouquet and set them on the coffee table. She sat down on the sofa, then withdrew the card that was stuck amid the blooms.

Gabe tipped the bellman, then turned in time to see Serena read the card, a blush sweeping over her features. "Oh, isn't that sweet," she murmured, more to herself than to him.

"I assume they're from Mr. Wonderful," Gabe observed, trying to keep any sarcasm from his voice, but having a hard time.

"Yes...from Avery," she replied. She jumped up, the card clutched to her breast. "He's going to pick me up at five." She looked at her watch. "I think I'll go take a nice, long bubble bath."

She nearly floated from the room, humming a lilting melody as she closed her bedroom door.

Gabe eyed the roses with distaste. How boring. How utterly predictable. Everyone sent roses. If he were going to send Serena flowers, he'd choose something wild and vivid, an exotic bloom as unique and vibrant as her.

He frowned, unsure if the disgust he felt was for the flowers, the man who had sent them, or himself for spending a mere second contemplating what kind of flowers he'd send Serena.

While Serena was taking a nice, long, hot bubble bath to prepare for the evening, Gabe thought perhaps he better take a bracing, cold shower. If he was going to spend the evening as a third wheel with Serena and Mr. Rosebud, he had a feeling it was going to be a trying, difficult night.

Two hours later, he sat with Avery Kintell and Serena at a table in a Chinese restaurant, listening to Avery tell Serena what it had been like for him to grow up in Vegas.

As she had planned, Serena introduced Avery to Gabe as an old family friend and explained that Gabe would be accompanying them that evening. Although Gabe had seen a swift flicker of disappointment in Avery's pale blue eyes, it had quickly been hidden beneath a pleasant smile and a welcoming handshake.

The man talked as though he had money. His chest puffed out each time he spoke of his success as an investment banker, and yet something didn't ring true about him. He wore an expensive suit, but the shirt beneath was frayed around the collar. Gabe had noticed his shoes, although shined to a high gloss, were old and worn.

Serena, on the other hand, looked more lovely than Gabe had ever seen her. Clad in a coral-colored silk dress and with her hair pulled up off her neck and twisted in an intricate fashion, she looked elegant, yet strangely vulnerable.

Dinner was relatively pleasant, with Serena and Avery talking about places they'd visited and places they would like to go. Gabe knew Serena was consciously studying every word she said, not wanting to ruin the image she'd created of herself as a salesclerk from Kansas City.

Gabe listened carefully to everything Avery said, still unsettled by a bad feeling where the man was concerned. He wasn't sure if it was specifically Avery or if he'd feel the same way about any man Serena appeared interested in.

"That store you work at back in Kansas City must pay you quite well," Avery observed when they'd finished eating.

"Why do you say that?" Serena asked.

"When I dropped you at your door last night, I couldn't help but notice you were staying in the penthouse," Avery explained.

"Oh…that…" Serena stuttered and Gabe could

see the wheels turning in her head as she sought a logical explanation.

"Gabe got the room," she finally said. "He has loads of money. His family is quite wealthy."

Gabe frowned at her, not approving of the web of lies she was spinning.

Avery looked at Gabe. "I was wondering what you did for a living."

Gabe shrugged. "A little bit of this and a little bit of that." He sensed Serena's audible sigh of relief at his answer. He supposed there was no real harm in playing her game for an evening.

"I couldn't help but notice the crest on your jacket," Avery said.

"Uh...my family crest," Gabe replied.

Gabe was relieved when dinner was over and the three of them left the restaurant. He didn't like Avery Kintell, and he wasn't sure why. All he knew was that the man gave him a bad feeling. Avery was smooth as butter, but Gabe sensed a slimy side that was disturbing.

From the restaurant, they went to a club, where the dance floor was huge, the music loud, and despite the early hour a large crowd had already gathered.

Serena and Avery settled at a table next to the bar, and Gabe took up residency on one of the stools at the bar. From his vantage point he was close enough to guard Serena, yet give her a little privacy with Kintell.

"Hi, handsome." The bartender, an attractive buxom blond, smiled at him. Her blue eyes gleamed flirtatiously as she leaned over the bar toward him. "What can I get for you?"

"Just a cola," he replied, then twirled his stool around so he had a perfect view of Serena's table and the dance floor.

As he sipped his drink, he watched Avery and Serena. He didn't like the way the man touched her so often, a hand on her hand, an arm around her shoulder, a touch to her cheek. They were light, casual touches intended to promote familiarity…intimacy.

"Here you are." The bartender placed his drink in front of him.

"Thanks." Gabe flashed her a quick smile.

"Big crowd tonight," she said and pointed to the dance floor. "Guess everyone is practicing partying for tomorrow night."

"Tomorrow night?" Gabe looked at her curiously.

"New Year's Eve."

"Oh yeah, that's right. It is tomorrow night, isn't it?" Somehow Gabe had managed to lose track of the holidays. Christmas had been a quiet day.

He took a sip of his soda, his mind whirling back to Christmas morning. Serena had awakened early and he'd found her sitting next to the Christmas tree. He'd known by the look on her face that she was missing her family.

Even solemn, she'd been beautiful. She'd worn an emerald robe and her hair had been sleep-tousled. As he handed her the small gift he'd bought for her, he'd wanted to wrap her in his arms and carry her to his bed.

She'd opened the present, exclaiming over the variety of scented soaps and bath oils. Gabe's mind had worked overtime, presenting him with an image of her in the bathtub, surrounded by bubbles, her body slick with sweet-smelling oil.

She'd surprised him with a gift, a leather shaving kit to replace the battered, torn one he normally used. He vividly remembered the pleasure she'd shown when he promised to use it every day.

For the remainder of the day, Gabe had fought a growing awareness of Serena not as a princess, but as a woman…a desirable, beautiful woman.

"So, are you alone or with somebody?" The bartender's question pulled him from his thoughts.

"I'm sort of with friends." He pointed to Avery and Serena's table.

"You're with Avery?" There was a distinct coolness in her voice.

Gabe looked at her. "You know him?"

She snorted indelicately. "Everyone knows Avery."

"Actually, I've only just met the man tonight. I'm friends with the lady he's with," Gabe explained.

The woman looked at Serena and shook her head with a knowing smile. "She's not his usual type. Normally Avery likes them very old, very ill and very wealthy."

Every muscle in Gabe's body tensed. "He's a con man?" he asked.

The blonde laughed. "Avery wrote the book on

con.'' She grabbed a damp cloth and swiped the top of the bar. ''If your lady friend has money, if you care about her at all, you'll warn her that Avery will wine and dine her right out of her fortune. He'll marry her, then leave her broke and broken. That's what he does for a living. Oh yeah, Avery is always looking to score.''

''Looking to score.'' The words echoed loudly in Gabe's head. Looking to score with a princess…Gabe's princess. Not in this lifetime, he vowed.

''He doesn't exactly look real prosperous,'' Gabe observed.

''Avery is good at getting money. He just isn't very smart about keeping it. The man has a major gambling problem and that's what keeps him constantly on the prowl.''

On the prowl. Gabe fought his impulse to rush over to Serena, throw her over his shoulder and carry her as far away from Kintell as possible. He knew as long as he kept her in his sight, nothing was going to happen to her.

He frowned thoughtfully. Poor Serena. She'd been so happy, so certain that her appeal to Avery Kintell was genuine, that he had no clue she was anything but a salesclerk.

Gabe would bet his sanity that Avery Kintell knew exactly who and what Serena was. Like the woman with her little girl the day before, Avery had known the minute he'd seen Serena that she was a Princess of Wynborough.

Damn him. Damn the man for putting Gabe in an

untenable position. As he watched Serena laugh at something Kintell said, Gabe's heart ached for her.

Gabe knew he had two choices: allow her to continue to see Avery for the remainder of their stay in Las Vegas and hope she didn't do anything foolish, or tell her the truth about the man and break her heart into a thousand pieces. At the moment, neither choice seemed the right one.

Serena wasn't having as good a time as she'd thought she would. Although Avery was as attentive, as wonderful as he'd been the night before, the excitement of the previous night was gone. She wondered if part of the fun of last night had been because she'd successfully snuck away from Gabe.

Gabe. Part of the problem was that his very presence distracted her from Avery. When Avery touched her hand, she wished it were Gabe's touch she felt. As Avery gazed into her eyes, she wished it were dark brown ones looking at her with such adoration.

Drat the man for confusing her so. She looked over to where he sat talking to the striking blond bartender. She frowned. What was he doing? What were they talking about? The woman wore a blouse cut so low her ample breasts were on display, and Gabe certainly didn't seem to mind the exhibition.

Emotion, rich and deep, flooded through her, an emotion she recognized as pure, unadulterated jealousy. It surprised her...and irritated her.

How could Gabe protect her if he had all his attention focused on the blond babe? Avery could throttle me right here and now and Gabe wouldn't even notice, she thought indignantly.

She knew she was being silly. Avery wasn't about to choke her, and if he did, Gabe would put the man to the floor before Serena could blink her eyes. Gabe might be enjoying the company of the bosomy bartender, but Serena knew that didn't mean he wasn't keeping a close watch on her. He was good at his job. Serena couldn't fault him there.

"Come on, Avery. Let's dance," she said.

She led Avery onto the dance floor, fighting for space amid the sea of gyrating couples. She and Avery had only begun to dance when Gabe and the tall blonde appeared next to them. Apparently the bartender was on break and had decided to spend part of her free time dancing with Gabe.

Serena had never seen Gabe dance before, and she was unsurprised to discover that despite his brawn, he was graceful and light on his feet. He flashed her a smile and her heart stepped up its rhythm.

She studiously ignored him and tried to do so for the remainder of the night. It was in the wee hours of the early morning when Gabe and Serena returned to their hotel suite.

Serena immediately went to bed, exhausted not only by the hours of dancing, but also by the knowledge that she had a wonderful man half-crazy for her, and a fixation on another man who she wasn't even sure liked her most of the time.

Thankfully, her sleep was dreamless and restful. She awakened at noon, to the scent of something delicious filling the air. She showered and dressed quickly, her stomach rumbling with hunger pangs.

"Something smells marvelous," she said as she left her room.

"Chicken Kiev," Gabe said. He pointed to the chair opposite him at the table, where a covered plate awaited her. "I wasn't sure what time you'd be awake, but I got hungry so I went ahead and ordered."

"I'm starving," she said. She sat and uncovered the dish and dug in. They ate in silence, and as the silence lingered, Serena sensed tension radiating from Gabe.

"Anything wrong?" she asked.

He hesitated a moment, then shook his head. "No, everything is fine."

But she sensed something bothering him. Whatever it was, it kept him quiet and introspective for the day. They spent the afternoon in stifling silence, waiting for the phone to ring, waiting for Lieutenant Breckenridge to call and tell them what he'd discovered about Betty Jo Parker's whereabouts.

The only interruption to their silence came when the bellman knocked, once again bearing roses from Avery. She read the note that came along with the flowers, then looked at Gabe.

"Avery has invited me to the New Year's Eve party here in the hotel ballroom this evening," she said. She eyed Gabe to see his reaction. "Dinner and cocktails begin at six. He says he's planned an extra special evening, one with the possibility to change my life. Maybe he intends to propose to me.''

''That's ridiculous. You hardly know the man,'' Gabe scoffed. A small tic pulsed in his jaw.

''Sometimes you meet somebody and within hours you know that's the person you'd like to spend the rest of your life with.'' Serena wasn't sure why she said this; she certainly wasn't in love with Avery Kintell, although she enjoyed his company.

''The man isn't right for you,'' Gabe said, the tic in his jaw more pronounced.

''You can't know that,'' she protested. ''He's nice, and he's sweet. He looks at me like nobody ever has before. And best of all, he likes *me*, not Princess Serena Wyndham of Wynborough.''

Gabe stared at her for a long moment, then turned away. ''If he's picking you up at six, hadn't you better start getting ready?''

''Yes, I suppose I should,'' Serena agreed. She frowned as she went into her bedroom, certain that Gabe had something on his mind…something weighty. But unless he decided to share it with her, there was nothing she could do about it.

She wasn't sure why she'd told Gabe that Avery might propose this evening, although a proposal from him wouldn't surprise her. He'd spent the night before talking about how well matched they were and extolling the virtues of marriage and life in Las Vegas.

Although she had no intention of accepting a proposal, she'd wanted to see what Gabe's reaction would be to such a possibility. His reaction had been decidedly underwhelming. Just that tic in his jaw…and she didn't know exactly what that signified.

At least tonight, when the clock struck midnight to ring in a new year, she'd have somebody to kiss her. She studiously refused to consider that the one man she most wanted to kiss her wouldn't.

She dressed with care, determined to have a good time no matter how taciturn, how moody Gabe remained. The outfit she chose to wear was a winter-white two-piece suit, the material shot through with strands of gold thread.

Once dressed, she eyed herself in the mirror with satisfaction. The tailored suit jacket hugged her curves, the deep neckline displaying just the right amount of cleavage. She looked festive and ready for a night of fun.

It was a quarter to five when she left her room. Gabe stood as she entered, his gaze dark and brooding as it raked over her from head to toe. The tic in his jaw was more pronounced than she'd ever seen.

"Get your purse," he said. "I've got the driver waiting."

"The driver? I don't understand. Avery will be here in just a few minutes."

"Avery will be here and you won't." He took her by the arm and propelled her toward the door.

"Gabe…" she sputtered in protest, wondering if he'd lost his mind, if somehow she'd managed to push him over the edge into insanity.

"Just don't say anything," he demanded, and

something about the look in his eyes warned her to keep her mouth shut.

She managed to stay quiet until he escorted her into the back of the awaiting car and he got in the front seat.

"Take us to Ye Olde Wedding Chapel," he instructed the driver.

"Would you please tell me what's going on?" she asked. "Why on earth are we going to Ye Olde Wedding Chapel?"

He turned in the seat and looked at her with a tight smile. "Why else would we be going there? We're going to the chapel and we're going to get married."

Chapter Six

"Whewee, sounds like that old song," the driver exclaimed. "You know, that one about going to the chapel of love…what was the name of that group that sang that song…one of them girl groups."

Gabe ignored the man and remained focused on Serena.

"We're getting married?" Her face radiated myriad emotions…confusion, bewilderment…and something else that Gabe refused to consider, something that looked amazingly like excitement.

"Hot damn," the driver exclaimed with a hoot of enthusiasm. "I knew the two of you were meant for each other the moment I laid eyes on you. Darned if I don't feel like Cupid."

"Just drive," Gabe demanded.

He wondered if his pronouncement had caused some sort of shock in Serena. He'd expected her to kick and buck, throw one of her royal fits, but she didn't say a word as they drove the short distance to the chapel.

Gabe knew he was definitely experiencing some sort of crazy shock. When she'd walked out of her bedroom in the white suit, with her hair all loose and curly and her cheeks flushed with color, he'd made an instant decision. She looked like a bride…he'd make her one.

If he married her, he'd keep her safe from Avery Kintell and every other man she might meet while in Las Vegas, and he'd never have to tell her the truth about Kintell and break her heart. He steadfastly refused to consider his king and queen's reaction to his marrying their youngest daughter. He'd face that hailstorm when it happened.

It was a desperate scheme to prevent dire circumstances. But Gabe knew one thing. If Serena was married to him, she wouldn't be available for any fortune hunters or a quick roll in the hay by a smooth-talking operator. And Avery Kintell was definitely bad news. A quick call to Lieutenant Breckenridge had confirmed that the man was trouble with a capital *T*. Gabe had to do something…and fast.

When the driver pulled up to the curb in front of Ye Olde Wedding Chapel, Gabe told him to wait, then he and Serena went inside the building.

She was more subdued than he'd ever seen her. He'd expected a royal protest of his plan, but as they stepped into the lobby, she simply looked up at him and smiled shyly. "Can I have a bouquet?" she asked.

The request, so simply, so sweetly asked, touched Gabe. Before he could answer her, the minister of the chapel greeted them.

"Welcome," he said and held out a hand to Gabe. "I'm Edward Doyle, minister of this church."

"I'm Gabriel Morgan and this is Serena Wyndham. We'd like to get married," Gabe blurted. He felt a sudden urgency to get this over and done with before he changed his mind.

On the one hand, he knew it was the most logical answer to the problem of safeguarding Serena. On the other hand, his nerves jumped and jittered in protest of what they were about to do. It felt too real, and he didn't intend for it to be real.

"Wonderful," Edward exclaimed, beaming at both of them. "There is nothing I enjoy more than uniting two people in love."

Gabe bit back his protest. He wanted to confess that he didn't love Serena, that this marriage ceremony had nothing to do with love. "Uh…we need flowers," he said instead. "And we don't have rings."

Edward nodded, his bulbous nose appearing to grow red with joy. "We provide everything you need for an occasion to remember." He turned to Serena and gestured to the flower case. "What kind of flowers would the bride like to carry?"

Serena appeared to be in a daze. Her eyes were more lustrous than Gabe had ever seen them, and her hand trembled slightly as she pointed to a lovely bouquet of orchids with a trailing ribbon of pale lavender.

A momentary thrill rushed through Gabe as he realized she'd eschewed the rose bouquets in favor of the exotic orchids. He'd been right and Avery had been wrong. She was more than a rose kind of woman.

"Wonderful," Edward exclaimed as he handed her the bouquet. "And now if the two of you would step into my office, we'll make the necessary arrangements and I have a variety of rings for you to choose from."

The next few minutes passed in a haze for Gabe. They chose the kind of ceremony they wanted, then he picked out a gold band for her. She surprised him by insisting that he get a gold band for himself as well.

All too quickly he and Serena stood before the simple altar, listening to Edward Doyle speak of love through eternity and cleaving unto one another. Gabe felt as if he'd stepped into a dream.

Serena looked every inch a true bride in her white suit. The scent of the orchids filled the air, mingling with her perfume and dizzying Gabe's senses.

Nothing seemed quite real as he faced Serena, repeated the vows of a man to a woman, and slipped the gold band onto her finger.

As she echoed those vows, her voice quivered and her eyes filled with tears. She looked so lovely, so vulnerable, and Gabe had a feeling he was making the biggest mistake of his life. He should have explained to her what he intended with the marriage. He should have told her the rules before they came to this place in time.

It was too late now. He'd have to explain after the ceremony. He needed to explain to her that it wasn't a real marriage. Oh, it was legal, but it would never be binding. He'd see to that. But at the moment it was difficult to think about rules or about good intentions; it was difficult to focus on anything but Serena's loveliness and the luminous shine of her eyes.

"I now pronounce you husband and wife." The minister's words pulled Gabe back from his thoughts. "You may kiss your bride."

Kiss your bride. Gabe looked at Serena. Her lips were parted as if in eagerness, and the last thing he wanted to do was to kiss her...because what he wanted to do most of all was to kiss her.

He leaned forward, intending a circumspect little peck on her mouth, but she apparently had other designs. With tears streaming down her cheeks, she wrapped her arms around his neck and pressed her body into his.

He didn't have a chance to protest, and in any case, whatever protest that might have flown through his mind was lost as her lips met his.

Sweeter than he'd ever imagined, softer than he'd ever fantasized, her mouth plied his with heat, and for a moment he was lost to the heady pleasure of kissing Serena.

When the kiss finally ended, Gabe stepped away from her, needing to distance himself from the beckoning invitation that remained in her gaze.

He took her by the arm. "Come on, let's get out of here."

She said nothing until they were out on the sidewalk next to the car. "Gabe?" There was a soft yearning in her eyes, a need to understand what they had just done.

Despite his reluctance to touch her, he grazed a finger down her cheek. "We'll talk later, in the privacy of our room," he said.

She nodded, apparently satisfied for the moment. When they got back to the hotel, the New Year's Eve celebration was in full swing, revelers spilling out of the ballroom and into the lobby.

"Let's join the celebration," Gabe suggested. He was eager to find Avery Kintell and see the man's face when he realized his attempted scam had been ruined.

"Okay," she agreed with little enthusiasm. Obviously she'd hoped for a more private celebration, but that was exactly what Gabe intended to avoid.

He couldn't tell what she thought about their sudden marriage, but he knew instinctively what he had to tell her later would probably make her angry...or make her cry. He dreaded doing either, but he could stand her anger far easier than he could stand her tears. Better to put it all off for as long as possible.

The live band was loud, the dance floor already packed, as they made their way through the crowd. They found an empty table, complete with party hats and confetti. Appropriately, the two hats on their table were a cardboard tiara and a top hat. Serena placed the tiara on her head as she ordered a bottle of champagne from the waiter.

The tiara, although flimsy and garish, sparkled

brightly and only served to remind Gabe of just how impossible a marriage between them truly was.

She was a princess. He was her bodyguard. He'd gone above and beyond the limit to do just that…guard her body. But he couldn't bind himself to her forever. Despite the obvious opposition to such an event, his heart rebelled at the thought of being hurt another time.

Besides, he reminded himself firmly, it wasn't as if he loved Serena.

No matter that they were, for the moment, married. No matter that kissing her had stirred crazy emotions he'd thought were dead. He refused—absolutely refused—to fall in love with Princess Serena Wyndham.

From the moment they had gotten into the car and Gabe had told her they were going to the chapel to be married, Serena had felt as if she'd stepped into an alternate universe.

When he'd kissed her, she knew somehow she'd transcended from earth and fallen into paradise. The kiss had been more…so much more than she'd ever fantasized, ever hoped for. His lips had been so soft, yet masterful, sweeping her away with love and desire.

The wedding had been all that she'd ever wanted in a ceremony…except she wasn't sure exactly why the groom had married her. She wanted to believe it was because he loved her desperately, passionately. She wanted to believe that thoughts of her and

Avery had driven Gabe over the edge and he'd suddenly realized how much he loved her.

But since the ceremony ended, he hadn't acted like a newly wedded groom who was madly in love with his bride. He'd been distant and seemed far too eager to join the New Year's Eve melee than spend private time with his wife.

She sipped her champagne and noticed how the lights caught and sparkled on her ring. Her wedding band. She was married…married to Gabe. Her heart trilled a song of joy. She was Gabe's wife. Serena Morgan. It sounded perfect, as though the two names belonged together.

As the band began to play a slow song, she looked at Gabe…her husband, and she wanted him to dance with her. She wanted to be held tight in his big, safe arms as their bodies swayed to the rhythm of the music.

"Dance with me, Gabe," she said. He frowned, and she had a feeling he was about to lodge a protest. She didn't allow it. She stood and grabbed his hand. "Please. Every bride should get the pleasure of dancing with her groom."

He hesitated only a moment, then with a nod, he stood and took her arm to lead her to the dance floor. The music was slow and romantic, and the ring on Serena's finger, coupled with the glass of champagne she'd drunk far too quickly, made her more bold than she normally would be.

She wound her arms around his neck and pressed herself against him. For a brief moment he held himself rigid, as if in an attempt to keep distance between their bodies. With a nearly inaudible groan, he relaxed and wrapped his arms around her waist, accepting her body molding to his own.

She lay her head against his chest and closed her eyes. For so long she'd dreamed of being in Gabe's arms and now her dream was a reality. She had other dreams…fantasies of making love to him, bearing his children, growing old with him. Was tonight the prelude to all her dreams coming true? Her heart thudded in anticipation at the very thought.

Her heart wasn't the only one beating rapidly. She could feel Gabe's heart pounding a frenzied cadence. Was it possible he wanted her as much as she wanted him? The thought thrilled her.

All too soon the song ended and the band picked up the tempo with a fast hit from the fifties. Together, Serena and Gabe made their way back toward their table. They had almost reached their seats when Avery Kintell appeared.

"Sarah…darling…I've been looking for you everywhere," Avery exclaimed. Worry lines etched deep in his forehead as he took Serena's right hand in his. "Where have you been?"

Serena emitted a little forced laugh. "Avery, you aren't going to believe what happened," she said. "Gabe and I got married."

Avery stared at her for a moment, then threw back his head and laughed. "Oh, darling, you're such a funny girl. Why don't you come over here where I have a table waiting for us?"

"She's not going anywhere with you, Kintell. It's

true. We're married,'' Gabe said as he stepped next to Serena and took her arm in his.

Serena watched the two men glare at each other. They looked as if they were passing secret messages with their eyes.

''Avery, I'm terribly sorry,'' Serena said in an attempt to break the tension. ''Gabe…it was all so sudden…so overwhelming.''

''I'm sure it was,'' Avery said thinly. His eyes, when they gazed at her, were no longer friendly, but rather filled with animosity. ''See you around,'' he finally said.

''I doubt it,'' Gabe returned evenly.

Serena and Gabe both watched Avery lose himself in the crowd, then Gabe smiled down at her. ''Come on, let's go back to the table and share a toast.''

The coldness that Avery's gaze had created in her dissipated beneath the warmth of Gabe's smile. They went back to their table where Gabe poured them each a glass of the bubbly champagne.

''To the future,'' he said and clinked his glass with hers.

Serena tamped down her disappointment. He hadn't said to ''our'' future, but rather to ''the'' future. Again, she wondered what had prompted the marriage. Suddenly she didn't want to go back to their room, where Gabe had said he would explain everything.

She wanted to stay right here and pretend that he'd married her because he loved her. She wanted to dance the night away in his arms, allow her fantasy of a future together to last for as long as possible.

When they finished the toast, Gabe signaled the waiter and ordered himself a glass of soda at the same time he poured Serena another serving of champagne.

"You don't drink," Serena said when the waiter had departed. "Other than the champagne you just had, I've never seen you have an alcoholic beverage. Why?"

"For several reasons," he replied. "The main reason is because I've always been on duty when I've been with you. The second reason is because there was a time in my life when I drank too much."

"You were an alcoholic?" Serena asked in surprise.

"Let's just say it was easy and appealing to lose myself in a bottle of scotch."

"Why would you want to do that?" Serena realized that although Gabe had been her bodyguard and despite the fact that at this moment they were man and wife, she knew very little about him and his past.

"For reasons far too complicated to go into at a New Year's Eve party," he replied, his eyes dark, forbidding her to push the issue.

Frustration nagged at her. How could she expect to develop any kind of intimacy with Gabe if he refused to share the pieces of his past that made him the man he was today?

What really frustrated her was that she had a feeling that was exactly why Gabe withheld pieces of himself, so that no intimacy could develop between them.

She twisted her wedding band around her finger. So why had he married her? Let him love me, she prayed with a hint of desperation. Let him love me just a little bit.

As midnight approached, Gabe placed the cardboard top hat on his head and together he and Serena joined the other partiers counting down the clock to midnight.

When the clock hands hit the hour, heralding in a new year, the band struck up *Auld Lang Syne* and Serena moved into Gabe's arms. She didn't give him a chance to protest, refused to consider that he wouldn't want to kiss her.

She raised up on her tiptoes, wound her arms around his neck and pulled his head down so her lips could meet his.

She felt his hesitation, but it lasted only a moment, then his arms wrapped around her, pulling her against his hard length as his mouth moved against hers.

Hot flames danced inside her, shooting up her arms, down her legs, exploding in the pit of her stomach like fireballs of desire.

She was vaguely aware of the hoots and hollers of the people around them, but they seemed distant and unreal as she reveled in Gabe's kiss. His tongue moved into her mouth, dancing erotically with hers, as he deepened the kiss.

All the sensations that had been missing when she'd kissed Avery were present with Gabe. Bells and whistles and smoke and fire—she was drowning in sensation and didn't want to come up for air.

All too quickly she did surface. Gabe ended the kiss and stepped back from her. For a moment his eyes appeared glazed and unfocused. He gave a tiny shake of his head and frowned. "We need to go upstairs," he said, his voice slightly unsteady. "We definitely need to talk."

They left the party and rode the elevator up to their room. Neither spoke, and Serena found the silence deafening. What did he think they needed to talk about? Whatever he felt he had to say, she instinctively knew she didn't want to hear it.

When they got into the suite, Serena headed right for her bedroom. "I'll be right back," she said to him. "Then we can talk about whatever you want."

Her hands shook as she closed the door to her room and contemplated what she intended to do. This was her wedding night and she wanted it to be as perfect, as special as any night she would ever experience in her life.

With this in mind, she undressed and slipped into the most luxurious, sexiest nightgown she owned. The mint-green gown slid down her body, caressing her curves in cool silk.

She reached up and unpinned her hair, then shook her head, allowing her curls to fall in a spill down her shoulders. She sprayed a spritz of her favorite perfume around her head, then checked her reflection in the mirror.

She was self-consciously aware that the deep, plunging neckline of the nightgown did little to hide her breasts, and the material was thin enough that each and every curve was visible.

Never before had Gabe seen her in anything so revealing, so sexy. But never before had they been married, she reminded herself. And the ring on her finger gave her courage…the courage to turn away from the mirror and leave the privacy of her room.

"What have you done?" Gabe said the moment he saw her, his voice once again thick and unsteady.

"What do you mean?" she replied, then gave a nonchalant shrug. "I just got ready for bed."

While she'd been in her bedroom, he'd taken off his jacket and tie and had loosened the collar of his shirt. He now tugged at the top of the shirt, as if still finding it too tight. "Do you always sleep in something like that?" he asked crossly.

"You don't like it?" She twirled around slowly to give him full view of the clingy, sensual gown. "I wanted to look nice for you, Gabe. I wanted to look beautiful for our wedding night."

He frowned and raked a hand through his hair. "Serena…about this marriage," he began.

She gave him no opportunity to continue. Walking to him, she slipped her arms around his waist and placed her head against his broad chest. "Oh, Gabe, this marriage makes me happier than I've ever been in my life," she said softly.

She could hear his heart beating a rapid rhythm. She felt his muscles grow taut, the stir of desire that filled him. With a deep groan, he pulled her away from him and held her at arm's length.

"Serena, the marriage isn't real." His eyes were

the deepest brown she'd ever seen as he gazed at her intently.

"Of course it's real," she protested. "You placed a ring on my finger and said vows before a minister and God. We have a license that states we are man and wife."

"That's true." He released his hold on her shoulders and took several steps back from her. "But I married you to keep you safe. Serena, I care about you and wanted to make sure you didn't make any crazy mistakes. As long as we don't consummate the marriage, your father can annul it when we get back to Wynborough."

"But I don't want an annulment," she said, fighting against tears that suddenly pressed hot and burdensome behind her eyelids.

"Serena, I care enough about you to make sure an annulment occurs." He averted his gaze from hers, as if he found it difficult to talk to her while looking at her. "I'm not husband material, Serena. I told you before I don't have a heart. You deserve somebody better in your life. Now, I'm going to bed. I'll see you in the morning."

Without waiting for her reply, he turned and went into his bedroom, closing the door behind him. Serena stood and stared at the closed door, the first of her tears trekking down her cheeks.

She loved him. The moment he had slipped the gold band on her finger, she'd recognized and embraced the love in her heart for him.

Angrily, she swiped at her tears and moved to stand at the windows. The night lights of Las Vegas glittered and shone, but the brightness only served to make her feel lonely.

It was her wedding night. It should be the happiest night of her life, but instead she'd never felt more lonely. Her husband was in his room, and he expected her to sleep in her own room...alone...apart from him.

He'd said he cared about her, a little voice reminded her. He'd said he cared, and the two kisses they'd shared spoke of an emotion deeper, more complex. He wanted her. She'd felt it when he held her while they'd danced; she'd known it when she'd entered the room in her nightgown and his eyes had glowed with a feverish light.

If they made love, there was no way an annulment could occur. If he cared about her, wanted her, then surely she could make him love her.

The tears halted as her thoughts raced. She wanted Gabriel Morgan, not just for a night, not just for a week, but for a lifetime. She was spirited and willful, and she almost always got what she wanted. Gabriel Morgan didn't stand a chance.

She went into her bedroom and grabbed her pillow from her bed, then padded back to Gabe's bedroom door. She could make this marriage real. She could make it work.

All she had to do was seduce her husband.

Chapter Seven

Gabe slid beneath the sheets of his bed, knowing sleep would be difficult. It would be impossible to surrender to slumber with the vision of Serena in that sexy nightgown still emblazoned on his brain.

The pale green gown had intensified the emerald of her eyes and had barely skimmed her breasts, revealing more than it concealed. It was a gown created to make a man want to take it off, a gown formulated to stir mind-boggling passion. It had worked.

Not only did he have her stunning image in his head, but the taste of her still lingered on his mouth; the warmth of her body pressed against his own still teased him with possibilities.

The marriage had been a mistake. He knew that now. But at the time it had seemed the only logical solution to the problem of Avery Kintell's machinations and Serena's own impetuousness. But, as usual, he'd not counted on Serena's response to the whole thing.

She was the most complicated, bewildering woman he'd ever met. She never reacted the way he expected, usually surprising him and reminding him of her complexity.

One thing was certain. He had to stay true to his original plan. He and Serena were married, but he intended it to remain a marriage in name only. As long as they didn't make love, King Phillip could annul the marriage as soon as they returned home.

Then Serena would be free to find a man whose heart was open and giving, a man who would love her to distraction. And Gabe…he'd continue alone, as he'd been for the last four years…alone and safe from any hurt life might throw his way.

He jumped upright as his bedroom door opened. He smelled her, although the room was too dark for him to see her. She smelled of the exotic, spicy perfume that always caused his head to spin.

"Serena, what are you doing?" he asked, tensed for any possibility.

"I know you don't intend to consummate our marriage, but that doesn't mean I can't sleep with my husband." The opposite side of the bed depressed with her weight.

Gabe wanted to protest. He wanted to rocket out of the bed to escape the scent of her, the knowledge that she was right next to him in that gown that would be cool and slick beneath his hands, and the skin beneath that would be invitingly warm.

"Relax, Gabe," she said as if reading his thoughts. "I promise I won't force you to make love to me." Her voice softened somewhat. "I just don't want to sleep alone, okay. A woman shouldn't have to sleep alone on her wedding night."

How he wanted to toss her out, lock the door behind her so she couldn't get to him. He heard the rustle of the sheets as she got comfortable. Every nerve he possessed was on guard, wary of her and more wary of his own control where she was concerned.

"Are you tired?" she asked, her voice a soft whisper in the darkness of the room.

"Exhausted," he replied.

"So I guess you don't want to talk."

The last thing he wanted to do was hear her voice. If he heard her, then he couldn't ignore that she was lying right next to him. "No, I don't want to talk," he replied.

In fact, he wished he didn't have to breathe, so he couldn't smell her. He wished he couldn't feel, so her body warmth didn't invade his space.

"Good night, Gabe," she said, her voice soft and sweet, as if she had no idea of the raging emotions her very nearness stirred in him.

"Good night," he replied and lowered himself back to the mattress. He was careful not to twitch a muscle, move a leg or an arm onto her side. He had a feeling if he touched her in any fashion, no matter how innocuous, it would snap the tenuous hold he had on his self-control.

She sighed, a soft sound that somehow spoke of

wistfulness, of yearning. Gabe squeezed his eyes tightly closed and prayed for sleep.

Within thirty minutes, Serena was fast asleep. Gabe remained tense, listening to her deep, rhythmic breathing. What was she doing in here with him? What had prompted her to come to his bed, knowing that he'd made it clear he didn't want to make love to her?

Sleep didn't come to Gabe until near dawn, and he awoke with the sun seeping around the edges of the drawn curtains. At some point, in the brief time they'd both been asleep, their bodies had sought each other.

Gabe lay on his back, Serena's head on his chest, her one arm across his chest. Her body was curled up next to his, one leg thrown across his thighs. It was obvious that at some point her nightgown had worked its way up her body, for the leg that was across him was bare.

He knew he should get up, get away from the sweet warmth of her, but she was still sleeping, and for just a moment he wanted the pleasure of her in his arms.

Her hair smelled like flowers, with a hint of sweet shampoo, and her body radiated a sleepy warmth that was bewitching.

He closed his eyes once again, fighting the overwhelming desire to awaken her with a kiss, to pull her to consciousness by stroking down the length of her. He could imagine the surprise and pleasure that would light her sleep-filled eyes as he caressed her breasts, then kissed each and every inch of her.

Desire surged inside him, a desire so intense it nearly stole his breath away. Heaven help him, but he wanted her. He ran a hand up her arm, her skin achingly soft. It was more than lust that stirred in him. Lust would have him take her without regard for her mental well-being. Lust would have him sate his need without thinking of the heartache he might inflict on her.

But reservations kept his lust in check, and the fact that he had any reservations about making love to her let him know his feelings for her were much more complex than mere want.

He needed to contact Lieutenant Breckenridge today to find out if the man had been successful in locating Betty Jo Parker. The quicker they found the woman, the faster they'd get back to Wynborough and the faster he would be released from the marriage he'd foolishly entered.

Serena stirred against him and he tensed, knowing she was leaving behind her dreams and surfacing to the new day. She raised her head and smiled, a sweet, open smile that soared through him. "Good morning," she said, but didn't move away from him. "Did you sleep well?"

"Not really," he replied gruffly. "You've been crowding me all night long."

"Oh, sorry." Languidly she moved away from him and stretched like a contented cat. Her motion caused the sheet to fall away, exposing to his gaze one perfect silk-clad breast.

He started to get out of bed, desire roaring in his

head, but she grabbed his arm. "Don't go," she said.

"I'm awake. I always get out of bed when I'm awake," he countered. Relief filled him as she pulled the sheet up around her neck.

"Please, stay here and talk to me for a little while." Her eyes held a soft appeal, and with the sheets completely covering her she was less threatening to him. "You were too tired to talk last night, but you can't be tired now."

"Talk about what?" he asked, still unsure it was wise to linger in the bed with her.

"Stuff. Anything and everything." She rolled over on her side to face him and propped a pillow beneath her head. She frowned, still managing to look sexy with her hair disheveled and her cheeks slightly flushed. "If you won't make love to me, the least you can do is talk to me. That's what married people do."

She had no clue what marriage truly entailed...the giving of hearts without reservation, the mingling of souls so that you no longer knew where you left off and your mate began. But if talking would make her happy, he'd talk.

He settled back and eyed her expectantly. "Okay, let's talk."

She smiled, flashing that quicksilver dimple at the corner of her mouth. "About what?"

He laughed despite his discomfort and shook his head. "It's your game, Princess."

"Tell me about you...you mentioned before that

you don't have any family. What happened to your parents?''

''They died in a car wreck when I was two.''

''Oh, Gabe. I'm so sorry.'' Her face radiated sorrow for him.

''Don't be,'' he said, touched by her empathy. ''I don't remember them, and it's difficult to miss something you never really had.''

''Then who raised you?'' she asked curiously.

''I was raised in foster homes.''

''Gabe...that's so sad,'' she said.

He smiled at her. Despite her stubbornness and willfulness, he knew she had a soft heart. ''It wasn't so sad,'' he replied. ''I stayed in some good places, and I stayed in some not so good places, but I survived.''

''Childhood should be about more than survival,'' she exclaimed.

''My childhood made me strong,'' he returned. ''It made me realize I couldn't depend on anyone but myself.''

''That kind of strength carried too far becomes a weakness,'' she said softly.

He eyed her sharply, surprised by her perception. ''Maybe,'' he agreed. ''But it's a safe weakness.''

''It's a sad weakness,'' she countered.

The conversation had spun out of his control, and was now touching areas he didn't want touched. He wasn't weak; he was smart and she'd never understand that because she'd never known tragedy, never known the ache of loss.

He'd learned in his early years that the people in

his life weren't permanent. Just when he'd start to feel safe, to let down his guard and care about the parents he'd been placed with, he'd be moved to a new family. By the time he was ten, he had already erected a barrier around his heart…a barrier that had been breached by only one woman, and in the end, she'd abandoned him, too.

He rolled out of bed, not liking the direction of his thoughts. Serena's questions had him thinking too much. "I'm going to take a shower," he said.

"Okay. I'll order some breakfast," Serena said.

He was grateful she didn't try to stop him as he went into the bathroom. He locked the door behind him, not trusting her. Knowing Serena, she'd decide she wanted to bathe with him. He could just hear her saying that she knew they weren't going to make love, but at least they could shower together. It was what married people did together.

Despite his earlier unhappy thoughts, he smiled and shook his head ruefully as he thought of Serena. She seemed to have very definite ideas of what being married entailed.

Although Gabe was thirty years old, only nine years older than Serena, there were times he felt a hundred years older than her in life experience.

As he stood beneath the warm spray of water, he thought of all the events that had led him to work for King Phillip. After LeAnn's death, Gabe had plunged into a despair so black, he'd thought he would never surface from it. A picture in a travel agency window of Wynborough's rugged cliffs and charming villages had prompted his impulsive trip to the small country.

During the days, he'd worked security at one of the casinos, and during the long, lonely nights, he'd drank himself into a stupor. Then he'd come to King Phillip's attention and had worked as head of security in the palace.

When the King had offered him the position as head of the Royal Wynborough Bodyguards, Gabe had a feeling he'd taken the job in an attempt to be redeemed. While he protected all the princesses, Gabe had made Serena his top priority, realizing that decision had been a further need for redemption. He had not been able to guard his wife and keep her safe, but in these past months of keeping Serena safe, Gabe had found a measure of forgiveness for himself.

Somehow, in the months of being with Serena, his deep, internal wounds had healed. He would always feel a natural sadness when he thought of LeAnn, but thoughts of her no longer ripped him apart.

However, just because his pain had dissipated didn't mean he was willing to make himself vulnerable again. He would never allow himself to love another person again. He would never be that kind of fool again.

He shut off the water and dried off, resolved that he could remain strong where Serena was concerned. He cared about her, he knew he desired her, but he would never really love her as she needed to be loved. He'd take her back to her father, have the marriage annulled, then she could get on with her life and find a man who would love her desperately, passionately, as she longed to be loved.

He left the bathroom, dressed for the day and found Serena already seated at the table, nibbling on a piece of toast from the breakfast cart. She was still clad in the bewitching nightgown, but thankfully, she'd pulled on a matching robe that covered her from neck to ankles.

"I poured you coffee," she said with a sunshine smile. "And I ordered you scrambled eggs. The morning paper is on the cart, too."

"Thanks." He fixed himself a plate, then grabbed the paper and sat down across from her.

She smiled and again he was struck by her beauty. With the golden light of the morning sun playing on her hair and her cheeks filled with color, she looked sexy and touchable and far too appealing.

"This is our first breakfast together as husband and wife," she said.

"Serena—"

"I know. According to you, it isn't a real marriage," she interrupted. "But that doesn't change the fact that for the moment we are married and this is our first breakfast together since our wedding."

"Okay…you're right," he agreed helplessly.

He took a sip of his coffee and opened the morning paper. He stared at the headline and the accompanying picture. "Oh my God," he exclaimed, a sinking feeling in the pit of his stomach.

"What's wrong?" Serena asked.

Wordlessly, Gabe shoved the paper over in front

of her. Serena stared at the front page. Did They Or Didn't They? the headline screamed. The picture was of the two of them in front of Ye Olde Wedding Chapel and it had obviously been taken as they had exited after the ceremony, for their gold bands on their fingers were easily visible.

"Who…how?" Serena sputtered with surprise.

"Apparently we were followed by a photographer or reporter who knew who we were and smelled a story." Gabe let loose an expletive and shoved away from the table to stand.

"At least it's a good picture of us," Serena said. Secretly, she was rather pleased. Other people knowing they were married made it all seem much more real.

"A good picture?" Gabe glared at her.

She flushed. "Don't be mad at me," she exclaimed. "I didn't take the photo and sell it to the paper." Serena scanned the article. "It's all speculation. Edward Doyle refused to admit or deny that we were there to get married."

"It doesn't matter whether it's speculation or not. We have to call your parents right away. It wouldn't be fair for them to hear it through the grapevine and not from us." Gabe's frown let Serena know he dreaded telling her parents.

"We would have had to tell them at some point," she reminded him.

"I know," he agreed, more calm than before. "I just don't like feeling manipulated by a reporter. I would have preferred to pick the time and place to tell your parents. But it appears the time has been chosen for me, and the time is right now."

He strode across the room and picked up the phone. Serena knew he had the number to her father's private line, and she assumed that was what he punched in. The connection took a moment.

"Sir, it's Gabriel," Gabe said when the connection finally clicked through.

As Gabe spoke with her father, Serena sipped her coffee and watched him. Waking up in his arms that morning had been the most wonderful thing she'd ever experienced.

She had feigned sleep for several minutes after awakening, allowing the sensations of his nearness to sweep over her, through her. His body had been toasty warm, and the feel of his bare skin against hers had made her want to weep with want.

When he'd run his hand softly up her arm in a caress that held infinite softness, a wealth of tenderness, her love for him had filled her. She'd hoped that he would continue touching her, let his touching grow more intimate, allow the passion she knew he felt for her to spin out of control. But he hadn't.

Now, standing near the window, with the sun playing on his features, he looked strong and determined and she loved him for his strength, and hated him for it as well. If he wasn't so strong, perhaps his desire for her would career out of control. If he wasn't so strong, maybe he'd find some little piece of love for her in his heart.

"Yes, sir," Gabe said into the receiver. "I have everything under control, but we wanted you to hear about it from us rather than from a news article. There were some complications and immediate action was necessary.''

Complications. Immediate action was necessary. The words arrowed through Serena's heart. Had Gabe's vows only been uttered in the line of duty? Without any emotion at all? Would he ever love her as she loved him?

Gabe looked at Serena and a slight flush colored his cheeks. ''She will be returned to you safely and the marriage will not be consummated so an annulment can be obtained immediately upon our return to Wynborough.''

Gabe averted his gaze from her and instead focused out the window as the conversation continued. ''No problem. Okay…here she is.'' He held out the receiver to Serena. ''Your mother wants to talk to you.''

Serena walked over and took the phone. ''Mama?''

''Darling, are you all right?'' Queen Gabriella's voice washed over Serena with love and concern. Serena closed her eyes, surprised to feel the heat of tears.

No, I'm not all right, she wanted to confess. I have made the stupidest mistake by falling helplessly in love with Gabe and my heart is going to be broken by him. She said none of it, knowing that there were some things a mother, even a mother who was a queen, couldn't fix.

''I'm fine,'' she assured her mom.

''Your father wanted to talk to you, but he had to

leave for a meeting. Serena, darling, have you been giving Gabriel a difficult time?''

"No more than usual," Serena replied and Queen Gabriella laughed.

Suddenly Serena wished she were home, where her mother could wrap her in a loving embrace. And yet she didn't want to go home, because going home meant losing Gabe.

"When are you coming home, Serena?" Queen Gabriella asked.

"Soon," Serena replied. "Probably in the next week or two." She forced a lightness to her tone. "You know we're all busy promoting Wynborough and the upcoming celebration of father's coronation." The last thing she wanted her parents to know was that the four princesses were hunting down leads to their brother's whereabouts.

After another few minutes of talking, Serena said her goodbyes and hung up the phone. She returned to the table and gestured for Gabe to do the same. "So, what was my father's reaction?" she asked when he'd joined her.

He shrugged. "Surprisingly well. Of course, I was quick to explain to him all the reasons for the marriage and the fact that it isn't a 'real' marriage. I'm sure he wouldn't be thrilled to have a royal bodyguard as his actual son-in-law."

Serena looked at him in surprise. "I can promise you that my father's first concern would be for my happiness," she exclaimed. "He wouldn't care whether I married a royal bodyguard or a shoe salesman, if that's what made me happy."

Gabe looked at her in disbelief. "Surely you don't really believe that," he scoffed.

A little niggling doubt entered her mind, but she shoved it aside. "I not only believe it, I know for certain that it's true." Serena leaned forward. "My father is a man who places great value on love, not on position or a person's station in life."

Serena's heart filled with love as she thought of her father, the most loving, just, wise man she'd ever known. However, she couldn't forget that her father was also king and never forgot what was best for his people, his country. But, she needed to believe that her father's first concern would be her happiness. She needed to believe that it wouldn't matter if she married her bodyguard.

"If my father didn't believe in true love, he never would have married a salesclerk."

Gabe's eyes widened in surprise. "When did your father marry a salesclerk?" he asked.

"When he married my mother," Serena answered with a sense of satisfaction.

Gabe's face radiated amazement. "Queen Gabriella was a salesclerk?"

Serena nodded. "In Aspen. She sold glassware and jewelry in the resort areas around Aspen." Serena smiled as she remembered how often she'd asked her mother to relate the story to her. "The first time my father saw her, he was completely smitten with her. He had to have her and he refused to take no for an answer." She shivered, wishing Gabe felt that way about her.

"I never knew that," he replied.

"The whole point of the story is that my father believes in the power and glory of love and I know as long as I'm happy and in love, he won't care who the man is or what he does for a living."

"Good. Then when you find that special shoe salesman, or whoever, you know you'll have your father's blessing." He stood, ignoring her look of frustration. He went over to the window and stared out, his rigid back making him appear stiff and unyielding.

Serena sighed. What he didn't understand was that she didn't want a shoe salesman. She didn't want a prince or a duke. All she wanted was Gabriel Morgan.

She wondered if the little pieces of his past that he'd shared with her that morning had anything to do with his continuous assertions that he didn't have a heart. Had growing up in foster care made him afraid to trust others? Afraid to love?

She'd meant what she'd told him. Being strong was a valuable asset, but taken to the extreme, it became a liability.

Was he afraid to allow his feelings freedom? Afraid to love her?

What a pair they made. He was afraid to love her and she was afraid he wouldn't love her.

She got up from the table and approached him. He didn't turn around, but remained staring out the window with his back to her.

She walked up behind him, put her arms around his waist and laid her head against his back. He tensed.

"Serena…what are you doing?"

"Just giving you a hug," she replied. "I think maybe when you were growing up, you didn't get all the hugs you needed."

He stood motionless, neither rejecting, nor accepting her hug. His stillness was so complete, for a moment she thought he'd stopped breathing.

Serena wanted to soothe all the hurt he'd ever experienced as a child. She understood the kind of empty loneliness he must have felt and she wanted to heal him.

Still not saying a word, Gabe gently disentangled her arms from his waist, then turned to face her. His features were softened and he reached out and drew a thumb down her cheek. "For a spoiled brat, you can be incredibly giving." His voice was deep, a soft caress as potent as his touch on her face.

Serena sensed his defenses were down, that at least for this moment his heart was open and available to her. She reached up and touched his cheek, as he had touched hers. She wanted to tell him how deep her love for him was, how complete loving him made her feel. She wanted to tell him not to be afraid, that she would love him until the end of time, but she was afraid she'd chase him away.

His eyes were dark and he lowered his head toward hers. She knew he was going to kiss her and she desperately wanted him to.

He'd kissed her at the end of their wedding ceremony and again at midnight on New Year's Eve, but this would be the first kiss initiated by him, initiated by his desire and not any other circumstances.

She raised up on her tiptoes to accept his kiss, then the phone rang.

He jumped away from her as if shocked by a cattle prod. Serena swallowed a scream of frustration. As he answered the phone, she stared out the window, bitterly disappointed.

It had been a single, shining moment. His heart had been unlocked, accessible to her. She'd seen it in his eyes, felt it in his touch. And now the moment had been lost.

She turned to face him as he hung up the phone.

"That was Lieutenant Breckenridge," Gabe said. "He found Betty Jo Parker for us."

Chapter Eight

It was almost two hours later when Gabe and Serena entered the Treasure Chest Casino in downtown Las Vegas. As they walked toward the office, Gabe could feel the nervous energy radiating from Serena.

The phone call from Lieutenant Breckenridge couldn't have come at a more opportune time. Gabe didn't want to think about what might have happened had the phone not rung. But he knew with certainty he'd been about to make a huge mistake.

Her hug had touched him deeply, more so than anything else in his life that he could remember. It had been such a simple gesture, yet he knew it had been a spontaneous gift from her heart.

As they reached the casino office, Serena placed a hand on his arm. "Give me just a minute," she said, and leaned against the wall to draw in deep breaths. She gave him a small, trembling smile. "All of a sudden, I'm so nervous. It's possible in the next few minutes we'll know where James is.'' Her smile fell away. ''It's New Year's Day. Maybe Betty isn't working.''

''Breckenridge said she's here.'' Gabe shoved his hands in his pockets, fighting the desire to kiss the nervous tremble from her lips, kiss her until her mouth trembled with another emotion. ''This is why you came to Las Vegas. This is what you've been waiting for.''

''I know…and that's why I'm so nervous.'' She reached over and tugged his hand out of his pocket and grasped it tightly. ''Oh, Gabe, I want this so badly. I want to give my parents back their son. I want James back in our lives.''

Gabe placed an arm around her shoulder, wanting to support her. She could be the most irritating woman he'd ever known, but she also had the softest heart of anyone he'd ever met.

He knew her need to find James wasn't just her own, but rather a desire for her to give her parents back the son they had lost so many years before.

''I just hope she knows where James is,'' Serena said.

''She won't know James by his real name,'' Gabe reminded her.

Serena nodded. ''I hope she knows where Bill Lewis is, and I hope Bill Lewis is James.''

Gabe gave her a quick hug, then released his hold on her. ''You ready?'' he asked.

She drew one more deep breath, then nodded and together they went into the office. They spoke to a supervisor, who eyed them suspiciously, then asked if Betty was in trouble.

"No trouble at all," Serena quickly responded. "It's a family matter," she explained. "We just need to talk to her for a minute or two."

The supervisor, a big man with a bald head, eyed her for a long moment, then nodded, as if satisfied there would be no trouble. "Betty is in the lounge. She's the bartender."

"Thank you," Serena said and was halfway out the office door before Gabe could catch up to her.

The lounge was connected to the casino through an inner door. Gabe and Serena followed the signs and entered the small, adjoining room. Despite the morning hour, there were already people in the lounge. Several men sat on the stools at the bar, and two couples sat at two of the tables that dotted the room.

A woman stood behind the bar, wiping out a glass as she talked to one of the men seated there. She was short, rather plump and wrinkles radiated from her sharp eyes. Her hair was short, with gray strands intermingling with a darker brown.

Before Gabe could approach the woman, Serena grabbed his arm and tugged him to sit down with her at a table. "Something's wrong," she said.

He looked at her curiously. "What are you talking about?"

She shot a meaningful glance to the bartender, then looked back at Gabe. "If that's Betty Jo Parker, then something is definitely wrong."

"I don't understand. What's the matter?" Gabe asked.

She looked at the bartender again, a worried frown marring the smooth skin of her forehead. She nibbled her lower lip worriedly, then said, "Katherine thought that Betty Jo Parker was Bill Lewis's lover, but that woman looks too old."

"Too old for what?" Gabe smiled at her. "Too old to love? Too old to be romantically involved?"

"If Bill Lewis is James, then he's only thirty years old, and that woman looks like she's in her mid-fifties."

Gabe smiled patiently. "Perhaps your brother is like your father and believes in the power of love…a love that transcends age barriers."

"I guess you could be right," she said, once again catching her lower lip between her teeth.

"The only way you're going to find out is to go over and talk to the woman," Gabe said gently. He knew she was afraid…afraid that once again the possibility of finding James would be lost.

Serena drew one last deep breath, nodded and stood. Gabe followed just behind her as she made her way to two stools at the bar. As she slid onto one, Gabe sat on the other.

"Morning, folks," Betty said as she moved down to stand before them. "What can I get you?" she asked with a friendly smile.

"A little information," Gabe said.

Betty's graying eyebrows rose slightly and the smile wavered. "Information about what?"

"Bill Lewis," Serena replied. "Do you know him?"

"Is Bill in trouble?" Betty asked, worry creating lines across her forehead.

"Not that we're aware of," Gabe answered truthfully.

Betty swiped the top of the bar once again. "Then why do you want to know where he is?"

Serena drew a deep breath before answering. "We're looking for Bill because we believe he might be my long-lost brother."

Betty shook her head. "That's impossible," she exclaimed.

"Why is it impossible? We know Bill was at The Sunshine Home for Children in Hope, Arizona, when my brother would have been. Bill is the right age. Everything points to him." There was a desperation in Serena's voice.

"Bill is an only child. He doesn't have any brothers or sisters. I should know. I'm Bill's mother."

"His mother," Serena gasped. She reached out blindly for Gabe's hand. He gripped hers tightly, knowing the bitter disappointment she must be feeling at that moment.

"Bill contacted me a couple of months ago," Betty explained softly, as if aware that Serena had been shattered by her news. "He found me through a private investigator. We talked to each other several times on the phone. Bill even gave me his partner's number in case I needed to find him. We had a lot of healing to do. He came out here to see me a while back. We had a nice visit, but recently I haven't heard or seen from him.''

With every word Betty spoke, Serena appeared to grow smaller, more fragile. Gabe had known that finding James was important. However, he hadn't realized just how much hope Serena had placed in Betty Jo Parker and Bill Lewis. It was evident now that Bill Lewis wasn't the crown prince and all of Serena's spirit seemed crushed beneath the knowledge.

''We're sorry we bothered you,'' Serena said dully. She let go of Gabe's hand and slid off the stool.

''Honey, I'm sorry I couldn't help you,'' Betty said. ''I hope you find your brother. I know how difficult it is to live each day when there's a piece missing from your heart.''

Gabe nodded their thanks to the woman and together he and Serena left the lounge. Serena managed to hold herself together through the drive back to the hotel and the short trip up in the elevator. But Gabe sensed the breakdown to come.

She was taut as a rope threatening to fray, as tight as a wire about to snap. For the first time in years, Gabe didn't want to run from the explosion of emotion he sensed she was about to release. Rather he wanted to be here for her, to hold her, to somehow ease the pain of her disappointment. It surprised him, this need of his to be her strength.

''I need to call my sisters,'' she said the moment they entered the suite. ''They need to know that Bill Lewis isn't James.'' She sat on the edge of the sofa and stared at the phone, as if reluctant to make the calls.

He nodded, fighting the desire to take her into his arms. She looked achingly fragile, but he knew Serena well enough to know that when she needed him, she'd reach out for him. Instead of following through on his desire to hold her, he sat next to her on the sofa.

He watched as she slowly punched in a series of numbers, then waited for her call to be answered.

"Katherine, it's me. Happy New Year to you, too." Serena twisted the phone cord around her fingers as she spoke. "I wanted to let you know that I found Betty Jo Parker. She wasn't Bill Lewis's lover as we suspected. She's Bill's mother. Bill isn't James."

As Serena explained the situation to Katherine, Gabe watched her. He'd seen Serena in a dozen moods in the past. He'd seen her fiery with anger or smoldering with aggravation. He'd seen her green eyes darken with hurt and dance with joy. But though he'd spent almost every hour of every day with Serena, he'd never seen her look as sad as she did at this moment.

It was a sadness that filled his heart, touched him in a way he hadn't been touched in a very long time. If it had been in his capacity, he would rush out and beat every bush, turn over every stone, never rest until he could present her with her long-lost brother.

He shifted positions as she dialed the phone again. Two more sisters to contact, he thought, then she would fall apart.

"Alexandra, it's me," she said, before relating her discovery to first her eldest sister, then to Elizabeth.

She unwound the cord and sat up straighter, listening to whatever Elizabeth was saying. "Really? That's great. I'll keep my fingers crossed." She shot a quick glance at Gabe, then looked back at the phone. "We'll probably be returning home to Wynborough in the next day or two. There's something I need to take care of. Yes, I'll keep in touch. Love you, too."

She hung up the receiver, then looked at Gabe once again. "Elizabeth has another promising lead to follow. While going through the records at The Sunshine Home, she came up with a few more names of boys who could be James. She asked Grandma Beulah about them and they've narrowed it down to one man. A man named Sam Flynn."

"That's great, but who is Grandma Beulah?" Gabe asked, sorry he hadn't kept up with all this from the very beginning. Besides, he thought, talking might give Serena an opportunity to calm down.

"I told you already. Grandma Beulah is a woman who used to work at The Sunshine Home. She'd been retired for years, but she's the one who found a blanket with our family crest and contacted Laura Bishop about it. She's the reason we started this whole search."

She stood from the sofa, her body still vibrating with energy, an energy that appeared unhealthy when coupled with the paleness of her face.

"Are you all right?" Gabe asked softly.

"I'm fine," she replied, and promptly burst into tears.

She was appalled. She hadn't even been aware the tears were coming. She was surprised when Gabe rose and walked over to enfold her in his arms. She buried her face into the crisp, masculine scent of his shirt. Her tears came faster, uncontrollably hard, and as sobs shook her, Gabe soothed her, rubbing his hands down her back and whispering words of comfort.

"I'm sorry, sweetheart. I'm so sorry you were disappointed." His deep voice caressed her, but instead of easing the flow of her tears, it only served to make her cry harder.

"Elizabeth told you they have other leads. We'll find James," he said.

She knew that he thought she was disappointed because Bill Lewis wasn't her brother.

He had no idea that she wasn't sure if her tears were for the brother she hadn't found or if her heart was breaking because now there was no other reason for them to remain in Las Vegas. Now they would travel back to Wynborough, where her father would grant them an annulment.

Somehow it had all become confused in her mind. But she knew one thing for certain. She was going to lose Gabe, and she knew losing him would break her heart forever. Although she knew now he'd married her for all the wrong reasons, she'd hoped that with a little time he would realize he loved her as deeply as she loved him.

Now they were all out of time.

This thought made her cry harder and she clung to Gabe, wishing he would hold her forever, through eternity. His arms were strong enough to protect her throughout her lifetime. His shoulders were broad enough to share any of her burdens. His laughter was deep enough, infectious enough to pull laughter from her. If only his heart was big enough, opened enough to love her just a little bit.

"Serena, honey, you've got to stop crying. You're going to make yourself ill," he finally said, worry deepening his voice.

She raised her head to look at him. "Kiss me, Gabe. Please, just kiss me."

His eyes darkened and he hesitated only a moment, then his lips claimed hers in a fiery kiss that stole every thought from her mind. His mouth was fire, and Serena wanted to be consumed by his flame.

Tears forgotten, she opened her mouth to him, allowing his tongue to deepen the kiss, at the same time she unbuttoned his jacket and attempted to shove it off his shoulders.

He aided her in the attempt, shrugging out of it and allowing it to fall to the floor. Her hands then found the buttons of his shirt. She fumbled to unfasten them, wanting—needing—to touch the heat of his skin. When she reached the bottom of the material, she tugged the shirt from his slacks and tore the offending barrier from him.

She was out of control and somewhere in the back of her mind, she knew it, reveled in it. Her only thought was of Gabe and her need to feel him next to her.

She knew he was out of control as well. His breathing came in quick gasps as his fingers found the buttons of her blouse. His mouth was everywhere, along her jaw, across her cheeks, then once again on her mouth.

Taking a step back from him, she pulled her unbuttoned blouse off, leaving her in only a pale pink lacy bra. She didn't want him to take her here, in the middle of the floor, or on the uncomfortable sofa. She wanted him in the bed...in their bed, where they had spent their first night as husband and wife.

She backed away from him, toward the bedroom as she reached behind her and unclasped her bra. She felt a brief moment of hesitation, of shyness, but reminded herself he was her husband. It didn't matter what had prompted the wedding ceremony. They were married, and she wanted her husband to make love to her. There was nothing wrong with that...rather there was something intrinsically right with it.

He appeared dazed, his eyes darker than she'd ever seen them before. Desire was written all over his features...a desire too strong to ignore, too potent to avoid.

As her bra came unfastened, she held it against her, still hiding her breasts from his view. She allowed it to drop to the floor as she stepped out of his view and into the bedroom.

She stood for a moment alone, heart thudding

frantically as she wondered if he'd follow her or if he'd find the strength to halt this loving process.

Her breath caught in her chest as he appeared in the doorway, filling the space with his overwhelming presence, filling the entire room with his masculinity.

As he stood there, his gaze burning into hers, she unfastened her slacks and slid them down her hips. She had never felt more feminine, more desirable than at this moment. Kicking the slacks to the side, she stood before him in nothing but a pair of silky panties.

Trembling with need, she held her breath as she waited to see if he'd deny her or accept what she knew had been inevitable for some time.

"Gabriel," she said softly, pleadingly.

Slowly, as if still dazed, his hands went to the fastening of his slacks. He unclasped, then unzipped them, the sound explosive in the otherwise silent room.

"Serena." Her name eased out of him with the reverence of a prayer. His slacks fell to the ground, exposing his long, athletic legs and the undeniable evidence of his desire for her.

And then they were in each other's arms, tumbling to the bed while their bodies pressed together and their mouths found each other's in a kiss that swept away all reason.

His skin was hot, heated with flames of desire. Serena ran her hands across his chest, tangled her fingers in the wiry hair, caressed down his flat, muscled abdomen.

Her heart sang with pleasure as his lips left hers and instead nipped at her breasts, taking the turgid tips in his mouth and creating sizzling sensations inside her.

Serena knew the intensity of her response to him was not only because of the mastery of his touch. It was because her love for him filled her up, made her whole, made her vulnerable yet unafraid to respond without reservation to each and every caress.

"I love you, Gabriel. I love you so much," she said, unable to repress what burned in her heart.

He froze, not moving a muscle. In that moment she realized that speaking her heart had been a terrible mistake.

She released a small cry as he rolled off her and stood. "I'm sorry, Serena. I shouldn't have let things get so out of control. This isn't going to happen now...or ever."

He turned and disappeared into the bathroom. She heard the click of the door locking behind him. Locked out. Out of his heart.

Her body ached with need, with want...with love. Tears burned at her eyes, pressing so hot, so thick, she couldn't swallow fast enough to make them go away. She gave into them. This time there was no confusion. She knew exactly why she cried. She cried for Gabe...because he didn't love her.

Chapter Nine

Gabe stood beneath a cold shower for an interminably long time, attempting to scrub away the feel of Serena's sweet, heated flesh against his own, to scour off the floral scent that lingered despite the soap and water.

His desire had spun out of control so quickly, he'd had no defenses. She'd been like a white-hot flame inside him searing away good sense and all reason, leaving behind only the incredible need to possess her.

Thank goodness good sense had prevailed. Her sweetly uttered words of love had returned sanity and halted what would have been an irreversible error on his part.

He finished his shower, wondering how he would be able to face Serena again and not think of the heat of her body against his, the honeyed taste of her lips, the perfect size of her breasts.

He dressed and left the bathroom, relieved to discover that Serena was no longer in his bed. In fact, she was nowhere in the suite.

Damn. Had she run off again? Had he shoved her out of his bed and into harm's way? He raced across the living area to her bedroom, then into her bathroom, but both rooms were empty. No sign of Serena anywhere.

He cursed her, then cursed himself. He hadn't a clue where to begin to look for her. Before he could fully work himself up, she walked through the door carrying a pizza box and a handful of tabloid papers.

"I thought we agreed you wouldn't leave here alone," he said as she set the pizza on the table.

"I was hoping to be back before you knew I'd left. I just went down the street. I was hungry for pizza."

She didn't look at him and he didn't have the heart to yell at her. Her eyes were red rimmed and slightly swollen, and it hurt him to know that he'd been the cause of her tears.

"You want some pizza?" She finally looked at him and he could see that she was struggling to keep things as normal as possible between them.

"Sure," he agreed. Although he knew nothing would ever be normal between them again. Every time he looked at her, he'd remember holding her in his arms. Every time he spoke to her, he'd remember the taste of her kisses. Despite the fact that he'd halted their lovemaking before the actual act itself could be accomplished, they had crossed a boundary and now could never go back to the innocent relationship they'd once known.

He sat down across from her at the table and gestured to the small stack of tabloids beside her. "I didn't know you went in for literary reading," he teased.

"I don't usually read them, but today you and I were fodder for several articles." She held up one with a headline that read Wild Princess Gets Her Man. A photo similiar to the one that had appeared in the morning paper accompanied the sensational article.

"You shouldn't read that garbage," Gabe said as he helped himself to a piece of the pizza.

Serena shrugged. "I'm going to cut out all the articles and pictures about our wedding and make a scrapbook. In lieu of wedding pictures, these will have to suffice."

"Serena, don't you think that when we get back to Wynborough and the marriage is annulled it would be best if you just put it all behind you?" Gabe asked gently.

"You deal with things your way, Gabriel, and I'll deal with them in my way," she replied. She traced a finger across his face on the front page of one of the papers. "Maybe some day I'll want to show my children the pictures of my first husband." She picked up a piece of pizza.

"You like children, don't you?" he asked, wanting to change the subject.

"I love children." The look in her eyes softened. "For as long as I can remember, I've wanted children of my own. Two…three…maybe half a dozen. The more the merrier.''

"You're good with children," he said, remembering the many times young boys and girls had approached her. She had the patience of a saint with the little ones. It was only one of the qualities that made her a favorite with the public.

Once again they grew silent. Gabe ate his pizza, his head filled with visions of the children Serena would one day have…little girls with flaming hair and dancing dimples or boys with stubborn chins and bright green eyes.

An emotion curiously like grief rose inside Gabe as he realized those children would be hers, but not his. She would have her children with another man, a husband that would be for keeps.

He'd wanted children…a lifetime ago. He'd once dreamed of a little boy who would carry on the Morgan name. Or a little girl who'd wrap her arms around his neck and call him daddy. But he'd put those dreams away, at the same time he'd decided he didn't want love in his life.

He finished his piece of pizza, which had turned to the consistency of sawdust in his mouth. He pushed away from the table, no longer hungry as he thought of Serena marrying another man.

Moving to the window, he stared outside, seeking the emotional distance that had always been his friend, his comfort. He'd always counted on his emotional detachment to keep him sharp, his mind uncluttered. But somehow Serena had destroyed any neutrality he might feel where she was concerned, and that was dangerous.

"Gabe?"

"What?" he asked sharply. He turned back to look at her, wishing his heart felt nothing where she was concerned.

She winced slightly, as if his tone of voice had slapped her. She gestured toward one of the papers opened before her. "There's an article in here about you."

He frowned and walked over to stand just behind her where he could read the headline of the piece. Tragic Past Haunts Bodyguard Groom.

He scanned just enough of the article to realize somebody had done their homework. It was all there, his past as a cop, his marriage to LeAnn and LeAnn's tragic death.

He felt the blood rush from his face, leaving him lightheaded and half-dizzy. "They are nothing but vultures, picking over the pieces of people's lives. I don't know why you read that garbage."

Serena turned around in her chair to look up at him. "Is it true? Were you married before?"

"Read all about it," he said with a touch of bitterness. He pointed to the paper. "They probably have a fact wrong here or there, but what the heck."

Her gaze was somber as she got up from the table and instead sat down on the edge of the sofa. "I'd rather hear it from you, Gabe, than read it in a tabloid."

He wanted to tell her it was none of her business, that it had all happened a long time ago and didn't matter anymore. But there was a part of him that wanted to talk about it, that wanted to explain to Serena what had happened. He needed to make her understand how those events so long ago had changed him and why he would never, ever allow himself to love her as she so wanted to be loved.

He started to sit on the sofa, then changed his mind, needing to walk, to pace while his thoughts carried him back in time. "I met LeAnn when I was working traffic and she sped by me as if begging me to ticket her."

"Did you?" Serena asked.

A ghost of a smile curved his lips as he remembered how LeAnn had flirted and cajoled in an effort to avoid the speeding ticket. "Yeah, I did. I gave her a ticket, then asked her out."

He moved once again to stand at the window and stare outside. "It was a crazy, whirlwind kind of courtship. We only dated for two months, then we got married."

Now, with the perspective of time, Gabe realized he and LeAnn had probably married too quickly and for all the wrong reasons. He had been lonely and LeAnn, reeling from a broken engagement a month before, had been desperate. Despite the odds, despite their differences, they were determined to make the marriage work.

He drew in a deep breath, fast forwarding in his mind to the day it had all ended. "We'd been married about six months on the morning I took her to the bank so she could deposit a check." He turned to look at Serena, the pit of his stomach burning with the memory of that day.

"Gabe...don't." Her gaze was tender, soft with emotion. "If it hurts too much, you don't have to tell me."

Her obvious concern for him and his emotional well-being was almost his undoing. It would be so easy to sweep her up in his arms, carry her into the bedroom and lose himself, his memories and his regrets in her sweet heat.

"No...you need to know," he replied. "You need to understand." Even as he said these words he wondered if she would. He wondered if he even understood all the emotions that had died on the day LeAnn had been killed.

"We'd only been in the bank a minute or two. I was standing near the front door, watching LeAnn as she waited in line." The muscles in his stomach tightened as the memory of that moment grew crystal clear in his mind. "It was a gorgeous summer day and LeAnn was wearing a short dress and sandals."

He shook his head, amazed at the peculiarity of memories a person's brain chose to retain. "She had a blister on one heel. I remember thinking we should stop and get some bandages on the way home."

Pacing back and forth in front of the window, Gabe drew in a deep breath. "I was watching LeAnn, and she was watching the teller when everything went crazy. A voice yelled 'Freeze,' somebody screamed, a gun went off and LeAnn was dead."

"Oh God, Gabe…" Serena stood and took a step toward him, but he stopped her by holding up a hand.

"Apparently a kid, high on drugs, had decided to pull a bank robbery. When he yelled and the teller screamed, he fired the gun. LeAnn was simply an innocent victim who was in the wrong place at the wrong time."

"I don't know what to say. It must have been devastating for you." Serena reached out and tentatively touched his arm, as if unsure how he would react to the physical contact. "You must have loved her very much."

Loved LeAnn? He stared at Serena. What he'd once felt for LeAnn was nothing compared to the emotions Serena had managed to stir inside him.

"Yeah, I loved her, but in the last couple of years, I've come to terms with her loss." The burning in his stomach intensified and he felt the hot press of tears behind his eyelids. Tears he hadn't cried when he'd been a lonely, unwanted child, tears that hadn't been released when LeAnn had died, tears he'd held inside for a lifetime.

He swallowed hard against them, refusing to let them fall. Instead he sought the anger, the self-hatred that had always kept him strong. He stepped away from Serena, so he could no longer feel her comforting touch.

"What I can't forget…what I'll never forget is that I was right there, a cop trained to protect people, and I couldn't even protect my own wife." The words tumbled out of him, a sea of guilt that threatened to drown him. "I was a trained professional. If I hadn't been so busy looking at LeAnn's legs, I would have seen the kid come into the bank. I would have sensed his intent and been able to stop him before anyone got hurt."

"You can't know that," Serena exclaimed. "You can't blame yourself for LeAnn's death."

"I could have stopped it." The words exploded from him. "But caring about her made me stupid and dull. Caring about her made me preoccupied and less perceptive. That's why she's dead. And that's why I'm going to call your father this evening and tell him to send another bodyguard for you. I'm not going to be your bodyguard anymore and I'm not returning to Wynborough with you."

Serena stared at him for a long moment, shocked by his words. Not returning to Wynborough with her? Getting her another bodyguard? Someplace in her mind, she'd known that Gabe would probably try to quit his job as her bodyguard, but she'd been certain before they returned to Wynborough she would be able to change his mind.

She couldn't imagine him not in her life, if not as her husband, then as the man she depended on for her security and protection.

"You can't mean that," she finally spoke into the depth of silence his words had created.

He raked a hand down his jaw, looking exhausted and wrung out. "I do mean it." He slumped into the sofa. Leaning backward he closed his eyes, as if in telling her of his past, he'd used every ounce of energy he possessed.

Serena stared at him, loving him with every ounce of her being. When he'd spoken of his past tragedy, she'd embraced it as her own, her heart aching for him and his loss.

But she refused to embrace the obvious guilt that ate at him. She had a feeling her enemy was not his memories of LeAnn, but rather the culpability he felt because of her death.

Frowning, she tried to climb into his mind, to understand the forces that drove him, the emotions that had dictated the choices he'd made with his life since LeAnn's death.

She sat down next to him. She didn't touch him, knew instinctively he would rebuff any simple touch, any loving caress from her. He leaned forward and buried his face in his hands.

"Gabe, when you took the job as my bodyguard, weren't you seeking redemption?"

He raised his head to look at her, his eyes so dark, so empty, Serena's heart once again constricted with his pain. "Redemption?" He said the word as if it were foreign to his vocabulary. "I wasn't seeking anything," he scoffed. "I needed work. The job fell into my lap so I took it."

"You saved my father's life," she exclaimed.

"A mere accident of fate," he retorted. He averted his gaze from her and instead stared at the surface of the coffee table.

"A mere accident of fate," she repeated with a nod. "Just like LeAnn's death."

Again his gaze found hers, this time burning with intensity, as if the fever of guilt raged hot inside him. "You don't know...you can't know."

She held his gaze, unflinching. "I know this... I've always felt completely safe with you. I've always trusted that you would protect me. I've never had a moment of doubt about that."

He sighed and some of the intensity of his gaze lessened. "I never had a moment of doubt until now, but now I know it's time to move on. I can't guarantee your safety any longer."

"Why? What's changed?" Serena asked desperately. "You haven't doubted yourself before today...before this moment. What's happened to change you?"

He stood, his features ravaged with torment. "I'm out of control where you are concerned," he yelled angrily. "I want you, and it's eating me alive. I can't keep my mind on anything else. Don't you understand, I'm a security risk now." He turned away from her. "I need a little time alone," he said and stalked to his bedroom.

Serena watched him disappear, stared at the door he closed behind him. He wanted her. He couldn't think of anything else. Her heart sang with the knowledge. And she knew beneath his desire for her was love. He loved her.

The joy that filled her heart was short-lived as she stared at the bedroom door. What good did it do for her to know he loved her, for him to want her beyond reason, if he didn't intend to spend his life with her? If he continued to fight against what was in his heart?

She had to figure out a way to get through to him, to ease the guilt that had eaten at him for far too long and now threatened to destroy any hope they had for a future together. But how? How could she make him forgive himself? How could she make him not afraid to accept their love for each other?

The afternoon brought her no answers. Gabe stayed in his room until dinnertime. When he finally came out, he appeared completely in control and coolly detached from her. "Why don't we go out for dinner," he suggested. "I think we both could use a little fresh air."

"Okay," she agreed, disheartened by the hours that had brought no easy answers.

They found a quiet little Italian restaurant not far from their hotel and were led to a secluded table in the rear by a friendly hostess.

They had not spoken on the short walk to the restaurant. It was as if both of them were afraid to say anything that might shatter the tenuous calm between them.

"It smells wonderful in here," Gabe said as he opened his menu. "Are you hungry?" He looked at her and in his eyes she saw his need to keep things normal, devoid of the emotions that had torn them apart earlier.

"A little," she replied. The light from the candle in the center of the table played on her wedding ring and Serena felt a helpless sense of defeat.

Was she wrong in believing that he loved her? Maybe she was fooling herself. Maybe what he felt for her had nothing to do with love. Was it only lust that made him want her, a lust with no basis for forever?

They ordered their meal, then once again silence grew between them. Serena sipped a glass of wine, trying to keep her gaze averted from Gabe. It hurt too much to look at him, to remember the heat of his kisses, the feel of his hands caressing her body. It hurt too much to know he intended to walk away from her rather than risk loving again.

"Serena? I'm sorry."

She looked at him then, saw the sorrow that deepened the hue of his eyes. She shrugged and took another sip of her wine. "Don't be sorry for me, Gabe. Be sorry for yourself. You're the only loser in this whole thing."

He flushed slightly and averted his gaze from hers. "Then that makes you the winner, and that's all that's important to me."

Anger rose inside her. "That's where you're wrong." She bit off what she was about to say as the waitress appeared at their table with their dinners.

"Here we are. Lasagna for the lady and spaghetti and meatballs for the gentleman," she said with a perky smile. "A meal fit for royalty." The waitress giggled with excitement. "I saw in the paper where you two got married and I just wanted to extend my congratulations." She giggled again and pulled a slip of paper and a pen from her apron. "Would you mind…could I have your autographs?"

"Of course," Serena replied with the graciousness she'd been taught from the cradle. She signed the paper, then pushed it to Gabe, who signed it as well.

"Thanks so much," the waitress gushed. "I've never met a prince and princess before."

"But I'm not—" Gabe began.

"You're welcome," Serena interrupted him.

"Enjoy your meal. Just let me know if you need anything." With another giggle, the waitress left their table.

"She'll be disappointed when she realizes I'm not a prince, but just your bodyguard," Gabe observed.

Just your bodyguard. How easily he discounted everything he'd become to her.

"She'll probably find that autograph worth a lot of money some day," Serena said. "After all, it will be the only autograph of a princess and her husband during the brief time they were married."

Once again silence prevailed. The low sounds of mood music floating in the air did nothing to break the stifling quiet as they ate.

As Serena shot Gabe surreptitious glances, she realized she'd been wrong when she'd thought to keep him as her bodyguard. If she couldn't have him in her life as her husband, it was better that he not be in her life in any capacity.

She would die a little bit each day seeing him, having him near, having him protect her as his job, as his duty, yet knowing there would never be a future for the two of them.

They had finished their meal and had ordered coffee when Gabe once again spoke. "I called your father this afternoon and told him you were ready to return home but needed a new bodyguard to escort you. He's sending a man named Lance Grayson. Grayson will be here first thing in the morning and your flight home leaves at noon."

"Tomorrow?" she echoed in dismay. Too fast. It was all happening too fast. She had hoped for more time…time to figure out what to do, time to figure out how to change Gabe's mind, to help him accept the love she knew that resided in his heart.

Up until this moment, she'd held on to her pride, but she felt that pride flitting away as desperation grew stronger. She wanted to give him one last chance, to try one final time to change his mind, but not here in the restaurant.

"I don't really want coffee," she said. "I need to get back to the hotel and start packing if I'm returning home tomorrow."

"Okay," he agreed. "I can always order up some coffee from room service." He paid their tab and they left the restaurant.

Outside, the lights of Las Vegas lit the night as if the sun had never set. But night was upon them, and Serena knew it was her last night with Gabe. In the morning a new bodyguard would arrive, and he and Serena would return to Wynborough.

She looked at Gabe as they entered the lobby of

their hotel. "What are your plans? If you aren't going back to Wynborough, where are you going?"

As they got into the elevator, he punched the button for their floor. "I'm going back to Kansas City." He leaned against the elevator wall. "I'm not sure what I'm going to do there, but that's where I'm going. My flight leaves tomorrow about the same time yours does."

The elevator halted and the two of them got off and entered their suite. Serena turned to Gabe just inside the door. "Gabe...I can't make you forgive yourself for whatever responsibility you feel about LeAnn's death. All I can tell you is that I love you with all my heart, with all my soul."

She had expected him to back away from her, but he didn't. Instead, he reached out and ran a finger down her cheek, his touch so sweet, so achingly tender, it caused tears of frustration to spring to her eyes.

"Serena, you're so young, such an innocent. You deserve much better than what I can offer you. Besides—" he allowed his finger to linger on her chin "—what do you know about love? It's only natural you believe yourself in love with me because I've been the only consistent man in your life."

"You pompous ass," Serena exploded as she shoved his hand away from her face. Anger swept through her as she glared at him. "How dare you."

"Serena," he protested with surprise.

"How dare you tell me what you think I really feel for you," she said. "I know what's in my heart, Gabriel Morgan, and it's real love, true love. I love you despite the fact that you're overbearing and arrogant. I love how I feel when I'm with you, how you make me want to be a better woman. I'm not confused about my feelings for you.''

The words tumbled from her, one after another, and when tears stung her eyes, she angrily swiped them away. "You act like you're the only person in the world who has suffered loss, like tragedy has never touched another person but you.'' He opened his mouth, apparently to protest, but Serena gave him no opportunity.

"Twenty-nine years ago, my brother was kidnapped...a terrible tragedy that haunts my parents still. Don't you think my mother blamed herself, wondered what she could have done differently to keep James safe? Yet she didn't stop living, stop loving. She went on to have four more children when she could have allowed that tragedy to keep her childless forever.''

Gabe moved away from her and sank to the sofa. But Serena wasn't finished yet. Emotion still pressed in her chest, myriad emotions of anger and bitterness, of need and grief, and the desperation of a woman in love.

"How arrogant you are to accept full responsibility for LeAnn's death. How egotistical of you to believe you're godlike and had the ultimate power to save her. Some things are just meant to be. They're out of our control and there's nothing to be done about it but have the courage to go on.'' She paused, half-breathless from the expulsion of words.

"Are you through?" he asked, his voice cool, his eyes blank…emotionless.

She drew a deep breath and shoved her hair behind her ears. "No, I'm not through," she said, her voice softer, more controlled. She sat on the opposite end of the sofa, her gaze not leaving him.

For a moment she couldn't continue speaking. She was so filled with her love for him, it made speech momentarily impossible. She realized she'd loved Gabe since the first day he'd become her bodyguard. She'd tried to tell herself it was a silly crush, an impossible case of puppy love, but that crush had transformed, and what she felt for him now was the mature, enduring love of a lifetime.

"Gabe, I love you, and nothing is ever going to change that." He stiffened slightly as if in defense. "Just tell me one thing…do you love me?"

The words hung in the air, and Serena's heart resonated with frantic thuds as she waited for his answer. If he told her he didn't love her, then she'd know it was truly over and she wouldn't fight the annulment. If he told her he loved her, then all bets were off and she would do her best to make him learn to trust in that love.

"Serena…" He averted his gaze from hers. "I've made up my mind about what I'm doing and—"

"Just answer the question, Gabe," she interrupted, feeling as if she might scream if he didn't tell her now.

"I told you before that I want you. I want to make love to you. I desire you." He stood and looked at her once again. "I also told you that I didn't have a heart.'' His voice was low, soft. ''And without a heart there can be no love.''

Serena's heart seemed to stop beating altogether. He doesn't love you, a voice cried in her head. You were wrong about him, wrong to believe that he did love you.

She stood, her legs wobbly and her head swimming with tears she refused to release. ''Well, then that's that. It's time for me to pack for the trip home tomorrow.'' She was glad her voice sounded normal.

She walked to her bedroom door, then turned back to gaze at him. ''You know, LeAnn's death wasn't the real tragedy.'' She swallowed hard, then continued, ''And you not loving me isn't really the ultimate tragedy. The real tragedy in all of this is that you died on that day in the bank. As long as you keep yourself closed off from love, you won't really live. You're a walking dead man, Gabriel, and you don't even know it.'' She turned and went into her room and closed the door behind her.

Chapter Ten

When a knock fell on the door at ten the next morning, Gabe assumed it was the new bodyguard arriving. He was surprised to open the door and find an older, balding man in a suit and tie. The man held out a badge.

"Lieutenant Breckenridge."

Gabe greeted the man with a handshake and invited him inside. "Nice to meet you, sir."

"You, too, Mr. Morgan," Breckenridge returned. "I'd like to thank you for your help in finding Betty Jo Parker. Princess Serena was pleased by the cooperation of your department."

"No problem." The lieutenant shifted from one foot to the other, obviously ill at ease. "Actually, I'm here about another matter."

Gabe looked at him curiously. What other matter could a member of the Las Vegas police department have with them?

"Actually, the captain sent me over as a sort of courtesy call. We're a tourist city, and we like to think we look after the tourists who come here. And that means we try to keep tabs on the nefarious characters who call Las Vegas home." He frowned and scratched his balding head. "The captain was quite upset when I told him about your phone call to me checking up on Avery Kintell."

Gabe shot a quick glance to Serena's bedroom door which was open, but he saw no sign of Serena. He gestured for the lieutenant to step out into the hallway, then he pulled the suite door closed behind him.

"I can tell you Avery Kintell is a dead issue. In any case, the princess and I are leaving Las Vegas today so Avery Kintell will have to find another mark."

Lieutenant Breckenridge nodded. "Good. The man is slippery as a snake and we try to keep tabs on him. Unfortunately, legally we can't do much about him."

"Tell your captain we appreciate his concern."

Breckenridge nodded. "We hope you and the princess will come back to visit again sometime."

The two men said their goodbyes, then Gabe returned to the suite. He was grateful there was still no sign of Serena. The last thing he wanted her to find out was that Avery had only been interested in her because she was a wealthy princess. Gabe knew that information would only serve to hurt Serena.

He poured himself a cup of coffee from the room service cart, then sat down at the table.

His eyes felt gritty with lack of sleep. All night long he'd tossed and turned, Serena's words echoing over and over again in his mind. He knew what he was doing was right. He knew she would be better off married to a prince, a duke, an earl. What he hadn't realized was that leaving her would be so difficult.

Already he dreaded the ride to the airport, dreaded the goodbyes they would say to each other as she got on her plane and he took off for his flight.

He'd only seen her once that morning, when she'd brought her suitcase from her bedroom and placed it by the front door.

She hadn't spoken to him, but had returned immediately to her room. No chatter, no smile, no nothing. The heart he had professed not to have ached with the absence of her generous warmth, her natural vitality.

He sighed in relief as another knock sounded at the door. Surely that would be the new bodyguard. He opened the door to reveal a tall, well-built man with black hair and cool gray eyes. "Gabriel Morgan?" the man inquired.

Gabe nodded. "And you must be Lance Grayson." He gestured the man inside. "Nice suit," he commented. Lance wore an exact copy of the navy suit Gabe wore.

Grayson smiled ruefully. "And the tailor told me it was one of a kind."

Gabe laughed despite the sick feeling in the pit of his stomach. Not only good-looking, but with a sense of humor as well. Why hadn't King Phillip sent somebody older…less handsome? Lance looked to be in his early thirties, just the right age for a princess looking for love.

"Would you like a cup of coffee? We have a few minutes before we need to get to the airport."

"Sounds great," Lance agreed.

Gabe poured him a cup, then the two sat at the table. Lance remained rigid, not relaxing despite the fact he was seated.

Gabe noted that his gaze swiftly darted around the room. The sign of a man automatically checking out the room's security, making mental notes of entrances and exits.

He should feel glad that Serena was going to be in good hands, but he found nothing vaguely similar to gladness in his heart.

Both men turned as Serena stepped from her room. Dressed in a pair of jeans and a vibrant yellow blouse, with her hair wild and curly down her back, she filled the room with her presence, like a shining beacon on the darkest night.

Gabe's heart, the heart he insisted he didn't have, did a peculiar lurch. He stood, as did Lance. "Serena, this is Lance Grayson."

"Ah yes, the new warden." She shook his hand, then gestured them both back to their seats. "Do I have time for a quick cup of coffee?" she asked.

Gabe looked at his watch. "We have about fifteen minutes before we need to get to the airport."

She poured herself a cup, then joined them at the table. "My parents are well?" she asked Lance.

"Yes, and eager for you to come home," Lance replied.

Serena studiously ignored Gabe as she made small talk with the new bodyguard. So much for her love, he thought, growing more certain that he was doing the right thing.

She'd apparently managed to get over loving him through the long hours of last night. She appeared cheerful as she talked to Lance, with no shadows of unhappiness or misery darkening the emerald hue of her eyes.

Young love, he thought ruefully. Deeply felt, quickly forgotten. Yes, it was best that he leave her. She had obviously mistaken trust and familiarity for love.

Serena was a survivor, with a joy for life and a romantic soul that would make her quickly forget the bodyguard she'd thought she loved.

They finished their coffee, then Gabe carried their bags to the awaiting car and they headed for the airport.

All too quickly they were not only at the airport but at the gate where Serena and Lance would catch their flight. It was time to say goodbye.

"I'll stay in touch with your father," Gabe said. "In case there are papers I need to sign or whatever." The animation that Serena had exhibited for the last hour in Lance's presence was gone, and a deep sadness darkened her eyes as she faced him.

Gabe gazed at Lance, who stood nearby, looking alert and attentive to the crowd. "You're in good hands with Lance. He appears to be quite competent." He forced a smile. "Your father would have sent only the best." He drew a deep breath. "So, I guess this is goodbye."

She nodded, then before he could guess her intent, she wrapped her arms around his neck and pressed herself against him as her lips sought his.

He had a moment to think about stopping the kiss, but the moment vanished the instant her lips touched his. He drank of her, relishing the sweet fire of the kiss, the bewitching warmth of her body intimately pressed against his.

Wrapping his arms around her, he tangled his hands in her fresh-scented hair, then caressed down her back, losing himself in the kiss, in her.

The kiss seemed to last both an eternity and a mere split second. It was far too long, and achingly short. When he finally ended the kiss, he murmured a goodbye, then turned and walked away.

He didn't look back. He couldn't. Funny, how a man who didn't have a heart could feel so utterly broken inside.

He went directly to the gate where his flight would be boarding within the next few minutes. Slumping into a chair, he tried to shove all thoughts of Serena from his mind.

Serena, in the pretty white suit when he'd married her. Serena, her head thrown back in laughter, eyes sparkling like expensive gems. Serena, in that damnable sexy nightgown, stretching languidly with her hair all tousled around her head.

Visions like snapshots exploding in his mind refused to let him forget a moment, a second of his time with her. Clad in her snow jacket, attempting to sneak out of the Aspen house. Legs and arms tangled with his and the morning sunlight radiant on her face.

It hadn't just been about desire, he finally acknowledged to himself. He'd been fooling himself, believing that desire was all he felt for her.

It had been about love. He loved her as he'd never loved before and had a feeling he never would again, but he knew his decision to walk away from her was the right one.

He didn't know how long he sat there, playing and replaying moments with Serena in his mind, telling himself over and over again that her love hadn't been real, would never have lasted. His thoughts were finally interrupted by a monotone voice over the loud speaker announcing the boarding of his plane. He got in line with the other travelers.

"Morgan!"

He turned to see Lance Grayson hurrying toward him, a tense look on the man's face and no Serena in sight.

"Don't tell me," Gabe said as Lance approached. "She gave you the slip."

Lance nodded curtly. "She went into a gift shop and disappeared."

It's not your problem, a little voice whispered in Gabe's head. It's Grayson's problem. You are no longer responsible. His head said one thing, but his heart said another.

"Damn," Gabe said succinctly and raked a hand through his hair. "I should have warned you that she is like Houdini when it comes to making great escapes.''

Gabe picked up his bag and slung it over his shoulder. "Come on, let's go find her. Surely one slip of a woman can't evade the pursuit of two trained professionals.''

Together, the two men walked back toward the gift shop where she had disappeared. While Lance checked the right side of the concourse, Gabe checked the left. Where would she have gone? Why in the heck would she ditch Grayson just before her flight?

Gabe's head raced with questions. As always, he found it impossible to second-guess Serena. They went into the gift shop where she had disappeared and discovered a side door inside that led to rest rooms, then back to the terminal.

Shouting a warning, Gabe went into the ladies' rest room, startling the sole occupant, an elderly woman washing her hands at the sink. He exited and caught up with Lance.

"This has never happened to me before," he said to Gabe, a frown creasing his brow. "What if she didn't just sneak away? What if somebody has kidnapped her?''

"Then heaven help them…they'll have their hands full," Gabe returned dryly, but the same fear had already knocked on his heart.

Where in the hell was Serena?

Serena boarded the plane and found her seat. Sinking into it, she swept the silly hat she'd bought in the gift shop off her head. With her hair tucked up, she'd managed to pass within twenty yards of Gabe and Lance without them spotting her.

Losing Lance had been easy. She had a feeling the man had never had a person he was guarding actively try to get away from him. He hadn't been expecting her to ditch him, and so he hadn't taken the kind of precautions Gabe would have. Gabe never would have allowed her to enter a store alone. Gabe never would have allowed her out of his sight for an instant.

Gabe. Her heart cried his name as she stuffed the hat beneath her seat, then leaned back. Her heart thudded rapidly, beating the rhythm of anticipation and uncertainty.

She closed her eyes, hoping she wasn't making the biggest mistake of her life.

There were two things that had happened to prompt her action. First, she'd been shocked when she'd overheard what Lieutenant Breckenridge had said about Avery Kintell. She'd been completely blown away when she realized Gabe had known about Avery and hadn't told her.

She'd spent the morning contemplating what it meant. Gabe had known Avery was probably only after her because she was Princess Serena. He could have told her that at any time, but he'd chosen not to.

Why? The only answer that made sense was that he hadn't wanted to hurt her. And a man who didn't care about a woman didn't do things to spare her feelings. It would have been so much easier to tell her about Avery than to marry her.

The second thing that had made her realize what she wanted—needed to do—was their kiss goodbye. Gabe's kiss had said to her all the things he'd been unable to verbalize.

The kiss had spoken of love.

He loved her. Serena knew she wasn't wrong. She prayed she wasn't wrong. She'd taken her ticket and turned it in for one on the same flight as Gabe's to Kansas City. She'd finagled and cajoled to get assigned the seat next to his. Now all she had to do was wait for him to board…wait to see if he surrendered himself to love…or threw her off the plane.

As the minutes ticked by, her heartbeat raced frantically and she wondered if it were possible for a twenty-one-year-old woman to have a heart attack.

Where was he? Why hadn't he boarded yet? She twisted her wedding band around and around her finger, a band she hoped she never had to remove.

Passengers filled the aisles, storing overhead bags, finding their seats. Doubts plagued her mind. What if she was wrong about his love? When she'd asked him if he loved her the night before, he'd not been able to tell her he did. But he hadn't said he didn't love her.

She closed her eyes, praying she'd been right, praying that she hadn't made a huge mistake.

"Going somewhere?"

The deep, sweetly familiar voice washed over her and she opened her eyes to see Gabe. His eyes burned with anger and his features were taut with tension.

She raised her chin and eyed him defiantly. "As a matter of fact, I am. I'm going to Kansas City with my husband. That's what married people do...they travel together."

"Your disappearance act gave Lance a near heart attack." Gabe sank into the seat next to her to get out of the way of other passengers.

She frowned, chagrined that she'd worried Lance. "I'm sorry I scared him. He seems very nice. But a woman has to do what a woman has to do. And this woman intends to follow her husband wherever he goes...to be with him whatever he does."

Some of the anger left Gabe's eyes, but the tension in his face didn't dissipate. "You crazy fool."

She flushed. "I'm not crazy. I'm willful and spoiled and I know exactly what I want and I don't intend to settle for anything less."

A tic appeared in Gabe's jaw. "You're supposed to be on a plane back to Wynborough with Lance."

She ignored him, intent on saying what was in her heart. "Let me tell you exactly what it is that I want. I want you. I want to be Mrs. Gabriel Morgan for the rest of my life. I want to have your children. I want to go to sleep at night and wake up in the morning with your arms around me. I want to dream with you, then work to build those dreams. I want to take your hopes and make them mine. I want to share all the big and little things that life brings...the joys and the sorrows."

She placed her hand on his jaw, where that muscle

ticked erratically. "I want to give you all the hugs you never had as a child, give you all the days of joy that were stolen from you. Gabriel Morgan, I love you and I intend to stick to you like tread on a tire."

At some point during her monologue, his muscle had stopped throbbing and his gaze had softened. "You make it sound like I have no choice in the matter," he said, a touch of indulgent amusement in his voice.

"You don't," she said with a conviction she didn't feel. "I've made up my mind. We belong together, and that's that." She held her breath, waiting for him to say something…anything.

The certainty she'd managed to keep in her voice wasn't in her heart. She still didn't know if he was going to carry her off the plane and out of his life.

"Gabriel, if you're worried that loving me will make you less sharp, less competent as my body-guard, then quit your job as my bodyguard…don't quit being my husband."

He stood suddenly. Leaning over, he scooped her from her seat and into his arms. "Gabe…please…" Tears sprang to her eyes as he carried her down the narrow aisle and off the plane.

"Please, don't put me on that plane to Wynbor-ough unless you intend to be on it with me," she cried.

"You are the most irritating, aggravating woman I've ever known," Gabe said as he put her down. He held her shoulders. "And I'm not putting you on the plane to Wynborough. I'm not about to spend my first night as a real married man on an airplane.''

"A real married man?'' Serena stared at him intently, her tears disappearing as a small flame of hope warmed her heart. "Gabe?''

He gazed at her, a tenderness she'd never seen on his face. "You said a lot of things to me last night that for the first time made sense.'' He dropped his hands from her shoulders. "I will always feel a certain amount of responsibility for LeAnn's death, but I can live with it. What I can't do is live without you.''

He placed a finger against her lips as she opened them to speak. "I want to live every moment of every day with you. I want to be beside you when you give birth. I want to share in the celebration when James is found…and he will be found.''

Again, his hands went to her shoulders, his touch gentle as his thumbs made tiny circles over her collarbone. "You asked me a question last night and I sidestepped it. Now I need to answer it. Yes, I love you.'' He smiled, a smile that transformed her hope into promise. "I love you madly, passionately.'' His voice trembled with emotion. "When Lance came running up to me and told me you were gone, I realized I didn't want to live without you. And when we couldn't find you, I thought I was going to lose my mind. I got on that plane hoping, praying you'd be there, hoping and praying that for once in my life I guessed what you intended to do.''

"Oh, Gabe.'' She melted into his arms and their lips met in a fiery kiss that spoke of hunger, and need, and the incredible love that had blossomed between them.

For the first time in her life, Serena felt that she was finally where she belonged, in his arms with his words of love ringing in her ear.

"So, if we aren't going to Wynborough and we aren't going to Kansas City, where are we going?" she asked when their kiss had finally ended.

"We're going back to the hotel, and we're going to spend the night making love, and building dreams and planning our future because..."

"That's what married people do," she finished for him.

He laughed and hugged her close. "Yes, my love. That's what married people do."

Epilogue

Serena awoke to the early morning sun streaming through the hotel suite window and Gabe's warm, muscular body snuggled against her own. For a long moment she remained unmoving, eyes closed, allowing memories of the night before to play through her mind.

It had been a night beyond her imagination. In her wildest dreams, she'd never envisioned that making love with Gabe would be so exciting and wonderful. She'd never fantasized that the man she'd married, the bodyguard she adored, would be such a tender, patient lover.

Even now, remembering the heat of his kisses, the magic of his touch, her entire body tingled with pleasure, and the anticipation of making love with Gabe again.

She opened her eyes and smiled as she saw he

still slept soundly. He was finally, truly hers, and never had she loved anything or anyone so completely.

For a moment she remained still, watching him sleep, her heart filled with the utter pureness of her love. The sunlight danced across his face, emphasizing the length of his dark lashes, the sensual curve of his mouth.

She thought about waking him up, then reconsidered. He was probably exhausted. They had made love for more than half the night. She'd let him sleep and order a breakfast fit for a king.

Carefully, she eased away from him and out of bed. In the adjoining bathroom she washed, brushed the tangles from her hair, then slipped on a dressing gown. She left the bathroom on tip-toes and headed for the door to the next room.

"Going somewhere?"

His deep voice sent a shiver of delight racing up her spine. She turned and faced him, her breath catching as he raised up on his elbows and the sheet fell away from his naked chest.

"I'm hungry," she said, wondering how it was possible that she felt shy after the night they had shared.

"So am I." His eyes glittered wickedly and a sweet rush of heat suffused Serena.

"I...I thought I'd order room service." Her mouth was suddenly dry as her internal temperature seemed to rise.

"They don't serve what I'm hungry for." His voice was deep and husky.

"And what are you hungry for?" she asked breathlessly.

"My wife."

Her eyes widened as he got out of bed, splendid in his nakedness. When he reached her, he scooped her up in his arms. "It seems I'm always chasing after you," he said as he carried her back to the bed.

She placed a hand on his cheek and smiled teasingly. "I promise I'll never run so fast that you can't catch me."

He laughed and together they tumbled to the bed. His laughter lasted only a moment, for his lips found hers in a fiery kiss that left them both breathless.

Serena was on her back, and her heart pounded furiously in her chest as his fingers danced across the dainty buttons of her dressing gown.

"Tell me, my beautiful, sweet Serena. What are you hungry for?" Her breath caught in her throat as his hand skimmed across the top of her aching breasts. "Omelets?" He unbuttoned the first button. "Pancakes?" The second button came undone. "Waffles?" With the release of the third button, the sides of the gown fell away, exposing her nakedness to his hungry gaze.

"You," she whispered fervently. "Always and only you, Gabe."

Again his mouth found hers, kissing her with a hunger she felt deep inside her. It was a deep kiss that stirred her to dizzying heights, and when his hands cupped her breasts, his thumbs teasing the swollen peaks, she moaned his name.

He pulled his mouth from hers, his eyes blazing

with flames of desire. "Do you have any idea how much I love you, Serena Morgan?"

She thrilled at the name...his name, now her own. "Show me," she whispered. "Show me how much you love me."

And he did. He made love to her with a passion tempered by tenderness, a desire born of their love. She matched him touch for touch, caress for caress, moving with him as tiny little cries of pleasure escaped her.

He loved her until she was incapable of a coherent thought, until there was nothing else in the world but him and their escalating need for each other.

When finally their need was spent, they remained in each other's arms, facing each other and gazing into each other's eyes.

"Will it always be like this?" she asked, her fingers teasing the hair on his chest.

"Like what?" He used his index finger to stroke down the side of her cheek.

"So...so...wonderful." She frowned, aware that the word was inadequate to describe what they'd just shared.

He smiled, an indulgent smile that not only curved his lips, but lit the darkness of his eyes. "Always."

"And will you love me madly, passionately, forever?"

"Forever." The word was a promise she knew she could count on.

The shrill ring of the telephone on the bedside stand broke the moment. "It must be one of my sisters,'' Serena said, then rolled over and grabbed the receiver. ''Hi, Elizabeth,'' she greeted the caller.

Gabe watched his wife as she talked, loving the expressions that swept over her face, loving the way her hair sparkled like flames in the sunshine. He paid no attention to the conversation, preferring to indulge himself by nibbling the sweetness of her shoulder.

He couldn't believe this woman, this sassy, sexy unpredictable woman was his. She'd healed his spirit, restored his dreams and he knew his future with her would be an exciting adventure of laughter and love.

She hung up the phone, an endearing frown wrinkling her forehead. ''Problems?'' he asked.

''I can't believe Elizabeth is about five months pregnant and won't say who the father is. I told her she should at least tell the baby's father.''

''It's not your problem,'' he said, once again kissing her shoulder.

''She's attending a fund-raiser in Phoenix, then she's going to try to find Sam Flynn.'' Serena looked at him. ''It's possible Sam Flynn is my brother, James. Maybe we should—''

''Forget it,'' Gabe exclaimed. ''I see the wheels turning in your head and that always means trouble. We are not going to Phoenix. Elizabeth is perfectly capable of finding this Sam Flynn.''

''But…''

Whatever she was about to say was lost beneath the kiss Gabe pressed onto her lips. He knew with certainty he'd never get tired of the taste of her, the feel of her body against his.

"If we aren't going to Phoenix, then what are we going to do?" she asked when the kiss finally ended.

"We're returning to Wynborough." He stroked the fire of her hair, loved the impish gleam in her brilliant eyes. "When we get there, we'll find ourselves a beautiful little cottage and we'll make lots of babies."

"Hmmm." She snuggled against him. "That sounds wonderful. I love you, Gabriel Morgan."

"And I love you, Princess Serena." Gabe's heart filled to overflowing as he once again kissed his princess, his wife.

* * * * *

0805/62/MB136

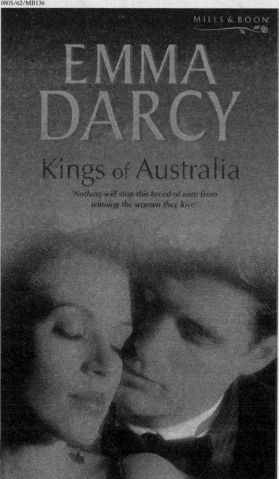

Logan's Legacy

Because birthright has its privileges and family ties run deep

ℒogan's ℒegacy

Because birthright has its privileges and family ties run deep

TWO FANTASTIC NOVELS IN ONE VOLUME

A Precious Gift
by Karen Rose Smith

On the surface, Brian and Carrie Summers had a fairy-tale marriage, but a crisis threatened their peaceful union. For Brian, his unhappy childhood made him believe he needed to be a father in order to be truly happy. But in these troubling times, could he see that their love was stronger than any obstacle and that his precious wife was all the family he needed?

Child of Her Heart *by Cheryl St John*

Meredith Malone was thrilled to deliver a healthy baby girl—even though little Anna happened to be a different race than her mum. To escape the media barrage due to the clinic's obvious mix-up of donor sperm, Meredith headed to the country…and into the arms Justin Weber.

Available from 19th August 2005

Available at most branches of WH Smith, Tesco, ASDA,
Borders, Eason, Sainsbury's and most bookshops.

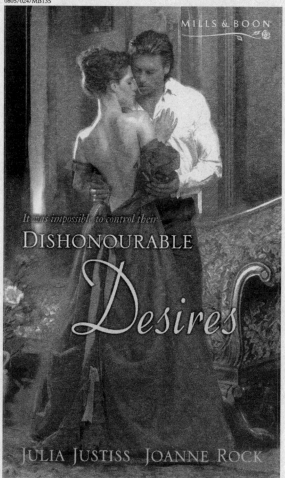

MILLS & BOON

It was impossible to control their

DISHONOURABLE

Desires

JULIA JUSTISS JOANNE ROCK

On sale 5th August 2005

Available at most branches of WHSmith, Tesco, ASDA, Martins,
Borders, Eason, Sainsbury's and all good paperback bookshops.

ANN HAVEN

PEGGY NICHOLSON

Homeward

Bound

Because when baby's on the way

there's no place like home...

On sale 19th August 2005

Available at most branches of WHSmith, Tesco, ASDA,
Borders, Eason, Sainsbury's and most bookshops.

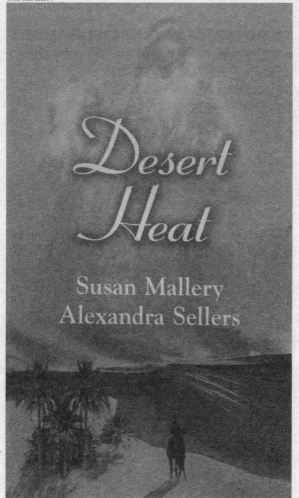

Desert
Heat

Susan Mallery
Alexandra Sellers

On sale 19th August 2005

Available at most branches of WHSmith, Tesco, ASDA, Martins,
Borders, Eason, Sainsbury's and all good paperback bookshops.

The *Regency*

LORDS & LADIES
COLLECTION

Two Glittering Regency Love Affairs

BOOK THREE:
Lady Clairval's Marriage *by Paula Marshall*
&
The Passionate Friends *by Meg Alexander*

Available from 2nd September 2005

MIRA
An international collection of bestselling authors

WORLD EXCLUSIVE!

You're invited to the celebrity wedding of the year — but things aren't quite as perfect as they seem...

ISBN 0-7783-0090-0

Jack Carlisle, media darling and wild-child heartthrob, has finally been tamed by PR exec Emma Hunter — or at least that's what the papers think. As what appears to be a fairy tale love story conceals scandalous secrets the tabloids would have a field day with...

'A hilarious first novel'
—OK! Magazine on Name & Address Withheld